OF DARK AND BRIGHT

MANDY BEX

DEAR READER:

TROPES
Fated mates, he falls first, yearning, secret identities, hidden magic, touch him/her and die, feminine rage.

TRIGGERS
This book features graphic battle scenes and violence. There are also mentions of torture, uncomfortable physical contact, and heavy themes of grief and trauma in the aftermath of child death (not depicted on page). If these are triggers for you, please protect your mental health and skip this one.

CONTENT WARNING
This book contains explicit sexual scenes, profane language, and violence.

If you've ever been told to smile more,
to be softer, to be less...
If your vulnerability hides behind
the strong walls you've built...
This one is for you.

She walks in beauty, like the night
Of cloudless climes and starry skies;
And all that's best of dark and bright
Meet in her aspect and her eyes;
Thus mellowed to that tender light
Which heaven to gaudy day denies
-Lord Byron, *She Walks In Beauty*

If I was born as a blackthorn tree
I'd wanna be felled by you
Held by you
Fuel the pyre of your enemies
-Hozier, *NFWMB*

Prologue

Death was coming for her. The Queen would meet it with fury.

Great and unending sorrow seemed to press down upon the kingdom of Eodia from the heavens above. The stars winked out one by one, casting the land in a deep and horrible darkness. Thunder boomed like the clouds themselves were wailing in grief. The skies cracked open with rain and blinding streams of lightning. Violent winds raged, tearing trees from the earth by the roots.

High in the bell tower of Lyra Castle, Queen Nyx, bloody and broken, stretched her arms and reached her straining fingers towards the ancient metal bell pull. Using her last rasping breath and all the strength that remained within her, she tugged the chain as her vision darkened, and her body went cold. Nesting white birds exploded into panicked flight from the tower at the sound of the bell. Nyx fell to her knees and watched them disappear into the abyss of the black sky above. Gone. She would follow them into the dark soon.

She fell forward on her hands and lowered herself to the cool floor. The Queen would not die on her knees. Teeth gritting, Nyx rolled onto her back and lay herself down for what she knew would be the very last time. She heard their footsteps approaching and knew they stood above her. Their laughter was the sound of metal scraping against stone, barely drowned out by the ringing of the bell.

Blood spread around her like a blanket, carrying what was left of her life into the cracks between the mighty rock that built the Castle. Seeping down, down, down into the foundation of the fortress, her blood flowed into the yawning earth below. Nyx's voice made no sound as her mouth spoke her last words. She reached inside for her magic, the sleeping giant of her power, and she brushed against it. It seemed to be grieving, but it answered– one final time.

It warmed her. She could no longer see its glow, but she felt it dance with the words she managed to release with her last breath.

A curse.

Then there was nothing.

The old gods wept. The Queen was dead.

PART ONE

Lady Nightmare

1

Neve D'Aeth descended from the sea-battered ship, and set foot on the forsaken kingdom of Eodia.

"I almost didn't believe this place was real," one of her black-cloaked companions said, stepping up next to her to survey the land.

"People say that about us, too," Neve replied.

It was true. Throughout the many continents they'd traveled, and all the gods and men they'd come up against, the most common reaction to Neve and her twelve companions was disbelief.

The tricky thing about myths was that sometimes they weren't truly mythical at all.

She knew that all too well. Neve and this kingdom were kindred in that way.

She planted her boots in the dark soil beyond the rocky shore, and gazed out at the expanse of land before her.

Eodia was an Island in the middle of the Great Sea, and it was cursed.

Once upon a time, it was the center of the world: a place of innovation, education, and art. People would come across the Great Sea on ships to visit and *marvel*. Skilled healers once called Eodia home, as well as some of the most famed scholars and wizards. It was a land of poetry and magic, an example to the world of what equality between classes and clans could be.

The books Neve read told the story of a beautiful, sprawling kingdom, lush with lakes and rivers, high mountain passes and forests so ancient that their beginnings were beyond memory. Rolling hills of heather often led to a crisp, burbling creek.

It was a wild place. *Alive.*

Villages and towns were scattered amongst the wilderness, most found along the sweeping King's Road, which stretched from one end of the Island to the other.

In the exact center of it all was Lyra Castle.

From where she stood, it was merely a shadow on the horizon, but Neve could see the phantom of its towers jutting up into gray skies.

The Castle was a massive, imposing monolith of lost beauty and power, now filled with nothing but infinite emptiness. A giant ghost clad in cream stone, it was covered in creeping green moss and vines that curled up the steep turrets like wisps of living smoke. Its towers reached into the heavens, piercing through the clouds.

It was also said that surrounding the castle was a vast hedge maze of brambles. Miles deep, the maze would take *hours* to trek through, even if they could make it past the bramble thorns, which were so thick and sharp any hopeful conqueror could easily impale themselves upon them. The bleached bones littering the maze told the story of the many who thought themselves worthy to pass and failed.

Legend had it that the brambles themselves were fortified with magic so that no weapon forged would be strong or sharp enough to cut them down. No man ever managed to make it through the maze to the palace doors. It was impenetrable.

There was a lonesome feeling to the kingdom; it was like the earth itself knew this place was forgotten, left behind.

But there was something else beneath the sadness.

Something ancient and sinister.

That was why Neve made the months-long trip across the violent Great Sea to reach the shores of Eodia.

She had work to do.

2

His sword was already in his hand as he stood over his wife, soundly asleep in their bed. The room still smelled like her, like them; like their sheets and their clothes, their life together. But there was another scent too, something dark and familiar. His wife was curled on her side, the blankets pulled up to her chin. All he wanted to do was slip beneath the covers with her and pull her into his arms.

But he could not.

There was no rise and fall to her chest as she slept. He moved closer, croaking her name through parched lips. She did not stir. Closer still, he reached for her and brushed her golden hair from her face. She looked asleep, peaceful even, but her lips were blue, and her skin was cold. She was no longer there. He spoke her name, quietly like a prayer. He lowered to his knees before the bed, his long fingers stroking the slant of her cheek. Chanting her name until it was the only word he knew, he found himself lost in her death.

But soon his blood went cold as he remembered something else. Something important. She wasn't alone in the house.

His children were there.

Killian Grey woke with a ragged gasp. His heart hammered in his chest and the muscles in his body coiled as if threatened. The dreams were always the same. His home. His family. Death. To relive the worst night of his life over and over again would seem like a fitting punishment to most, but although they were awful, Killian knew they weren't nearly enough punishment. He deserved worse for what he'd done, for his failure. Much worse.

Sweat dripped down the small of his back. The pile of rags he used as a blanket to ward off the wet coldness of the cell twisted around his ankles, dirty and moth-eaten. Everything here was filthy. It was just as well. He had become a part of that filth long ago.

Five years in this dank, forgotten dungeon.

He blinked the sting of tears from his eyes and sat up, rubbing his hands over his face and through his thick, greasy hair. Killian looked around his cell. It wasn't much. It wasn't anything. Everything reeked of mold, the stone walls were covered in it, the corners thick with cobwebs and worse. Some distant part of him knew it was his last day in this place, but he couldn't seem to summon the will to care. He was numb to nearly everything except the ache. The loneliness. It settled into his bones like an illness, became a part of him as common and essential as blood and air.

There was also fear.

He feared that the time he'd spent alone would never absolve him of what he'd done or what he might do once he was released. Killian Grey was a dangerous man. Now, his wife and children were gone, and there was no one to anchor him, to inspire him to goodness. There would be no more balance, no one to keep him grounded. No motivation to keep his rage tethered.

Five years in a dungeon was not enough for his sins. They should have executed him. Instead, he was thrown into the dungeon, a weapon cast aside to be picked up again later.

Now, the Highborns thought it was time for Killian to get back to work. Time to spill more blood in their name, for the glory of Eodia. Time to put their favorite weapon to use again.

Killian wasn't being released into freedom. He was simply trading one prison for another.

The clattering of keys and thud of boots against a packed-dirt floor drew Killian out of his thoughts. He was filled with unease, haunted by the dream that still clung to the air, barely dissolved, and the knowledge of what awaited him outside these walls. He stood, yanking on a filthy and tattered brown shirt that was once an entirely different color. Pulling on his boots, he looked around the cell, as if searching for anything else he might need to bring with him. There was nothing but the clothes on his back and the sickening weight of guilt on his shoulders.

A Cavalry soldier, dressed in pure, clean white, approached the bars of his cell. The man's nose wrinkled as he peered inside and saw Killian, probably catching a whiff of his stench.

"Grey. Let's go," the soldier said, pulling an iron ring from his hip, selecting a large black key, and sliding it into the lock. It clunked as it turned. The Cavalryman stepped aside and pulled the cell door open with a rusted creak.

Killian stepped over the threshold for the first time in half a decade. The soldier's eyes widened, drinking in Killian's height, his broad shoulders, the pure lethality of his size. The man took a small step backward. Killian couldn't help it as the corner of his mouth tipped up in a smirk.

"Don't worry, boy," Killian said, his voice gritty and rough, having forgotten the last time he'd spoken to another person. "I'm reformed."

The Cavalryman's cheeks went a bit pink, and he lifted his chin in defiance. "This way," he said, then stepped in front of Killian, leading the way.

Killian tracked the angle of the soldier's body, the way he wouldn't fully turn his back to him. Smart man.

The fetid hallways twisted and turned like a maze. The dungeon was constructed that way by design to thwart potential escape attempts. Though he'd never seen another prisoner. In Eodia, justice was often served in more savage ways, which made it all the more uncommon that he'd been left without freedom rather than without his head.

Ahead, he could see light streaming in through the front gates. Sunlight. Some sweet, mournful emotion twisted in his chest. Five years without the sun, and he'd never let himself believe he missed it.

Oh, but he did. That golden midday glow reminded him of pure, innocent things: a kiss, the smell of grass, the twinkling laughter of his sons.

Killian swallowed past the lump in his throat.

The soldier used another thick key to open the dungeon gate, which creaked and yawned. Killian took a deep breath and closed his eyes, letting the stale prison air fill his lungs for the last time, then he walked through the door.

The sun was so bright that he had to shield his eyes with his hand. It took a good, long moment for his vision to adjust. He squinted through the sunlight. Just beyond the gates was a cluster of black leather and steel atop horses.

The Cadre. The group of warriors tasked with meting out the Highborns' darker forms of justice upon the unlucky criminals and dissenters of Eodia.

They were the only family he had left.

Killian was once their leader, their Commander, a title since passed down to his brother Rory. He'd received a handful of short correspondences from them over the years. They had to bribe the guards to bring the letters, and money was in short supply. Still, he was somewhat surprised to see them there, waiting for him. It made something in Killian's chest clench with emotion.

As he approached, he spied his horse, saddled and ready for him, and his heart broke open a little. He brushed his hand down Willow's dark, coarse mane.

"Hello, girl," he murmured in her ear, leaning into her.

She gave him an encouraging nudge with her head as if to say, "*Nice to see you, let's get on with it.*" So he did, mounting her with practiced ease.

The Cadre's First General, Arran, bent across the space between their horses and clasped Killian's forearm in a rough yet affectionate gesture that Killian immediately returned. A long scar raked down the left side of Arran's world-weary face, but his brown eyes shone with good humor and relief. There was much more gray in his hair now, and the wrinkles around his mouth were deeper, the texture of his dark olive skin having turned leathery. But he was still Arran, Killian's closest friend, his mentor.

"It's good to have you back, lad," he said. Arran handed Killian his sword and its worn leather harness. Without even thinking, he slipped it on and fastened the buckles.

Killian Grey's sword rested with a familiar and comforting heaviness on his back and shoulders. Sitting atop his horse felt good, too. Somewhat surreal, but good. He looked around at the faces of the men who'd come to greet him.

Everything else in his world was different, and the men who'd seen him through the worst and the best of his life were no exception. They were all older, weathered, haunted. Somehow, though, the humor in all of their eyes remained, at least as they looked upon Killian. Their expressions were welcoming and warm. As warm as they could muster.

Killian gave a nod, not trusting that his emotions wouldn't get the better of him if he opened up his mouth to speak.

"I've never heard him so quiet," muttered Logan, his lips tight with held-back laughter. When Killian went to prison, Logan's hair had been more pepper than salt, but now his dark skin stood in stark contrast to his snow white hair. Time had moved forward, indeed.

"This must be setting a record." This came from Fraser, a tall and lean warrior with dark hair cropped close to his head and even darker eyes. Gone was the boyish roundness of his cheeks and chin, replaced with hollows and lines that made the youngest man of the Cadre look severe and jaded.

"I'm not complaining. I got used to the quiet without his majesty's constant barking," Gillis added. A brawny, red-haired bear of a man, he was easily the largest of the six of them, which was quite a feat in itself considering Killian's own size.

A low chuckle rumbled through the group of men and they watched him closely.

Five years might as well have been one hundred. He hadn't spoken to anyone except the occasional guard since he'd been imprisoned, and he found he was out of practice with conversation.

It seemed that his friends were eager to get the "old" Killian back. The deadly warrior with a swagger, tenacious wit, and relentless ambition. Their fearless and ruthless leader. He steeled himself. The Cadre, *his* Cadre, waited for him all these long years. The least he could do was pretend to be the man they thought he was, despite his doubts that the "old" Killian still even existed.

It wasn't as hard as Killian may have thought to slip into the mask. He turned on the dangerous, mischievous light in his cold blue eyes, squared his strong shoulders, and let a cocky smirk play on his lips. Tilting his head to the side, he sized each of them up, reminding them with simply a look that he could take each of them down without breaking a sweat.

"Careful, boys. I'm just a stone's throw from the dungeon, and it'd be a damn shame to end up back there for bloodying your ugly faces in public. Tempting, though."

They all seemed to breathe a collective sigh of relief and offered him satisfied, gruff laughter in return.

All except his brother, Rory, who sat furthest away, and eyed him with something that resembled resentment, maybe even hate. That look wasn't new. Killian considered all of the men in the Cadre to be his brothers, but he and Rory truly were. They shared a mother and father, yet that was as far as their similarities went.

Rory was the kind of man who'd climb over the body of his best friend if there was something in it for him. He was selfish and entitled, but more than that, there was a shade of darkness to him even deeper than the most devious of men Killian had ever met.

He'd need to deal with that later.

~

Eodia wasn't always the way it was now; it once was a utopia full of life and new ideas, but that ended with the Queen being killed three centuries ago.

A civil war within castle walls.

An internal battle between progress and decline.

A Queen who could have changed the world, cut down by her own.

The royal family was left in ruins, scattered to the wind like so much ash. Leaving the people of Eodia open and vulnerable.

Killian, riding atop Willow down the deeply familiar King's Road, could not imagine Eodia as anything other than what it was now. A place where the chief priority for all citizens was merely survival. The fabled monarchy of Queen Nyx ended three hundred years ago. Without a ruler, without a leader, the kingdom was cut off from trade. Foreign nations would no longer dare or bother to make the treacherous journey across the Great Sea to Eodia's shores.

No one visited Eodia.

No one left.

Soon, men who'd been born into wealth before the death of the kingdom were the only ones to retain any resources after the kingdom fell.

Then, they'd hoarded it.

Then, they'd leveraged it for power.

They called themselves the Highborns.

Now, in the kingdom without a ruler, the citizenry was at the mercy of the men who inherited that power. Two brothers, the last of the Highborns, controlled all industry and used the threat of starvation and homelessness as a means to bring the people of Eodia to heel. The brothers established strict laws against what they deemed treason. Any defiance of their dominance would result in imprisonment, slavery, torture, or, most commonly, a swift execution.

The Highborn brothers' version of justice was terrifyingly brutal and, more often than not, was doled out by Killian and his Cadre. They were skilled warriors, all born and raised for battle.

Killian and Rory's family roots could even be traced back to the honored Knights who once served the Queen. Killian tried not to think about how far from that reputation he and his brother had sunk. How they had sullied it with the dark deeds they were now commanded and paid to do. Not that his ancestors were truly remembered anymore, beyond legends and songs crooned off-key after too much ale at the tavern. Not that Killian and his brother had any choice about becoming what they did.

No matter.

The Cadre lived in the village of Lowbarrow, along the King's Road. A place that once had been considered charming with its quaint cottages and the thick blanket of forest surrounding it, but was now just another struggling village falling into disrepair and decay. Although the money the Cadre made from serving the Highborns afforded the village comforts other places did not have: a small market, a good tavern, and a roof over the head of every townsperson.

They rounded the corner into Lowbarrow proper, and Killian felt his chest tighten as faces turned his way, eyes widening. There was a sickly combination of fear and pity on those faces. Fear, because they knew who he was and what he was capable of. Pity, because they knew what had been done to him, to his family. Mothers put their arms around their children and ushered them away as the Cadre passed. Old men nodded.

Courtesans lounged outside the tavern, and Killian knew that they could nearly *hear* the sound of coin. Killian was finally home and that meant there would be a Cadre-funded feast and celebration in the pub, The Cross, that night.

But first, he needed a bath.

He nodded his thanks and farewell as the Cadre all went off to their own homes, leaving him to face the moment he'd been dreading for five years.

Willow rounded a corner and came to a stop in front of Killan's cottage. The Cadre had been meticulous about the upkeep while he'd been away. Not a weed in the garden or a single creeping vine up the brick walls. Not a cobweb or a stone out of place.

But, no life either. This was a dead place. A *violated* place.

Killian hopped off his horse in an easy motion, leading her to the stable where there was plenty of fresh hay, no doubt courtesy of his friends. He turned toward the walkway that led to his front door and found he could go no further.

The plain yet pretty face of his wife flashed in his head. In truth, they'd not been a love match. Lilith's father and brothers were branded as traitors to the Highborns and killed in a Cavalry raid. If not for Killian, she would have been banished from her village and left to fend for herself along the King's Road, surely to find a fate worse than death. So, on a desperate impulse, Killian married her.

She was a good woman, and she gave him his sons.

Liam and Sean.

His muscles tensed, every instinct in his body told him to *run*, to not face this. Avoid. He clenched his jaw, closed his eyes, and raised his face to the sky, feeling the dapples of the sun between treetops dance across his skin. His heart was a thunderstorm behind his ribs.

Steady now, old boy.

He flexed his hands over and over, reminding himself of the earth beneath his feet, the smell of pine and woodsmoke in the air. Reminded himself of who he was. *I am Killian Grey. Leader of the Cadre. Warrior. I yield to no man and nothing.*

He took a step.

I yield to nothing.

I am Killian Grey.

He opened his eyes and took another step toward the door.

~

The homecoming feast was in full, loud swing and The Cross was at capacity. It seemed that everyone in Eodia was aware of Killian's return. The air was a thick haze of ale, pipe smoke, and unwashed bodies.

There was a small minstrel band playing drinking songs on lute, fiddle, and drum. The beat of the music rolled through the tavern in a raucous rumble. A few of Lowbarrow's finest courtesans were dancing to the rhythm amidst the delighted cheers of salivating men. Ale and whiskey flowed like water. Fights were already starting to break out. Countless just-met couples were pawing at each other with no regard for anyone who might be watching.

Killian sat at a worn, high-top table nursing his fourth glass of whiskey and watching the chaos around him. A slow calm was beginning to spread through his nerves. Business as usual. There was something astoundingly comforting about being at a perfectly normal tavern, where perfectly normal folks were enjoying themselves, as if they had no cares in the world.

He'd experienced what felt like hundreds of nights just like this over the years. They all looked the same. Mead and ale, whiskey, smoke, sex, and violence. All of the underlying rumblings of what motivated men like them, men like him, in a world such as this, on full display and without inhibition.

A strong hand slapped down on his shoulder. He looked up. Arran nodded and slid yet another drink in front of Killian. He raised his cup. "So good to have you back, lad," he said in his deep, raspy voice.

Killian took a swallow. "Good to be back," he said, and thought perhaps he meant it.

Mostly.

Fraser and Logan joined them at the table. Both seemed halfway to the moon. Killian clocked the obvious absence of Rory, but his relationship with his brother had always been... difficult. It was probably better that Rory made himself scarce. The initial welcome hadn't been warm, and it was easy to imagine that his brother would have preferred for Killian to never have returned at all.

Rory Grey spent his life in his older brother's considerable shadow. Certainly, Killian's absence was a reprieve Rory must have reveled in. Now that it was over...well, it wasn't a homecoming Rory would celebrate.

The rest of the Cadre, though, were dizzily drunk and red-faced with whatever passed for mirth in men who killed people for a living.

Fraser pointed behind Killian. "You see that?" he asked. Killian turned, following Fraser's gaze. Gillis was on a settee in a dim corner with two blonde courtesans crawling all over him with enthusiasm. The man had a look on his face like he'd just seen the gods.

"It must be the red hair," Killian remarked.

They laughed and took another drink. Then another.

Killian gazed around the room. He saw the looks being aimed his way by dozens of eager women artfully draping themselves around the tavern as if on display. Heaving corsets, pink blush on creamy skin, painted lips.

Before going to the dungeon, Killian was very accustomed to the look of a woman who'd zeroed in on exactly what she wanted. He'd become quite good at appreciating the attention from afar while he was with his wife, and before that, he'd indeed been a master of taking advantage of those looks. Now, the heated gazes that leveled on him gave him the confidence to know that he'd at least *looked* like the old Killian Grey, despite feeling like another man entirely.

The man he was now was different.

Logan seemed to notice the contemplative way Killian was staring off into the fray of the party and mistook his quiet for interest. "Want me to see if the madam can round up a couple of girls for you?" Logan offered.

Killian clenched his jaw. "I may be a little rusty, but I'm certain I can still do the rounding up on my own."

He took a thick gulp of his whiskey and scanned the room again, if only to avoid looking his friend in the eye, the edges of his vision becoming deliciously fuzzy.

Then everything seemed to come to a dizzying and sudden halt.

He spotted her across the room. His eyes locked on her immediately and unerringly.

Long, dark hair fell in waves around her face and down her back. Her dress was little more than cobwebs and mist. Midnight blue gossamer embroidered with what looked like small gold constellations draped over her soft body like an invitation, secured with a cord of the same color looped around her curved waist. A cord that looked as if it would be so, so easy to slip a finger beneath and unravel with the barest touch.

No corset, no layers of skirts. Just that flimsy fabric floating around her. Her shoulders and arms were bare, her skin gleaming like pooled silk, and the neckline of her dress plunged low enough that Killian could imagine that one small shift of gossamer would bare what was underneath to his thirsty eyes. Each step she took revealed a smooth, strong leg, a soft thigh, the dress sighing around her.

Killian sat up a little straighter, sucked in a lungful of air, and didn't take his eyes from her.

She moved through the room like water over rocks. Slow, graceful, deadly. A predator. She seemed quiet in a way that eluded the gaze of other men, and strong in a way that made the women she passed step aside without realizing what they were doing.

25

Killian leaned forward on his elbows, ignoring the conversation at the table. He watched the way she lifted her hair off her neck, then let it fall back down around her shoulders.

"Killian!" Arran shouted, waving his hand in front of Killian's face, forcing him back into the conversation.

"Who's that?" Killian asked, nodding toward the woman. She'd stopped moving, leaning against the bar, searching the room with eyes that looked calculating and hungry.

Logan shrugged. "Some woman. Never seen her before."

It made sense. She wasn't desperate for attention. Not the way the other women at the tavern were.

But somehow she commanded all of Killian's interest, every shred of it.

She shifted slightly at the bar, getting more comfortable. The gossamer slipped down her shoulder, revealing a soft collarbone and a violent hint of skin. Without realizing it, Killian sucked in a sharp breath. The movement of that fabric felt like a challenge. Like a promise.

Fuck.

He shook his head and looked away. Maybe he was drunker than he thought. Not having a drink for five years could surely alter a man's tolerance.

He hadn't even noticed that all but Arran were gone from the table.

"You alright?" he asked, peering at Killian cautiously.

"I think the whiskey is hitting me harder than I thought."

Arran snorted, tossing back the rest of this drink, standing up. "That dungeon turned you soft." He clapped Killian on the shoulder and sauntered off into the depths of the party.

Killian gave a short, humorless chuckle. The dungeon had turned him into something, that was for damn sure.

"May I?" an impossibly smooth voice asked.

He looked up.

It was her.

She gestured to the chair next to him with an unbothered hand. It wasn't an invitation, the way most women would ask that question. It was an off-the-cuff demand. She barely even looked at him.

Look alive, soldier.

He gave her that Killian Grey smile. The one he'd realized long ago could make anyone of the fairer sex blush and swoon for him.

"Of course." He pulled the chair out, leaned towards her a little, and was rewarded with a closer vision of her face.

Gods, those lips.

She nodded a nonchalant thank you at him and turned away. He felt immediate defeat at her dismissal.

"Quite the party," he half shouted at her, like a desperate asshole.

He winced at himself. Maybe he'd been wrong. Maybe he was a little more rusty than he thought. But she turned around and regarded him. There was an expression on her face that Killian could barely read. Annoyance? It quickly melted away into an amused smirk. Progress. That was something. He leaned back in his chair, relaxed, waiting to see where this would go.

She nodded. "Quite." She looked around the room, eyes dancing with that predator's light again. Green eyes, Killian thought, maybe hazel, shining golden in the candlelight. "A few too many people for my liking."

She brought her gaze back to him, and it settled on his face in a way that made his palms itch to reach out to her.

He laughed through his nose. "I tend to agree."

She watched him in another stretched moment of silence, sizing him up. Killian licked his lips. He tried to keep his eyes on her face, but on their own agenda, they moved over her body like a caress.

"Can I get you a drink?" he asked, just to put words into the air between them.

She gave him an unreadable quirk of her lips. Without ceremony, she wrapped her hand around his glass, raised it to her lips, and took a mighty swig. It may as well have been water, the bite of the strong whiskey going unnoticed.

She didn't give an inch. She looked into his eyes. "Thanks."

Not to be outdone, he took a swig himself. "What brings you here tonight, love?"

Her eyes narrowed slightly at the honorific, but the curve of her perfect mouth grew a little bigger. She gestured at the cup between them. "Free drinks and good company. You?"

He cocked his head to the side, and froze for a moment. Did she not know who he was? If not, what was she doing at The Cross? His interest in her piqued, and now another feeling washed over him. A feeling he'd learned not to ignore. Distrust.

He let his smile fade, and he let her watch as it did, revealing the dangerous man that lived behind the charm. "I'm Killian Grey," he said in a low voice.

Her face blossomed into a full smile that nearly stopped his heart. A smile more deadly than any of the weapons in the tavern.

"I know who you are, " she said.

Interest took distrust's place in his head again.

"The Great Killian Grey." The way she said his name sounded like naked skin in a whisper of consonants.

This was ridiculous. He wasn't sure if he should ready his sword or pull her across the table, and kiss her.

"Do you belong to someone here?" he asked, giving her a pointed glance around the room.

She shook her head. "I belong to no one."

"What's your story?"

She stood up, moved around the table, and stood close to him. Close enough that he could smell the clean scent of her hair, like clover after the rain, and the smoke on her skin. Close enough that if he moved his arm just an inch, he could touch her. The air between them was thick and electric.

"My story is that it is past my bedtime." She licked her lips and looked into his eyes for an impenetrable moment.

He could almost taste her breath. His hand nearly stretched out to touch her. He clenched his fists on his lap.

"Do you have a name?" His voice was low and husky.

She tilted her head. "Everyone has a name, Killian."

Before he could breathe, she turned on her heel, walking away.

He was too stupid to move.

He just sat there like an idiot and watched her go. Her hips swayed so rhythmically that it made him forget what language he spoke. She didn't even look back over her shoulder at him. Like he hadn't even mattered.

Like he wasn't Killian Grey.

3

His children.

Two small boys, tucked into bed together. The blankets around them held the same acrid scent that permeated the rest of his home. Burning metal. The smell of magic.

Too still. Too quiet.

They were gone.

Some distant part of his addled brain remembered seeing Mages on the King's Road as he'd traveled home that night.

Every thought after that disappeared into a thick, red mist of fury.

Killian woke up, hungover and heart racing, in a bed at the Inn above The Cross.

Head swimming, pushing the thoughts of his children from his mind, he squinted at the early morning sunlight drifting through the window.

A blonde-haired woman was sprawled and snoring softly next to him. Bare skin beneath the worn sheets.

The only thing he remembered about taking this woman to bed was that when he was inside her, and closed his eyes, he saw someone else's face.

Hers.

He imagined being smothered in dark blue gossamer, the scent of clover, and a set of impossibly full lips saying his name over and over again.

Killian.

I belong to no one.

Killian.

Killian...

The whiskey had ruined him. Never in his life had he been so at a loss for common sense.

Somehow, he knew if she'd met him with those green-gold eyes and asked him to give up all of his earthly possessions just for a taste of her skin, he would have done it.

Drunk, off-balance, back in the free world after five years in prison... perhaps he was owed a bit of allowance for falling all over himself.

She'd found him at a vulnerable moment; that was all.

Remembering the way she prowled through the tavern as if searching for her next meal. He wondered if that was *why* she'd approached him. The thought was unsettling.

A brusque knock nearly rattled the door off its hinges. The woman next to him stirred, and Killian pulled the sheet higher over her naked body before answering, "Come in."

Gillis opened the door, looking just about as worse for wear as Killian felt. The big man's red hair was a wild mass on top of his head, and he swayed a little, so he put a reassuring hand on the doorframe. "A messenger came by just after dawn this morning."

Killian fought the urge to roll his eyes and groan. "And?"

"We're meant to head off to Hythe. Reports of thieves."

A smile played on Killian's lips. Handling thieves was always a good way to release a little tension.

There wasn't any guilt in the business of taking down a group of raiders. It nearly felt heroic. Much more heroic than delivering justice against well-meaning, simple folks. Much more heroic than torture.

Killian was overdue for a good, old-fashioned fight.

~

Hythe was a two-hour ride south from Lowbarrow. The King's Road could be a terrifying place. Bands of raiders and worse used the King's Road as their hunting ground. Beasts, sharp of tooth and claw, haunted the forests on either side. Not to mention that the eyes of the Highborns were everywhere, just waiting to spot a wrong move. But for Killian and the Cadre, it was as safe as anywhere else.

Killian knew no peace that could match going at a gallop atop his horse, surrounded by pines and willow trees, with his brothers at his back.

This was freedom.

The wind whipped at his cheeks, his body tilted and straightened like he was an extension of the horse itself. All he could hear was white noise; his thoughts were drowned out.

He saw their turn coming up; Rory was at the lead and raised his hand to signal the others to slow down behind him. They pulled off into a clearing and would stop for a moment to get their bearings, then head up the road to the Hythe.

The minute the horses stopped, Killian heard it.

The distinct noise of clashing metal came from around the bend.

It sounded like a battle.

"Shit," he muttered.

"Are we walking into a trap?" Logan asked.

Kilian clenched his jaw. "Somebody walked into a trap, but it wasn't us. Let's go, nice and slow."

He didn't miss the way Rory stiffened when Killian spoke, didn't miss the look of loathing in his brother's eyes as the rest of the Cadre wordlessly followed his lead. Rory may have taken Killian's role as Commander upon his arrest, but it was clear that the Cadre still considered Killian to be in charge.

They quietly rounded the corner and Killian drew his sword.

The hot thrill of danger shot through his blood. The feeling was almost nostalgic, almost comforting.

They dismounted with a practiced and deadly silence, leaving their horses behind. Killian led the way, walking slowly and defensively into the sounds of shouting.

They walked against the outside wall of an old stone building at the far end of the village and stopped when they reached the edge.

Steeling himself, he planted his feet, his arms straight and solid, sword at the ready. He leaned forward and looked around the corner.

The first thing he saw was a dead man. A thief.

And then a trail of them.

Someone had taken this job into their own hands.

He tightened his jaw and huffed a curse under his breath, eyes searching the rest of the scene for answers.

Figures in hoods, ruthlessly swinging weapons into the group of raiders.

Killian could smell blood. His heart was racing. Although whatever was happening here would inevitably cause a serious mess for the Cadre to clean up, a deadly smile formed on Killian's lips.

If being on his horse was euphoric, being in a good brawl was a relief. His hands were itching to get busy and feel his knuckles collide with flesh.

"These men in hoods, who are they?" Gillis wondered out loud.

Killian shook his head. "I have no idea."

"Looks like they've got a little one among them. We could pick that one off and question him," Rory said, nodding towards someone in a black hood who was at least half a head shorter than the rest. He was fighting a massive bear of a man with scarred hands and a mean face. The raider kicked the smaller man in the gut so hard he went sprawling into the dirt, and his hood fell off.

That's when Killian's heart jumped right into his throat and got stuck there.

The smaller man in the hood was not a man, after all.

"What the fuck?" Fraser whispered.

Killian couldn't make sense of what he was seeing.

A woman.

A woman with long, dark hair and hungry predator's eyes. The woman from the party.

The thief lumbered down on her and dragged her back to her feet by the collar of her tunic. The look on his face was one of amusement.

He pulled back his arm, winding up to drive his fist right into her face, but she jerked free of his grip in a swift, expert move and threw a surprisingly powerful uppercut into his chin that had him staggering backward, stunned.

The raider's face turned from amused to furious. Killian knew that look. It was the look he, himself, often gave someone before ending their life.

Killian shifted his weight from one foot to the other. His breath was coming out in short, angry rasps from his nose.

The raider lunged at the woman and wrapped his large, lethal hands around her neck, sending them both to the ground. She scrambled underneath his weight. Rage-filled spit dripped from his lips onto her. He squeezed. And *squeezed*.

"What do we do here, Killian?" Arran asked with a nervous edge to his voice.

Suddenly, neither the thief nor the woman was moving.

Which meant one of them was dead.

There was an emotionless, serene look on her face; her lips were pursed like she was waiting for a kiss.

"Shhhh...." she whispered to the man on top of her.

Then she slowly, *very* slowly, dragged a buried-deep knife from the man's navel to his sternum.

She rolled out from underneath him, leaving him and his guts spilling onto the ground.

"Ho-ly fucking gods," Killian said, in shock.

He's seen some cold killings in his life. Some brutal bloodshed. But he'd never seen something quite like this.

This woman was a killer without mercy. She'd killed him like she was breathing, like it was breakfast.

The thieves were dead, littered around the clearing like errant garbage.

It was time to get to work.

Killian gestured at the Cadre and they followed him.

The hooded men drew swords on them as soon as they were visible. Killian and the Cadre responded accordingly, with their own steel.

"Sheath them," the woman commanded, her voice firm and cold as glass. Without hesitation, the people behind her sheathed their weapons.

Interesting.

Killian sheathed his sword and walked with purpose toward the woman. She regarded him with that same cool look she'd given him at the feast.

He, on the other hand, couldn't remain calm. His confusion led to an anger so full, he was nearly vibrating with it.

He stood face-to-face with her, raised his eyebrows, and stared her down.

"What the hell is going on?" he asked in a low, carefully restrained voice.

She didn't falter under the weight of his gaze. She still held the knife in her hand, dripping blood on his boots. A muscle feathered in his jaw as he pointedly glanced at her weapon, at the raindrop sound of blood on leather.

The corner of her mouth lifted.

It took every ounce of restraint in him to keep from flinching as she pulled the fabric of his tunic from the waistband of his pants and wiped her knife clean on it.

It was hard to swallow, his heart beating with such fury against his bones, he was sure she could hear it. His skin flushed with rage, and some other, more complicated thing. A curious desire.

His mind was as thick as a swamp.

"I suppose," she drawled, slipping the knife into her belt and taking a step back from him, "that you wouldn't have allowed these vermin to walk away if they ambushed you, either."

He took a step back himself, took a breath to calm his ire, and looked around.

A clean, modest camp stood beyond the carnage, with raised white tents and a few hearty fires crackling. There were thirteen people in hoods, some of them men and some women. They all stood behind her, casually lethal and not at all fazed by the pile of dead bodies or the imposing group of warriors behind Killian.

Each wore a black, hooded cloak with an emblem embroidered on the breast: a white crescent moon held by a black, raised hand. He *knew* this symbol; it tugged at the corner of his memory, but all the blood had rushed out of his head, and he found himself unable to think.

Rory stepped up to Killian and stood close. "They wear the sigil of the Maere," he murmured. Killian's eyes snapped to his brother's face, which was stricken with shock and wariness.

Yes. That's exactly what it was. However, the Maere was just a myth. A tale told to young warriors to give them motivation and fortify dreams of might.

According to legend, the Maere was a group of assassins trained in the art of shadows and secrets whose purpose was to keep the balance between gods and men.

They were god-hunters.

As far as Killian had known up until that very moment, they were entirely made up.

The dark-haired woman stood before him patiently, watching the war on his face. The war between logic and fairy tales, between confusion and awe. Rage and wanting.

"Who are you?" he growled, clenching his fists to keep his hands from shaking.

She gave him a calm, deadly smile. "How rude of me, of course. My name is Neve D'aeth and these are my companions."

Neve.

She told him her name, and the word felt like a stab to the heart for no other reason than it was beautiful and it belonged to *her.*

"Are you—" he couldn't say the words. Couldn't ask her if she and her *companions* were a bedtime story. The Maere. Gods, he couldn't say it.

She seemed to read his very thoughts. Her graceful hand gestured to their camp. "Come. We have much to discuss."

~

Sitting on a tree stump near the fire, Killian's knee bounced in annoyance. Neve led them into her camp, told them to make themselves comfortable, and then disappeared into a tent. The rest of her group went about their business as if the Cadre was invisible, as if they weren't sitting there in a clump of grumpy, hunched muscles and barely contained violence.

When he'd heard that they'd be spending their day hunting thieves, it energized him in a way he hadn't felt in five years. He'd been born to be a warrior. From the moment he could walk, he was in combat lessons.

In Eodia, a person was born into their fate.

If a person were born into a family of bakers, they'd be a baker. If a girl's mother was a courtesan, she'd grow up to warm the beds of paying customers.

The very path of his life had been decided for him before he was even old enough to utter a word.

Killian knew no other life.

He was *good* at his job. Very good. His body was as lethal as the weapons he carried, forged, and honed to perfection. Tall, covered in hard muscle, with a talent for violence, he was unquestionably the archetype of danger.

All that coiled-up aggression had been *dying* to be unfurled upon unsuspecting thieves, but now the job was done, and that tension had nowhere to be released.

It was easier to be angry at this group of people for stealing his thunder than it was for him to face the thought of who they could be.

He'd grown up absolutely enchanted by tales of the Maere.

In the old tongue, "Maere" was often translated as "nightmare". They were the world's best hunters, known to be the only force able to outsmart the gods. Their number was always thirteen, no more and no less.

 It was said that they could speak every known language, move with the shadows like smoke incarnate, were immune to minor magics, and each had the might of ten men and therefore never lost a battle.

It was also said that they were the size of titans, but looking around the camp, Killian saw that this was untrue. They all looked... normal. Maybe they moved with a little more grace than the average person, but perfectly normal.

So, either the legends about The Maere were largely overblown, or these people were wearing the emblem as imposters.

Killian had so many questions, and he was at the end of his patience. He ran a hand over the coarse texture of his short beard and released a quiet rumble of frustration from his throat.

He was eyeing the tent Neve disappeared into, weighing how reckless it might be to storm in there uninvited and demand answers, when the canvas door flap parted, and she emerged.

His back straightened, and every thought fell right out of his head.

She wore a loose white linen shirt that, despite its shapelessness, did nothing to conceal the devastating hint of her breasts beneath it. She'd tucked it into a pair of light brown leather breeches that were molded to the curves of her waist and hips, the beckoning roundness of her ass. Her hair was piled high on her head, showing the milky swoop of her neck, and when her eyes rested on him, he realized his mouth had dropped open, and he was openly gaping at her.

"What's the matter with you?" Arran whispered, and Killian elbowed his First General in the ribs with a satisfying jolt.

He stood as she approached and the Cadre once again followed his lead. Killian could feel their uncertainty; it rolled off of them like waves of heat. He just hoped that Neve couldn't sense it as well.

She gestured towards a table laden with food: fruit, cheese, crusty bread, and wine. "Can I offer you something to eat?" she asked.

Killian felt Gillis and Logan take a step towards the table, but he kept his eyes on Neve as he raised his hand- a command for his men to stop, which they did without question.

"I think we'll take some answers first."

A small smile touched her lips as she poured herself a chalice of wine, so vibrantly red that it looked like fresh blood. Turning back to him, she raised the cup to her lips and took a sip, never moving her eyes from his face.

She nodded. "Certainly."

She lowered herself down onto a tree stump and *lounged* on it, resting her cup on her knee, the picture of relaxation. Such ease only served to make Killian and the Cadre more unsettled. But they all sat back down around the fire without being asked.

She looked at each of the men in turn, sizing them up, as if measuring their strength against hers. The woman regarded Killian last and touched her tongue to the corner of her mouth where there was a small cut. A closer look had Killian noticing a bruise forming on her cheekbone and darker bruises blossoming on her neck where the man she'd killed had strangled her.

Despite himself, he felt a twinge of rage at the hands that marred that beautiful throat. Kilian swallowed hard and, with monumental effort, reminded himself of why he was here, the job he needed to complete.

He leaned forward, his elbows on his knees. "What business do you have in Hythe?"

She didn't miss a beat. "My companions and I are traveling."

"Where?"

"We're following the changing leaves of Autumn." She gestured at the tree-tops, which were indeed beginning to burnish around the edges.

Killian bristled. "Horse shit."

Neve laughed, a sparkling and amused sound. "Perhaps you're right."

"So?"

She tilted her head. "So what, Killian?"

He clenched his fists. "You assured me of answers."

"You haven't asked the right questions."

They stared at each other for a moment, the air between them was thick with challenge.

Her finger circled the rim of her chalice slowly, waiting.

He blew out a breath and decided to leave all pretense behind. "Are you The Maere?"

Something in her eyes changed, like a lake turning to ice upon a sudden winter deep freeze. There was no smile now. No mischief played on her face. Nothing but cold, resolute calm as she uttered just one word: "Yes."

A chill ran down his spine and the hairs on the back of his neck stood on end. There was no lie in that word; he could feel in his bones that it was true. He sensed his Cadre fighting to maintain their composure.

Out of the corner of his eye, he saw Rory's hand drifting toward the sword at his hip.

Killian watched as Neve noticed it, too.

She made a tutting noise with her tongue and gave Rory the slightest shake of her head. "We're not going to do anything careless today, are we, friend?" she asked.

Rory looked to Killian, perhaps as backup or permission to strike. His brother's ears were flushed red with fury, but Killian gave him a pointed look and a head shake of his own.

"No," Killian answered for his brother, who begrudgingly moved his hand back to his lap. "No, we're not going to do anything careless today."

"Good," she said and waited.

"I think you owe us an explanation."

Neve D'Aeth chuckled, actually *chuckled*. "I'd heard you were arrogant, but I must admit I didn't expect you to be quite this presumptuous. I wouldn't exactly say that we *owe* you anything, would you?"

Killian's blood heated. "Presumptuous? From a woman who *presumes* to know anything about me?"

"Are the rumors of your arrogance untrue?"

He felt utterly out of his depth. In an admittedly feeble attempt to take control of the situation, he gave her an arched eyebrow smile, defaulting to charm in the hopes of disarming her defenses a little.

"Would you like to find out, Neve?"

Despite himself, her name felt like a blessing on his tongue.

She drained her chalice of wine, a glossy sheen left on her lips which she lazily licked off. She wordlessly held her cup out and within an instant, the biggest man in her group refilled it for her and then went back to his business.

Killian observed it all.

She was showing her power, showing him and his Cadre that she was in charge. He imagined that the group behind her would do much more for her than simply fill her wine; he was certain that, without hesitation, they would slaughter each and every one of his men just as they had done to the thieves.

"I think," she drawled, "You're quite good at showing us all your cards at once."

His gaze rested again on the black and blue bruises dancing around her throat, simply to remind himself that she was human.

"Why are you here?" he asked.

She paused, watching him. It was the first time that she seemed not to have an immediate answer, as if she had to stop and weigh different options in her mind.

Her eyes flicked to his men, who were all growing restless, and she rested her gaze on Rory. Killian assumed it was to make sure his hand didn't once again drift to his weapon.

"We're hunting," she replied, leveling that cool stare at his brother for another moment before returning her attention to Killian.

He packed that observation away for later.

"Who are you hunting?"

"Not who. *What.*"

He swallowed. "You're going to make me beg for answers, aren't you, love?"

She set her cup on the ground and gracefully shifted in her seat, spreading her knees and leaning forward on them with her elbows. "I don't mind a man who begs."

Lightning shot through his spine and he heard Gillis choke out a surprised cough.

It was a monumental task to try not to show his feelings on his face.

Inside, he was a thunderstorm; all of his nerves were sizzling. He didn't know whether he wanted to draw his sword or grab her by the shirt and haul her closer to him.

Recovering, he cleared his throat. "*What* are you hunting?"

She leaned back, satisfied with herself. "Gods."

Every fiery feeling that flooded him seconds ago immediately froze and his deadly warrior instinct returned.

"Impossible. There haven't been gods in Eodia for centuries."

When Queen Nyx died, not only had Eodia been cut off from foreign nations and trade, but it was also the precise moment that the old gods stopped listening.

The screaming prayers of Eodia went unanswered until, finally, the people just stopped praying.

To Killian, the gods were more folklore. Myth. Bedtime stories.

Neve shrugged. "In my experience, nothing is impossible and nothing is ever as it seems. Sometimes myths are true," she gestured at herself and the rest of the Maere.

A shiver crawled up Killian's back. "How do you know there are gods here?"

"It's what we do. What we've always done." She gazed up at the sky, searching the clouds. "Something is stirring here. Unbalanced." Neve turned her gaze back to Killian. "You haven't felt it?"

He shook his head and deadpanned, "I've been in a dungeon for five years."

"How did you get here?" Rory asked out of turn.

Killian clenched his teeth; his brother had zero finesse and worse impulse control than his own. They were finally getting somewhere in this conversation, and Killian wasn't too keen on Rory's big mouth being the thing that ended it.

Neve's lips quirked, but there was no humor there. She regarded Rory with an indefatigable coldness. "What does it matter to you?"

Killian watched Rory's knuckles go white as he clenched his fists. "No one comes to Eodia, and no one leaves. The tides of the Great Sea around make a voyage to the Island impossible. So, how did you get here?"

Unbothered, she examined her fingernails. "As I already said... nothing is impossible."

"That still doesn't answer–"

"Stand down, Rory," Killian interrupted in a low, warning voice. He cut his brother with a brutal glare.

Red-faced with rage, Rory shot to his feet and stormed off to the horses.

Killian might have been mercurial, but his brother was an entirely different breed of hothead. The fact that Killian seemed to be unintentionally usurping Rory's command only made matters worse.

Killian stifled his groan and sighed, returning his attention to the striking and terrifying woman before him. The rest of the Maere seemed to pay no mind to Rory and his outburst, but Killian sensed that they'd move in a heartbeat to put his brother down should it happen again.

The line between friend and foe here was very, very thin.

Neve stood, moving toward the table of food and drink. All eyes watched her as she took the platter of fruit, cheese, and bread and brought it to the Cadre.

She held it out to Arran, who looked first to Killian for permission and, upon a subtle nod of approval, accepted the platter from her with a gracious bow of his head.

The barest smile graced her full lips and she turned to the table again, filled her cup with that vibrant wine, pouring a second as well. Killian sat ramrod straight as Neve stepped into his space.

Her legs brushed against his knees as she stood before him, above him.

She offered him the cup and he looked up into her face. This close, in the natural light of day, he could indeed say that she was the most beautiful creature he'd ever seen.

The curls of her dark hair were like a vapor around her head, with a few unruly tendrils falling from their pins. A delicate nose that was slightly upturned, with just a handful of freckles like stars across her nose and cheeks. Skin like cream with a natural peach blush around the edges from spending days out in the elements.

And those green-gold eyes... and, fucking hell, that mouth.

She was all soft curves, not a sharp angle on her. But beneath, inside, he could see she was hard and cold and deadly as ice. Unmovable. Unbreakable.

Neve held his gaze steadily. Killian didn't know how long he'd been lost in his head, lost in her. He swallowed and took the chalice from her hand, feeling her finger trail against his and the faintest scrape of her long, sharp nails.

An offering and a threat.

She raised her wine, "To possibility," she said.

They drank deeply together, watching each other over the rims of their cups as they did.

The wine was like nothing he'd ever tasted. Sweet, yet dry and full-bodied. It was vivid like he could taste the sun that had warmed the grapes and the vines they'd ripened on. Neve gave him a look like his pleasure in the taste of the wine was written all over his face. He was sure it was. She seemed almost content to see it.

Moving smoothly as mist, she bent and took an apple from the tray that was being greedily passed between Logan and Fraser as they stuffed food into their mouths. They barely noticed as she slithered past them, but Killian was watching her intently.

He couldn't stop watching her.

As she walked, he could see the outline of hidden daggers, one in each of her boots. A feeling he couldn't name, something between distrust and envy, came over him as Neve approached Rory near the horses.

A graceful hand brushed along Willow's mane as she greeted Killian's mare, who immediately lowered her head and relaxed easily into the stranger's touch.

Neve stood with her back to the camp, speaking so low that Killian couldn't hear a word. He watched his brother's face regarding her in naked defiance. She reached out her hand and offered him the apple resting in her palm.

Rory looked as if he might be so bold as to slap it away. But, then, she said something else that leeched the color from Rory's face, melted away any arrogance and bravado, and left him looking utterly unnerved, terrified even.

He cast his eyes to the ground and gingerly took the apple from her hand. When she walked away, turning back to Killian, her face betrayed nothing of the words she might have spoken an instant before, stoic and cold with just the faintest sparkle of mischief in her eyes.

The restless groan of thunder rumbled in the distance, startling Killian from his watchful gaze. He looked up at the sky and indeed saw angry, dark clouds rolling in. It was just as well.

Full days and nights without cold or rain were few and far between in Eodia, keeping the landscape green, the sea raging, and the skies almost permanently gray. It made the dapples of the sun in between downpours that much more precious.

The ride back to Lowbarrow was going to be stormy and uncomfortable. More uncomfortable still would be the report he'd have to make to the Cavalry, who served as the middlemen between the Cadre and the Highborns, about not having vanquished the bandits themselves and instead spending the afternoon eating and drinking with the Maere.

There would be punishment in store for him and his warriors. The Highborns would certainly not believe this tale. He might as well tell them that they'd ridden off into the sunset on unicorns; they'd accept both stories with equal incredulity.

Another crack of thunder, closer now.

As if she'd read his thoughts, Neve nodded toward the sky, holding his stare with that relentless, predatory focus of hers.

"Your ride back to Lowbarrow will take hours in the storm and that pretty horse of yours won't be too happy about it," she said. "I think it's time to say farewell."

He wanted to argue, but he bit his tongue against it. She was right. No matter how much he wanted more answers, he could see that she'd given him everything she'd been willing to today. The ride back to Lowbarrow would indeed be arduous.

Still, it was an effort to stand and peel himself away from her. He opened his mouth to say something, but she turned from him and walked back to her tent, without so much as a glance over her shoulder. Just as she'd left him the night before at the tavern, he remained wanting more and feeling seven shades of inferior.

Right, then. Onward.

4

Neve D'Aeth peeled off her wet clothes as fat, fierce raindrops pitter-pattered down on the roof of her canvas tent.

The Maere moved their camp after the warriors left, just as the skies opened up and poured down onto them. The rain was cold, but she didn't mind.

She and The Maere moved quickly, traveling northwest to the edge of the Dark Forest- a place of untold dangers, vicious beasts, old magic, and death.

Neve was unbothered by such places.

She chose it on purpose.

Tomorrow, at first light, they would enter the forest and see for themselves which grim legends were still alive amongst the gloom.

Once undressed, she wrapped herself in a thick blanket, the wool was so old and worn from use that it was soft as down against her icy skin. She sat at a small table where a single candle burned, a map was spread across the surface before her in the center of the table, and a small stack of ancient books rested near her elbow.

Neve tip-toed her nimble fingers along the path on the map they'd already explored: from the southeastern coast of Eodia, through the Blackstack Mountains, and to the fork of the River Fyne, where The Maere had gone west to Hythe and Neve had gone north to Lowbarrow.

To meet the *famous* Killian Grey.

In her experience, famous men were usually never as impressive as the stories made them seem. Usually, they were

lackluster, dull around the edges, and worn out like the wool of
the blanket she held close around her shoulders.

Famous men were usually the type to tell her how *strong*
and *brave* they believed themselves to be while trying to sneak a
hand up her skirt.

Famous men usually thought of themselves as heroes.

Alas, Killian wasn't famous for being a hero.

No, his *lineage* was famous for being heroic.

The Great Greys, knights of House Lyra, had served the
royal family with honor for millennia until it was all snuffed out
on that fateful night three hundred years ago.

Killian, in his own right, instead, was quite famous for
being savage on the killing field. Unrivaled in brute strength and
combat skill, people spoke his name on every continent she'd
traveled.

Killian Grey bested one thousand men at once.

Killian Grey destroyed a village with his bare hands.

No one could beat Killian Grey in combat.

Killian Grey was a torturer.

Killian Grey was a murderer.

It made her wonder, if he was such a force to be reckoned
with, why was he doing the bidding of lesser men?

The killer she'd met at the tavern certainly looked the
part. He was huge, a wall of muscle, and at least a head and a half
taller than her. He had a scruff of beard along a sharp jawline,
long-fingered hands adorned with simple silver rings, and the
ghost-white outline of scars. His mid-brown hair was long
enough to fall across his brow, just above a pair of steel blue eyes.

She'd lounged in the shadows watching him that night in
Lowbarrow, and while he was certainly arrogant, he was not like
most of the famous men she'd met.

He was gracious to the barmaids who brought him his
drinks, gave his companions genuine smiles, and winked at the
girls who blushed as they passed his table.

But it was in the quiet moments, when he thought no one
was watching, that she'd seen his mask slip. Beneath the
bravado, he was someone else entirely.

Deep sadness and a loneliness with no end seemed to consume him; it swirled around him like a ghost. He looked like a man who'd lost everything. Rudderless.

She'd watched him glance toward the door a handful of times as if desperately wanting to leave, yet he stayed.

Perhaps because there was nothing for him to go home to. Perhaps because he'd spent five years in the solitude of a dungeon and he couldn't stomach the thought of spending another endless night alone.

Moving through the room to approach him had been deliberate. She'd captured his eye immediately, as she'd known she would, and she felt the weight of his stare as she let him watch her.

The desperation came off of him in waves so thick, she could almost smell it.

Orchestrating the meeting today was just as easy.

A group of raiders had been following the Maere since the Blackstack Mountains.

So, Neve herself left a message for the Cadre, pretending to be the Cavalry, and sent them to Hythe.

Encouraging the thieves to strike The Maere was as simple as flashing a bit of gold and jewels when she knew they were watching, letting it glint in the brief sunshine of the early afternoon.

She smiled to herself. Her timing was *impeccable* today.

Neve opened a book from the top of the stack before her, the binding creased and cracked. Its gilded title long since worn off, the cover was dark blue and threadbare, and the pages inside were brittle and smelled of time-worn paper and, faintly, of vanilla. The title page was adorned with a simple line drawing of a crescent moon and clusters of stars above an ivory tower.

This book had traveled with her across the world, had been in her possession since she was born, and had been written long, *long* before

She sensed movement outside her tent before she heard the mud-squelched footsteps. A steady female voice quietly called her name.

"Come in," Neve replied easily.

Ducking through the tent door, balancing a stack of dry clothes in her hand, was a tall woman with braided copper hair and dark, golden skin.

Neve did not have many friends.

No, friendship was complicated and intimate, dangerous. Tender feelings for others made a person an easy mark, something she could not afford in her position.

But, she supposed, the effortless rapport she found with Cara was the closest thing to the friendship she had.

Cara set the stack of laundry in front of Neve on the table. She gestured for Cara to sit down on the chair opposite her. The redhead gave Neve a faint bow of the head and sat, sighing with pleasure after a day on her feet.

"Where is he?" Neve asked.

Cara shook her head and offered a low chuckle, her brown eyes glittering with amusement in the candlelight. "A quarter mile east of us. Making camp in the cave we passed."

Neve smiled. "Stealth was never part of his legend."

"Is recklessness part of his legend? What man in his right mind would follow The Maere into the Dark Forest?"

"A man whose curiosity outweighs his fear of death," Neve responded.

She'd known that he was following them immediately. She could hear him in the rain, his boots in the mud, his horse huffing at him in annoyance.

More than that, she *sensed* him, feeling the weight of his eyes and the shift of the air as he moved through the storm.

Above all, she'd anticipated his pursuit. Neve had given him just enough information to pique his interest without satisfying it and Killian Grey was not a man accustomed to being left unsatisfied.

She was luring him into the forest.

~

The cave was dank and offered little warmth. Torrential rain soaked Killian to the bone, his drenched clothes now laid out on the stone floor near his bedroll in the hope that they might be dry enough before morning.

Perhaps he hadn't thought his plan through, especially now that he realized he'd followed The Maere straight to the edge of the Dark Forest.

Admittedly, following them was a last-minute decision. A thought that came to him suddenly, but with a power so intense, he could focus on nothing besides the need to pursue. The urge sank its hooks into him and he found he was inexplicably and infuriatingly unable to compel himself to do anything but give in.

Perhaps it was curiosity.

Perhaps, on a more basic level, the conversation with Neve at the campground was the first time in five years he'd felt anything besides numb grief. And that... was worth its weight in gold.

Perhaps it was as simple an explanation as Killian wanting to taste freedom for once in his life. To make a decision that belonged to him alone. An opportunity for agency in a world in which choice was denied to even the most mighty of men.

The Cadre had ridden for perhaps twenty minutes before the nagging in the back of Killian's mind got the best of him and he abruptly stopped.

Hands reached for weapons as the Cadre looked around the King's Road for threats, unsure why their leader had come to a halt.

"I'm going to follow them," he stated, rain plastering his hair to his head and running in rivulets down his angular face.

"Why?" Arran asked.

"She knows more than she's telling us."

"Of course she does. But what's that got to do with us?"

Killian shook his head. "I'm not sure. But I need to know more."

"No," Rory interjected. He'd been quiet since he'd taken the apple from Neve's hand. He still had the look of a haunted man, pale and shaky, but the intrinsic defiance was returning to his eyes. "No. I'm in command now and you're not following them."

Killian's anger flared and he shifted in his saddle so he was facing his brother.

"You've been acting like an embarrassment all day," he said in a low, lethal voice.

"And you've been thinking with your cock."

In an instant, Killian's fist backhanded across Rory's face, sending his brother off his horse and crashing into the mud.

Killian dismounted Willow with fluid grace and prowled toward Rory. He reached down, grabbed a good handful of his brother's hair, and hauled him to his feet, holding him there.

"You forget yourself, *brother*," Killian growled. "You forget who *I* am. You don't command me. Keep your fucking mouth shut or you'll be swallowing your teeth."

Rory's face was bleeding from where Killian's rings had ground against his flesh, his eyes were twin flames of rage, but he kept quiet. In Killian's heart, there was no love for his brother in that moment, only fury.

He yanked harder on Rory's hair, causing a hiss of pain to release from behind clenched teeth.

"Say you understand."

Rory swallowed hard, outmatched, and his lip curled in disdain as he said: "I understand."

The rest of the Cadre knew not to say a word, not even Arran uttered a sound of caution or question as Killian left them on the King's Road.

But he felt their eyes on him. Their hurt. Their confusion.

For that, on some level, he felt remorse. But it was not enough to drown out his need to make a choice of his own for once. Even if it killed him, he'd die knowing it was a mistake he owned.

Something deep inside of him was stirring, his mind swirling around Neve's words...

Nothing is impossible.

Nothing is ever as it seems.

Sometimes myths are real.

Now, alone in a musty cave just on the perimeter of the Dark Forest, shivering against the storm, Killian had to concede that he wasn't exactly prepared for whatever journey he'd set himself on.

He wasn't concerned about food or water; he could easily hunt and forage along the way. But all he had was one set of clothes, his armor, and a handful of weapons.

He supposed a man of his talents didn't need much else. But he knew the terrors that dwelt in the Dark Forest. If that was where The Maere was leading him, he feared his reckless choice to follow could indeed lead to his doom.

He'd cleared a corner of old leaves and brush for his bedroll and settled in for the night. Outside, the storm was still raging; great sheets of rain, heavy wind, and thunder sounded like the stomping feet of an angry god.

He was thankful for shelter, thankful that there was a cozy bank of trees just outside of the cave for Willow to rest beneath, but this cave was less than ideal. Everything about it reminded him of the dungeon: the smell, the cold stone, the hard floor, the solitude.

Perhaps it was too soon to have brought himself into another bout of isolation.

But if he was being honest, being alone in a cave was better than being alone in his cottage.

The night of his homecoming, he could absolutely not bear the thought of spending the night there. Could not fathom what it would do to him to sleep in the bed where his wife had died, to pass by his sons' room ... no.

No, the cave was better.

His cottage once was as sweet and idyllic a home as any man in Eodia could imagine, but now he'd sooner see it burned to the ground than live there.

On top of everything else, there was Neve.

His brother hadn't been wrong; Killian certainly *did* want Neve. Indeed, he could scarcely remember a time in his life when he'd felt so absolutely stumbled with want.

He felt a deep and oddly primal need to know her, to understand her, to make sense of her. In all of his days, most of which he'd spent with the most vicious of warriors, he'd never met a person so unmovable.

Neve D'Aeth seemed to be made of cold steel and secrets. He knew he could not bend such steel, could not break it. But he wanted her secrets nonetheless.

So, he followed.

5

Neve sat before a crackling fire as the first gray light of dawn began to break. The rain finally stopped and a thick mist lingered behind. The heat of the fire before her was hearty and welcome after a cold night. The scent of wet earth and woodsmoke clung heavily to the oppressive, cool fog.

She held a cup of near-boiling mint tea in her hands as she watched the world around her begin to wake. She drank deeply, the steam warming her face, enveloping her in its scent, scalding her mouth happily.

She loved this time of day, loved to watch the great awakening of the morning. The Maere shifted in their tents, birds balanced on high tree tops complaining to each other, and the Dark Forest just ahead began to stir.

She could see movement in the forest through the ground clouds, slithering and skittering darkness. Faint growls and snarls could be heard in the distance, which was barely muffled by the heavy foliage and primordial trees.

Eodia as a whole felt off, *wrong*; Neve sensed it the moment she and The Maere approached its rocky and impossible shores. It was as if a veil clung to it, a mighty spider's web of sticky wickedness keeping the entire Island wrapped up like a fly waiting to be swallowed.

The forest felt hungry.

There were fell creatures inside; beasts and wraiths, banshees and goblins, and monsters with no names.

Yet Neve knew that whatever lived in the Dark Forest bent its knee to some even greater evil. The very evil that she'd come to Eodia to hunt down.

The very evil that she believed had also been hunting *her* since the day she was born.

Neve D'Aeth was not afraid of evil.

She was ready to welcome it with the cold embrace of her violence.

The sun was rising, but the murky sky promised no warm light today. It would remain gray and ominous until nightfall.

She rose on nimble legs and, with her cup of tea in hand, sauntered toward the entrance to the Dark Forest- a gaping maw formed by two twisted, great trees curved inward toward each other like an archway.

Sipping her tea, letting it singe her tongue, she took a steady step into the mouth of the forest. The temperature dropped around her and the wood seemed to take a deep breath, like the anticipation of a lover in the night.

Malevolence beckoned to her.

Come to us, it seemed to say, *you belong here.*

All of her senses were wildly alert, excited, even. She knew that the eyes of the forest were pinned on her and waiting.

The forest was so lush with trees that the sky was barely visible through the umbrella of branches above. Early autumn color was beginning to pepper through the blanket of green, leaves falling in a drowsy pattern to the wet ground.

She'd learned long ago that there was beauty to be found even in the most villainous of places..

There was a faint trail down what appeared to be the center of the forest floor, but it was overgrown with reaching roots and vines, sure to wrap around an unsuspecting foot.

A slinking shadow moved beside her, with the sound of chattering teeth. Neve let it come to her.

She took another lazy sip from her cup, as a bony hand crawled up her shoulder.

She glanced at that hand; skin the color of ash, sharp and rotting black fingernails tickling along the details of her leather armor. Neve did not flinch.

"I know you," the wraith whispered, its breath a cough of dust against the length of her neck. She did not shiver. It stood behind her and moved its other scraping hand across her lower back, around her waist, to rest against her stomach, holding her close to it like a paramour. "Where have you been?"

She took another sip of her tea, letting the wraith sway gently back and forth with her in its arms, rocking her as if in a lullaby.

"If you truly know me, you would know where I've been," she said to the creature.

The wraith's laugh was another plume of dust as it nuzzled its face into the hair at the top of her head, scenting her.

She knew what that face looked like; if she cared to turn around, she'd see a skull covered only by a thin layer of soot-gray skin, empty eyes, no nose, and a mouth full of yellow, spiked teeth.

She didn't need to look, she had seen its kind before.

"You have been gone," it said. "There are many who have searched for you. And look! Now you are here. With me." Its fingers caressed her like a prize.

"I bring you a gift today," she said. "A gift for you and the others of your forest."

The wraith groaned hungrily, pressing her body against it. "You offer yourself to us, Neve D'Aeth? At last?"

Neve sipped her cup and shook her head. "I belong to no one. But I do offer a gift."

It tightened its grip on her, a threat and a warning. "Oh, but we want *you*..."

"You cannot have me," Neve said firmly.

The wraith gave her a monstrous hiss and licked its black tongue up the side of her neck.

"What could you offer us of any value besides yourself?"

"A challenge," she replied, speaking loud enough for all the forest to hear.

She knew every creature was listening, lurking. Her free hand found the wraith's, interlacing her fingers with those gnarled knuckles, gently drawing its claws away from her body. Her touch relaxed its rigid bones.

"A warrior has followed us here. He will follow us into your forest," she said.

"Bah. We care not for *men*."

"You care for blood. It is blood I offer."

"You want us to destroy him? For you?"

"I want you to try. The Maere will not interfere. *I* will not interfere. Do your worst and unleash upon him."

She slipped her fingers out of the wraith's hand and finally turned to face it. Nothing but ash and bone and gnashing teeth.

"You offer this to us freely?" It asked with utter yearning.

She could feel the other dark beasts waiting, the forest itself leaning in towards her with greedy want.

Neve reached up, caressed the wraith's empty skull face, and cupped its chin in her hand.

"There is always a price," she said.

She drew the blade from her thigh and cleanly thrust it up through the wraith's jaw in the space of a breath.

In her experience, dead things could always die again.

And the wraith did, choking out one final word, "*You,*" before disintegrating into a pile of dirt at her feet.

Turning back to the forest, she spoke to those still in shadow, hiding their faces from her brutality.

"Do as I ask. What's left when you're done with the warrior belongs to me. If you refuse..." She wiped her dagger clean and took the last lingering sip of her tea, which had remained steady in her other hand amidst her casual slaughter. "I will turn this place to ash and you all with it."

~

His family was dead. Murdered.

The stench of lethal magic polluted his home.

Without thought, some primal instinct commanding his every move, he prowled to the stable and leaped onto his horse.

The Mages. It had to have been the Mages he'd passed along the King's Road on his way home.

Perhaps he'd wronged one of their kind and they'd come for revenge. It was likely. At the behest of the Highborns, Killian's hands were often covered in the blood of people who didn't necessarily deserve it.

He could not think about it. His sole focus in that foggy instant was on the Mages.

Because he'd smelled the magic.

Because there was no one else upon whom to find vengeance.

He found them easily enough.

Huddled together in a makeshift camp not far from where he'd passed them on the Road, the Mages were settling in for a cold night, oblivious to the swift hand of death that was coming for them.

His approach was soundless and he unleashed himself on the sleepy camp. Sword out, teeth bared, letting loose every savage and dark part of himself.

Seeking. Raging, the blood pounding in his head as his blade found purchase again and again and again.

They were all dead before a single one of them could scream their terror to the night wind.

He was covered head-to-toe in Mage blood when he was found wandering the next morning.

If he and his Cadre weren't so important to the Highborns' judicial system, Killian's sentence for murder would have been his execution.

As it was, he was sentenced to five years in the dungeon for what they called an "unsanctioned kill".

Nearly feral with grief and madness, they'd kept him in chains for the first year of his confinement. He still had the scars around his wrists and ankles from that time. Eternal, inimitable proof that he once lost himself, lost everything.

Five years for his frenzy.

The dark cool of his cell became his only friend, his only constant. Aside, of course, from the endless grief. And guilt.

Dawn came and went, and Killian woke late. The damp hadn't fully lifted from his clothes and he fought a cringe as he pulled them up his body and over his skin.

The world was blanketed in fog as he emerged from the cave, a vicious cold humidity that did nothing to warm his already chilled bones.

There was no way to know if The Maere had already moved on; the mist was so thick he could barely see three paces in front of him.

He packed up his meager belongings and took Willow's reins, leading her along with him as he made his way west toward where he last scouted them the night before.

His footsteps thunked wetly in the mud as he walked. Noting it, he tried to walk more softly. Spying on them wouldn't be very easy if the noise of his boots carried and alerted the Maere to his lurking.

The brume was so full it felt like he was swimming through clouds. Eyes searching, he relied on the faint trail beneath him and the even fainter position of the sun above to orient himself, although the sun was little more than a ghost in the nebulous sky.

The storm left a clean scent on the autumn-turning foliage; the green smell of fading summer mixed with the crisp, papery perfume of dying leaves. Indeed, the cold air promised a swift autumn and a frigid coming winter.

The ground was suddenly thick with tracks, and as he moved further, he saw the remnants of small bonfires. This must have been where The Maere spent the night, already packed up and deserted.

How long into the morning had he slept? How far gone were they? Cursing under his breath, he paused, peering through the mist.

Just ahead was the great yawning entrance of the Dark Forest, and beneath that ominous archway, he spied the outline of a horse and a rider.

Lethal focus slowed the blood in his veins and he reached for his sword. The steel in this palm was cold comfort. A gust of wind shifted the fog, clearing the path of his vision.

Even without a glimpse of her face, he knew exactly who the rider was.

Sitting atop a brilliant and beautiful white horse, Neve D'Aeth appeared to be lagging behind the rest of The Maere. Not too far behind, as he could see the rest of them a few paces ahead.

Her dark hair was plaited in an intricate braid down the length of her spine. She wore leather armor that was perfectly fitted to her form with ornate epaulets on her shoulders that looked to be adorned with a mixture of shards of metal and sharp stones that glittered like diamonds even in the paltry daylight. He could see twin daggers, one sheathed to each of her thighs in holsters decorated with the same metal and stones as her shoulders.

She looked wicked and ready for war.

Killian swallowed hard as she moved deeper into the forest, following The Maere. The sight of her both thrilled and unnerved him.

What unnerved him further was the Dark Forest itself. It was a foreboding place. The trees themselves were gnarled like great hands of the dead, at once beckoning him and warning him to stay out.

He'd heard stories of the things that called the Dark Forest home. Beasts so huge and ferocious they could take out a whole army as easily as blinking, sprites that could wield their mischievous magic to make a man forget his own name, vicious banshees whose screams had been known to cause madness, wraiths that hungered for souls to join them in the dance of death. And worse.

Despite the certain doom that awaited just ahead, an eager and deadly smile crept across Killian Grey's lips. Fighting was as natural to him as breathing, and he hadn't had a proper battle in half a decade.

A reckless part of him hoped that the Dark Forest would unleash its worst upon his sword. His muscles craved the strain and his knuckles were eager to become battered and bloody.

He watched as Neve casually moved deeper into the forest, her body swaying invitingly with each step her horse took, until both she and The Maere were too far beyond the trees for him to see.

Killian waited a few moments before mounting his horse and following, giving enough space between himself and The Maere so as not to rouse their suspicion.

His skin prickled with warning as he crossed the threshold into the Dark Forest; the air was colder within and felt charged with evil.

The journey through the Dark Forest, from what he'd heard, could take days. It was lush and thick, and every step was treacherous- the forest floor covered in ancient roots and vines, the path through often hidden or non-existent. As much as he wanted to charge forward into the gloom, he'd have to go slowly and carefully, if not for his own sake, but Willow's as well. His horse didn't seem nearly as spooked as he was by the forest, a fact that he took comfort in.

Inside the forest, there was a cacophony of sound: the rustling of leaves, the creaking of old trees leaning against one another, and the skittering of small animals in the underbrush.

But his spine stiffened when he heard other things, blackish things. Growling, snarling, the uncomfortable noise of sharp teeth grinding together. Killian peered around, trying to determine where those sounds were coming from, but the forest was too dense to see anything but the woodland itself.

His senses sharpened with each slow mile he descended into the thicket. Killian had the distinct feeling of being watched...no, being *hunted.*

His hand rested on the pommel of his sword, reassured by its weight and the battle-worn notches in the metal. He ran his long, calloused fingers over the grooves again and again, heartening himself against the pressing gravity of being *prey* in this place. He knew he was being followed, just as he was following The Maere, but it was the anticipation of the attack that was gradually bringing him to the edge of reason.

And yet, no attack came.

Morning faded into the afternoon, the awareness of being stalked only increasing as each hour passed. He'd entirely lost track of the Maere ahead of him. He could only hope he was still going in the right direction, that he was still following their path.

What a waste it would be to make it through the Dark Forest only to find them gone and he would be left with nothing but nagging questions and yearning.

But first, the task of making it out of the Dark Forest whole.

He didn't dare look behind him, not because he feared what might be following, but because the wildwood was so dense and dark that a simple glance elsewhere could completely disorient him. And then he'd be well and truly lost. There was no true north in this jungle, no way to see the sky or the sun, a place where not even the wind could move freely.

Despite the chill in the air, a sweat broke on Killian's brow. The forest was closing in on him. It had been hours moving in the same slow and endless direction, and yet he felt as if he'd barely covered any ground. Every curve of the trail resulted in more forest that looked exactly the same and it was smothering him.

The scent of dry leaves was beginning to feel like a hand around his throat. This forest was as much of a prison as the dungeon. He loosened the collar of his tunic beneath his leather armor, his Adam's apple bobbing, and still found no relief from the relentless feeling of suffocation.

He pulled back on Willow's reins and she came to a grateful stop. Killian raised his face to the sky, gulping down a deep breath of air. And another.

He wondered if Neve and The Maere felt as choked and small here as he did, or if this was a special hell saved up just for him. He took a swig from his water skin and poured a little over his hair and down his face. The cool trickle sent an instant iciness through his body and for a moment, he was able to breathe easier.

That's when he heard it.

The incessant muffled growling that had accompanied him along his journey so far was suddenly louder. Much louder.

Slowly, so slowly, Killian dropped his water skin back into his saddle bag and laid his hand on his sword, straightening up and rolling his shoulders back. His heartbeat slowed and a murderous calm took the place of the claustrophobic panic from a moment ago.

The danger was like a home; danger was family.

From the darkness emerged a mighty paw. A huge paw covered in black, tangled fur with yellowed claws. The paw itself was enormous, but a breath hitched in Killian's chest when the beast fully revealed itself and appeared from the shadows.

It was the largest creature he had ever seen.

Twice Killian's height on its four legs, it reminded him of a massive bear- but worse. Its eyes were glowing black coals and below its wet snout was an ugly gaping mouth with four rows of razor-sharp teeth between which were rotting strands of its last meal.

The beast smelled of death. On its hulking back stood a pair of tremendous, spiked wings, their tissue frayed and shredded with age.

Never taking his eyes from the monster in front of him, Killian drew his sword and leaned forward.

"Go, girl," he whispered to Willow.

He dismounted, dead leaves crunching underfoot, and his horse did as he asked, galloping off into the forest.

The beast paid no mind to the horse; its sole focus, it seemed, was on Killian.

He pinned his heels to the ground and stood tall, securing his grip on the worn and trustworthy leather of his sword hilt. The beast huffed through huge, wet nostrils and pawed at the dirt. Killian's eyes searched the behemoth for any obvious weaknesses, but it stood solid and menacing.

He wondered if those wings were strong enough to make the animal fly and he quickly decided that he didn't want to find out.

A growl rumbled from its throat, a growl that grew into a ghastly, nightmarish roar that split Killian's eardrums. He ground his teeth and bared them at the beast, staring at that toothsome, filthy mouth as it let loose its sounds of fury, snapping its jaws at him.

Here we go.

It charged at him. The great lumbering thing was slow, which was good news, but its size certainly made up for its lack of speed. Killian would have to be faster and more nimble on his feet.

He stood his ground, gripping his sword with two hands, his blood pulsing faster and faster the closer it came to him.

Steady now, steady.

He braced himself, fingers twitching, he could feel its reeking breath on his face. Just as it was about to barrel into him, Killian ducked and rolled on the ground beneath it, between its paws. He sliced into its front leg, spilling first blood, before popping back up to his feet on the other side of it.

It roared again. Killian guessed the sound was more from rage than pain, despite the trail of red spurting from its underside.

The beast charged and Killian shifted towards the same maneuver, but it guessed his move and pivoted. It swiped him with a giant paw, a claw ripping into his side as the impact sent Killian flying into the unforgiving trunk of an elm tree.

The air *whooshed* out of his lungs as he crashed to the ground. His wound bloomed and bled warmly right beneath his ribs. If the claw had caught him any higher, he'd be for the worms.

Scrambling to his feet, he wasn't able to form a thought before the monster crashed into him and bore him back to the ground. Unleashing a roar of his own, Killian blindly thrust his sword upward, driving it into the beast's belly.

For a bare second, it retreated, giving him enough time to get his legs beneath him and go after it. He brought his sword down and plunged it through the top of the thing's mammoth foot, bearing down and ripping through as much muscle and sinew as he could, hoping to render it useless and give himself an advantage.

Enraged, the beast screamed and used its other front leg to slam down on Killian's chest. Pain rocketed through his whole body and a rush of nausea hit him as he felt himself being crushed under the weight of the creature.

It was off balance now, its right leg entirely useless thanks to the onslaught of Killian's sword on its thigh and foot. A fact that would have been brilliant if it didn't mean that more of its weight was being held up by the left. The left leg that was now pressing him into the earth, wrecking him.

Its mouth lunged for him, biting the air mere inches from his nose. Killian took a ragged gasp and struck with his sword. He couldn't even see where he'd hit; he only knew that he had because of the stinking blood that rained down on him. It wasn't enough. The mouth lunged again and Killian was able to move just enough to shove his blade inward, breaking a few of those wicked fangs. He pulled his sword down, mangling its jaw.

The beast howled and shuffled backward just barely enough for Killian to roll out of its grip and to his feet. He was panting; he couldn't get air into his withered lungs fast enough. He was covered in sweat and blood, both his and the beast's. Gripping his sword with both hands, he bent his knees and readied himself for another attack.

With one ruined leg and a gushing, ghoulish mouth, it came at him with unrelenting force. Killian slashed and spun, spun and slashed, as quickly and brutally as his aching body would allow. More blood flowed, his boots sloshed in it, and yet the beast kept coming.

He had the vague sense that he was screaming, all of his muscles were on fire and he knew that soon the initial adrenaline would wear off and he'd be feeling the full damage of his injuries.

He needed to put this beast down before that happened. If not, he'd be a dead man.

With the flick of a claw, the beast flung him backward, sending him crashing into a tree again. Killian heard something crack as he hit the ground, and a sharp pain lanced through his left shoulder. He crawled to his knees, then, mercifully, back to his feet. Everything hurt.

Killian and the beast faced each other once more. Circling.

One last time.

They bared their teeth at each other, both snarling and feral.

Killian knew nothing at that moment but pain and bloodlust. There was nothing else.

This time, it was Killian who charged, sprinting toward the beast with everything he had left in him. Instead of striking, he *climbed.* He shoved his sword in his belt and grabbed handfuls of fur and climbed up that terrible, massive body.

Bucking and thrashing madly, the beast didn't make it easy. But somehow Killian made it onto its shoulders, between the ruined wings, and then up to its neck. Bracing himself, he unsheathed his sword, raised it high above him, and with a war cry ripping from his raw throat, drove it down deep into the beast's skull.

Just as he dislodged his blade and pulled it free, the ancient thing gave up the ghost and collapsed upon the forest floor. The boom of its fall caused Killian to lose his balance and tumble to the ground.

There, he lay on his back, his chest rising and falling with panting breaths. Victory. A hard-won victory.

Killian willed himself upright and sat with his elbows on his knees, pushing back his sweat-damp hair and forcing himself to calm down until his thrashing heart slowed and his breathing became normal again.

But then, he heard the snapping of twigs, the shuffle of branches, and a low growl.

Fuck.

Killian turned his head just in time to see yet another black-furred, winged beast appear out of the forest and step towards him.

6

The depth of night was quiet and serene. Wrapped in her cloak with the hood hiding her face, Neve was nothing more than a shadow in the pitch-black as she wove silently through a copse of pine trees.

The Maere had traveled far into the belly of the Dark Forest today, only stopping when nightfall came. Now it was past midnight, her companions slumbered peacefully in their camp a few miles north of where she now wandered.

She often spent time on her own. The Maere did not belong to each other; each belonged to themselves and could come and go as they pleased. Her companions trusted her with their lives - and deaths -as she trusted them with hers.

Neve had grown up among them, on a continent far, far away from Eodia. When she heard gentlefolk speak of *family*, she often thought that The Maere might be her family...but different.

They were not gentlefolk. They perhaps resembled a family in how they lived together, hunted together, took their meals together, and would protect and defend one another. But there was no soft-heartedness amongst them. Nothing loving or warm.

The Maere knew her plans.

They'd sailed to Eodia because there were indeed gods here, but they'd made the journey because the Island was where Neve needed to be, where she would soon leave them.

There was no protestation or tears when she'd declared her intentions, and no one worried about the lonely sojourn she was going to embark on.

"Very well," they'd said. "As you wish", and touched their palms to the emblem on their cloaks in silent blessing.

They knew who she was.

They understood.

And that was all she needed.

Neve breathed in the fresh scent of evergreen but instantly noted a different odor beneath. The sharp, muddy tang of blood. Moving like a phantom through the night, she followed the scent. Soon, she could see the faint light of a campfire flickering just beyond a bank of thorn bushes.

Despite the cold, Killian Grey was covered in sweat. Sweat and blood and all manner of gore.

His dirty tunic was in shreds and he hissed in pain as he pulled it off over his head. From her place in the shadows, Neve took in the considerable damage that had been done to his body.

His left shoulder looked like it was dislocated and he'd forced it back into the socket. A still-bleeding gouge dripped on his right side, the wound looked angry and like it'd been made with a claw. *The Magham*, she marveled with fascination, *he'd come up against the Magham, and by the looks of it, more than one.*

Neve D'Aeth was not easily impressed, but having fought the Magham herself a few times, she knew they were not easy to kill. It appeared, then, that at least some of the legends that made Killian Grey famous were, in fact, true.

She watched as he pulled one of his daggers from the fire where it was resting, gathering heat. He ground his teeth, a muscle feathering in his jaw, took a deep breath, and pressed his red-hot dagger against the wound on his side. It sizzled against his skin and he struggled to keep from crying out-managing to only grunt as he cauterized the laceration.

She could smell his burning flesh.

His horse, tied to a tree nearby, huffed at the scent from the shadows.

He dropped to his knees in pain, tossing his dagger off to the side. Bent forward on his hands, he dug his fingers into the earth, his breath releasing in shallow pants. The ridges and mountains of muscle on his shoulders and back were taut with the strain of his agony.

She watched and admired from afar his resilience, the beautiful mold of his body, his strength.

Moving slowly, he finally crawled backward and sat. He leaned against a tree, closed his eyes, and raised his face to the sky.

Without a sound, she shifted her weight from one foot to the other and watched as Killian immediately snapped to attention.

The corner of her mouth tugged up, pleased. Good.

He sensed her there. Despite being absolutely wrecked, licking his wounds, he was alert enough to sense the danger of her. He was on his feet, sword in hand, and his wide eyes searched the darkness.

Appeased, at least for the moment, Neve left him in peace and once again disappeared into the gloom.

~

Surely, he was dead. When Killian fell asleep, he didn't completely expect to wake up. Those fell beasts nearly killed him and he was certain even after cauterizing it, the wound in his side was infected.

He had no shelter and if he fell asleep, he would be easy prey for whatever else was prowling out there. But staying awake in such exhaustion felt like dying, too.

Despite *knowing* something was out there watching him, and against his better instincts, his body gave in and he slept.

When his eyes drifted closed, his last thought was that he was going to die tonight.

And yet, he awoke.

He was alive and somehow made it through to greet the morning.

His whole body was stiff, his muscles cramping and his wounds stinging. Still, satisfaction bloomed in his chest- the warmth of victory after having so many losses felt almost sublime.

For a warrior, victory was always holy. It was good to know the years in the dungeon hadn't softened him, hadn't robbed him of his instinct and skill.

But now, he needed to regroup. He needed food and water, as well as a bath to get the layers of blood and carnage off his skin.

He knew he was risking losing even more ground behind The Maere, but he wouldn't make it through the forest without seeing to his most basic human needs.

Killian gathered his weapons and what was left of his clothing and set out in search of fresh water.

The sun was shining this morning, warm dapples of light through the treetops made the Dark Forest look nearly unrecognizable, charming even, if it weren't for the menaces that lurked in the shadows.

Killian stretched his limbs and muscles as he walked, leading Willow at a gentle pace. There was a dull ache in his shoulder where it popped out of joint, and the wound on his side still felt like it was burning. His knee was twisted and he was certain one of his toes was broken.

All things considered, he fared pretty well. At least he hadn't been entirely butchered.

Killian walked along the faint trail on the forest floor, following the unconcealed footprints left by The Maere. The prints seemed relatively fresh, with some luck, perhaps he wasn't that far behind them.

Soon, he could hear the sound of water- and the sound of voices. He moved in the direction, down a steep bank, into an ancient gorge, and came upon a tenderly moving spring.

It glittered in the morning sun like a thousand stars lit the waters.

He knew the Maere must be near, enjoying the spring themselves, but the watercourse was winding and lush with tree cover, so if they were here, he could not see them.

And hopefully, they also would not see him.

Carefully, he moved to its shore, finding a well-hidden spot behind the weeping leaves of a clan of willow trees, out of sight. Cupping his hands, he slid them into the cool, clean water and then lifted them to his lips, drinking deeply.

Parched, he could feel the chill hydration of the water bloom inside his chest as he drank and drank.

With a sigh, he sat down on the rocks, unlaced his boots, and kicked them off. He peeled off his clothes and left them in a haphazard pile.

Killian was nearly brainless with relief as he sank his sore body into the water. The spring certainly was cold, but, by the gods, did it feel good. Divine, even.

He dunked beneath the surface and as he emerged, smoothing the water out of his face and slicking back his hair with it, he saw movement through the willow branches. Not close, but someone was out there nonetheless.

He warily waded to the curtain of leaves and peered through. At first, he saw nothing in the water and thought perhaps it had been a trick of light or an animal...

But, no.

Rising from the waters, the sun shining golden in the tendrils of her dark, wet hair, was Neve D'aeth.

Her back was to him, her hands running down the length of her hair, coiling it around her hand, twisting the water out of it. Droplets trickled down her bare back, sparkling in the morning light.

Killian swallowed hard, a breath hitching in his chest, as she rose higher.

The bell curve of her hips appeared and he felt heat prickle across his skin. With effort, he looked away, averting his eyes from the splendor on the other side of the trees.

His heart was hammering against his ribs like it was a panicked and caged animal. The sight of her made him dizzy.

He'd like to chalk it up to hunger or exhaustion, but no, this particular unsteadiness was singularly because of her.

He'd never thought of himself as a true gentleman, but he was honorable. He would rather cut off his own hand than take what wasn't freely and enthusiastically given.

And yet...

If he were indeed a better man, he would have kept his back to that devastating woman in the water. He would have gone about his washing, dried, and moved on with his morning, despite the sizzling of all of his nerves.

But he was not a better man.

The same compulsion that drew him to follow her into the forest returned. It told him to look, to feed this strange hunger that was so sudden and so consuming.

Cursing himself, he turned around once more and gazed through the willow branches.

What he saw nearly ended him.

Neve was facing his direction now, arching backward and dipping her hair into the water.

Fuck.

The sight of her naked body, all curves and gleaming skin, made him forget his own name.

He was lost. He was a lost man, watching her.

He didn't know who he was, where he came from, or what day it was. There was nothing in his mind but her.

The softness of her, the strength, the bends and sweeps of her. Killian's mouth was watering and his hands trembled. He was frozen on the spot and even if she somehow were to notice him spying on her, he wouldn't be able to move away.

He'd never seen such coolness, such self-possession.

The way she moved, casual and confident, disarmed him completely.

He dragged his gaze all over her as if he could devour her with his eyes alone. He wanted her, wanted to fit his hands into the curve at her waist, in that perfect dip just above her hips. He wanted to taste her skin. Crush her body against his. Rove his hands and mouth over every inch of her. Feel the warmth of being inside her.

Wanted to see if he could crack her impenetrable nonchalance, if he could make her writhe for him, beg for him.

He watched her as she moved through the water. She seemed... content. There was a slight smile on her full lips and she dragged her hands against the current of the spring.

She kept arching backward and wetting her hair, or dunking beneath the surface and rising back up slowly, as if she couldn't get enough of it, that sensation of being immersed. Every time she did it, Killian's breath caught in his throat. The sun made her glistening skin glow as her body bowed and bent.

Neve waded back and forth, luxuriating in the brook, while Killian stood there watching like a captive idiot.

His blood was a heavy roar in his head, slugging through his veins.

On some level, he knew he was behaving like a boy who'd never once seen a naked woman in his life, sloppy and stupid with lust.

But what else could he do? From the very moment she'd prowled into his line of sight in The Cross, he'd gone mindless. And every time he'd seen her since, it had been the same- he'd instantly been rendered moronic.

Killian was no stranger to the pleasures of a woman's body. But never had he encountered one that captivated him so completely.

Never one that made him lose every sense of himself.

She swallowed him down into her darkness with a mere glance.

Killian thought that if she asked him to give her everything he owned in exchange for one night in her arms, he would do it without a second thought.

Who *was* she?

How could she possibly have this kind of power over him?

Certainly, she wasn't a Mage or a sorceress. No, he wasn't bewitched.

It was more that there was a primal *pull* toward her. Something deep and animal and ancient.

Like her blood and body called to his own.

Ridiculous.

She flowed through the water and was soon rising out of it to walk onto the rocky shore. He watched as she was utterly bared before him, inch by inch, as she exited the water.

Anything and everything. He would give it all up just to touch her. Cut out his beating heart and offer it on a platter for her to drag her teeth across. He would go back into the dungeon for the rest of his life in exchange for the taste of her mouth. Lay his sword and shield at her feet, just to bury himself between her legs.

He may as well drown himself now, here in this beautiful spring, because he'd obviously lost his mind. It was the only explanation for this madness.

As she faded from view, walking up the bank and away from him, he sank lower into the water and closed his eyes, willing his heart to slow and his brain to start working again.

Killian Grey lost count of how many minutes, maybe hours, passed as he fought to regain his senses.

Interlude I

This kingdom was theirs.

The world, too.

But something was stirring.

Something unexpected, and yet... not.

Cut off. Isolated. Without power. Well... true power.

They'd done this to themselves, of course. But they shouldered no blame. The bloodshed had been magnificent. Thunderous.

A death so catastrophic that it became a masterpiece, a work of art. Everything had gone perfectly.

Until it didn't.

But something was stirring.

A rising.

A joining.

They could feel it in the sticky mire of their blood. Their hands itched with it.

Something was stirring.

Something to bring them what they'd been searching for all these centuries.

Release.

Vindication.

The throne.

But, perhaps most cruelly, something that also sought their ruin.

Two sides of the same blade.

Matched.

So, they would do what they'd always done. They would wait. Hide and wait and watch and scheme.

And when it came for them, this *thing*...

They would drink the very life out of it until they had what they wanted.

Drink it until oblivion.

7

On the other side of the Dark Forest, like a prize, was a sweeping heather moorland. An open plain of rolling, rocky hills blanketed in soft purple and white heather and endless green grasses. A jarring opposite to the forest's dim confinement, the moor was an uninterrupted expanse of spacious liberty. The gray clouded sky above was never-ending and the view was boundless, barely a tree in sight. Nothing but clean, open air and the scent of sweet meadow.

Killian Grey collapsed, sucking down great lungfuls of that air. He'd run out of the Dark Forest. Sprinted until he thought his heart might burst. When he finally emerged into that beautiful lilac-hewed field of freedom, he nearly wept with relief. When his legs finally gave out, he fell into the tall grass.

They'd come for him.

All the nightmares and villains of legend came for him in those final days in the forest. The morning watching Neve bathe in the spring was a distant memory now after the horrors he'd endured.

First, it was the sprites. Mischievous and wrathful little faerie folk who used their magic to render him blind. Killian could not begin to describe the depth of the panic that infected him when he could no longer see. It forced him to move through the treacherous forest on feel and sound alone, trusting Willow to lead the way. They'd gotten turned around at least twice.

Then came the banshees. His vision was still dark when the banshees began screaming. Perhaps they allied with the sprites to bring him to his knees. Their shrieks nearly split his head in two. Blinded, deafened by relentless otherworldly wailing, Killian could do nothing. Willow wouldn't move and he could not find his way on his own.

So he'd stood there. He endured. *For hours.*

It nearly drove him mad. But he was determined that it would not break him.

The blindness, the noise, he would not yield to it. Would not kneel or falter. He gripped Willow's reins, digging his fingernails into the leather. The screams were driving blades of pain into his head, still, he held firm. Withstood.

After an eternity, he blinked and could see again.

After another eternity, the screaming stopped and nothing was left but a violent ringing in his ears.

Now, Killian lay amid the heather, gasping for air and feeling his entire self filling with an emotion he could not name. Relief? Gratitude? Anguish? All of it? Yes, all of it.

After the sprites and banshees, the Dark Forest marched upon him with all the creatures dwelling within. One after another, or sometimes in groups, they came for him. A relentless surge of attack after attack, each with its own challenge, its own torture.

The night before visiting the spring was the last time he'd slept. They'd come for him day and night, whether with magic or deception or sharp teeth and claws.

There was a sweet, tender pause for several hours. He hadn't dared to make camp or rest. He learned that the forest was tricky and its horrors didn't sleep. So, when it all stopped, Killian was unsettled. The longer it lasted, the less he trusted that the forest was finished with him. But, it stayed quiet and serene. When nearly a day passed, he finally allowed himself a spark of hope.

Precisely at that moment, when his mental and bodily tension eased the tiniest bit, the final terror came for him. He'd felt the forest grow colder, and then he'd felt the hand on his shoulder.

Killian whirled to behold a wraith. Ancient and nearly faceless, all bones and shadow and ash. Its teeth and nails, though rotting, were razor sharp. From behind him, another bony hand crawled up his back to rest on the nape of his neck. A fierce shiver shot up his spine. He drew his sword and whirled again.

Two. Two wraiths.

"You," they hissed in unison, clouds of bone dust and dirt escaping their mouths as they spoke.

"Me," he replied, gripping his sword with two hands, ready to strike.

Four skeletal, groping hands reached for him. Not to attack but to *caress.* Killian's throat bobbed as he waited, letting them touch him.

"Are you following *her*?" They asked, the sound was like a crackling wind.

"Who?"

Rasping laughter. "You know who."

They were circling him slowly, petting him; running those filthy fingers over his chest, playing with the ridges on his leather armor, brushing his cheek, combing through his hair. He planted his feet in the dirt and stood strong.

Raising an eyebrow, the picture of unbothered arrogance, he replied: "I don't know what you're talking about."

"We've seen you. Watching her, wanting her."

He shrugged, "You can't blame a man for admiring a beautiful woman."

More laughter, more petting. "Oh, he doesn't know," one of them drawled.

"Of course, he doesn't," whispered the other.

"What don't I know?"

They tutted at him. "No, no, no. Not our secret to tell."

Killian became impatient, his hands eager to swing his sword. "Are we done here? I've just about had enough of this place."

In an instant, the grazing and groping hands became violently firm, clutching him with a strength he wasn't sure he could match. He willed his body to stay relaxed, to show that he wasn't afraid despite the hammering of his heart.

"How did it feel, *Killian Grey*," they growled, "to know that you killed your family?'

Everything ceased. Dread sluiced through his veins and his stomach dropped.

"I...I didn't." He was suddenly cold, so very cold.

"Oh yes, you did," they murmured. "They are dead because of you. Because of the *company* you keep. Because of your hubris."

"I wasn't- I wasn't even there that night. I didn't kill them." There was a roaring in his head, not of anger, but of deafening despair.

"Oh, but don't you think if you *were* there, you could have saved them? A big, strong, brave warrior. If only you'd been there... if only they didn't have to wonder where *daddy* was when death came for them..."

Killian's eyes blurred with tears. He tried to open his mouth to say something, but all that came out was a broken croak.

"Did you know," they continued, closing in on him until their bodies were touching his, like an embrace. "That your wife was asleep when it happened? A sweet mercy indeed. But... your children.."

"No," Killian managed, his voice cracking.

"Your children did not slumber."

"No," he said again, this time it came out like a sob.

"Oh yes. They were awake. *Playing* together. Giggling under the covers late into the night. They saw it coming for them..."

"Stop," he begged. He would do anything to make them stop talking. He couldn't move; they held him tight and close.

One of them wrenched his sword from his hand and he did not fight it. He let them disarm him.

"They weren't giggling when their bedroom door opened that night. They thought it was *you*, home, at last, come to kiss them goodnight and chide them for not being asleep."

"Please stop. *Please*," he was crying now, in earnest.

In his mind, he could see it. Those two golden-haired boys, trying to hold in their laughter and pretend to be asleep as their door creaked open...thinking it was him...thinking they would get an embrace from their father, and then...

"They missed you while you were gone. They kept saying to your wife 'When is daddy coming home?'. So imagine their *joy* when they thought it was you coming to see them that night."

"Stop. Stop talking." All he could feel was anguish.

The wraiths held him close as he wept, as his knees buckled.

"But it was not you that came to them that night. No. And their joy went quickly. Fear. It was fear that they felt in the end."

"No," it was a whispered prayer on Killian's lips.

"And you... Now you live in such pain. Such guilt must be heavy, is it not?"

Killian felt himself nod.

One of their hands settled around his throat.

"Think of the *relief* you would feel. To set it down. Give it up," the wraiths replied.

He shook his head. "I can't."

A rapturous gasp exploded from their mouths. "Oh, but you *can*. It would be so easy. Lay down your burdens. Let it all go. You can be finished with it."

He shook his head again, but with no conviction this time.

"All you have to do is embrace us and we can make it all end. All the guilt, the shame, the heartbreak."

It may have been the most feeble and cowardly moment of his life when he quietly asked: "How?"

The hand at his throat tightened. "There is, of course, always a price. But this one... it seems you may be willing to pay..."

He knew they meant his life. They could end his suffering, his guilt, in exchange for offering them his life.

Despite his agony and the thunderous cracking of his heart, despite the guilt and the torture of these new revelations, he would not pay this price.

"No," he muttered, through his tears.

"Speak up, *boy*."

Killian ground his teeth and lifted his chin, fumbling his hand towards the sword one of the wraiths now held. He looked into its face, its empty eye sockets and fanged, black mouth, and yanked his sword out of its hand. It hissed, squeezing its hand around his throat, cutting off his air.

"I said, *no*," he ground out.

Rage replaced sorrow and a red cloud of fury- familiar and welcome- spread across his vision.

He swung his sword and unleashed his violence upon them.

Here, now, in the wide field of heather, Killian's chest rose and fell unevenly as he lay there. He was utterly shattered. Physically, mentally. And heartbroken anew, like a wound reopened and bleeding freely.

Slowly but surely, his heart slowed and his breath returned to its normal rhythm. He took in the scent of the grass and flowers around him and centered himself more and more.

"You made it," a cool voice said.

Startled, he gasped and sat bolt upright, pulling a knife from his boot.

Neve D'Aeth lounged in the heather in front of him. She sat, leaning forward with her elbows on her knees, and she was resting her head on her folded arms, her dark hair pulled to one side and cascading down. She looked at him with clear green-gold eyes, calm and waiting.

His nerves were shot, he was completely spent, and he could barely put a thought together. "What--how long have you known I was here?"

The corner of her mouth lifted. "I've known the whole time."

He blanched. "The whole time?"

"Yes."

He swallowed, mustering as much of himself as he could, letting a smirk play on his mouth that he knew didn't reach his eyes.

"You could have come to say hello," he remarked.

Her eyes sparkled. "Hello."

He huffed a laugh and nodded. "Hello."

"You did well," she offered.

He stiffened. "What do you mean?"

Neve leaned back, rolling her shoulders, and regarded him coolly. "You followed me here and you did well."

He clenched his jaw, the pieces slowly falling into place. "You knew I would follow. You led me here."

"Yes," was all she said.

"Did you know... did you know that they would come for me?"

A pause, and some small, quiet thing changed in her eyes. Something close to sympathy, but barely. "Yes," she replied.

"Did you want them to kill me?"

"I was hoping they wouldn't."

Killian swallowed. "And if they had?"

"I would have had to adjust my plans."

His ire rose and he pressed his lips into a thin line. "Your *plans*? You risked my life for your plans?"

She lifted her chin and all the warmth left her face. "You chose to follow me. The risk was yours."

Killian moved to his feet, his muscles screaming, and took a step towards her. His hands balled into fists.

"Were you...testing me?"

She rose, too, and stepped forward, closing the space between them. They were nearly chest to chest and she looked up into his face.

Despite being a head taller than her, the look she gave made him feel so small.

"I wanted to be sure that the rumors of your strength were true."

He took a deep, steadying breath through his nose, catching the clean, clover scent of her. "And?" he said through gritted teeth.

She tilted her head. "It's rare that a person can live up to their own legend. But it turns out, Killian, that you do."

Something like pride bloomed in his chest, despite his confusion and agitation.

"Why does it matter to you whether or not I live up to the stories about me?"

"I'm going on a journey," she replied. "And I would like you to join me."

He took a step back. Nearly stumbled. Of all the things he'd expected her to say, this was not one of them. "Where are you going?"

"I seek the Oracle of Ula."

All the hairs on his body stood up on end. "Ula is far from here. And a dangerous trek."

"Yes."

"And after Ula?"

A cold fire sparked in her eyes. "We'll go hunting."

He stilled. "Hunting for what?"

A fragrant, warm wind blew through the moor, moving through her hair. There was something regal about her, surrounded by that sea of purple flowers, with the breeze lifting and blowing her hair around her head.

And something very, very dangerous.

She offered him a dark smile and said, "Gods."

8

Neve had always been, more or less, alone.

She was born to a quiet pair of nomads in a kingdom far, far north of the one she now traveled. From her memory, it was a wild place, a *blue* place. Snow and glaciers, seas and lagoons, wide cerulean skies. It was cold there, but beautiful.

The couple she was born to, her parents, were kind but they did not keep her for long. Neve was barely able to walk or talk before she was left at the Citadel with the Maere, never to see her parents again. The only reminder that they even existed was the book tucked into her blankets as they'd forsaken her.

The old book with the worn cover and the etching of the stars and moon and tower inside. Neve's tiny fingers had traced the lines of that etching countless times. Even now, grown and without any lingering longing for her lost parents, she found herself tracing those lines...particularly on nights when she could not find rest.

Nights like this one.

Killian was too drained to travel further than the heather moor after escaping the Dark Forest. And he hadn't given her an answer as to whether or not he'd accept her invitation.

If he'd immediately said yes, without any consideration, she likely wouldn't have trusted him. If he'd immediately said yes, she would have left without him under the cover of night.

It was not the anxiety of waiting for his answer that kept her awake that night. No, Neve was certain he would decide to go with her. Despite seeing that look of betrayal on his face when he realized that she'd deliberately led him through the horrors of the forest, she knew he would still go with her.

No, what kept her awake that night with only the stars above and the heather below as company was the idea of not being alone.

Of course, she'd always been with The Maere, and they'd always been with her. But she'd never *needed* them. She did not depend on any of them for her survival. The loss of them would not impede her life. After all, the first and most important lesson in training at the Citadel was to learn self-sufficiency and self-reliance. To learn to need only yourself. To be smart and skilled enough to have no need for another person to come to your rescue.

It was a brutal lesson and a hard-won skill, especially for a child. But that was what made The Maere so powerful and so good at what they did. Each member was an army unto themselves.

Neve sensed that this pilgrimage with a man she did not know would feel much different.

For her to take this path, to do what she had to do, Killian's particular skills would be of great use to her. *He* would be a necessity. It was why she'd sought him out to begin with, and why she'd tested his tenacity and strength in the Dark Forest.

If she was going to offer up her *need* to this person, she had to be sure he was worthy.

Letting another person, one she barely knew, be a part of this with her, to be a part of her life… felt deeply uncomfortable.

So, she lay awake under the stars, cold autumn air chilling her to the bones, and she traced the etching in her book with her fingers.

Periodically, she would glance in Killian's direction. He camped alone several yards away and he'd fallen into an angry yet exhausted slumber. She'd given him his space after offering the invitation and told him to come find her in the morning if he wanted to join her.

Even from so far away, she heard him muttering to himself in frustration. Furious gruntings about how stupid he'd been to follow her, what a snake she was to have tested him.

She smirked now, thinking about it. His agitation amused her. He seemed to be an easily ruffled person, passionate about the here and now, while she was singularly focused on the big picture and did not offer her energy to things that did not matter long-term.

He was a burning flame, raging and snapping at the slightest breeze.

She was ice, like the glaciers she'd grown up amongst. Cold and steadfast, moved only by the influence of her own weight and gravity.

This would certainly be interesting.

~

The sun rose in layers of amber, pink, and crimson over the rolling green and lavender hills of the moor. It was the most beautiful sunrise Neve had seen in months.

She stood, pulling on her leathers over a flimsy linen tunic, careful not to cut her fingers on the rough stone and metal epaulets decorating the shoulders.

She then took the thick, velvety fabric of her black cloak in her hands and admired the embroidered cloth emblem of The Maere. She touched it almost reverently for a moment as the stunning morning broke over the horizon.

At peace, she took her knife and cut the emblem off, letting the wind take it like a leaf, carrying it across the moor until she could see it no longer.

A new day.

A new journey.

Neve settled the cloak around her, tying it at her neck, and pulled her braided hair out from under it. She paused to drink in the vibrant sky, feeling its warm glow on her skin. The pure endlessness of that sunrise unlatched something deep in her chest, if only for a moment. Something that felt close to excitement, to hope.

She knew he was watching her. She'd sensed him coming long before she heard the sound of his boots and his horse's hooves on the rocky terrain.

Neve turned her head to look at him and found that he seemed frozen in place several feet away, his throat bobbing up and down, blue-gray eyes swimming with some emotion she couldn't name. Perhaps he, too, was stunned by the colors of the rising dawn... but Neve knew his eyes were on her and not the sky. On her face, illuminated in the warm radiance of the morning, on her body dressed in black, on her very presence standing there before him. His attraction to her was palpable, a living thing, and it had been since the moment she'd walked into his field of vision in Lowbarrow.

She hadn't yet decided what she'd do with it.

Neve turned her body to face him fully and regarded him, waiting.

He seemed to pull himself together and squared his shoulders, making himself appear even larger than he was. Killian Grey was a veritable mountain of brawn and muscle. It would certainly be of use to her on this coming quest.

"I've made my decision," he said, his voice a deep rumble across the distance between them.

Neve tilted her head to the side, the tiniest smile on her lips. "And?"

"I will go with you."

Wordlessly, she crossed the distance between them, her steps slow and deliberate. She watched him tense, clenching his jaw as if preparing for the onslaught of her in his personal space.

Up close, he towered over her, but it did not make her feel small. His eyes looked tired but eager.

"I'm giving you my trust in this because you've earned it," she said.

A glimmer sparked in his eyes as if it was the last thing he expected her to say and the very thing he'd been hoping to hear.

In turn, she expected him to swagger or smirk or even snap at her for having put him through hell in the Dark Forest. But, instead, he appeared humbled and gave her a nod.

"I won't betray it."

Killian's earnestness as he spoke those words reassured her. He spoke true.

"Good," she replied, leaving it at that.

They mounted their horses just as the sunrise began to fade into a soft and lingering orange. Together, they rode north, traveling for hours in silence as the sky changed from orange to soft blue to dismal gray when the clouds returned in the afternoon.

Neve and Killian left the Dark Forest and the purple moor behind them, heading into an unknown future side by side. The day moved along just as they did, steadily and without incident.

Halfway into the afternoon, they stopped to eat and water the horses in a quiet orchard. The leaves were starting to change color on the trees, their limbs heavy with fat, pink apples. The ground was littered with fallen fruit, which the horses found delight in.

Neve cleared a place for herself and sat beneath one of the trees, her back against its trunk. The air was fragrant with the scent of drying foliage and sweet apples.

Killian sat next to her and buried his teeth into one with a crunch, its juice trickling down his chin. He wiped it with the back of his hand.

She could feel Killian getting restless. He was bobbing his knee as he sat; he kept glancing at her like he was mustering the courage to strike up a conversation, but didn't know what to say.

Hiding her amusement, she pointed at the sword on the grass near his outstretched legs. "A family heirloom?" she asked.

He glanced down at the weapon and then back at her.

"It is. How did you know?"

She moved nearer and sat next to him. Leaning in close, she felt him tense and could hear the quiet intake of breath through his nose as the scent of her hit him.

She touched the knotwork on the metal of the pommel, an intricate curving and twining of lines with no beginning or end, like a circular vine or root system.

The sigil of the Greys was synonymous with the knights who once guarded Eodia's royal family and their ivory palace, Lyra Castle, for millennia.

"I've seen this symbol before," she responded simply.

He raised an eyebrow. "Have you?"

She settled back against the tree. "Yes."

He smiled and rolled his eyes, huffing. "You don't give anything away, do you?"

She shook her head and leveled a look at him. "Never."

He laughed. "All right. So what's it going to take to get you to have a normal conversation with me?"

"Define 'normal.'"

"The kind where I say something and then you say something and it carries on like that for a bit until we know each other a little better."

There was a light in his eyes, and his playful arrogance was returning. Neve liked that better than the haunted husk of a man she'd found outside the forest a day before.

"You need to learn to ask the right questions."

He scoffed. "Fair enough."

Killian pinned her with his gaze, eyes roving her face to search for a path through her walls. He wouldn't find one, but she admired that he was trying.

"*Where* have you seen this symbol before?" He touched the metal knot on his sword.

"Books," she said.

"Books? Somehow, I have a hard time imagining you with your nose stuck in a book."

"Why's that?"

"Because you're one of the most terrifying people I've ever met." His eyes danced with humor and interest, watching her, trying to read her.

Neve offered him a shrug. "I like stories."

His eyes widened playfully. "Now we're getting somewhere. Lady Nightmare likes *stories*. What kind of stories?"

She didn't hate the nickname he threw at her. *Lady Nightmare*. It wasn't exactly... *incorrect*, all things considered. She weighed her next words as she did all things, carefully.

"Old stories," she said. "Lost stories."

He took another bite of his apple, licking the juice from the corner of his mouth, and stared at her for a moment as if he, too, needed to be deliberate with his words.

A game, then.

Good.

"Tell me what your books say about this sword," he drawled.

She let a dangerous light shine in her expression as she looked him dead in the eye and wrapped her hand around the hilt of his sword. He visibly bristled, his face turning stony, eyes flitting down to the grip of her hand. She casually lifted it and set it across her lap.

He was wholly rigid and she suspected that if she were anyone else, he would have ripped it from her grasp and hauled off on her with his fists. Instead, he just pressed his mouth into a hard line and swallowed.

It felt weighty against her thighs, heavy and old. Much older than the man who bore it. Her fingers danced delicately along its length and then she sketched her nails over the complicated sigil. Indeed, the blade was ancient and had so much history living in its steel that it nearly thrummed with it. Neve wondered if Killian could feel it, too, the vibrating age of its tale.

"According to legend, this sigil belongs to House Grey, and this sword has been in their–your– family since nearly the dawn of time. I read that it was made by the goddess of the battlefield herself and that whoever it belonged to would be blessed with great and mighty strength," she said.

Killian was silent, trying to force his expression to be impassive and failing. His eyes were burning into her.

"It's said that a sword-bearer, your ancestor, was at the foot of the bell tower the night Queen Nyx met her end. That he died defending her, and that the sword was lost, buried beneath the wreckage, and locked away like everything else in the palace. And yet…" She examined the gleaming, well-smithed metal. She looked at Killian again. "And yet here it is. With you."

They held each other in a deadlocked stare for a moment, and the world around them went silent. Not a bird or a gust of wind dared disturb them. Neve ran her finger along the razor-sharp edge of the blade, light as a ghost, so it drew just the faintest scrape of her skin, the barest hint of blood.

His eyes flared at that and he was instantly on his knees, facing her, looming over her, as he took the sword from her hands. He paused there, looking down at her, chest rising and falling unevenly.

"I'd rather you didn't hurt yourself with my sword," he said, his voice quiet and just on the fringe of being lethal.

The way he was looking at her told her that he wasn't angry that she was playing with his sword, but rather that she'd drawn her own blood with it. There was something in that action alone that pulled him out of the back-and-forth they were having and into an entirely different mindset.

Some deep instinct had taken over and he seemed surprised by it himself.

Interesting.

She looked at the tiny droplet of blood rising on her middle finger and raised it to her lips, sucking it into her mouth. His eyes twitched and he audibly swallowed. Neve pulled her finger from her lips and showed him her hand. No more blood, just a barely visible red line on her finger.

"I'm not hurt," she assured.

He stood and slipped the sword into the scabbard at his back. She watched as he gave his arms a shake as if ridding himself of some unwanted feeling.

"How much farther do you want to travel today?" he asked. He was finished with her stories now, seemingly unnerved by his own reaction.

Neve looked to the sky for the position of the sun, and thought for a moment about how far they'd come.

"There's a tavern we can reach by nightfall."

"Good," he said, gently pulling Willow away from her bounty of fallen apples. "I could use a drink."

"What's its name?" She called after him. He froze and slowly turned back toward her. "The sword. What's its name?"

Before he uttered the word, she knew what he would say.

She just wanted to hear him say it.
"Celesta."

9

Neve paid for their rooms at the tavern in advance and promptly went up the curving back stairway to find her space without a word to Killian.

He watched her go until he could no longer see her and found a table in the corner, where he put his back to the wall and had a clear view of the door.

It was a long day. He was hungry and could use a mug or two of whatever swill they served here. The bed upstairs was calling to him, too, especially after a week of sleeping on the cold ground.

The barmaid placed a steaming bowl of beef stew and a hunk of fresh, crusty bread in front of him, along with a mug of ale filled to the brim, foam spilling over the edge. She gave him a wink, a blush on her cheeks and Killian offered her a smile and a wink back.

"Thanks, love," he told her and watched her blush deepen.

He took a bite of the stew, thick with meat and root vegetables swimming in a silky, salty broth, and nearly groaned.

Days of foraged food made this meal taste like ecstasy. He ate voraciously. The bread and ale were just as good, and as he was nearing the bottom of his bowl and mug, the barmaid reappeared with more stew and ale.

Grateful, he handed her a coin for her trouble and she left her hand in his, lingering. The look in her eyes was an offer, an invitation.

He wasn't sure where the night would take him quite yet, so he gently squeezed her hand and pulled away with another smile that said *maybe*.

The tavern was well-kept. Clean and busy with good food and plenty of ale. As the night went on, and Killian sat at his table with a cup that never seemed to empty thanks to the heart-eyed barmaid, the space became more and more crowded, with more and more people becoming deeply drunk. The volume of voices increased until he could barely make out a single conversation within the din.

He watched gruff, road-dirty men grab at courtesans, travelers, and barmaids. Most of the women laughed and let themselves be groped, and didn't seem to mind the sloshing of ale on their shoes and dresses. Those who didn't laugh were the ones Killian's eyes stayed on a little longer, just to ensure he wouldn't have to step in.

He had a real problem with men who *took* what they wanted without being offered.

It wasn't long before he started noticing the whispering and pointing in his direction. The hushed sound of his name spoken from ale-slurred mouths. No one approached him, at least not yet, but they all knew he was there.

Killian Grey, warrior. Killian Grey, murderer.

No matter where he went, he was either revered or hated, or both. Which always made traveling interesting.

He minded his own business and actively ignored the gawking, his belly warm and full of stew, the fourth mug of ale finally relaxing his nerves from the past week. It felt good to sit and do nothing but eat and drink. He stretched his neck and rolled the tension from his tight shoulders.

When Neve asked Killian to join her on this journey, he'd been so disarmed that he almost just blurted out an emphatic "yes". But somehow he'd had the wherewithal to remember that she'd not only led him through the forest but had done it to *test* him. He went to bed furious with her, rageful even.

Then, the sight of her in the amber glow of the sunrise that morning, clad in sharp black leather, unmoored him.

His pull to her felt like the tide to the moon. He couldn't explain it. He could only choose to follow it or leave it.

He wasn't willing to leave it.

Neve D'aeth had many secrets. In the orchard, she'd also proven that she already knew some of his. There was an imbalance between them. He was mightily outmatched, but for the first time in his life, the thought did not rankle him.

Movement on the staircase across the tavern caught his eye, and there she was.

He sat up straighter and leaned forward with his arms folded on the table before him. His pulse instantly quickened. She strode down the steps, moving just as she'd done the first night he'd seen her, in another tavern.

She'd freshened up and changed out of her leathers, reemerging in a simple gray cotton dress with an unremarkable but well-fitted black linen corset over it. How the corset hugged her waist and put her full breasts on display made Killian's skin light up with reckless burning.

She was beautiful, but to anyone else, she must have looked completely anonymous. Effortlessly blending in and able to weave through the crowd mostly unnoticed. No one had any idea who she was or what kind of terrifying presence they were sharing space with.

The Maere was trained in the art of shadows and secrets- this ability must have been part of that. The skill of blending in, hiding in plain sight.

Killian found himself envying that she was able to employ deliberate obscurity at will. There were many times in his life and work when such a talent would have come in very handy. And he couldn't help but smirk, knowing that he was the only one here who knew that she was anything but invisible. It felt almost like a privilege to be in on the secret of her.

Neve approached his table and gave him an amused smirk. He couldn't control the wide smile he returned. He tipped his cup at her and nodded.

"Lady Nightmare," he said, by way of greeting.

Her green-gold eyes sparkled. She took the mug from his hand and raised it to her lips, just as she'd done the night they met. She drank down the rest of his ale and set the mug back on the table.

The blushing barmaid immediately returned to him with another mug, this time with a much less pleasant look on her face. Her eyes pointedly surveyed Neve from head to toe and the maid stepped into Neve's space in an attempt to stake her claim on him.

The girl shimmied a little closer to his seat, trying to insinuate herself between them.

"I can get you your own ale, dear. There's plenty to go 'round," the barmaid said, in a voice he'd often heard women use with each other. Sickly sweet on the surface, with nothing but bitter hatred beneath.

Until the girl spoke, Neve hadn't even noticed her. At the words, Neve turned to face her, stepping closer. The air around them changed and turned colder. Neve's eyes roamed the barmaid's face and Killian saw a visible shiver shake up the girl's back. He didn't know whether to watch this play out like entertainment or to get between them to avoid something bloody.

He stayed put.

Neve didn't say a word, didn't make any threatening movements, just regarded the barmaid with that icy gaze, the promise of danger radiating from her. Killian knew that he now shared something with the barmaid- the girl could see Neve as she was. Not an anonymous traveler, but something else entirely.

Something that very much felt like a wolf among sheep.

The barmaid swallowed nervously. "I'll bring your ale straightaway. Can I offer you anything to eat? We've got fresh stew. No charge, of course," she rambled, unable to look Neve in the face.

"That won't be necessary," Neve replied. She reached into her pocket and pulled out two coins. The barmaid flinched when Neve pressed the money into her hand. Dismissed, the girl was gone instantly.

Killian raised an eyebrow when they were alone again. "Impressive," he said.

Neve shrugged and the corners of her lush mouth lifted conspiratorially. " I don't know what you mean."

He snorted a laugh. "Right."

"There are a lot of curious whispers in here tonight," she drawled. "About you."

It was his turn to shrug. "I don't know what you mean."

"Well, I'd better go take a listen for both of us, then," she responded. "Enjoy your ale." Neve turned on her heel and disappeared into the still-growing crowd.

Killian's spirits fell just a little. He'd hoped that perhaps she'd join him.

For the better part of the night, he sat and observed.

And became more and more agitated.

Killian was tired, but he hadn't seen Neve head back upstairs to her room and, regardless of her own prowess, he couldn't find it within himself to leave her alone in the tavern that soon became volatile.

Several fights broke out and each time fists started flying, he searched the crowd for her, just to make sure she was away from the melee. He continuously watched for her and she kept catching his eye as if to remind him that she was indeed still there.

Worse than the chaos around them, he'd watched drunken hands reach for her as she passed through the mob.

Over and over again, all through the night, hands reaching and cloudy eyes leering at her body.

No hand touched her; she was too smooth and swift to allow that. But the *reaching* for her itself, the hungry, demanding fingers, was enough to make his palms itch with the promise of violence.

Eventually, she made her way back to his end of the tavern, which made him feel a semblance of relief.

She leaned her back against the bar but did not look in his direction, did not catch his eye. No, her gaze was locked on the warrior advancing on her.

The man wore no sigils, but there was no mistaking that he was a soldier. He radiated pure brutality, his face pockmarked and scarred, and his singular focus was on Neve.

Killian cursed under his breath.

The warrior pulled up a stool to the bar and plopped down on it right next to Neve. She ignored him, which only seemed to pique the man's interest and ire. He reached for her and Killian thought his heart might stop with the restraint it was taking to keep himself seated.

There was a roaring between his ears as the brute dragged his knuckles down the front of Neve's corset. Bile rose in Killian's throat and his hand was on his sword as he stood.

Neve caught Killian's eyes and gave him a subtle shake of her head.

No, she didn't need his help. Didn't want it.

Did she want... this man to touch her? This wiry-haired ogre? Killian was shaking under the weight of his jealousy, hand still on his sword, body still poised to strike. *Begging* to strike.

The soldier wrapped his meaty hands around Neve's waist and pulled her onto his lap. She let it happen, but Killian saw the way her face changed, saw the darkness rise.

Killian was vibrating with fury as the warrior began lifting Neve's skirt, moving his hand up and up and up...

Over the man's shoulder, Neve settled her gaze on Killian.

Everything happened so fast.

One moment, the warrior was sliding his hand between Neve's thighs and the next, his hands were pinned to the bar in front of him, her twin daggers buried deep into the flesh and the wood beneath. The man's mouth was open in a roar of pain.

"You bitch!" he screamed.

She smiled serenely at him and twisted both daggers at the same time. Slowly.

"Say something nice," she murmured.

The man growled at her.

Killian sat back down, released his grip on his sword, and watched.

She twisted the daggers again, leaning closer to the man despite another ear-splitting wail of pain.

"I said, say something nice," she repeated.

Sweating, drooling, and red-faced, the warrior bared his teeth at her. "Fuck you," he hissed.

Neve tutted her tongue at him, as a parent would do to a misbehaving child. Slowly, oh so slowly, she pulled the daggers out.

No, not out.

Through.

Instead of pulling them up and out, she dragged them through his hands. Inch by tortuous inch, slicing muscle and sinew and even bone. Splitting both hands precisely in half, from wrist to knuckle to fingernail.

When she was done, when she'd wiped her daggers clean on the man's shirt and slid them back into her boots, the warrior's hands were an utter ruin, nothing but blood and flaps of skin and cleaved bone. He would never have use of those hands again, which was as good as a death sentence for a warrior. He passed out and collapsed to the floor with a wet clatter.

The whole tavern had gone silent, each person pale-faced and mouth agape.

Neve eyed the blushy barmaid from earlier and called out to her in the crowd, "I think I'll take that stew now, *dear*."

Killian couldn't hide his wide-eyed grin.

Lady Nightmare, indeed.

10

There was a fire still crackling in the hearth when Neve awoke in the morning, embers popping soundly. Her room at the inn was sparse but cozy, with clean, crisp sheets on the bed, a threadbare rug laid across the creaking unfinished wood floor, and a curtainless window overlooking the meager settlement that hosted the tavern. A white wash basin holding cold but fresh water sat on a well-used oak dressing table in the corner. She could make out the cracks in the old porcelain from where she lay in the bed, like gray veins up its sides.

A thin frost bloomed on the window glass, the dim morning light cloudy behind it.

Neve stretched her limbs, luxuriating in the feeling of the goose-feather mattress beneath her. She couldn't remember the last time she'd slept in a proper bed. She slept deeply and part of her was tempted to nestle back under the covers until the morning grew late, but a noise outside her door promptly halted her leisure.

A hushed, sighing sound.

Pulling a dagger from beneath her pillow, she slid from the bed and padded towards the door. Despite the fire, the air in the room was cold and it pricked at her skin. Autumn was truly arriving in full force.

She paused with her fingers on the doorknob, listening, greeted by that same muffled whooshing, and she quietly pulled the door ajar.

Lying in a heap at her feet was a sleeping, softly snoring Killian Grey.

It looked like he'd drunkenly curled up on her doorstep to sleep instead of bothering to find the room she'd purchased for him. Curious, she nudged him with a bare toe.

Startled awake, he shot to his knees and spun to face her. He was close enough that his nose was nearly touching her chest and he slowly raised his eyes to hers.

The look in them kindled something low in her body, low and surprising.

She was wearing nothing but a thin white nightdress, which she knew he could see right through thanks to the light from her bedroom window illuminating her from the side. Her hair was a dark and wild tangle around her face and down her shoulders.

Neve knew exactly what he saw when he looked at her. She could see it in the way he wet his lips, the way he struggled to keep his eyes on her face.

She did not mind the sight of him on his knees before her.

She gave the dagger in her hand a lazy spin and raised her eyebrow.

"Hello," she said.

His throat bobbed as he swallowed.

"Hello," he replied, his voice low.

Something in that voice felt like rough velvet along her skin. He made no move to rise to his feet as if he did not mind being on his knees before her either.

"What are you doing?" she asked softly.

"I…slept here," he responded, finally, almost reluctantly, standing.

She tilted her head. "Why? Did you get lost?"

He huffed a sheepish laugh and ran his hand through his hair.

"No. I just... the warrior you maimed, there were other men with him. I was worried they'd come looking for you."

Her smile dissolved. "I can handle men."

He looked down nervously. Clearly, he hadn't meant for her to find him there.

"I couldn't," he said. "I couldn't handle them. The thought of them. Coming here. To find you. To..."

He took a breath. She waited.

He finally met her eyes again. "I just wanted to make sure you were safe. That you stayed... safe."

Everything inside of her paused at the sincerity in his words. The *care* in his words. Tenderness and worry were highly unfamiliar sentiments, especially when the care was for her. She could not recall a time when someone had expressed concern for her safety, because until now, there had only been the Maere, and they did not worry.

"I tried," he continued. "I tried to sleep in my room, but every time I closed my eyes, I saw his hands going up your skirt..." he swallowed and looked down again.

"He has no hands now," she replied coldly.

"He has nothing now. *He* is nothing now," Killian looked at her, that nervousness dissipating, replaced by a resolute malice that could devour the world.

"You went after him?"

A firm nod. "I found him."

"And?"

"Ended him."

"Finishing my projects for me?"

He smiled. "For my own sake. My peace of mind."

"Not enough peace, apparently, if you still couldn't sleep in your room."

"Like I said, there were others with him."

Two thoughts warred within her.

One: the icy bristling that, despite the considerable power she'd already shown him, the depth of which he still could not truly fathom, he seemed to think she required rescue. And that she required it simply because she was a woman.

Two: the affection he was offering felt... *good*. Warm. Which was new and disconcerting.

"You understand that *I* was unconcerned?" she asked. "That even if a drunkard had walked into my room, he wouldn't have walked back out. If he'd left at all, he would have *crawled*."

Killian's jaw clenched. "I know."

"I need you to understand that I do not break."

He stilled and looked her in the eye. "I understand. I see you. But still, I find myself wanting to be here, near you...in case."

She didn't dislike it.

"In case," she repeated, giving him an inch of good humor.

He smirked, blue eyes dancing. "Just in case."

"Fine," she said.

"Fine, then," he responded with a nod.

She stepped aside and gestured to the room beyond. "Come in."

He followed her in and closed the door behind them. There were no chairs in the room, so he sat on the edge of her unmade bed. It felt strangely intimate, his sitting there amongst her tangled sheets. Still, she sat next to him and began braiding her hair.

"There were many whispers about you last night," she said, aware that he was watching the way her fingers moved as they plaited her dark waves.

"More rumors and stories for you to collect?"

"Some. And something new."

He tensed beside her. "New?"

She wrapped her braid around her head like a crown and tucked it into itself so it would stay put. She turned to him. There was a woodsmoke and pine scent to him that seemed to draw her nearer. Just slightly. "A new word to include on your list of titles," she purred. "Warrior. Legend. Killer. And now...*Deserter.*"

Something dangerous flared in the iron blue of his eyes.

Neve stood and sauntered to the dressing table, his gaze followed.

"They say you were released from the dungeon and immediately fled." She cupped her hands in the cold water of the basin and splashed her face with it, droplets falling onto the front of her nightgown. "They say you cast away your sense of duty to the Cadre and fled."

His nostrils flared. "I did not flee."

"You were eager to leave them and follow a woman you'd just met into the Dark Forest. Some might see that as you finding an excuse to escape." She reached into one of her packs and pulled out a clean pair of pants and a shirt, and dropped them on the bed.

A muscle feathered in his jaw. "Oddly specific rumors. Are you certain it wasn't you who was whispering?"

She shook her head casually. "I'd prefer if no one knew anything about us. These rumors are... inconvenient."

"And they've traveled fast. Much faster than we've traveled ourselves, it seems," he said.

"So it seems."

He was quiet for a moment. She could tell he was angry, trying to silently work out how folks out here knew about him going to the Dark Forest.

Neve had an idea about how the story spread so fast, but wasn't prepared to share it with Killian just yet. They needed to be further along in their journey for that conversation.

So, in the meantime...

She heard the sharp intake of his breath as she began lifting her nightgown and pulled it off over her head. Killian immediately turned his back to her and cleared his throat.

"Oh, such a gentleman," she murmured. "But you've seen it all before."

Neve watched his back go absolutely rigid and a pink blush appeared on the edges of his ears.

"When?" he managed to choke out.

"In the forest springs."

He turned his head towards her, still averting his eyes. "You knew I was there? That I was... watching you?" his voice was nothing more than a rumble.

Neve dropped her nightgown to the floor and pulled her pants up her legs and over her hips.

"I *let* you watch me."

Slowly, his eyes turned towards her as she slipped into her shirt. The look on his face was dark with want. Keeping her gaze locked on him, she pulled on her leather armor and closed the distance between them. He stood, jaw tight, hands clenching and unclenching.

"Will you tighten the laces at my back?" she asked, turning away from him. He was a wall of heat behind her. His fingers found the leather laces at the back of her armor and he did as she asked without a word. With each tightening tug, she let herself be pulled closer to him. She could feel his warm, unsteady breath on her neck and she liked it. His hands were rough as they yanked on the laces, tightening them from the top to the bottom, where he finally tied them off.

His hands were on her hips then. Resting there, waiting. She leaned into the touch ever so slightly. Neither of them moved. It felt like a moment suspended in time. There was nothing but the thrashing of his heartbeat against her back, the feel of his thumbs making small circles on the swell of her hips.

She knew she would have to be the one to break the moment.

So she did.

Neve took a step away from him and he nearly staggered. She turned and met his eyes, finding bare and utter desperation. She steadied herself.

"This town seems to like rumors. Let's get out of here before we give them more fodder."

He blinked and swallowed hard. "Of course," he croaked with a nod. "Wouldn't want that."

11

A fortnight passed as they traveled along the northern plains of Eodia. It was a good and proper October, the countryside awash in tall grasses that turned golden as autumn took hold. The trees were painted in bright reds and oranges, and the air jostled between blessedly crisp and downright cold.

The nights were full of frost. Inns were few and far between out in the endless plains, so most evenings Killian and Neve found themselves sleeping under the cold blanket of stars. They had begun their journey sleeping platonically and somewhat distrustfully, positioning their bedrolls with plenty of distance in between. But by now, as the season advanced with cold and their friendship took wing, they were nearly sleeping on top of each other for warmth. They shared their bedrolls and slept nestled next to each other, back to back.

Sometimes Killian would roll in the night and wake to find himself wrapped around her, pressed against her from behind. His arms would curl over her body, hands pressing against her ribcage, feeling her move with each steady breath. Her hair would be in his face, tangling in his beard, filling his world with her scent.

When he woke and caught himself holding her, he would always apologize and roll back over. She never made a noise to acknowledge his embarrassment, she just let it be. He almost wished she would say something, to know if she liked his touch, but he wasn't sure if he could bear knowing if she felt the opposite.

It was becoming more and more difficult to hide his feelings. His desire for her was a living, breathing thing. A dragon sitting on his chest, hot and heavy and deadly.

She was utterly unreadable and gave nothing away. No blush on her cheeks, no hot spark in her eye. Nothing on her face but cool confidence and, often, that smirk on her mouth.

That fucking mouth. He had dreams about that mouth.

But he wasn't about to risk the trust they were building by putting his hands on her, as much as his body begged him to. He wouldn't touch her unless he *knew* she wanted him to.

And, if that never happened, he'd have to be fine with it.

Or die pretending he was.

Around their campfire, Neve often told him stories. Tales of her god-killing conquests on far-away continents, places that were so wild and different he had a hard time believing they were real. Lands that were covered in nothing but sand and heat, or ice and cold.

What he really loved, though, was when she held her old blue-covered book in her hands and spoke about Eodia's royal bloodline and the knights that had once defended it.

The Island had once been a place worthy of such reverent stewardship. Its monarchs were just and fair, believing in progress and balance, and truth above all things. They were ruthless in warfare, cunning and smart, and would lay waste to any enemy that threatened their way of life and the freedom of Eodia's people. Victory belonged to them in each and every battle, until eventually, rival nations learned that pursuing war against them would be fruitless and fatal.

Defending the bloodline and the kingdom, often to their demise, were the men and women of the Grey family. Noble knights who were as deadly as they were loyal. The head of the family was known as the Sword-and-Shield Bearer: the greatest possible honor.

Killian did not deign to believe that the blade he carried was *the* sword and despite being a Grey himself, he'd never even *heard* of the fabled Bearer's shield until Neve told him about it.

Of course, old stories were notoriously inaccurate. None of it mattered anymore, anyway. The royal bloodline was long dead and what was left of the Greys was Killian, a soldier for hire who had now deserted his station, and his brother Rory, a man who didn't know the meaning of honor.

But it was a pretty tale that helped warm the night.

Deserter.

Perhaps it was the fact that he'd spent five years alone in a dank and moldering cell, but Killian was surprised to find that he didn't exactly care what the gentlefolk of Eodia thought of him.

He felt a semblance of guilt for not immediately returning to the Cadre. They'd been his family his whole life, his brothers in arms, his support, his *people*. But it was the thought of returning to Lowbarrow and settling back into an unabridged life as if the last five years hadn't happened... It was that thought that kept him from turning back.

He was not the same man as he once was.

Each day that passed, he recognized that man less and less. Something about Neve's quest, as mysterious as it remained, felt *right*. He couldn't explain it in any way. Like he was meant to do this.

There were countless times he'd been sent out on a mission by the Highborns and it had felt *wrong* as if it went against some ancient and deep instinct within him, but he'd done it anyway. This felt like the opposite. Like that instinct was sighing with relief at him.

Finally, it seemed to whisper, *something good.*

The stars were cascading across the sky. Killian lounged on his back, staring up at them with Neve next to him, a shared blanket pulled up to their chests.

Neve called this a "star shower," and he thought that there was no better way to describe it. Some stars simply winked in and out, like cold silver sparks in the sky, while many others streaked across the wide, dark canvas of night. It was a celestial storm dancing above them. Killian had never seen anything like it.

"I was born during a star shower," Neve said quietly.

He looked over at her and saw the reflection of the falling stars glittering in her eyes, the flickering light above playing across her face.

It almost looked like she was glowing with starlight.

He didn't think he could tire of gazing at her, but the way she looked on this night was... something else entirely. He swallowed the lump in his throat and moved slightly, feeling the line of her thigh against his under the blanket, and the knuckles of her hand casually grazing his fingers.

"Does this happen often? A star shower?" he asked.

She cut him an amused glance. "At least once or twice a year. But always on this night."

"What's special about this night?"

She smiled at the sky. "It's my birthday."

A strange glee climbed up his spine and he rolled to his side, propping his jaw on his hand and looking down at her. "Your birthday?" he mused.

She turned her face towards his, eyes sparkling. Gods, she was so close he could taste her breath.

"That's what I said. My birthday."

Perhaps it was a trick of the light, but Killian could have sworn her gaze ticked down to his mouth and lingered for a moment before she turned back to the stars.

He smiled. "Imagine that."

"What?"

"The very stars above celebrate your birth. Pretty impressive."

She looked at him again, her expression was unreadable, but it felt to him like she wanted to say more, like she wanted to let him in on one of the many secrets she carried with her. She paused for a long beat and seemed to search his eyes. Despite the cold, the air between them was thick and warm, taut with a tension that Killian couldn't tell if it was real or imagined.

The corners of her mouth lifted. "I'm glad you're impressed," she purred.

"Most things about you impress me," he responded, and immediately wanted to cut out his tongue for it being the dumbest line that had ever fallen out of his idiot mouth.

But her features softened just a little. "I know," she responded almost gently.

He froze. Her words were full of meaning and weight. He knew she meant more than just the fact that he was impressed.

She knew how he felt about her, a fact that was more terrifying than it had been to watch her quite literally eviscerate a man in front of him back in Hythe all those weeks ago.

"You know?"

"Yes, I know."

He sighed and lay back down, staring up into the night.

"I suppose I haven't exactly been secret about it."

She didn't say anything and they lay there next to each other in silence, the stars like flurries of glowing snow above them.

Beneath the blanket, he felt her hand move and soon slip into his, their fingers interlacing. His heart faltered and skipped a beat.

An offering. A kindness.

He was certain she did it to save him from shame, a gentle reassurance rather than as a confession of her feelings, but he wasn't about to pull away.

If a tender act of mercy was the only way he would be welcome to hold her hand, he would take it and savor it.

He brushed his thumb along hers, reveling in the softness of her skin. He felt his chest crack and he couldn't bear to look at her.

This had to be enough.

He would let this be enough.

"What did you get me for my birthday?" she asked, a playful lilt in her voice.

He huffed a grateful laugh. "Nothing. Of course, that's your fault for keeping it secret until now."

"Pity. I love gifts."

"Noted," he laughed again. Her hand was a warm comfort in his, sending thrill after thrill through his blood. "If you could have any birthday gift, Lady Nightmare, what would it be?"

The stars were beginning to slow their dance above. A short-lived phenomenon, star showers.

Neve gave a contemplative sigh before responding. "Anything?" she asked.

"Yes. If you could have anything at all."

"A kingdom."

He knit his brows and looked over at her. "To call your own? A place to put down roots?" He knew she'd never put down roots, never had a place that was hers in this wide-open world.

She looked at him with that same expression as before, like there was more to the story. But she just smirked and nodded.

In the sky, the stars ceased falling and simply peppered themselves across the sky as if they hadn't just put on the most magnificent show he'd ever seen.

Killian smiled and squeezed her hand. "I'll see what I can do about getting you a kingdom. Maybe by your next birthday."

12

Morning came, and she awoke with his arms around her. Again.

His snores were soft and steady against the nape of her neck. After the star shower, the night turned cold- very cold- and Killian enveloped her in his embrace many hours before dawn. And there she had stayed, thankful for the warmth.

As her eyes fluttered open for the day, she could feel his fingers moving.

The hem of her tunic had ridden up during the night and now his hands were on the bare skin of her stomach. His thumbs were caressing the softness he found there.

His breath changed and she knew he was awake, but neither of them moved from their position. The touch of his hands on her skin ignited something low in her belly and she found herself scooting closer to him under their shared blanket, spooning into him.

She could feel the hardness of his cock against her as she pressed nearer, a low and barely audible groan rumbled in his chest.

Within the weeks they'd traveled together, Neve had grown fond of Killian. He was loyal and dedicated despite knowing very little of the truth about her plans. He made her laugh and beneath the blustering warrior bravado, there was a playfulness to him that she enjoyed.

He was also beautiful. Deadly and handsome, a mountain of pure strength, and she found herself wondering what all that strength could offer her body- and not only in battle.

At first, she'd planned to use sex as a piece of leverage with him; if he started to stray or to consider turning back, she would have manipulated him into staying by offering herself.

But he hadn't strayed. He was steadfast, seeming to care less about the *why* of her journey and more about just being on it. With her.

As it turned out, unlike most men, he didn't need any sort of incentive for him to do what she wanted, he just followed because he chose to.

The choice of it all, *his* choice, turned out to be one of the most appealing and convincing things about him. It was something she'd never experienced before.

Another person *chose* her for no other reason than the fact that they wanted to.

He would follow her to the edge of the world.

And she would let him.

Neve arched her lower back slightly, bringing their bodies even closer together, and heard him release a hiss between his teeth.

His heart was hammering against her spine, thrumming in his fingertips, and she could feel her pulse quickening in response. His nose grazed along the length of her neck and the feeling sent a shiver down her spine.

He must have felt her reaction and, encouraged, gently pressed his lips against the same spot.

Another thrill shot through her. He trailed a line of tender, soft kisses up and up until his mouth was on the sensitive skin behind her ear. Yet another tremor of pleasure burst open, she felt it down to her core and couldn't control the desperate gasp that released from her.

The sound she made spurred him on, one hand slowly dragging down her side, over her ribcage, into the dip of her waist, up the curve of her hip where he *gripped.*

Her back arched again, this time of its own volition, and she felt his arousal pressing hard and eager against her.

Mere fabric separated them.

Her lower stomach clenched in anticipation as she felt his fingers slipping just the tiniest bit beneath the waistband of her pants. He paused there, giving her a chance to stop him. And when she didn't, his fingers moved a little lower. And lower.

And lower.

And.

Hoofbeats in the distance.

They both froze.

His hand was nearly at the apex of her thighs, but all of that primal need halted and an entirely different instinct took over. They were both on their feet in an instant. A wordless flurry of movement, yanking on leathers and gathering weapons, packing up bedrolls and securing them, eyes searching across the rolling, rocky plain for signs of movement.

"How far from here?" Killian asked brusquely..

She listened for a moment. "Not far. A mile, maybe two." As if on cue, they appeared, blurry figures cresting over a craggy hill in the distance.

"Fellow travelers?"

She looked at him and knew that he was likely asking out of hope rather than logic. "No, I don't think so."

Perhaps if they hadn't been wrapped up in each other, she would have heard them, sensed them, and tasted them on the wind much earlier.

She and Killian very well could have been long gone by the time they arrived. Then again, she trusted herself enough to know that even arousal couldn't dull her weaponized senses.

No, there was something else at work here. Something that had cloaked their visitors from her until now.

They waited.

She let a familiar ice fill her veins as the riders finally came upon them. Twenty-five guards approached. Most wore expensive white garments beneath shining metal armor, meticulously polished.

The Cavalry.

If Killian's Cadre was tasked with the Highborns' dirty work, the Cavalry was in charge of official orders: the high crimes of Eodia.

Namely, high treason.

And there, at the head of the formation, decked out in his own pristine Cavalry whites, was Rory Grey.

Neve could feel the way Killian stiffened, the way the heat of his instant anger rolled off his skin in a wave.

There would be a bloodletting this day.

A different and more familiar thrill crackled in her spine.

Rory dismounted his armored horse and took a few decisive steps toward Neve and Killian with dull eyes - no light at all in them. He regarded them with a haughty curl to his lips.

Drunk on power and cruel to the bone.

Rory looked at both of them, but his glare rested on her. T here it was. The light in his eyes that was absent a moment ago, now burning with disdain and hatred. He looked at her like he'd love to drive his fist into her face.

She answered his ire with a smile.

The loathing in his face sparked brighter. "Command Sergeant Rory Grey, at your service," he etched a sarcastic bow.

Through the corner of her eye, Neve caught Killian's hand moving over the hilt of his sword.

"Someone got a promotion, it seems," she taunted.

Rory took two steps forward into Neve's personal space so that he was nearly standing toe-to-toe with her.

"It turns out being able to track your traitorous brother earns you a good amount of credibility."

He looked down at her without lowering his chin. If she wanted to, she could end him right now.

He was utterly too arrogant to realize the danger he was in.

Killian was coiled and tense next to her. She could tell that he didn't like his brother's proximity to her or the threat in his stance.

Neve was without anxiety.

After a moment of failed intimidation, Rory stepped back and turned his attention to Killian.

"Your employers seek your return, *brother*," he stated.

Killian shrugged nonchalantly. "They can come for me themselves."

Rory's nostrils flared.

"They're otherwise occupied. So they sent me instead." He looked at Neve and then back at Killian. "I think it's best if we bring you both."

Killian was vibrating with barely contained violence.

Neve side-stepped Rory. The Cavalry was already in formation, she strode along their front line, examining each face that stood before her. Their eyes were all forward, avoiding looking at her, but she knew they felt the weight of her gaze.

"No," she said over her shoulder, petting a Cavalry horse. "We won't be going with you."

Rory turned. "I'm afraid that isn't up to you."

She paused and spun slowly on her heel to face him, standing squarely between Rory and his guards. Neve raised an eyebrow.

"Isn't it?" she challenged.

In a move too fast for any of them to see, never taking her eyes off Rory, she grabbed the daggers at her hips and flicked her wrists, sending them flying behind her and lodging resolutely in the chests of two guards on the front line.

Before anyone else could move, she pulled another pair of blades from her boots, threw them, and laid waste to two more men.

Four bodies slid from their horses and thunked to the ground in near unison.

"Remember what I told you, Rory Grey," Neve said to Rory in a low, steady voice. "You're a coward."

Rory Grey's lip curled in a furious sneer. "Seize them," he hissed.

And all hell broke loose.

13

Killian had seen and participated in hundreds of battles, if not more. He'd fought amongst and against the very best warriors of the age, been trained by the most ruthless experts in warfare.

And in all his days, he'd never seen someone fight the way Neve did.

She moved like a shadow, so fast and smooth that her opponents barely had time to take a breath before she was on them. She seemed to be one step ahead of each attack, anticipating blows as if they'd already happened.

She danced through the Cavalry like a death storm. Neve was vicious with her daggers but seemed to enjoy disarming the guards and using their own swords to end their lives. One after another.

Killian watched as a particularly large guard came at her like a bull, full force, with his greatsword flashing in the dim light of the gray morning.

Neve spun out of reach, untouched. The soldier growled, spit flying from his mouth in rage, and lunged again, cutting at her with brutal strength. He missed.

She side-stepped him, that fucking smirk playing on her lips, and swiped his legs out from under him with the mere toe of her well-placed boot.

The guard crashed to the ground and lumbered back to his feet with a roar that sounded a lot like: "You little cunt."

Neve caught Killian's eyes across the plain and a wicked grin spread on her mouth, making her whole face glow. Killian returned the grin, thinking that he'd never seen something so beautiful or terrifying.

Neve reminded him of a cat, pawing at a mouse until she was ready to swallow it whole. This guard was as good as dead.

She began circling the Cavalryman, her hands loose at her sides, taunting and waiting. He went for her again, swinging his greatsword high, aiming for her pretty neck.

Neve bent and spun in a crouch until she was behind him. Faster than his eyes could follow, she swiped her daggers across the tendons between his calves and heels, severing deep and sending the guard to his knees. A scream ripped through his throat and his sword fell from his hands as they instinctively reached for his injuries.

Neve wasted no time, the greatsword was hers. She stepped around the guard and stood in front of him.

The look on his face changed. Gone was the rage and vitriol. His eyes looked up at her from where he was on his knees and they were filled with fear.

"Please. Mercy."

She turned the greatsword, hefted it in one hand, and looked down her nose at the guard.

"Say it louder. So your friends hear."

He hesitated but raised his voice. "Mercy," he begged.

She leaned forward and Killian watched the guard flinch as Neve reached out and caressed his cheek, cupping his sweat-drenched chin in her hand. The man seemed to sag slightly with relief.

It was then that she struck.

Gripping his chin in one hand, she ran him through using his own sword with the other.

She looked him in the eye as she pushed the blade through his chest and said: "This *is* mercy."

Killian could have watched her fight all day, but, alas, he had guards coming for him as well.

The Cavalrymen were well-trained. But not the way he was. They were trained while wearing armor and helms, and with blunt-edged blades. Killian was trained in naught but his skin, to the death.

Many of the boys in the Warriors Keep didn't make it to adulthood because of the sheer ruthless brutality of their training alone. These men, in their shining steel and white clothes, were not the same as him.

His brother should have known better than to bring soft men to come up against Killian Grey.

They came at him in groups of two and three. He cut them all down while barely breaking a sweat.

Now, a group of four surrounded him. Killian cracked his neck, releasing the tension coiled in his muscles, and unleashed himself on them.

"All right, lads, let's get on with it," he casually taunted.

The two nearest to him charged him with their swords, and Killian deflected both, parrying the blows with sharp twists of his blade. Killian drove his weapon through the ribcage of the guard on his right, then spun and slashed, opening the throat of the one on his left and spilling it into the dirt. The tang of blood was a thick odor in the crisp fall air.

Of the two remaining Cavalry guards surrounding him, one was sneering and eager. Young. The other was as large as Killian and battle-scarred. That one bided his time. The young one attacked Killian with a speed that seemed almost greedy. He lunged with a clumsy move that Killian easily struck against, sending the boy's weapon flying onto the reddening ground.

Killian made that death quick, the boy didn't even see it coming.

He turned to the older, more patient guard. "Second thoughts? Or shall we?"

The guard smirked and sheathed his weapons. "Heard a lot about you, Killian Grey." He stretched his arms and bounced a little on his toes.

Right, then. A man out to prove his mettle and beat Killian Grey with his bare hands. Killian was almost impressed.

He sheathed his sword and closed the distance between them, sizing the guard up as he strode forward. Killian could smell the man's sweat and the freshly laundered linen he wore as they stood face to face.

"Show me what you've heard about me," Killian said in a low, deadly voice.

The guard swung a quick, heavy fist into Killian's gut and he let him. Although he was sure he'd have a bruise there tomorrow, outwardly, he didn't move. No flinch, no sound, not even a blink to acknowledge his opponent's effort. He just took the punch like it was nothing and watched the surety drain from the soldier's face when he realized he'd probably bitten off more than he could chew.

Killian stepped back and delivered a brutal right hook to the guard's cheekbone, feeling bone crunch beneath his knuckles. He stumbled back and Killian waited, watching as the man's eye swelled shut.

The guard straightened and came at him swinging. He landed a feeble hit on Killian's chin, and as soon as his fist connected, Killian grabbed the man's wrist and bent. Bent until he heard a snap, not unlike the sound of a branch cracking in half. The guard howled.

"Is this what you've heard about me?" Killian snarled.

He bent his knees and used his full power to bestow an uppercut to the man's jaw that sent him flying backward. Killian stalked forward and had his hands on either side of the man's head before he could even try to stand.

With a quick and brutal twist of his hands, he broke the guard's neck.

Killian turned to face what was left of the Cavalry and the air changed; the scent of coal and hot steel overwhelmed his senses, like the smell of a blacksmith. A smell that brought him crashing back into the memory of the worst night of his life.

The smell of magic.

Panic flooded him and his eyes searched for Neve. He found her across the killing field, standing at attention.

She locked her eyes on him, giving him a nod that seemed to say: *I am here. I am all right.*

His panic slowed a little. He watched her eyes flick to something behind him. Killian spun on his heel to see his younger brother striding his way, not a drop of blood dirtying his shiny armor or white clothes.

"Time's up," Rory said, the unmistakable look of presumed victory curling his lips.

Killian tried to take a step but found he was frozen in place. An unnatural heaviness spread through his limbs, his body utterly unmovable. His heart jumped to his throat. He wanted to turn to check on Neve, but his neck, even his eyes, were immobilized.

Magic.

Magic was paralyzing him.

14

"I'd hoped we could have handled this business like civilized men. Like brothers, even," Rory drawled.

From across the field, Neve could see the frantic rise and fall of Killian's chest. That was the only part of him that was moving. The sight of him immobilized and defenseless made a cold-blooded serpent of rage uncoil in her belly.

"If the girl hadn't started throwing weapons, we could have avoided this nonsense."

The girl.

She should have known there would be magic. After all, that would explain why she hadn't sensed the Cavalry coming for them until they were a mere mile away.

Even now, as Killian stood motionless, his eyes panicked, Neve could feel the tingle of that same magic knocking against her body, looking for a way inside.

Two guards advanced on Killian, links of heavily clinking iron in their hands.

They were going to put him in chains. Rory simply stood and watched. A coward, of course.

Neve stood as still as the dead, for all onlookers, she was just as paralyzed as Killian, which seemed to make the half-dozen or so remaining Cavalry find their comfort.

Indeed, the magic was strong. She could feel it. But she was stronger.

Her eyes searched the plains for the source of the power. It wasn't coming from the Cavalry, certainly not from Rory Grey: worm among men.

No, someone else was out here with them.

There weren't many places on this wide expanse of earth to hide. There was nothing but rolling hills peppered with tall golden grasses and the occasional tree, along with plenty of rocky outcroppings.

It was those upon which she focused her quick attention. Sure enough, there they were.

Her eyes narrowed on the two hunched figures, clad in brown hooded cloaks and nearly camouflaged against the rocky bank their backs were against.

Mages.

Tricky, indeed. She wouldn't have known they were there if she hadn't been looking for them. Their mouths and dirty hands were moving, furiously working a spell. Neither looked like they'd had a proper meal in months. Gaunt with beady eyes, lost in dark, exhausted hollows. Where their teeth should have been were only recessed gums and rotten nubs, making them look more like goblins than people.

Neve chanced a look at Killian. The Cavalry hadn't brought proper manacles, so now they were attempting to wrap the chains around Killian's wrists and ankles. Surely, they wouldn't need much more than that, given the magic had him paralyzed.

For now.

When she was certain the Cavalry was relaxed into the arrogance of thinking they'd won and their attention was not on her, she moved.

She prowled toward the Mages. Sheer terror crossed their worn faces when they saw her coming, and yet they continued working their spell. They did not break from their chanting, and they did not try to run. For that, she could commend them.

She made their deaths quick.

One moment, Killian was watching lesser men wrap his wrists and ankles in irons, feeling his heart thrashing in his mouth. And the next... the next moment, the unbearable heaviness of his limbs was very suddenly gone.

He staggered but found his balance quickly and sneered at the guards. The chain around his wrists was soon in his hands and he twisted it deftly around the neck of the nearest guard, strangling him while shocked gasps exploded amongst the Cavalry.

It took Killian a moment to realize they weren't gasping at his prowess with a chain.

No, they were gasping at what was sauntering across the plain toward them.

Neve. Her round hips swished back and forth as she confidently strolled in his direction. Her black leathers were spotted with other people's blood. The battle had ripped her hair free of its braid and it caught in the wind, flying wildly around her face. Her hands were at her sides and in them...

Heads.

One head in each hand, held by a casual grip in their hair, a trail of fresh blood following.

The look on her face was one he had never seen, despite having spent many hours staring at her.

Her endlessly amused smirk was gone, replaced by an expression of icy violence. Killian swore he could hear the men around him gulp down their fear. Even Rory looked uneasy.

Pure death. That's what walked across the killing field.

When she reached them, she stepped right up to his brother, who flinched despite himself as she dropped the heads at his feet, splattering the white pants that were tucked into his pristine boots.

Looking him in the eye, she set her hands on his shoulders and wiped her bloody fingers down the length of his arms. She wiped until her hands were clean and his white shirt was well-reddened.

"It will be more convincing," she purred. "If you return to your masters looking like you fought in the battle that your Cavalry lost. Perhaps they'll even spare your life."

All the color drained from Rory's face and he bared his teeth at her. "You fucking bi-"

She interrupted him with a loud whistle. The sound made the younger Grey nearly jump out of his skin.

Killian smiled.

Sure enough, Willow trotted across the plain with Neve's horse, Giselle. Both looked unbothered and like they'd spent the better part of the day gorging themselves on grass.

"You will let us pass without further incident," she said casually. Finding the bedrolls and supplies they'd stashed in the wreckage of what had, only hours ago, been their campsite and was now a blood-stained mass grave.

"Lay down your weapons," she commanded.

The five remaining Cavalrymen looked spooked and utterly out of their depth, and despite Rory's apparent seething rage, each man dropped his sword. The iron clattered on the ground.

A sword remained holstered across Rory's back. The traitor was a vibrating pillar of bitterness. Killian's lip curled in disgust. He stepped into his brother's space.

"The Lady asked you to lay down your weapon," Killian said in a gravelly voice. He circled the man and roughly yanked the sword free of its sheath.

A good, expensive blade. Brand new.

Smiling, Killian turned to Neve and offered the sword to her with a nod of his head. "My lady."

The cool smile he loved so much returned to her plump lips.

"That's a pretty holster he has," she remarked with an arched eyebrow.

So, Killian relieved Rory of his holster as well and slipped it over Neve's head and across her back. He took the sword and sheathed it for her.

Neve smoothly mounted her horse and Killian did as well, giving Willow a loving pat.

"You're both dead," Rory growled. "The Highborns will hear of this treason."

Neve looked down on him from where she sat atop Giselle.

"Why do you think I'm letting you live?" she asked in a near whisper. Rory blanched. "Tell the Highborns that *the girl* who took you down today is named Neve D'Aeth." A grin spread across her mouth. "And I'm coming for them."

15

They rode until evening, when they reached the edge of the plain and found a thicket of maple. The trees were all burning red and orange, the fire and flush of deep autumn. Against the amber setting sun, it looked as if some great painter washed the whole world in warmth.

Neve loved autumn; the burning colors always felt like good magic.

But there was another burning inside her.

She and Killian slowed and came to a stop. Without speaking, they settled on the perfect spot to make camp for the night.

His eyes were on her as he dismounted and let Willow trot off. There must have been a look on Neve's face because Killian tilted his head to the side curiously.

Neve dismounted and slung her newly-won sword and sheath off her back. Giselle strode away to find Willow.

Beneath her skin, Neve's blood was on fire. She'd never felt such heat.

It had been a good battle. Thrilling. Victorious. It felt good to fight alongside Killian. Both of them were utterly beautiful and brutal. She'd released her terror upon the Cavalry to devastating effect. She should have been well-sated after such a thorough fight.

And yet, she was not.

Her whole body was thrumming with wicked and resounding unrest. Normally cool as northern river water, her blood now slammed through her veins like hot lava.

Concern crossed Killian's face, a sharp and protective kind of worry that made the burning all that much worse.

"Are you hurt?" he asked.

She stalked towards him and, in a move too quick for him to see coming, shoved him against the nearest tree.

"What the fu–"

She didn't let him finish.

Instead, she grabbed him by the collar and crushed her mouth against his. For a split second, he froze with shock.

Then she felt a purely male smile cross his lips as she kissed him.

His hands found her hair and he *yanked*- hard enough to send a slice of delicious pain through her nerves- and pulled her away to get a look at her face. What he saw there made his cocky smile disappear, replaced by a dark and burning need to match her own.

He slammed his mouth back onto hers, biting and pulling her bottom lip, hands moving down her back and gripping her ass. He pulled her thighs apart and easily lifted her. She wrapped her legs around his waist, grinding against him. She took a handful of his hair and pulled his head back so she could lick up the side of his sweaty neck and take his earlobe between her teeth.

A low groan rumbled through him.

He spun them and slammed her back against the tree, pinning her between him and the trunk. She could barely breathe, but it didn't matter. She reached her arms up and grabbed onto the branch above her, squeezing her thighs around him and pulling him closer with her legs alone.

Realizing she was supporting her own weight, his hands explored her body with an expertise that rivaled only his skill in battle.

Groping and kneading like he would touch all of her at once if he could. His tongue stroked alongside hers in the tangle of their mouths. He wouldn't be able to get her out of her leathers at this angle, so she held tight to the branch above her as he used his strength to yank down the front of her corset.

Cold autumn air and the weight of his gaze washed across her skin and she moaned.

He leaned back to drink in the sight of her.

"Fucking hell, Neve, look at you," he growled.

His hands squeezed her breasts before he lowered his mouth to one, his teeth finding her nipple and then sucking it into his mouth.

She couldn't control the noise that came out of her throat or the way her hips bucked against him. A lightning current of pleasure rocked through her entire body, curling her toes in her boots, and he moved and gave the same relentless attention to her other nipple.

He slid his hands to her thighs.

"Down," he said, his face now buried in the valley between her breasts.

For the first time in her life, she did as she was told.

Her hands gripped the back of his neck and he slowly lowered her to her feet. With his hands on either side of her face, he looked at her for a moment. His expression was enough to make her combust, before capturing her mouth in a kiss that made a low purr rumble in her chest. His tongue licked the inside of her mouth and his teeth nibbled again on her bottom lip.

One hand was still on her face, the other traveled achingly slowly down the length of her body until he was undoing the laces on her waistband. He paused and looked at her before roughly shoving his hand down her pants and running a finger along her wetness.

He groaned and the sound had her rolling her head back in pleasure. Instantly, his hand was gripping her chin, pulling her face back to him.

"Eyes on me," he commanded.

She locked her eyes on his and he deftly spread her with his fingers and began rolling them in steady circles against her clit.

"Oh fuck," she moaned.

Her legs went nearly boneless. His rhythm was slow and the pressure he applied to her was devilishly perfect. She leaned forward and licked his bottom lip.

He smiled against her and moved the hand on her chin down to her throat, holding her in place.

"I want to watch you fall apart for me," he said quietly.

There, against the tree with one hand on her throat and the other down her pants, Killian was a storm of strength and Neve let herself become completely undone for him.

She barely remembered her name as he kept his fingers moving at that same unrelenting tempo. She felt her pleasure building and building.

Her eyes locked on his, surely her face was begging him for more.

"Come for me," he whispered. "I want it."

That was enough for her and she completely shattered.

A sound close to a scream ripped from her mouth as she came for him. Her whole body was shaking and she didn't even notice as Killian lowered her to the forest floor. His mouth found her breasts again and the pleasure already demolishing her only intensified.

Killian stripped off his leathers and the shirt beneath and she licked up his chest, hands roaming the ridges of muscle on his back and shoulders.

She reached between them and gripped his cock beneath his pants.

Hot, hard as stone, and throbbing for her.

Her hands went to work unbuckling his belt and unlacing the waistband. His hips firmly seated between her thighs, she used her feet to shimmy his pants down his legs. He gave her a gruff laugh and moved to finish the job.

It allowed her enough room to shove down her pants and kick them off.

When he was back between her thighs, he found her bare and gasped as his cock pressed against her needy entrance. His chest was heaving with need and she urged him forward, curling her legs around his lower back.

He restrained himself. His jaw tensed and a vein in his neck pulsed. He kissed her deeply, hungrily, and then pulled back and looked her in the eye, caressing her collarbones with shaking fingers.

"I need to hear you say yes," he said, his voice like gravel.

Something cracked in her heart at the same time as her lower stomach clenched with need.

"Yes, Killian. Yes."

His eyes darkened and with one brutal stroke, he plunged into her.

They both gasped.

Time was suspended. They watched each other with need and knowing. He was searching her eyes and she was doing the same.

Something was happening here. Something that would change them both.

Their mouths collided hungrily.

He began moving inside of her. She moaned into his mouth and met him thrust for thrust. They moved faster and harder, hands clenching flesh and leaving bruises behind. She raked her nails down his back.

She was a whirlwind and he was lost in her.

"More," she begged. "Deeper."

He groaned and gave her a nod.

"On your hands and knees, love."

A wicked smile melted onto her mouth and she turned for him. Watching him watch her as she did.

He looked as if he could die at any moment and be happy about it.

She leaned forward on her elbows, hips up in the air, teasing him. Looking over her shoulder, she smirked.

"Do your worst, Grey," she said.

Some sort of carnal, animal instinct seemed to take over and he gripped her hips before slamming into her so hard and deep that she cried out.

"Like that?" he breathed.

Her eyes rolled in pleasure as he thrust again, giving her all of his strength.

"Yes," she breathed, losing herself in his punishing brutality.

Her corset was still halfway on, and she felt him grip the laces at her back with one hand while taking a handful of her hair with the other, using both to pull her into each powerful thrust. A sound she'd never heard before erupted from her throat.

Pain and pleasure. So much pleasure. Her body was shaking around him, her internal muscles clenching and unclenching in a way that was making him groan repeatedly.

It was his turn to unravel for her.

She supported herself on one arm, looking over her shoulder at him. He watched as her other hand disappeared beneath her and began rubbing against her clit.

"Oh gods," he hissed.

She could feel him trembling, watching her pleasure herself as he rammed into her over and over again.

"Keep going. Touch yourself for me."

He was close; she could feel it.

So was she.

"Together," she breathed.

All he could do was nod, giving her all of himself, thrust after thrust. Her pleasure crested and she looked at him, begging, just as it was about to free–fall.

"Now," she groaned.

Her orgasm ripped through her and a mere second later, he went with her, calling her name.

Her body was an earthquake.

Killian leaned forward, wrapping his arms completely around her from behind. They were both still bent on their knees and Neve felt him pressing tender kisses against her shoulders.

He held her.

And she let him.

16

Above her was a wild canopy of red and orange. The trees were so lush that she could not see the sky between their fiery foliage and branches. Leaves fell from the treetops by the hundreds, floating idly to the ground where she lay. She could see nothing but burnished autumnal glory.

And Killian's head between her thighs.

Her eyes had opened at his first touch when he woke and crawled down the length of her body, kissing her dewy-cool skin as he went.

He settled himself between her legs, gently pulling her thighs over his shoulders. They'd slept naked together under the maple trees, so there was not a scrap of fabric in the way as he gazed reverently at her cunt, laid bare and eager before him again.

"Gods, I am a lucky man," he murmured, nuzzling his face against her, breathing in her scent. He said it more to himself than anything, but the rumble in his voice made her writhe.

Neve hissed when she felt his tongue begin to move against her, tasting, and she plunged her hands into his hair.

She became lost in feeling. The crisp air against her naked skin, the strength of his shoulders forcing her legs apart as she moved with his rhythm, the whisper of leaves as they fell around her and onto her.

Each stroke of his tongue brought her more and more outside herself and into some glittering, nebulous headspace where only pleasure existed. Like the stars in a star shower, like the very leaves swaying around them, she, too, was bound to gravity. Falling, deliciously falling.

He flattened his tongue and licked up the entire center of her before circling her clit. He groaned again.

"You taste so fucking good," he said, and burried his face deeper.

Neve's hips bucked against him, her fingers flexed in handfuls of his hair. Killian dove in, sucking her clit into his mouth and pulling with his lips, flicking with his tongue.

Pleasure moved like a shiver through her body. She ground her hips against his face again.

"Tell me what you want, love," he murmured.

"More." It was the only word she could find in the mess of her mind.

She felt him brush the tip of his finger against her entrance, teasing. Her body writhed, seeking more, needing more.

"You want my fingers? Use your words. Say it."

The rumble of his voice made her feel like begging, so, heart thrashing in her chest, she did what he asked.

"I want your fingers."

Slowly, he slid his long finger inside of her and latched his mouth around her clit. She could feel the cold metal of the rings decorating his knuckles against the heat of her skin and her entire body began to tremble.

"Can you take another one?"

"Yes," she hissed.

"*Fuck.* I can't tell you how many times I've imagined doing this to you."

Killian slid another finger inside of her and curled them both slightly. Then he began to fuck her in earnest, with his hand and with his mouth.

He was greedy with her, hungry, and all she could do was ride his face and the waves of thundering pleasure he offered.

The pressure built and built until finally, her orgasm crashed through her with such force that she found herself crying out, her head spinning and dizzy with it all.

Killian shifted so that his head lay on her chest, listening to the pounding of her heart, his hand cupping her breast.

"Good morning," he said.

She could *hear* the proud grin he was wearing, she didn't even have to look at him to know it was spread across his face.

"Indeed," she breathed. Her fingers lazily played with his hair and moved across the stable lines of his shoulders. She liked the weight of him against her, on her. It felt...secure.

As her heart slowed and her head came back to her, her thoughts moved to the journey ahead and how far they still had to go.

The next part of their trek would be, by far, the most dangerous yet.

For many reasons. Threat to life and limb, of course, but there was more. More to learn. More secrets that would have to be released. More trust would have to be given.

Neve moved, hoping to give Killian the hint that it was time to get on with their day. But he was immovable and held her firmly in place.

Shifting slightly and raising himself on his elbow to look at her, he said, "I have a feeling that this might be the last bit of peace we have for a while. Let's not rush to leave it."

"What makes you say that?"

His lips quirked. "The look on your face, for one. And, of course, there's the whole business of now being wanted for high treason."

"True, there is that."

He pointed in the distance and made a show of squinting his eyes. "Once we're beyond this forest, we'll be able to see the ridgeline of Mourner's Pass. Which happens to be the last barrier between us and the Oracle of Ula. So I'm sure we have a mountain climb ahead of us."

She nodded. "We do."

"So," he said, "I think I'd like to take our time this morning."

Killian leaned in and kissed her. She could taste herself on his lips and it momentarily drove her thoughts back to what he'd just given her, and what they'd shared the night before.

Reluctantly, he pulled away and stood.

She wrapped one of their blankets around herself as she watched him pull his pants up over his hips and set the kettle on their fire to fix her a cup of tea.

This was becoming a ritual for them. Through their travels together, Killian did this nearly every morning—he made her a cup of tea.

But today was the first day she saw it for what it was. Something he did for her as an act of affection. He didn't drink tea in the morning. But he knew that she did. And he would take the time to make it for her, giving her a few moments at the start of each day in which she could sit still without a task to complete.

So, when he gave her a steaming and fragrant cup today, she took his free hand in hers and said, "Thank you," and meant it.

Something quiet and gentle passed over his face, an expression she'd never seen and didn't have a name for. He nodded.

"Of course," he said, sitting down next to her. He shrugged his tunic on and ran a hand through his tousled hair. Killian looked at her, eyes searching her face. For what, she didn't know. "And thank you."

She tilted her head and took a sip of her tea, happy with the way it burned the edges of her tongue.

"For what?" she asked.

He looked away. It was then that Neve realized Killian was *nervous*.

"For last night," he replied. "And this morning." His brow arched at that, eyes glinting with mischief. Still, the disquiet was rolling off of him in waves.

When she didn't respond, he continued.

"You were... I don't have the words for what you were, what it meant to me."

Everything inside Neve tensed.

This was unexpected. Not only his words but the solemnity with which he said them. For her, she'd kissed him last night as a means of necessary relief. It was bodily. The pressure of battle and adrenaline and attraction felt like it would keep building until it killed her if she didn't do something to release it. So she'd done something.

She wasn't surprised that he was a good lover, but she'd been surprised by how quickly she'd let go for him, how she'd trusted herself to him without a moment's hesitation. Which indeed meant something to her.

But what he was talking about, the emotion in his eyes, this was something else.

"Say something," he said softly, looking down at his wringing hands.

"I am not... good at this," she admitted.

He smirked and nudged his shoulder against hers. "Beg to differ, my lady."

She resisted rolling her eyes at his attempt to lighten the mood.

"I've only ever taken men to my bed that I knew I would never see again," she said. "This is new to me."

Killian reached out and took her free hand, bringing it to his mouth and pressing his lips to her knuckles.

"I'm not asking for anything from you. If last night was the end of it, that would be enough for me."

The ice within her thawed just a bit. She felt it like a subtle shifting beneath her ribcage, some little change that made breathing a little easier.

"You're certain?" she asked.

"I am. It was enough," he replied earnestly. Then he gave her a wicked smirk and eyed her, still naked beneath the blanket wrapped around her shoulders. "That being said, if you ever wanted more, I certainly would not deny you."

Neve took a long sip of her tea to hide her amusement. "Good to know."

17

Mourner's Pass was a mighty range of mountains in northeastern Eodia, with over one hundred peaks spearing into the clouds. Nothing existed beyond the Pass save for Ula Lake, home of the Oracle, followed by a jagged coastline that marked the edge of the Island.

The mountains stretched the length of the northeastern peninsula from end to end. There was no way around the Pass; there was only up the mountains or through the equally treacherous valleys.

From where he sat on his horse, a few miles now from the foot of the Pass, Killian could see snow covering the peaks and the rest of the mountains were awash in the crimson brown of dying greenery. Winter arrived earlier here in the north and with their meager supplies, Killian didn't think they were prepared to weather it.

"We'll freeze to death if we try to go further with only the supplies we have left," he said.

Neve seemed, as usual, unbothered. Yet there was a blush high on her cheeks and on the tip of her upturned nose that told him she wasn't immune to the cold of the winter-spiked air.

He liked that rosy color on her skin, it reminded him of what she looked like when he was inside of her.

It had been nearly two weeks since the first time, and it hadn't happened again.

It played on a non-stop daydream loop in his mind, though.

Her creamy skin and the way her body moved beneath him. The sounds she made. The silky and sweet taste of her, the way she felt on his hand, around him.

It was bliss and torture all at once to be plagued with the remembrance of it every time he looked at her.

Something had changed between them, though.

She looked at him differently and spoke to him in a softer voice as if the cruelty in her was now only reserved for those who were not him. He felt like he'd been let into a secret club where only he and she were members. He said nothing about it, though, out of fear that she'd raise her guard back up.

During the night, he held her. Not just unconsciously, anymore. She let him begin the night with his arms around her and often nestled in close to him when the cold winds blew.

That was enough.

Perhaps not truly. Because in his heart and his body, he wanted more. He wanted all of her. Every hidden piece of her. But he would only take what she offered.

And the fact that she offered him this much... it would have to be enough.

"Neve, there is no outpost between here and the Pass. We will die without the proper supplies," he called out.

He loved her confidence and bravado, but her constant nonchalance and surety grated on his nerves.

Just once, he'd like to see her flustered, if only to validate his sense of anxiety.

She gave him a sly look. "Have you been here before?"

"No. But I've studied the maps."

She waved a dismissive hand. "Maps can be wrong."

He bristled. "Have *you* been here before?"

Neve smiled, a playful light dancing in her eyes. "No. But I've read the stories."

He rolled his eyes. "To our doom, then."

"No," she said, shaking her head. "Not to our doom." She pointed to the mountains. "Just past the foothills, in the first valley, there will be a place for us to spend the night and gather supplies."

"How do you know?"

She paused and pinned him with a look that seemed to read him. As if there was a secret he should be in on but wasn't.

"I have some old friends there."

A chilled sense of foreboding skittered up his spine at her words. He tried to ignore it, but the closer they moved toward the foothills and the valley beyond, the more intense the feeling became.

They crested a hill and soon they were truly at the foot of Mourner's Pass. Killian craned his head back as far as it would go and he couldn't see the top of the peaks from this angle. He hoped their path would take them through and not up, but each option was equally dangerous.

His eyes scanned the terrain for the outpost she said would be there and saw nothing. "Where--"

Neve approached the rocky expanse of the mountain base and dismounted Gisele, giving the white mare a reassuring pat. Killian followed her lead, hopping off Willow and looking around cautiously.

"Look," Neve whispered, pointing at the wall of stone before them. He was about to remark that there was nothing there when he saw it and his breath caught in his chest.

There, perfectly camouflaged, was an ancient archway and two ornate granite doors carved into the side of the mountain itself. Two tall, strong pillars stretched upwards on either side of the curved archway, decorated with scrollwork that must have taken the carver ages to complete. On the doors themselves, engraved with deep care and precision, was a familiar curving knotwork with no beginning or end.

The sigil of House Grey.

His stomach dropped and he reached out his hand to touch the carving. His fingers shook. A feeling of reverence and fear nearly took him to his knees.

"This is..." he croaked out, but was unable to finish his thought, overcome with feelings he could not utter.

Neve stepped up next to him, a deep *knowing* glittered in her green-gold eyes.

"The Grey's Stronghold," she said quietly. "The place your people lived and trained for millennia, before setting off to serve the Castle. If things were different," she paused, taking a deep breath and letting it out slowly. "If Nyx hadn't been murdered and the curse hadn't fallen on Eodia... this would have been your home."

His balance wavered and he pressed his forehead to the cool stone before him, as if he could embrace the place itself.

"I'd always heard the location of the Stronghold was a guarded secret; that only the Greys could find it and the knowledge was lost centuries ago. How did you know where it was?" he asked, his voice barely above a whisper.

Her chest rose and fell with another deep breath, but Neve's face betrayed nothing.

"Old friends," she said simply.

"What—"

"We should get inside. It will be dark soon."

He knew her well now, well enough to know that when she wasn't ready to tell him one of her secrets, there would be no coaxing her into offering it. So he took a shaky step back from the stone doorway.

"There's no handle. How do we open the doors?"

She touched a deep slit in the rock, just below the sigil on the right-hand door.

"Your sword," she replied. "Your sword is the key."

Moving as if underwater, dazed and nearly unbelieving, Killian drew his sword and slid it into the crack.

Sure enough, it fit, and as he pushed it in, a force of power crashed into his blade, moved up his arm, and into his body. It was a sizzling, hot fire and brute violence that felt like a horse kick to the chest. He gasped and yanked his sword out of the stone, and when he did, a great rumbling resounded deep within the mountain.

The door cracked open with a crumbling yawn and a blast of old air came out from within as a ghostly sigh.

This was a holy place.

A dead place.

Killian was sure that Neve could sense how completely overwhelmed he was and she placed her hand on his shoulder. Her touch somehow stabilized him and brought him back into his body. His vision cleared and he steeled himself. He searched her eyes and found them gentle, if not slightly eager.

"One day I'll need answers," he told her.

She nodded. "You'll have them. I promise."

That was as good as he could hope.

He took a step into the mountain.

~

Upon entering, immediately to their right, was an ancient stable. It once housed a hundred gallant horses, but now stood empty, covered in cobwebs and dust. The stalls still smelled of horse despite the centuries that stretched between now and the last time one was sheltered here. Killian and Neve left their horses in the stable.

A glance to their left revealed nothing but a narrow dark hallway, wide enough for one person at a time, and not suitable for their equine companions.

Neve moved to take the lead, but Killian placed a hand on her lower back, shook his head, and stepped in front of her. She let him. Whether it was the look on his face or the knowledge that this place was somehow *his*, she let him lead the way.

The hall was tight and suffocating, narrow enough that his broad shoulders brushed against the walls as he walked. It was dark and became darker the further they moved from the stable.

"We need a torch," he murmured, senses on high alert. The dense darkness felt claustrophobic.

Neve placed her hand between his shoulder blades and kept it there.

"We've both been in darker places than this."

He gritted his teeth and kept moving. She was right, of course. But it didn't ease the dread weighing down his guts.

He could see nothing. Each time there was a sound, his heart hiccuped; Neve's quiet breath behind him, water dripping in the distance, the scurrying of small rodents underfoot trying to avoid his boots. The deep moaning of old stone.

There were other sounds, too.

Footsteps against rock.

Killian halted, feeling Neve, a steady presence against his back, wordlessly do the same.

Indeed, the footsteps he'd heard were not their own. It sounded like they were everywhere. In the distance ahead of them. Above them. Below. Unhurried, lazy movements in the dim. The hair on his arms and the back of his neck stood on end.

"Keep moving," Neve said quietly.

Leading with his sword, gripped by both hands in front of him, he walked on. Soon, the shadows began to dissipate and the air became thinner.

They rounded a corner and the hall opened up into a wide and breathtaking chamber.

The walls were high, covered with carvings, scrollwork, and deep green moss. Light broke through the cracks in the stone in sharp, straight beams. In the center of the chamber was a great, oval table, around which were dozens of mismatched seats.

Carved in the middle of the dark-stained wood of the table was the sigil of House Grey.

On the north end of the chamber was a huge, soot-stained hearth, and along the walls stood suits of armor, so many that Killian lost count. The suits seemed to stand as sentries for the space, eternally at attention.

Killian lowered his sword and wandered the room in curious awe. Neve followed his steps silently.

Hanging above the hearth was a crumbling old flag, its insignia faded and covered in dust. He stepped closer and looked up at it, squinting his eyes to try to make out the design.

The tattered fabric was dark blue and at its center, barely visible, he could make out the edges of what was once woven there. A simple line drawing: a crescent moon and clusters of stars above an ivory tower.

The very same drawing from the title page of Neve's storybook.

Brow furrowed, Killian turned to look at her. She did not return his gaze. She was staring at the flag, her beautiful face was a mask of neutrality, but he could see it, the change in her eyes.

He swore the color in them was brighter, almost glowing, and they were filled with a particular longing that made something in his chest crack open and bleed for her. His fingers reached for her, his mouth opened to ask the question–

And something moved behind her.

18

At first, it was only smoke. A cloud of black vapor floated and swirled behind Neve, advancing towards her. And then it was more. It churned and rolled and grew, taking shape. The shape of a man.

Behind the first, dozens of other shadows gathered and changed form until the chamber was full of warriors that had quite literally appeared out of thin air. Some wore fighting leathers, some wore armor. Most bore the remnants of old wounds. Fatal wounds. Their faces were all menacing, scarred, and solemn. Their bodies were somehow there and also not as if they were the whisper of memory made corporeal.

Killian's breath caught. They all looked like *him*. Not identical, of course, but the way siblings and parents and children belonging to the same family looked alike. The same eyes on one, the same sharp jaw on another. His insides were a boiling cauldron of fear and confusion and some other emotion he had no name for.

Ghosts.

Ghosts of the Greys.

The first one stepped forward and faced Neve. Killian pointed his sword at the ghost protectively. He had no idea what these spirits wanted, but he and Neve had wandered into what was surely a sacred place, a tomb, uninvited.

"Easy," Killian warned, his voice low.

Killian watched as Neve's back straightened and she slowly raised her chin. She stared down the ghost with poise and authority, her eyes still shining with the same strange luminescence they'd had as she'd gazed at the flag above the hearth.

Killian's fingers itched around the hilt of his weapon.

The ghost drew his sword, making Killian tense and move closer to Neve. But the ghost held the blade before him, pressing the tip into the floor, then bowed his head and gracefully dropped to one knee in front of Neve.

The roomful of phantom warriors all followed suit until every man in the chamber, except Killian, was bending the knee.

Wild-eyed, Killian looked at Neve for answers, but her focus was on the ghosts kneeling before her, a small and gracious smile on her lips. His heart was pounding in his chest, making his whole body shudder.

The first ghost spoke, his voice deep and dusty. "My Queen," he said.

Killian swayed on his feet.

"My Queen," repeated the chorus of ghosts, the words echoing off the high stone walls.

The edges of Killian's vision blurred. He reached out for her. "Neve?"

She looked at him and in her eyes, he found his answer. They were beautiful and bright and full of relief, like she could finally let go of a secret she'd held onto her whole life.

"On your knees, boy," the first ghost growled at him.

Without thought, Killian pressed the blade of his sword to the floor and bowed his head, moving to kneel.

But she touched his arm. He raised his face back up to her and she gave him a subtle shake of her head before turning her attention back to the ghosts.

"Rise," she said. Her voice was the same melodic yet husky sound he'd come to love, but now it was... different, somehow. Regal.

Queen.

Their Queen.

Therefore, *his* Queen.

Neve was Nyx's heir.

So many things clicked into place in his mind. The secrets, her obsession with stories of Eodia despite being born on some faraway icy continent, her power and strength, his own internal *need* to follow her, to know her.

From the start, he had known she was different. Despite his loyalty to the Cadre, he'd left them without a thought to follow her. When she'd asked him to accompany her to the Oracle, he hadn't asked why; he'd just said yes.

His ties to her were ancient. As ancient as the very Island upon which they stood. For thousands of years, his bloodline guarded hers. And now here he was, compelled to do the same, without even knowing it.

The need to be at her side was instinct.

Blood-deep instinct.

Watching her stand before the ghosts of his family, he knew two things for certain: he would follow and protect her to his doom. And he was hers, forever.

His head and heart were a storm.

His body stumbled.

He found a chair at the oval table and fell into it, resting his elbows on his knees and his head in his hands.

He heard her make a *tsk* sound with her tongue before she said, "So dramatic."

A ghostly chuckle moved through the room.

Neve lowered herself into the chair next to him, at the head of the table, with Killian to her right. She gave his thigh a reassuring squeeze.

"Look alive, soldier," she said quietly. "I swore you'd have answers and you're about to get them."

Killian straightened up and took a deep breath to clear his head. Her hand was still on his leg, so he covered it with his own, enfolding her fingers with his.

The first ghost sat at her left and the rest of them found seats around the long table.

"We've been waiting centuries for you, Your Highness," he said.

"What's your name?" she asked.

The ghost gave her a nod of his head as if honored she'd asked. "Sir Gawyn Grey, Sword-and-Shield Bearer of Queen Nyx Lyra."

A chill went through Killian's body. "You were with her. In the end," he said.

Sir Gawyn's ghostly eyes filled with sorrow. "I was."

"What happened?" Neve asked.

"It's not pretty, Highness."

"I don't need pretty," she said, her voice like ice. "I need truth."

Gawyn nodded. "Very well," he said. He paused as if to gather his strength to tell a story that was still painful for him, even after centuries.

"Her half-brothers were coming for her. She knew it. Had known for weeks before it happened. She wanted to protect the bloodline. She had time to get her daughter out and used magic to make everyone believe the girl was dead. Everyone except me, because I got the princess out of Eodia and to another continent."

"I suppose I should thank you for that. I wouldn't be here now if you hadn't succeeded."

"I began to think the bloodline had died out despite the effort. But then, about thirty years ago, there were whispers that a Lyra girl was born under a star shower, on the very continent I'd sent Nyx's daughter off to. On that same night, here in Eodia, as the stars fell in the sky, the Island shook on its foundation. The very earth quaked, and I began to hope."

Killian remembered that night. Barely four years old and already training in the warrior camp. He remembered the earth moving, he remembered the screams of the boys in his barracks and his own wails of fear. His brother, Rory, was terrified in his arms. They were mere babies. It was over as unexpectedly as it started.

No one explained what happened, but the commanders claimed that they'd made the gods angry by not training hard enough.

From that day on, Killian spent each day training as hard as he could.

"Why did they come for her? Her half-brothers?" Neve asked.

"Many reasons," Gawyn said. "They wanted the throne, her power. They didn't like her politics or the way she ruled. But most of all, they hated her. They believed that she was favored unfairly by the gods while they were not favored at all."

"How fragile," she drawled.

"Indeed. They decided to kill her. They were warned, however. Mages, soothsayers, and even the Oracle of Ula all warned the half-brothers that killing Nyx would mean their demise. She truly was favored by the gods. They loved her and blessed her with magic and godly power of her own. And threatening such power, *murdering* such power, would only mean disaster."

"They did it anyway."

Gawyn nodded. "They poisoned her wine that night."

"Cowards," Neve whispered.

Centuries-old rage curled the ghost's lips. "The poison didn't kill her. But it slowed her down enough for them to reach her. They'd raised an army of their own, brutalizing everyone in their path. Down to the servants and the scullery maids. They killed everyone to get to her. She wanted to go to the tower, to ring the bell and alert the Island - and the gods - to what was happening. I ran with her through the castle. She and I battled the army as we went. Our swords, hers and mine, brought many to their deaths that night. But it was not enough.

"Her half-brothers found us. Just as we reached the tower. They may not have had the favor of the gods, but they had power of their own. Devastating power. That's where they ended me. Then they cut her down once I was dead. It is...my greatest failure. The rest I only know from stories and legends."

Neve made no move to comfort or absolve the ghost, whose guilt and shame were a palpable tension in the air around them. Killian knew the weight of such guilt. He bore it himself for his family. He would bear it again if he somehow failed Neve the way Gawyn failed Nyx.

"When Nyx cursed the Island and cut it off from the gods, where did the half-brothers go?" Neve asked, a deadly light glinting in her eyes.

Gawyn shook his head. "No one knows."

"Someone knows," she shot back.

"Apologies, Highness. Perhaps I should rephrase. *I* don't know. *We* don't know. We came to rest here after our deaths, and we only know what we hear in whispered rumors across the continent."

"What are the whispered rumors about the half-brothers?"

"Many different suggestions. Some say the gods struck them down before the curse took effect. Some say they ran. Some say they disappeared. Some say... that they are still here. In hiding."

"They would be over three hundred years old."

"As I said, they had power of their own. I do not know where such darkness comes from. So perhaps it's possible that they still live."

"Perhaps," Neve repeated quietly.

"And now? What do you plan to do, Highness?" Gawyn asked, hope lighting his eyes.

"I plan to find a way to take what's mine," Neve said simply. "And undo the rest."

Gawyn gestured at the ghosts around the table. "We are mere shadows now. But we are at your command, in whatever way we can serve." He seemed to swallow hard. "Seeing you here today makes me think... that perhaps all is not lost."

Neve gave the ghost a small smile. "Not lost at all."

Interlude II

The rat-like man came sniveling to their throne room.

His clothes were covered in streaks of blood.

Unacceptable.

"What news?" they hissed in unison. So many centuries together, they'd nearly melded into one being.

It was just as well.

The man smelled of fear and blood and failure.

"We were unsuccessful, I'm afraid. They got away."

"They?"

The man swallowed. "Yes. He had a girl with him."

"A child?"

"No, a woman."

"You had an army," they said.

"They are gone."

"Fled? We thought you were a better Sergeant than that."

The man was shaking. "No, they did not flee. They are dead."

Rage. Deep and undying rage.

"All of them?"

"Nearly. She spared me so that I could tell you her name."

"*She?*" Their voices were like the sound of so many snakes, rolling around each other, the brushing of scaly skin, the lashing out of forked tongues.

"Her name is Neve D'Aeth. And she said she is coming for you."

Rotting laughter came up from their throats.

"Find her. Bring the Mages. More this time. Then do your worst to her until you have answers."

The smell of fear left the man, and he grinned at them.

"My worst?"

"Oh, yes. Your very worst."

19

The ghosts of the Greys were good hosts. Excellent. By some magic, they'd set Neve up with a hot meal in her room and an even hotter bath, which she'd luxuriated in until the water turned cold and the skin on her fingertips puckered. The meal was a whole roasted chicken with root vegetables, and Neve ate until only licked–clean bones remained.

The bedroom they'd offered her was large with a high canopied bed, laden with fluffed pillows and thick blankets. The ghosts cleaned much of the dust and cobwebs from her accommodations, but not all, a fact which they apologized for profusely. She'd reminded them that simply having a bed was enough after months of sleeping on the ground.

They doted on her like she was precious and, despite her gratitude for their shelter and hospitality, she didn't care for being treated like porcelain.

They knew who she was, but didn't know *her*.

Soon they would.

The whole kingdom would know.

Gawyn invited Killian to go with him. Neve was sure it would be for a history lesson within the very walls his kin had trained in for thousands of years. That was between Killian and the Greys.

After supper and her bath, she'd dressed in a simple cream linen dress and piled her wet hair into a bun on the top of her head. Then, she'd gone to explore the stronghold.

She padded along the halls in bare feet. The floors were made of cold stone, covered with ancient rugs. Sconces along the walls burned dimly, illuminating as much as they could of what was essentially a less-primitive cave.

She felt phantom eyes on her as she went. Her ghostly army. Some watched her pass in their corporeal forms, others deigned to remain invisible to her, but she felt them nonetheless.

Neve knew that now she was here, things would start to move quickly. The secret she'd kept for thirty years, the secret The Maere also kept for her, was finally uttered out loud. Now that it was out, there was no putting it back. There was no *turning* back.

She'd never considered it for herself, but after seeing the hope in Gawyn's filmy eyes, the hope that sizzled amongst all of the ghosts who knelt before her today, what she needed to do was entirely cemented. If these dead men were hanging their faith on her shoulders with such earnest anticipation, she could not imagine how the living people of Eodia would feel when they heard that their lost Queen had returned.

She would not fail.

No, she would bring hell upon the heads of anyone who stood between her and the Castle.

Neve took a cramped, spiral staircase up, and the narrow hall opened to reveal a space that made her heart slow.

A library.

The smell of paper was as close to a sense of home as she'd ever known, and in this cavern filled with books, the scent was nearly overpowering. Books. Hundreds of them. Perhaps more. They covered the walls with shelves that were carved into the rock; they were in piles on the floor, strewn across the two writing desks that were crowded into the corner of the room. She could spend days in such a library. Years, even.

Sconces on the walls came to life as she walked deeper into the chamber—more old magic. Candles in golden holders on the desks spit into flame as well. Open pages fluttered as she walked past. She ran her fingers along the dusty paper, and a feeling settled into her that was something like peace.

Her eyes scanned the shelves, seeing some titles she was familiar with and some that she was not. There were many books on battle and war. Many history books as well. Neve's gaze settled on a small tome that could be the twin of the one she'd carried with her since birth. A worn dark blue cover, but on the title page, instead of the sigil for the royal house of Lyra, were the words *Astrea and Ewan.*

Neve settled into a chair at one of the writing desks and lost herself in the story.

If you would hear a tale of love and death, here is that of Astrea and Ewan. Of duty and service, cleaved in half by that ever-sharp blade of love.

Queen Astrea the Silver of the royal house of Lyra, named so for both the gleaming silver locks of her hair and the power of pure starlight she wielded.

Sir Ewan Grey, Sword-and-Shield Bearer to her reign.

Both were born in Lyra Castle and grew up together as children. Astrea grew into a mighty and great ruler. Ewan grew into a valiant warrior.

The story went on to describe the respective childhoods and training of each of them. More a manual on the raising of Queens and Knights than prose. Pages and pages on how to turn a child from a wee thing into something mighty and deadly. Each was born and bred to be a weapon in their own right. One to rule the kingdom and one to protect it.

Upon their adolescence, Astrea's mother, Queen Selene, died, placing the heavy weight of the ancient crown upon the 16-year-old's head. As part of her coronation, it was her duty to choose a Sword-and-Shield Bearer of her own.   She chose Ewan.

It was also her duty to find a Prince to marry to secure the Lyra bloodline.

Since the day he understood the word, Ewan loved Astrea. Loved her with the clumsiness of a boy. Loved her with the quiet of a man who grew up to understand that he could never have her. At her side, he stood, as suitors from continents near and far came to compete for her hand.

None were worthy, and he told her so, as she looked to him for his opinion as each new man darkened her doorstep.

Soon, Astrea grew fond of Ewan. That fondness, as it often does, turned to like, and like turned to love.

Until one day, a wholly worthy man arrived in Eodia and sought Astrea's hand. When the Queen turned to her Knight, seeking his opinion, she hoped he would once again quietly decline. But, with a tear in his eye, he nodded his head for this Prince.

And so, with a heavy and jilted heart, Astrea married the southern Prince, and Ewan stood as witness.

The story stretched years, decades filled with longing looks and mournful sighs. Ewan watched as his Queen fell in love with her Prince. Watched as she was happy with him. Watched her bear beautiful children. To him, she was a wonderful parent, and he bore a deep and unending ache to know that she would never mother his children. So he tended to hers as if they were his own. Becoming a teacher and an uncle to the babies whose eyes matched those of the woman he loved.

For her part, Astrea loved her husband. Loved him well and deeply. But could never offer him her whole heart, as part of it would forever be owned by Ewan. A secret she could not, would not, tell a soul.

Eventually, the years brought age upon them all.

One day, Sir Ewan called for his Queen.

She arrived in his chamber to find him ailing in his bed. An old man now.

"It seems I will not have a warrior's death, after all, my lady," he said to her.

"Surely you will not die today," she replied.

"Surely, I will. Before I go, let me hold your hand and tell you a truth that I've kept all these years."

So, she sat on his bed and gave him her hand. He held it lovingly, like a prayer, bringing it to his lips for a kiss.

"There have been two great joys in my life. Serving you and loving you. One has prevented the other. But it has been there nonetheless. I loved you when we were children, and I love you today, as we are old and gray. So I say to you now, that while you have never been mine, I have always been yours."

Tears fell from the Queen's eyes, and she leaned forward to bestow upon her faithful knight a kiss.

When she pulled away from his lips, he simply smiled and said, "Joy." And then, in her arms, he took his last breath.

The Queen wept, and in the magnitude of her grief, the foundations of the castle shook and her power of pure starlight broke free from the reigns she'd long controlled it with. It sprang from her fingers, her hair, her eyes, and her skin until she was consumed by her celestial magic. Until she became an explosion of starlight that outshone even the sun in the sky.

When the light of her power faded, there was nothing left in the Knight's chamber but furniture, for she, in dying, delivered them both to the heavens above. Where they, at last, could be together.

"Nose stuck in a book." Killian's smoky voice brought Neve out of the pages before her and back into the present moment.

He stood leaning in the doorway, looking much more tired, perhaps even a little older, than he had been a few hours ago. Despite the dark circles under his eyes and the weariness tensing his shoulders, his expression still lit up for her. A fact that she enjoyed, even if she didn't know what to do with it yet.

"I can't remember the last time I was in a proper library. Too long," she said.

He sauntered into the chamber and took a seat in the chair next to her at the desk. Killian released a sigh that told her he'd been on his feet for much of the day and was now relieved to be off them.

"You may be living the greatest story of our time, and yet you still need to read about other people's lives?"

Neve smirked. "I don't *need* to. I *want* to. There's a difference."

He offered her a smile. "Fair enough."

Words unspoken and questions unanswered hung heavy between them. He had a curious mind, particularly when it came to her.

She also knew that what he wanted, more than anything, was for her to open up to him. She could see it in his eyes, the way he looked at her; he was practically begging her to give him her trust.

What he didn't know was that she'd already given him as much of herself as she could.

The rest would either come with time.

"You look tired," she stated.

He leaned back in his chair and tilted his head to the side, cracking his neck. "It's been a long day. Traveling. Conversations with dead people. Finding out the woman I –" he caught himself and swallowed hard. "Finding out that you're the lost heir of Eodia. It's a bit much for one day."

"Since we met, you've been seeking answers, and now that you have them, it's too much?"

He arched an eyebrow at her. "How long have you known?"

"Known what?"

"About who you are, your lineage?"

She shrugged. "I've always known. I was left with the Maere when I was born, and they kept my secret."

"It's quite the secret," he said quietly, with just the hint of a smile at the corners of his lips.

"It is," she replied.

"I will also keep it, for as long as you need it kept." The sincerity in his tone and his face made Neve's chest clench.

She nodded. "I expect it won't need to be kept for much longer. But thank you."

"Can I ask you something?"

"Yes."

He took a breath, and it seemed like he was having a hard time looking at her, but he did it anyway.

"Why didn't you let me kneel for you?" There was a touch of something mournful in his question, something that felt like it was balancing on the edge of rejection.

Neve settled in her chair and gently closed the book in her hands.

"You're a warrior," she said. "You've been conditioned your whole life to follow orders. If you kneel to me, I want you to choose it for yourself. Not because someone else demands it of you."

He sat looking at her for a moment, his throat bobbing and the muscles in his jaw twitching. His blue-grey eyes looked fogged over with an emotion that felt sharp, sacred.

After a deep breath, he reached over and slid the book from her lap, setting it delicately on the desk. In a fluid motion, he shifted from his chair and onto his knees before her, taking her hands in his. He looked deeply into her eyes.

"I am yours to command," he said. "My body, my sword, my whole self. I am yours." He bowed his head and brought her hands to his lips and kissed her knuckles before pressing his forehead against them in what felt like silent devotion.

The thing that had clenched in her chest for him earlier now cracked, letting in the whisper of a warmth she had never once felt in all her years.

A new feeling entirely.

Something soft, something...fragile and tender and entirely foreign to her. She felt it physically, in a tingle deep in her ribs, in a flush of gentle heat on her skin. It was a feeling that made her want to touch his face and reassure him, a feeling that made her want to press her lips to his.

Instead, she sat quietly and let him kneel before her, offering himself to her service, offering himself to her.

20

The icy wind bit at their skin with sharp teeth. Despite the fur-lined coats and heavy wool underclothes they'd taken with them from the Grey's Stronghold, the cold of the vale was relentless. Neve and Killian decided they'd need to go through Mourner's Pass rather than climb it; while the valleys were filled with fell creatures, old magic, and forces of nature, it was still the path of least resistance when all things were considered.

Deep and dark, the vale of Mourner's Pass was a veritable wasteland of terror. The mountains surrounding it were so high that the sun could not breach their barrier, casting everything below in eerie shadows. Yet somehow, the ruthless north wind found its way through the towers of black cliffs, making it just as frigid and inhospitable as the mountain summits above.

Nothing green could grow in the valley. The ground was pure obsidian as if the stone melted long ago and spilled down the mountains to coat the landscape in cold rock.

There was nothing in the valley save for stone and violent rivers that, even this early in the season, were already becoming covered with a thin sheet of ice. And, of course, the shadows, along with the creatures and angry, ancient magic that made such a place their home.

Neve didn't mind the cold. But she knew what lived in the vale. And she knew they were waiting for her.

It was a rare thing that anyone ever made it to the Oracle of Ula beyond the mountains. The peaks and canyons were littered with the winter-bleached bones of those who tried. If the wolves, wyverns, and other beasts of Mourner's Pass didn't cut hopeful pilgrims down, the magic certainly would.

There weren't many things in this world that could make Neve hesitate, but the ancient and sinister conjury that was spelled upon Mourner's Pass was notorious. There were stories told in which even the hardiest of men were reduced to nothing. Monarchs from her own family had been driven mad or destroyed on the way to the Oracle. One Queen was even set in a continuous circle, a spell which confused her and ruined her senses. It was said that this Queen wandered in circles in the mountains for years and years, just trying to find her way out, until she finally succumbed to starvation and lunacy and lay herself down to die. It seemed the magic here delighted in crushing the powerful.

Neve was not immune to this magic.

"Keep your wits about you, Killian," she said quietly. "We're not welcome here."

He instinctively took a step closer to her.

They'd left the horses at the Stronghold, assured by the ghosts they'd be well taken care of, and would return for them after they'd finished with the Oracle. This place was not suitable for any living thing, so it was a kindness to leave the horses behind in the care of the Greys.

Neve and Killian loaded themselves up on as many supplies and provisions as they could fit in the big rucksack that Killian now carried on his back. He'd insisted that he carry it, merely giving Neve an incredulous roll of his eyes each time she'd offered to take it from him. They'd packed food, wound care supplies, and as many blankets as they could manage. Beneath their heavy coats, they were strapped with weapons.

As prepared as possible for the journey ahead.

She could feel Killian eyeing her, so she looked over at him from around her hood and found him smirking.

"What?" she asked.

He shook his head. "Nothing. I've just never seen you like this."

Neve raised an eyebrow. "Like what, exactly?"

"It seems that even Lady Nightmare can feel fear." His eyes were bright with humor, and his tongue touched the corner of his mouth in arrogant appraisal.

She gave him a slow blink, feigning annoyance, but in truth, she was thankful for his light-hearted distraction.

"I'd be dead by now if I didn't feel fear. I'm just better at managing it than you."

He huffed a laugh. "Oh, is that so?"

"Absolutely. You get all... strange and jittery when you're afraid."

He laughed again. "Strange and jittery? I do not."

"You do. Your fingers start twitching toward the nearest weapon, and your jaw does that funny ticking thing."

"Funny ticking thing? What funny ticking thing?"

She stopped walking and turned toward him. She stood close to him, her chest against his, and the warmth between them was welcome and beckoning.

"Grit your teeth," she commanded.

He couldn't hide his amusement as he followed her direction. She took off her glove and touched his jaw, tracing the muscle that protruded when he clenched his teeth together. His eyes darkened at her touch, and his gaze drifted to her lips.

"Here," she said. "This muscle starts ticking when you're afraid or feeling out of control. It's a wonder you don't break your teeth."

Killian took his glove off as well and covered her hand with his, sliding his fingers between hers to feel the muscle she was talking about.

"I'm always in control," he said in a low voice that somehow managed to send heat straight to her skin beneath the layers of wool.

Neve felt a dark light shining in her eyes as she looked at him, stepping even closer so that he could feel her breath on his lips. "I don't think that's true."

He followed her pursuit and took her chin between his thumb and forefinger to lift her face.

"Do you need evidence?" he asked, his voice was all gravel and quiet thunder.

She was about to respond by licking his mouth with her tongue when an entirely different type of growl broke them both from the moment.

Neve turned slowly to find a wolf stalking toward them from the shadows of a sharp cavern about a dozen yards ahead of them.

"Fuck," Killian muttered.

It was huge, and upon a second glance, Neve knew it was no ordinary wolf. This creature was gnarled, with long, twisted limbs. Even at this distance, Neve could see the rocky spine protruding from its curved back. Its reflective eyes shone in the dim canyon light, hungry maw open and dripping with fangs and frothy drool. Black fur covered its lanky, thin body. It looked as if it was once a starving man who transformed into a beast. Perhaps it was.

According to legend, men who made it to the Oracle and were deemed unworthy of her attention were turned into wolfish creatures and trapped in the vale for the rest of time, doomed to wear their unworthiness on their flesh and never return to their homes.

This was a lycanthrope. And it was hungry.

Killian stepped lithely in front of Neve, and she watched him slowly draw his sword, the gleaming metal scraping against the sheath.

"Know any stories about this creature? How to kill it?" he asked in a low voice.

"Everything dies the same," she replied.

He looked at her over his shoulder and raised his eyebrow. "You truly are terrifying. You know that, right?"

She smiled. "Yes."

"Allow me the honor of dealing with it?" his eyes were full of dark humor and an eagerness to get his hands bloody.

She waved a sarcastically regal hand. "By all means." She'd let him have this one, knowing that lycanthropes were pack animals and she could feel the rest of them slinking around in the darkness. They would have their hands full of beasts at any moment.

Killian stalked toward the wolf, his sword at the ready. Neve liked the way he walked, with an even swagger and determined purpose. He rolled his broad shoulders to release the tension in them. Hackles rose on the creature's neck, and it began to snarl. A horrid, choking sound like it hadn't had to use its voice in years.

In an instant, it lunged at Killian, who easily side-stepped it and threw out his leg in a stomping kick. His foot made contact with the side of its knobby knee, connecting exactly right with the joint to dislocate it, sending the beast to the ground with an ear-splitting yelp.

Neve watched as Killian circled it, sheathing his sword with a cocky smirk on his lips.

Killian truly was a magnificent man. The way his body moved. His well-earned swagger. The look on his face during battle made her blood heat. Even through his clothes, she could see the coiling and bulging of his muscles as he wielded his weapon.

The creature tried and failed to get to its feet. Killian stood above it for a moment, watching it struggle, before reaching down and putting a hand on each side of its big, writhing head. In a swift, strong motion, Killian twisted his hands and snapped the wolf's neck.

He straightened and looked at her across the field. "Well, that wasn't so hard–" The color drained from his face.

She knew why.

Neve could feel them behind her, creeping silently. Her expertly honed senses told her that there were at least six coming up on her, but likely more. The shadows behind Killian shifted and moved as well, the other half of the pack prowling toward him.

"Behind you," she said in a mild voice.

The lone wolf was a decoy. Probably their weakest link was sent out as a sacrifice to separate her from Killian. That was the thing about beasts who were once men, after all. Beneath the fur, they still thought like men.

Neve pulled two daggers from her thigh holsters and turned. The stench of death hit her nostrils as she beheld the loping creatures coming for her. Her assumption of their number had been wrong, but not by much. Eight of them had her in their sights while across the field, another ten advanced on Killian.

The lycanthrope closest to her licked its chops, as if her scent were an appetizer, and bared its teeth.

She bared her own and smiled at it.

For a brief second, it hesitated, but then decided that the meal would be worth the struggle. It leapt for her.

Neve crouched and let it come.

It was a blur of patchy black fur and tangled limbs. She could see flashes of brittle, jagged claws and yellow fangs that were as sharp as knives. She angled the daggers in her hands and waited for her moment. Just as its rank breath whispered against her face, she thrust both daggers up under its jaw and sliced, spilling its throat onto the ground in a hot, dark spray.

The rest of the wolves came for her quickly and with a vengeance.

~

Bile rose in Killian's throat at the sight of the wolves descending upon Neve across the barren field. Ten of the foul creatures were at his back and beginning to circle him; he would have no time to get to her before both sides launched their attack.

He needed to ground himself, force himself to remember that she could hold her own, because his instincts screamed at him to run for her despite the danger he was also facing.

Valiantly, he compelled his unwilling eyes to look away from that beautiful, vicious woman and focus on the growling lycanthropes surrounding him.

Killian drew his sword and turned slowly, eyeing each of them to determine which one would strike first. They were stalking him slowly, closing ranks around him, but the first one to move met a swift death on his blade.

Upon the first bloodletting, the rest of the pack went wild and surged for him. They were leaping, rabid, and aiming their teeth for his throat.

Killian needed to keep moving and stay on his feet.

If they took him to the ground, he'd be a dead man.

Swinging his sword, he delivered brutal killings to the next four that came at him. The obsidian ground became slick and slippery with wolf blood, and Killian found his boots skidding in it.

A memory of Neve's voice was in his head: *Look alive, soldier,* reminding him to pay attention, to not lose himself to the rage of battle, to not lose his footing.

As he sank his blade through the mouth of one beast, feeling it slice clean through the back of its head, another's jaws clamped down on his outstretched arm. Killian roared at the searing pain and then offered up a feral snarl of his own as he drove his other fist into the wolf's snout, crunching bones until its teeth released his arm and the bewildered beast went sprawling. Killian, fueled by the rage of injury, went after it and used both hands to bring his mighty sword down on its neck to sever it completely. The wolf's head and its body hit the ground on either side of Killian.

Blood was soaking through his coat and thick layers of wool from where the lycanthrope's teeth ripped into his skin. The smell of it made each of the remaining wolves lift their faces to the sky and howl before returning their attention to Killian.

All three leapt onto him at once.

The force of their bodies colliding with him had Killian wavering, his legs straining to keep himself upright. The smell was awful this close. They smelled of dirt and dead things. A flurry of filthy fur, yet he noticed each of them had a symbol branded onto the flesh of their necks. One long straight line, bisected in the middle with an "X". He would have to ask Neve about it sometime. For now, he was occupied. All he could hear was the snapping of jaws and the guttural, hungry growling from deep in their creatures' throats.

His boots slipped on the bloody stone ground.

Stay on your fucking feet.

He heaved a heavy and brutal elbow into the chest of the one to the right of him, sending it flying backward. This gave him the space to thrust his sword down onto the back of the wolf at his front. It sliced through fur and skin, and Killian felt the impact sing up his arm as the blade severed its spine.

The wolf he'd thrown off of him came back and barreled into him with surprising force. It nearly took Killian down, his knees buckling with the power of it. The beast's teeth scraped at the skin of Killian's neck, and he strained backward to avoid the bite.

On his left, the other wolf dug its claws into the flesh around Killian's ribcage. Growling himself, Killian cursed the beast and grabbed its ear, yanking as hard as he could until he felt the cartridge tear in his fist. The wolf yelped and tried to get away, but Killian held firm and delivered a violent slash of his sword that opened the animal up from belly to chest.

The last lycanthrope was still trying to sink its teeth into Killian's neck. Full of fury, he let his sword drop to the ground and grabbed the wolf's mouth with his hands, one on the upper jaw and one on the lower.

He pulled.

The beast roared in Killian's face, and Killian roared right back, using his strength to pull and *pull* the wolf's jaws apart until he felt the bones break, and the beast fell to the ground. Killian picked up his sword and put an end to it with one last swing of his blade.

Finally, he allowed himself to look across the field, eyes searching for Neve.

She'd taken out four of the abominations already and was fighting the final four with her bare hands. Somewhere along the way, she'd been disarmed. He could see her six daggers glinting on the blood–spattered ground.

Her shadowy speed didn't count for much when there were four wolves on her and nowhere to go.

What happened next nearly stopped his heart.

He watched the lycanthropes work together to take her down. The one behind Neve crouched low as the other three leapt on her, just as they'd done to him on his side. But because there was one crouched behind her, right against her legs, her balance was ruined, and she toppled backward onto the ground as the beasts careened into her.

They had her.

There was no thought in his head.

No breath in his lungs.

A near-catastrophic panic gripped him in its fist. The edges of his vision blurred with horror. He could no longer see Neve beyond the bulky bodies of the wolves that had descended on top of her.

He'd only ever seen her taken down once- during the fight with the bandits in Hythe- and that was by her own choice, to get the edge on her assailant. This was different. She hadn't seen it coming, and that in itself was terrifying.

If they hurt her, would she scream? Would he even know that she was injured, or worse, until he hauled the creatures off her?

His heart was in his mouth.

Killian launched himself forward and sprinted as fast as he could across the field. His brain was filled with a red fog of panic and wrath. He jumped on the back of the closest wolf, a primal sound releasing from his mouth as he snapped its neck. It was like his body was moving on its own.

Anything to get to her, to save her.

He couldn't see her beneath the last three lycanthropes; they were completely covering her in what felt like a triumphant frenzy. Killian wasted no time. He unleashed himself upon them, making frighteningly quick work of their deaths. Slashing, he beheaded one and kicked its carcass off to the side. He ended the next with an almost careless thrust of his blade through its back.

For the last wolf, he hauled it off of Neve with one hand, gripping coarse black fur. Then, he sat over it, straddling it between his thighs, looming down on it menacingly just as it had done to her. It snarled and bucked, and Killian growled at it as he slowly drove his sword into its chest and watched the life drain from its eyes.

He stood and moved to Neve, his heart hammering.

She was on the ground, dusting herself off. Gracefully, she sat up from her prone position and looked up at him.

His eyes desperately raked over her body, searching for injuries. A claw mark raked down the side of her neck onto her shoulder, staining her skin and clothes with blood. She'd gotten lucky. If those claws had met her throat with a little more force, she would have bled out almost instantly.

But she didn't even seem to notice.

There was a wild light in her eyes. Bloodshed excited her. This woman loved to fight, and she loved to win. But this time, that spark in her eyes, he realized, was for *him*.

He swallowed hard, closer to losing his balance simply by the look on her face than he'd been when the wolves were on him.

He reached his hand down to her.

"My lady," he said.

That smirk of hers lifted the corners of her pretty mouth as she took his offered hand and let him help her up.

Knowing that she was safe, alive, and looking at him with that strange glow nearly unmanned him right then and there. And the feeling of her hand in his had him taking a deep, steadying breath.

She stood close to him and looked up into his eyes.

"Thank you," she said, her smoky voice entirely calm and unfazed despite having just been mauled by a pack of starving lycanthropes. "I'm glad you were there."

He tried to hide the way her words unsteadied him. He took her face in his hands and looked her over once more as if to convince himself that she was truly alright.

"Me too."

21

Night fell, impossibly deepening the inherent darkness of the vale. Neve and Killian found a small, empty cave and decided it was as good a place as any to spend the night. Killian started a roaring fire near the cave's entrance and laid out their bedrolls as Neve began peeling off her layers of clothes to inspect her wounds. The cave became cozy once it was filled with the heat of the fire, and the shelter of it protected them from the barbarous north wind.

Neve stripped down to just her flimsy cotton underclothes, a camisole, and a pair of knee-length shorts. She sat on her bedroll and ran her hands over her body, feeling for injuries and lacerations. Neve found the rake of claw marks on the side of her neck and down her shoulder, and another across her belly. She'd been in far worse shape. This was manageable.

Leaning over, she hauled their rucksack onto her lap, digging her arms into it until she found the wound care supplies.

"Let me," Killian said. He stood above her, holding out his hand for the bandages and cleansing alcohol. She handed them to him, and he sat next to her, wincing as he did. "I'll likely need you to return the favor."

Neve breathed out a laugh. "It's only fair."

For such a big, brutal man, it always surprised her how tender his hands could be. He poured some alcohol onto a cloth and gently dabbed it against the wound on her neck. He was so careful with her that she almost rolled her eyes, but still, she let him help.

"Does this hurt?" he asked quietly. His mouth was tight with concentration and worry as he cleaned out the gouges in her flesh.

She shook her head. "No."

His throat bobbed as he finished cleaning her shoulder and started unrolling a strip of linen for a bandage.

"Those beasts...when you were on the ground, I lost myself. If they'd killed you—"

"They didn't," she reminded him.

He looked at her with a grave, raw expression. "I wouldn't have survived it. If they'd ended you."

The pit of her stomach dropped. She would never get used to the all-consuming care Killian held for her. It unsteadied her each time he offered it, which he did with ease and generosity as if it was as natural for him to care for her as it was for him to breathe.

His eyes, like the sea, raged with a strong and sad tide. She could almost see the hypothetical scenarios running through his mind, the thoughts of her death, of losing her. There was nothing dormant or hidden about this man. He wore everything for the world to see. And in that moment, the pain he felt for what simply *might have* happened seemed to completely overwhelm everything else.

Before she knew what she was doing, she reached for him and touched his face. He leaned into her hand and closed his eyes. His relief at her touch was palpable. She drew her thumb over his beard and across the skin on his cheek. He covered her hand with his, pressing it against his face more firmly, and turned his chin to kiss her wrist, a quiet, needful brush of his lips.

"I'm right here," Neve said softly, barely recognizing her own voice. She heard sweetness in her words, which was certainly a sentiment she'd never given anyone else.

Neve D'aeth was many things, but *sweet* was not one of them. Until now, it appeared.

He nodded and went back to work bandaging her shoulder and neck. Killian cleared his throat.

"Where else?" he asked.

She lifted her shirt to show him the wound on her stomach and leaned back on her elbows to give him space to care for it. He rested one of his hands comfortably on her waist as the other cleaned her cuts. His fingers felt good on her skin.

Neve watched him as he poured all his attention into playing healer for her. Two lines formed between his eyebrows as he concentrated; his hand moved expertly, knowingly. Of course, he'd dressed and cared for hundreds of wounds, probably thousands, throughout his decades as a warrior.

But perhaps none that marred skin was ever so dear to him as hers.

As Neve watched him, something peculiar fluttered in her chest as surely as the familiar flushing heat of lust spread around her hips and down her inner thighs. The two different feelings seemed to match pitch and energy with each other in harmony.

Was this care? She wondered, was this affection?

Killian finished caring for her wounds and exhaled before giving her a genuine, if not still haunted, smile.

"Good?" he asked.

She nodded. "My turn," she replied, holding her hand out for the supplies.

Their fingers grazed, lingered, and paused in some humming spark, as he gave them to her. Neve caught his gaze, noticing how the last of his fear melted slightly to make way for that same feverish warmth invading her body.

Kneeling in front of him, she began unbuttoning his shirt. His hands rushed to take over, but Neve gave him a look that stopped him.

Moving closer, she peeled the shirt off his strong shoulders, his nose grazing the side of her neck. She heard him take a deep inhale of her scent while somehow his body both relaxed and tightened at the same time beneath her hands.

Once he was shirtless, Neve saw that his arm was a wreckage of red, and there were deep claw marks around his ribs. He smelled like blood and sweat, his natural woodsy pine scent nearly completely masked under the stench of gore.

Neve went to work cleaning and dressing his arm first. He was lucky the animal's teeth hadn't torn clean through muscle and bone. She moved on to the claw marks on his chest. As she cared for them, she could feel the rough pounding of his heart against her fingers.

"Your heart is racing," she remarked. "Am I hurting you?"

When he didn't answer, Neve tore her gaze away from the bandage she wrapped around his midsection and looked up at him.

His eyes were full of fire, his jaw tight.

"No," he said.

Finished with her work, she sat back and looked at him. The muscles of his broad shoulders and thick arms stood in sharp relief against the shadows cast by the glowing firelight.

His tongue wet his lips as he watched her, chest rising and falling in unsteady rhythm with his thrashing heart. Deep in her ribcage, Neve could feel her pulse speeding up as if to match his.

Moving slowly and gracefully, she approached him and straddled his hips.

She could feel the heat and hardness of him already straining against his pants. His eyes raked down her body before settling again on her face.

Gently, almost hesitantly, he rested his eager hands on her waist.

His breath skated across her neck, sending a shivering thrill down her spine. Searching his face, Neve ran her fingers through his thick, sweat-dirtied hair, watching his eyes close in pleasure. She dragged her hands across the back of his neck and then cupped either side of his face. His eyes flew to hers, and she watched his throat bob up and down.

Something like confusion furrowed his brow, his gaze seemed to ask a desperate *why?* She knew he was not expecting such softness from her; truth be told, it surprised her, too.

But it felt right. It felt necessary for both of them.

She suddenly wanted nothing in the wild, violent world more than a gentle moment with this man.

Leaning forward, she brushed her lips across his. A quiet moan sprang from his throat as his fingers flexed and tightened on her waist.

Neve kissed him slowly and deliberately. The fluttering in her chest from earlier exploded and sent a vibration of warmth from the tips of her toes to the top of her head. Killian wrapped his arms around her lower back and pulled her closer.

She wanted to be closer to him. As close as possible.

Their mouths and tongues slow-danced, rising in intensity each time their lips parted and dove back in for more. His hands were slipping beneath the thin fabric of her camisole, caressing the soft skin of her back as her hands once again found his hair, combing through it with her fingers. Breathless, she pulled her mouth from his, and he trailed delicate kisses down her jaw, onto her neck. The feeling of his mouth on her throat sent a tingle down to her core.

Killian lifted his face back to hers, eyes stormy. He swiped his thumb across her bottom lip, then cradled her cheek in his hand.

"What do you want, my lady?" he asked earnestly, his voice rough and deep. "I'll give you anything."

She squeezed her thighs around him, drawing him impossibly closer, causing his breath to hitch and shudder.

"Just you," she said.

He raised his eyebrows, twirling a strand of her hair around his finger. "Me?"

She gripped his shoulders. "You."

He brushed his lips against her cheek and spoke softly into her ear. "Say it again."

Neve smirked and stood, looking down at him. She pinned him to the spot with her eyes and pulled the waistband of her shorts, letting them drop to the floor. His whole body tensed, and his stare froze at the apex of her thighs. He slid his hands up her legs worshipfully. She lifted her camisole over her head, and it floated down onto his lap.

She stood before him utterly bare and certain.

"I want you, Killian. Just you."

Neve lowered herself back down onto him, and he wrapped his arms around her, tugging her against him and burying his face in the valley between her breasts.

She brought his mouth back to hers and kissed him deeply, eliciting another one of those desperate moans from his throat that made her pussy clench with a tortuous ache. She reached between them and tugged at his belt. Killian made quick work of taking off his pants, barely letting his mouth leave hers.

When his naked arousal pressed against hers, they both took a sharp breath. Their eyes were locked on each other as Neve slid down onto his cock slowly and she released a deep purr of pleasure as he filled her up.

"You're perfect," Killian gasped, his eyes rolling back at the feel of her.

She wrapped her arms around his strong shoulders, pulling him as close to her as possible, riding him. His ragged breathing was in her ear, one arm circling her waist and the other on her back, his hand cradling the nape of her neck.

He crushed his lips against hers, tongue swirling inside her mouth, his hips moving in rhythm with hers, plunging his cock deeper and deeper. His kiss was burning and full of a need that mirrored her own.

Neve angled her body to take from him what she needed, feeling her pleasure building with each thrust. He noticed and pressed the heel of his hand against her pussy, griding firmly against her clit as she rode him, increasing that divine pressure until she was moaning and delirious with it.

"Look at me," he said. "I want to watch."

So she did. She looked him in the eyes as her pleasure rose to a grand crescendo. His name was on her lips as her world exploded, and all she could see was stars and the ravenously pleased look in his eyes.

She sagged against him as the final tremors rocked through her body.

He shifted gently, putting her on her back and settling between her thighs, never breaking his tempo. He smoothed the hair out of her face and thrust into her, slow and deep.

"That was the most beautiful thing I've ever seen," he breathed, lowering his lips to her nipple and sucking it into his mouth. Her back arched, and she wrapped her legs around his hips, encouraging him to drive deeper and pick up his pace.

Neve grasped a handful of his hair, bringing his face back up to hers and kissing him with abandon.

"I want to watch you too," she whispered.

His eyes blazed, and he pulled her legs up onto his shoulders, going so deep that she let loose a long, low groan.

He leaned down and gazed at her as he moved, her pleasure rising again just as he began to tremble above her. The look on his face was reverential.

In that instant, the tenuous threads between them wove themselves into a strong rope. Something inside of each of them recognized the basest, most fundamental, and primal part of the other and welcomed it with vigor.

It somehow broke Neve's icy heart and melded it back together all at once to become another, stronger thing altogether.

They were nothing but a tangle of trembling limbs with needy breaths ripping from their throats. Soon, both of their bodies were brought to their highest, most aching peaks.

And then they submitted to the free fall together.

22

Killian knew deep down in the milky marrow of his bones that he was well and truly fucked.

This woman was his Queen, but she was everything else to him as well. She was the stars, the moon, the whole bloody universe and he was lost in her.

He woke in the early morning and ran his palms down his face. The intoxicating scent of her arousal still clung to his hands, and it sent a bolt of lightning through his spine, nearly cracking him in two with the force of it.

He turned to his side to look at her. Her back was to him, the rolling ocean of her dark hair fanned across the pillow beneath her slumbering head. His fingers reached out and traced the small of her back and the curve of her hip.

Neve stirred under his touch. She rolled onto her back, languidly stretching her arms above her while turning her head.

She opened her sleepy eyes and looked right into him.

Not just at him, but straight into the heart of him.

The intensity of the feeling overwhelmed him, and his gaze floated over her body, her bare breasts peaked in the cold morning air. Without thinking, he ran his hand over them, then pulled the pile of blankets back up to their chins.

"What are you thinking about?" she asked.

He shook his head, forcing himself to meet her eyes.

"I can think of nothing except you."

She smirked. "I'm sure you have other thoughts."

"None."

"Hard to believe, all things considered."

Beneath the blankets, he flattened his hand against her chest, feeling the strong, steady, and violent beat of her heart.

"It's only you," he replied. "How to please you, how to serve you, how to make you laugh or moan or look at me the way you're doing right now."

"Who knew such a brute was a romantic underneath?" she mused.

He pressed his lips in a thin line. "You mock me."

Her eyes flared with a dangerous light. She put her hand over his and pressed it more firmly against her chest.

"No. I'm *learning* you. Tell me more."

He nodded and gave her a grateful smile.

"I'm not sure how much of this you want to know..."

"Listen to my words. I said: Tell me more."

He huffed a laugh.

"As you wish, my lady. You want more? Here it is: I'm terrified."

She stilled, and he swore he could feel the steady beat of her heart trip.

"Terrified of what?"

"You," he said. "The power you have. Over me. I'm terrified of failing you. I'm terrified of how very easily you could break me. I'm terrified of losing you."

"That's a lot of fear."

"It is."

"What are you going to do about it?"

"Just keep going and hope none of those fears come to life."

Her smirk returned. "Breaking you is no longer part of my plan. I think you had enough of that in the Dark Forest."

Killian laughed again. "True. But, there are other ways to break a man."

Breaking his heart. His hope.

"That's not part of my plan, either."

"Plans can change."

"Not mine," she said resolutely, and he believed her.

"I'm lost here, Neve. You're in my gut. In my throat. I'm drowning in you."

She touched his face.

"I'm not going anywhere. I chose you to join me. Chose *you*. You're with me until the very end, whenever that may be."

He clenched his jaw to keep the emotion from spilling out of him in a wave. "I am yours."

"I know."

"Not just as your sworn protector–"

"I *know*," she said firmly.

She knew, then. Of course, she did.

She knew that he was endlessly and torturously in love with her.

Neve offered him no similar vow, but the way she looked at him, her mere nearness was enough.

He understood that she'd never known love of any kind and that he could never ask her to yield that hidden part of herself to him if it even existed at all. He also understood that she was on a journey to take back her throne and save a lost kingdom- surely he did not expect something as small as love to take any precedence.

Though for him, his love for her was not a small thing at all.

"I will never ask the same of you. I need you to know that I would never expect more than what you already give me," he said.

"I've never belonged to anyone but myself," she said gently.

"I don't need you to belong to me. But, I want you to know that I am yours. Until the very end."

She kissed him then, his heart leapt, and his body sparked alive.

"Will that be enough for you? Truly?" she asked.

"I swear it. This is enough."

~

The air felt heavy; the sharp wind from the day before died out, leaving a dense fog in its wake that seemed to roll down from the mountain summits above. Neve hadn't wanted to leave the warmth of the cave or Killian's arms, but they needed to start moving.

She had the distinct feeling that, sooner or later, she and Killian would run out of time.

After clashing with the Cavalry, what felt like years ago instead of merely a month, she was certain that the Highborns were hunting them. On top of that, they'd woken the ghosts at Grey's Stronghold.

It was only a matter of time before some whisper of her would reach the ears of her enemy. An enemy whose name and face were unknown to her. Suspected, but unknown.

That was why they were traveling to the Oracle, after all.

She hoped the Oracle would reveal the truth, which she had only guessed at. Neve needed to get there before the whispers of her turned into roars and others tried to come for what was rightfully hers.

Neve and Killian walked with determination, their strong legs carrying them miles across the obsidian terrain.

She'd told him some of the reasons for their journey to the Oracle, but didn't want to say more until she knew for certain. If her guess was accurate, the truth would level the kingdom. Indeed, it would lay waste to everything Killian thought he knew about Eodia.

They would deal with that when it came.

Much of the day's travel looked the same. No trees. Nothing green. Only the endless black rock underfoot and stretching up around them to the clouds. They walked along the edge of a river, its surface a mirror of thinly accumulating ice. It was impossible to tell how far they'd come or how far they had left to go when the vale seemed to stretch on before them endlessly.

Neve looked to the sky, hoping to glean some marker to differentiate the mountains above, but there was none. They were identical, or near enough to appear that they were. The pure sameness of it all gave the illusion that they weren't making much progress whatsoever.

Almost as if they were marching in place. It was a disorienting feeling that filled Neve's bones with unease.

She and Killian made light conversation as they walked, or moved together in companionable silence. She felt comfort in his nearness, not only because of his skills as a warrior or that rageful protective instinct of his, but mostly because it was *him*. His swagger as he walked, the way his eyes scanned the environment with intelligence, the stories he told when silence was too much for him. Neve was fond of all of it.

It made an interminable task feel less tedious.

There was no way to determine what time of day it was. The sun was absent from the sky, leaving only plumes of fog and thin clouds. A wash of black and gray, as if the vale were a painting and the artist left all of their colors behind.

The edges of the valley were peppered with shadowy caves, much like the one they'd found shelter in the night before. Neve searched each one as they passed for markers or signs of life in this barren place. Nothing.

Nothing, that is, until a pile of ash at the mouth of one cavern stopped her in her tracks.

Killian stepped closer to her, eyes roaming her face with concern. "What is it?" he asked.

She tilted her head and pointed at the cave. "We spent the night there."

His brow creased. "Impossible. We've been walking half the day."

"And yet, here we are. Back where we started our morning."

"No," he said. "Someone else must be traveling the vale." He stalked toward the cave with the confidence of a man who thought he was right.

Neve followed.

He crouched down and touched the ash. "It's lukewarm. They must have left this morning. Hours ago."

"It was us, Killian. We left this morning. This was our cave, our fire." She'd been certain of it from farther away but was even more convinced this close. This cave was the exact size, shape, and dimensions as theirs. What was more, it still smelled of them.

"Impossible," he repeated.

Neve brushed past him and swept into the hollow, straight for the corner where an errant cloth sat in the shadows. She picked it up, gave it nothing but a cursory glance, and handed it to Killian. He looked at it like it was a dream, and his eyes widened. It was nothing but a strip of linen covered in blotchy red stains.

"My blood. From when you cleaned my wounds," she said. He opened his mouth to speak, and she interrupted him. "Tell me again that it's impossible, and I'll leave you here."

He shook his head, fighting a smile despite the situation. "Wouldn't dare, Lady Nightmare. But... how? It's not as if we've been standing still, walking in place. We've been moving for... six hours at least." He ran his hands through his hair in frustration.

"I'm not sure. Perhaps it's a trick. Let's keep moving."

Neve dipped her finger in the ash and marked the exterior wall at the cave mouth with the shape of a star. She knew that they would likely pass it again and again, but deeply hoped they would not.

~

Seven times.

They passed the cave marked with a star seven *fucking* times.

Killian was seething. He was exhausted and hungry; the heat of his panic turned to rage and boiled over each time he saw the mouth of that cavern. It seemed to grin at him, taunting him with its very existence. The favorable memories he kept of that space, the taste and feel of Neve during the night, and their perfect, sleepy moment the morning after were lost to him now. When he saw that cave, all he could feel was hate.

The light of day was quickly leaving them. Early evening arrived around the sixth time they passed the cave, and upon the seventh, night was becoming a cloak over the valley.

Such an endless place suddenly felt like a prison. Dark. Claustrophobic. Repeating over and over again.

Not unlike his five years in the dungeon.

It was making him dizzy and nauseous. The edges of his vision were blurred. He couldn't tell if it was because of the pressure of the blood roaring in his head or if it was part of the curse they were swimming in.

Everything felt thick and confusing, making his ire turn hotter, burning him from the inside out.

Neve was quiet and composed but lost in her own unreadable thoughts. He could see the tight set of her jaw and her rigid movements as they walked.

Her muted tension spilled out of her and into him, making reason and logic escape his brain to be replaced by the sneering urge to burn the whole world down around them.

Killian didn't like seeing her this way. He'd so rarely seen her emotions affected by anything that this silent stewing made him unbelievably anxious. He clenched his teeth so hard he thought they might crack.

If *she*, of all people, could come up with no confident solution to end this torment, he began to believe they would be stuck in this interminable loop for the rest of their lives.

"Any ideas?" he asked, utterly unable to veil the desperate edge in his voice.

She shook her head.

The misery of this agitation was a living, breathing thing inside him. Like spiders burrowing under his skin. He rubbed at his sternum in an attempt to ease the panic, but it didn't work.

Nothing worked.

"There has to be a way to make this stop," he said.

He was met, once again, by her silence.

As they continued walking, the darkness of the vale became nearly complete.

They'd need to find shelter, a place to spend the night, soon. The devils of this forsaken valley were sure to start clawing out of the shadows in no time. Part of Killian wished for it. Perhaps if there was something to fight, he'd find a way to channel all his tension and fear into something useful. He clenched his fists until the knuckles went white.

The eighth time they passed the cave, Killian's guts churned, and he let loose a rumbling groan of frustration.

Neve stopped walking and pinned him with a long, cold stare. As he opened his mouth to speak, she turned from him and strode into the cave.

"What are you doing?" he called after her.

When she didn't respond, he stalked her to the mouth of the cavern but refused to set foot inside. She, on the other hand, quietly gathered leftover wood and debris and made quick work of starting a fire on the ashes of the one they'd left the night before.

Crackling flames stood between them. Her features were cast in a lovely amber glow, but he was too worked up to enjoy it.

Finally, she spoke. "We can't do anything else tonight. Come in here and sleep. We'll start again in the morning."

"I don't want to start again in the morning. I want this spell broken," he replied in a low and furious voice.

Her very indifference to how terrible a situation they were in made him want to drive his fists into the stone of the mountain.

She squared her shoulders.

"Then find a way to break it. I'm going to bed."

Her voice was so icy that the hairs on his arms stood on end. The flicker of annoyance in her eyes cut him to the quick, like prying a knife under the surface of his pride and scooping out any confidence he'd had about her fondness for him.

He wanted to react. Perhaps to yell and lash out, or perhaps to beg her on his knees, never to look at him like that again. He wasn't sure. So he reined in his hurt and fury and instead took the rucksack off his back. He reached into it, taking a blanket for himself, and then held it out for her across the threshold of the cave and the campfire.

Her expression changed almost imperceptibly as she took it from him.

"You're not going to sleep?"

"I'm not sleeping in *there*. For all we know, this curse could have been put on us when we slept in this fucking cave last night."

Neve's pretty mouth tightened. "That's absurd."

"Everything is absurd!" he snapped, his voice coming out closer to a roar than he intended, echoing off the mountains around them. So much for not lashing out, then. "We spent all day walking and got nowhere!"

She tilted her head. "Your anger is useless."

He felt himself snarl at her. "And what are you doing that is so *useful*?! You've barely said a word since we realized what was happening, and you hardly seem to care. So tell me, *Queen*, what use are you bringing to the table?"

The moment the words fell out of his bumbling idiot mouth, he regretted it. Gods, he was exhausted and scared and so frustrated he couldn't see straight.

A profuse apology was at the tip of this tongue when the fire at their feet flared violently with a sudden white light.

He startled and stumbled back, but Neve was unmoved and unsurprised, as if she'd somehow made the flames burst colorlessly herself. There was a strange glow in her eyes when he looked at her.

Something powerful and terrifying.

"Raise your voice at me again," she dared. Her words were cool and calm, but they betrayed the utterly frigid brutality beneath the surface. The sound of it sent lightning down his spine.

She was a pillar of frightening strength standing before him, and in that instant, he was suddenly all too aware that if she wanted him dead, there would be no stopping her.

He was outmatched; it was a truth as certain as the stars. His eyes flicked to her hands just to make sure she wasn't palming her daggers.

Not that she would need them. He knew there was something within her that could end him without a single weapon.

This face, this beautiful face, was the last thing all of her foes had ever seen.

And, standing across the fire from her, Killian knew without a shadow of a doubt that it would one day be his last as well.

He swallowed hard. "Neve, I —"

She lifted her chin in dismissal. "Goodnight, Killian."

23

Each day that followed was the same. Each night, too.

Hours of walking the same stretch of valley, passing the cave too many times to count. Neve's eyelids started twitching intermittently, from either exhaustion or the strain of watching the same landscape underfoot on an eternal loop.

She was completely stumped. None of the stories she knew instructed how to break the curses of Mourner's Pass.

Perhaps because no one ever had.

At night, Killian continued to sleep outside the cave despite the creeping cold. To prove his theory wrong, that the cave itself had not cursed them, Neve had even chosen different caves as shelter several nights in a row.

It strangely gave her no pleasure to prove him wrong, because he still refused to sleep within the same walls as her.

Neve's unyielding steel resolve was admittedly becoming brittle. She couldn't sleep at night, her mind racing to try to put all the pieces together, to suss out the shadows of thought she may have missed. She obsessed over anything that could be a clue from twilight to dawn.

What was worse, sleeping alone left her with an *ache*.

At first, she thought it might have been hunger, the need for water, the desperation for slumber that seemed just out of reach.

But after the third night, she realized it was the ache of absence.

The absence of *him* by her side.

She missed the smell of his skin and his soft, rhythmic breathing in the middle of the night. She missed him.

They'd barely spoken in days. There was a wildness and a madness to him now that she did not want to touch. He was nearly feral with ever-growing rage.

Twice, she'd caught him screaming into the void and smashing his sword against the mountains. All muscle and sinew and a roaring, spitting mouth. When he noticed her watching, both times he sank to his knees in shame.

She'd never met a person so alive with feeling.

For her part, Neve struggled to maintain any shred of herself. Every single waking moment was a battle. Her body had never felt so tense, her chest had never felt so tight. Everything within her was coiling in on itself, just waiting to be released like a spring of chaos.

She could no longer hide the trembling that moved through her body in waves. Sometimes, deep in the night when she was alone, the shaking was so violent that she could do nothing but let it ride through her.

Last night, it was so bad that she thought that it would surely kill her.

Killian noticed. The first time he saw the tremors in her fingers, he'd asked if she was all right. She hadn't responded. She couldn't decide if it was because her cruelty was the only thing she could control or because she truly didn't have the words for it. He didn't ask again.

But he watched her, his already stricken expression growing even more deeply worried each time he saw her tremble.

For that, at least, she was glad he was sleeping separately. If he knew how bad it truly was, especially in the dark hours past midnight, it would break him.

Time had no meaning any longer.

Her internal clock told her when it was morning and when it was evening, but beyond that, there was nothing but the relentless abyss.

Each time they passed the cave with the star, something died within her.

They'd tried everything; if they went separate ways, they would both somehow end up back in the middle, if they tried retracing their steps they would get spun around and end up where they started, if they sat still the wind would pick up then slam against them viciously until they began walking again.

It was all beginning to blur like ink spilled into water.

It was nearly dusk on the fifth day when Killian abruptly stopped, pulled their rucksack off his back, and slammed it on the ground.

The sound was like a thunderclap.

A shudder ran up her body. Neve squeezed her eyes shut to try to get control of her nervous system before the shaking could descend upon her in earnest. She hid her hands in her pockets.

"I can't do this any longer," Killian ground out from between gnashed teeth. He crouched down and ran his hands through his hair. "I can't. I can't."

Neve's knees were threatening to buckle, so she planted her feet firmly on the stone beneath her.

"There's no choice but to keep going," she said coolly. Her throat burned with the effort it took to keep her voice level.

Something was wrong.

Aside from being cursed.

Something was wrong with *her*.

Killian was beside himself with weary panic and didn't seem to notice how hard she was working just to keep upright.

Good.

That meant she still retained some control over herself.

Neve hated how utterly desperate he looked. His eyes were rimmed with red, his hands were curled in tight fists, and he looked frantic, crazed, and devastated.

That devastation did something violent to her heart, making it clench in a way that had her hoping her next breath would come on its own.

He rose to his feet in a lithe movement and stalked toward her.

"How can you be so calm?" he demanded. "This is fucking killing me."

Her heart clenched again with such force that she nearly gagged on it. Still, she waged war against herself and forced her shoulders to loosen just enough to appear that she wasn't wound up so tight that a light breeze might snap her in half.

"Killian, we just have to keep going and hope this will run its course."

"Hope?!" He nearly screamed the word at her. "We are going to die here in this black wasteland, and you talk of hope?!"

Her body betrayed her again, trembling like a teacup on horseback. She fought for control. Swallowed. Grit her teeth.

"We will not die. Not here," she said steadily.

She knew that, at least, was true. They would not die here. She would not let them.

"I've failed you already, and we're barely out of the shadow of the Grey's Stronghold. I swore an oath-"

"Killian..."

Something deep and vital within her was breaking. A dam. A wall. Some important part of her internal foundation was about to be in ruins.

"No. I swore an oath, Neve. And we are going to die here. In this endless loop." His eyes were misty, and she watched a single tear shoot down his cheek.

He shook his head, a broken man.

Neve could barely breathe beyond the earthquakes inside of her, beyond the excruciating cracking of everything within.

"We will not die," she repeated.

He took another step toward her, baring his teeth.

"How can you be so calm? So sure? We are lost in hell, and you are *fine* with it."

"Stop," she commanded.

She was so close to completely losing control, so close to unraveling entirely.

He did not stop.

He took another step into her space. She couldn't even will her body to obey enough for her to step back.

"I have failed you. It's killing me, Neve. I can't save us from this. I can't." His voice broke. Another tear shot down his cheek.

"Killian, please."

Breaking. The very core of her was breaking.

He reached for her and clutched her shoulders. Surely now he would know. Surely now he would feel how her body was shaking. Surely he could see the great wrenching within her eyes.

"Neve!" Her name was a violent shout from his lips.

"What do you want me to do?" she asked, every ounce of strength left in her danced on tiptoes along the edge of a knife.

"I want you to feel something!" he sobbed.

The dam finally broke. Her last vestiges of control disappeared. A great rending tore her apart from the inside.

Without a thought, her mouth opened and the words came out in a scream. "I feel *everything*!"

Her vision filled with a flash of white light, gone as quickly as it came. Then the sky above them opened up. Cold, hard rain poured down on them.

Inside of her, something burst wide open.

Her chest was heaving.

Her voice was screaming.

"I feel everything, Killian! All the hate, despair, and pain in this world: I feel it. I feel each life I take as it slips across my dagger. I feel lonely. Sad. Afraid. All of it! I feel the way you hurt and the way you love me, and how desperate you are to be worthy of your name. All of it, Killian. All of it."

Her trembling body gave out, and she fell to her knees.

The carefully built wall inside of her was nothing but rubble.

And then she was weeping.

She couldn't remember the last time she shed even one tear.

Now, here on her knees in front of Killian Grey, the rain pelting her from above and her very soul ripping in half like so much paper, she wept.

Sweet release.

Everything that was coiled within her sprang forth and emptied. She cried and cried, unleashing everything she'd locked up so tightly inside of herself upon the earth.

Slowly, she noticed that she was no longer shaking.

And soon, she had no tears left to cry, no pain left to let loose.

The rain slowed and then came to a stop.

It was then that Killian slid his hands under her arms and pulled her to her feet. She let him. Just as she let him wrap himself around her in an embrace that filled her with warmth and comfort. The strength quickly returned to her limbs, not a tremor in sight, not even in her fingers. She curled her arms around his shoulders and pulled Killian closer.

He kissed the top of her head.

"Neve?" he said gently. "Look around."

As she pulled back, the first thing she saw was his face. Handsome, streaked with tears, those blue eyes glittering and full of something that looked very close to joy. His hair and clothes were dry as if the rain hadn't happened at all. She glanced down at herself and saw that she was also dry.

Then she looked around.

Flurries of snow.

Thick, fluffy flakes floated in the air around them. Above, the sky looked like a black blanket covered in salt, with too many stars to name.

And the terrain...changed.

They were still in the vale, but it had opened up, and they were far enough along the trail that Neve could nearly see the other side of Mourner's Pass.

The spell was broken.

They were free.

24

Killian wasn't a man who'd been educated in magic, so he couldn't begin to guess how the spell was broken.

Honestly, he didn't care. All he cared about was that it *was* broken.

With the light of the next day dawning, he could barely recognize the man he'd become over the past week. It was as if all of his worst, most toxic qualities were brought to the surface. In an unending state of panic, he'd become lost in pure emotion. Frustration turned into rage. He hadn't been able to see anything beyond the fury and despair.

More than once, the edge of his sword looked like an inviting way to end it all. The only thing that kept him from coming completely undone was Neve.

He hadn't slept. He'd lain awake outside the cave, listening to the way her body was betraying her night after night. She'd made it clear that she didn't want him near her, so it took every fiber of self-control he possessed to keep from running in and holding her until the trembling stopped.

He wasn't sure what happened to her or what kind of sickness the curse pressed down on her. He just knew that he wanted to fix it, and he couldn't.

When she finally broke and laid herself bare...words could not describe what it did to him.

His rage was instantly erased at the crack in her voice.

Some flash of white light blinded him, and when he could see again, she was on her knees letting herself break. In some hidden part of him, there was satisfaction in seeing her completely shattered, as if validating that she was human after all.

But mostly he wanted to scoop her up and mend her so that he'd never have to see her cry again.

The sight of her tears wrenched his heart as if her very hand reached through his ribs and squeezed it.

When she was done, the snow fell, and the curse was lifted.

Perhaps the vale required an offering, and Neve sacrificed the protective fortress of strength within her to save them both.

It didn't seem to affect her drastically. She was back to her old stoic self in no time.

Still, when he looked at her now, there was a spark of something *other* in her eyes and a new, nearly imperceptible lightness with which she moved.

Something certainly changed *in* her, but somehow it didn't manage to change *her*. For that, among many other things from the past day, he was grateful.

After waking, Killian made Neve a cup of tea over their dying fire as they readied themselves for the day.

He watched her closely as she dressed and braided her hair into a crown around her head. He liked the way her lips pursed when she sipped her tea, followed by the satisfied way she always closed her eyes after the first swallow.

He longed to touch her, to kiss her. He'd slept next to her for the first time in nearly a week but was too nervous to take her in his arms. It seemed like being at odds with her for days and days wrecked his confidence, despite the attention she'd lavished on him the night after they'd battled the lycanthropes.

He could face a great many horrors, but facing her rejection was something he wasn't sure he could do.

The end of the vale was in sight. As they emerged from their shelter, Killian could see that ahead of them, within miles, the vast valley ended and opened up to what lay beyond.

Mourner's Pass would soon be a memory they could leave behind.

The sky above was virtually hidden by the final massive mountain peaks. The air was thick with gray fog that rolled down from the summits and blanketed the valley. Killian could hear a distant rumble that sounded a lot like thunder.

It was now early November. The cold around them tasted of winter. If the weather turned against them, a rainstorm could lead to icy trails that would make these final miles take all day. His warm breath came out in a puff of steam as another rumble sounded in the clouds. He hoped they were out of the valley before the storm came for them.

Killian watched Neve tilt her head to the side curiously, eyes narrow. She heard the thunder as well.

"It's too cold for rain," she said.

"I was thinking the same. What's beyond the mountains? Perhaps we can get out of here before the storm comes and find a place to shelter. Do you know of an inn on this coast?"

She shook her head. "There is nothing except the Oracle beyond the mountains."

"Gods, what I would give for a real bed."

She smirked. "I know. But we won't find one until we're back at the Stronghold."

The thought of the return trip through the vale filled him with dread.

"Will there be more curses on the way back? I don't think I can do that again."

She lifted her chin, eyes searching the sky, when another rumble vibrated down the mountains.

"A curse here means to test our worth before the Oracle. I don't believe we'll have to deal with them on the way back. More wolves and creatures, perhaps. But not curses."

"Do you think we are worthy of the Oracle?"

She gave him a sly smile. "We're still alive, aren't we?"

Killian chuckled. "It appears so."

"Once we're back to the Stronghold, I want to sleep for a week."

He sighed, imagining such restful, safe slumber. "Can I join you?"

Neve pulled her bottom lip between her teeth, sending a slice of craving through the center of Killian's body.

"I don't think there would be much sleeping if you joined me."

"You underestimate my self-control, Lady."

"Perhaps you overestimate mine," she replied.

He raised an eyebrow. "Is that so?"

She gave him a shrug. "Perhaps."

Another roll of thunder ripped his attention from her. This one came as a great *boom* and caused a cascade of small rocks to loosen and roll down the side of the cliff.

"I've never heard thunder so loud without rain."

Neve's eyes were glued above them. "I don't think it's thunder, Killian."

His body went tense. "An avalanche?"

She shook her head slowly, squinting up at the dense mist.

"No. This is something else..."

Another *boom* rumbled, followed by a sharp, grating sound, not unlike that of a crow's caw, but bigger.

Much bigger.

From the corner of his eye, Killian saw Neve's hands go to her thighs, palming the handles of her daggers.

"What is it?" he asked, following her cues and drawing his sword.

A shadow passed above them, rippling the fog.

"I don't suppose we packed a bow and arrows?" she asked quietly.

His spine stiffened. The sky darkened, another shadow blotting out the light. "No."

Neve squared her shoulders and planted her feet, never taking her intense gaze from the mist hovering above their heads.

"We'll have to make it count with our blades, then."

"Neve... what is it?" he asked in a low voice.

Her eyes cut to him, filled with predatory ice.

"Look up," she whispered.

He did and saw nothing but a billowing shadow in the fog.

A shadow that grew darker and darker as if descending on them. The wind blew, shifting the smog to reveal an enormous shape within.

A shape with wings.

Killian's blood turned hot with adrenaline. The wings, tipped with claws, gave a mighty beat, clearing more of the mist and sending a rush of air into his face.

It reeked of fire and ash and decay.

Then Killian saw it.

A massive wyvern, its scales gleaming like molten obsidian. It was a fearsome beast, with razor-sharp talons and a venomous tail that could bring swift doom to them with a mere flick in their direction. Its intelligent eyes were a glowing golden color, and the beast regarded them with a promise of violence.

No, not them. *Her.*

The wyvern seemed to have a singular focus on Neve. It stared her down, Neve stared right back, meeting its gaze without a hint of fear.

It bared its teeth, each fang as big and deadly as Killian's sword. In its grinning maw, behind those teeth, its throat was covered in smoldering embers, just waiting for a strong exhale to ignite them into flame.

It gave another beat of its wings, creating a powerful gust of wind that could have knocked them off their feet if they were unprepared.

Killian watched the silent showdown between the wyvern and the Queen, his hands gripping the hilt of his sword. It moved forward and hissed in Neve's face, its hot breath pulling strands of hair from her braid to float around her cheeks.

Neve responded with a smile, her eyes darkening with a brutal challenge.

All of Killian's instincts screamed at him to grab Neve's hand and run, to drag her away from the dreadful danger standing before them. He allowed himself one step closer to Neve, forcing himself to follow her lead despite the lump in his throat.

The moment he moved, the wyvern's head snapped in his direction, and it released a roar filled with white-hot fury.

The beast swooped down and lunged at them. Killian's grip on his sword tightened, and he moved with purpose, stepping in front of Neve and positioning himself to shield her from the wyvern's wrath.

He felt the ferocity of Neve's gaze, matched only by the raw power of the monstrous creature coming for them, and ignored it.

Let her be angry at him, as long as she was angry at him *and* alive.

They moved swiftly as one, sidestepping the attack. Killian slashed at its wing as soon as it was within range, and the impact of the blow ran up his arms. The wyvern let out a deafening screech, blasting a mouthful of fire in their direction, but they were already moving. Neve was sprinting for the cliff wall, and Killian rolled, dodging the flame.

He kept one eye on Neve as she climbed the mountainside, ascending to meet the wyvern in the air above them. It turned, lashing its venomously spiked tail at Killian, who moved again. The tail crashed into the cliff so hard that rocks avalanched down from the top.

Killian's breath caught when he saw how the impact jarred Neve's balance and nearly threw her from the perch she'd found on the hillside.

That one-instant glance to make sure she was all right was a deadly mistake.

He didn't see the second cascade of rocks coming.

One moment, he was standing, and the next, he was on the ground, pinned beneath a pile of stone.

His head was dizzy with the force of the collision. He could have sworn he saw the wyvern's wicked mouth spread into a grin. And then Neve was there above him, crouching down with a mixture of concern and wrath in her eyes.

"Still whole?" she breathed.

He blinked to clear the disorientation and did a mental inventory of his body. Nothing broken, just stuck.

"Still whole," he croaked.

Her attention cut to the stones on top of him. They both knew she wouldn't have time to clear the rock before the wyvern struck again. Their eyes met. Horror climbed up his throat. She reached down and gave his cheek a caress before taking the sword from his hand and turning away from him.

Panic surged through him like a torrential wave, and the world seemed to blur around him. His heart pounded in his ears, drowning out the sounds of the snarling wyvern. He desperately tried to free himself, to rejoin the battle and help Neve, but the rock was unyielding, trapping him like a helpless insect.

He watched Neve stalk towards the beast, casually turning his sword in her hand as if it were as light as one of her daggers.

They began to slowly circle each other.

The wyvern lunged. Neve moved faster. It snapped its jaws at her, and she sliced at its open mouth, clipping its long tongue. It screeched and huffed a blast of furious fire. Neve dropped to the ground and rolled beneath the blaze, dragging the sword along the thick scales under its chin, spilling a thin line of black blood. It roared again and thrashed its giant head. Neve couldn't avoid the blow as the wyvern's face crashed into her and sent her flying backward.

With a surge of despair, Killian watched as Neve quickly got back to her feet but stumbled and had to fight to find her balance again. But then she straightened and her lip curled in a sneer. She pointed the sword at the wyvern as a threat.

"You're mine," she said, her voice a low purr of malice.

It screamed at her, flapping its wings as she came for it. It turned, lashing that lethal tail straight for Neve's chest. She spun and delivered a mighty blow to its tail, severing one of the poison-tipped barbs with a mirthless grin. It let loose another eruption of fire from its mouth, managing to singe Neve's hand, but the Queen barely seemed to register the pain.

Every moment felt like an eternity as Killian watched her dance with danger, but each swing of the sword was a symphony of lethal grace. He longed to call out to her, to offer words of encouragement or scream her name in warning, but his throat felt constricted with fear. Killian's heart was torn between the urge to fight and the agonizing reality of his immobility. He could only watch, aching with helplessness as Neve and the wyvern engaged in this deadly waltz.

The wyvern rose into the air, slashing at Neve with its talons. The first attempt missed completely, but the second landed, opening up a wound in her thigh that sent her to her knees.

Killian struggled beneath the rocks, fighting to get loose, but it was fruitless. There was no worse torture than helplessly watching the woman he loved bleed.

With a roar, the wyvern wasted no time. It was on Neve before she could clamor back to her feet. It lunged and pinned her to the ground with its knife-sharp claws. Neve lifted her chin in defiance and looked up at it as its mouth opened wide.

"Neve!" Killian screamed, his voice echoing in a raw cry.

Despite the jaws of literal death bearing down on her, she turned her head to look at him.

Neve was trapped beneath the wyvern, just as he was trapped beneath the pile of stones. His chest lurched, his heart utterly breaking, and he tried again to move the rocks, grunting and straining.

Neve turned her face back to the wyvern, whose dripping fangs were grazing against her skin. She locked eyes with it, just as she had when it first revealed itself. There was no fear in her regard, not a single ounce.

If she felt the eager kiss of impending death, she did not show it.

Rather, the look on her face nearly *dared* death to come for her.

The embers in the wyvern's throat glowed hotter and hotter. It was going to incinerate her. Killian couldn't bear to watch, but he also wouldn't dare look away.

He wouldn't let her meet her end without a witness.

He was vaguely aware that he was screaming, but his whole world was pinned on the woman about to die. He knew nothing else. Terror chewed at his very soul.

Flames erupted.

25

Neve D'Aeth Lyra looked death in the face and breathed in a great lungful of smoke that billowed from the wyvern's waiting throat.

The desperation in Killian's eyes was enough to send a flutter of regret straight to her gut. There was still so much she needed to do. She did not want to die. She wanted to live. To fight and battle until her knuckles were raw. Take back the throne and rule gallantly like her ancestors.

She wanted her name to be immortalized in books and stories that some other woman centuries from now could read.

She wanted Killian.

She wanted a decent fucking meal before the end.

But she shoved it all down- the trembling, the roaring, the want. Shoved it down and down until it was just another part of the dark stillness within her.

She met the gaze of the mighty beast above her without wavering. Neve forced her breath to be even and her face to remain neutral. Then, she looked right into its knowing, golden eyes as it opened its monstrous jaws.

At the last second, some curious consideration shifted in the wyvern's glare, and before burning Neve to cinders, it lifted its chin high and belched out that powerful fire into the mist above them instead.

The smell of sulfur and ash assaulted Neve's senses, the heat of the blaze licking her skin.

Once it was done, the wyvern lowered its face to her again, *sniffing* her. She swallowed every emotion besides brave steel and waited, willing her body into total calm even as she felt its breath brush across her mouth.

The wyvern straightened and then paused. Almost delicately, it moved off of her, careful not to harm her with its talons despite the near bloodbath they'd just engaged in.

Neve wasted no time and climbed to her feet.

She and the beast regarded each other for a long moment. It suddenly seemed to know her, who she was at her core. Those golden eyes were almost human, almost *speaking* in some quiet voice that only the most primal part of her could understand. A starkly glowing gaze that seemed to say: *Well played.*

It must have smelled something on her. Perhaps it noticed her lack of fear and understood her as a worthy opponent. Perhaps it just decided, in the end, that it didn't feel like killing something smaller than itself today.

Neve had the overwhelming urge to say something, to ask *why*. But as she opened her mouth, it tilted its head to the side, and then with a single flap of its massive wings, it was soaring into the air.

She watched it disappear into the fog, far beyond the mountain peaks above, before finally letting out a single, shaking exhale.

Undiluted, pure relief flooded into her blood, the sudden force of it nearly knocked her back off her feet.

She'd faced death countless times, from the hands of both beasts and men, but facing it here in the mouth of that ancient, near-mythic creature with Killian watching felt... different. Some feeling akin to grief touched the edges of her spirit at the thought.

Neve rushed to Killian's side and wordlessly began hauling rocks off of him.

"Still whole?" he asked, his voice tender and shaky.

She looked at him then. His face was stricken, yet he forced a smile for her, so she gave him one in return.

"Still whole," she said. Her hands clawed at the rocks, throwing them off to the side. "I'm not going to find a bloody mess under here, am I?"

He huffed a laugh. "Gods, I hope not."

Once his arms were free, they made quick work of the rest of the rocks, then Neve helped him to his feet. Her eyes roamed his body, looking for injury, but he seemed mostly just bruised.

In an instant, his hands grabbed her face and yanked her into a rough kiss, slamming her body against his. She held onto his wrists to keep herself steady and submitted to the desperation of his mouth. He moaned against her lips, a sound of agonizing need rather than lust, and she dug her fingers into his wrists in response.

Killian pulled back, her face still in his hands.

"You were fucking magnificent," he breathed, his brow knit, eyes full of fire and feeling.

"I don't recommend fighting a wyvern on your own," she replied, already feeling the adrenaline slipping, making way for the ache of sore, abused muscles.

He laughed. His thumbs caressed her cheeks, and he pecked at her mouth and jaw with a series of kisses, as if assuring himself that she was truly there. He then wrapped his arms around her, cradling her head with one hand and burying his nose in her hair.

It felt good to be adored this way. She knew he needed to touch and hold her, to know without a doubt that she was alive. Truthfully, she needed to be held for the same reason. That had been close. Too close.

"Being trapped, having to watch…" he murmured. She felt a shiver of dread move through his body. "I don't recommend that, either."

"I'm sorry I couldn't free you before... I didn't have time."

"No," he said firmly. "Don't ever apologize to me. Especially not for fighting to stay alive."

Neve moved her hands along his shoulders, fighting the well-hewn instinct to shut down. She'd seen how well keeping everything behind a wall had served her when they were under the curse. With effort, she let herself melt a little.

"Your face... You were screaming–"

He stiffened. "Do you think I'm a coward?"

Neve stepped back and looked him dead in the eye, gripping the collar of his shirt in her fists.

"Never," she replied with such conviction that she could have sworn he wavered on his feet.

"Then, what?"

Neve braced herself and let herself feel. "No one has ever cared for me the way you do. That's what I saw on your face."

He clenched his jaw, kissing her forehead so that she wouldn't see his emotion, but she felt it. He cleared his throat.

"You really were magnificent. If I wasn't nearly shitting myself in terror, I would have been cheering you on."

An unexpected laugh erupted from her mouth, and it was rewarded with Killian's bright, warm smile. The one that made the corners of his eyes crinkle.

A smile, she realized, that she would fight one hundred wyverns for.

He brushed an errant strand of hair from her eyes. "I think, perhaps, you might like me."

She raised an eyebrow. "Perhaps."

His smile turned arrogant, and he gripped her chin between his thumb and forefinger.

"Say it," he demanded.

"I might like you," she conceded.

"Good." He nodded and ran his hands down her waist, over her hips and thighs.

He paused and lifted his hand, which came away slick with her blood.

She'd almost forgotten that the wyvern's attack opened up her thigh. Almost.

He turned his head to look at the battlefield, and she followed his gaze. There was a wide puddle of her blood pooling where the wyvern pinned her to the earth, followed by a thick trail of it leading to where she now stood in Killian's arms.

Neve felt it then, the cruel lightness of blood loss.

Not good.

She felt herself swaying, but she did not move. Killian's strong arms were there, keeping her on her feet. Worry creased his forehead again, but it was quickly replaced with a look of gentle, protective stoicism.

"Let's get this cleaned up, yeah?" he said tenderly.

She knew he was fighting to swallow his nerves, a fact that she appreciated even more once she lowered herself to sit on the ground and examined her thigh.

The wyvern's talon had ripped her open. Neve took a deep breath. Ignoring the pain, she prodded at it with her fingers, examining where the blood was flowing from. Thankfully, she didn't think it had severed an artery. If it was a mere inch to the right, however...

"Do we have a needle and thread?" she asked. She leaned her back against the cliff wall, the edges of her vision filled with dark speckles.

Killian was on his knees in front of her with what was left of their meager medical supplies. He dug in the bag, finding only a few drops of cleansing alcohol in the vial and a handful of linen strips. He shook his head with a frown.

He ripped the tear in her pants wider so he could get a better look at the injury. His jaw tightened. He took her hands and pressed them to her thigh.

"Keep pressure here."

A wave of dizzy nausea moved through her, but she did as he asked. She could feel herself fading. It wouldn't have been so bad if she'd treated the wound immediately. But she'd lost time in fighting, and even more afterward. Stupid mistake.

Neve watched with heavy eyes as Killian started a small fire. His hands moved quickly and expertly.

She knew what was coming next.

"The dagger," she said, keeping her voice smooth. "In my boot."

His gaze cut to her, knowing and solemn. Killian reached into her boot and removed her dagger, then held it over the popping flame. She watched the cold steel glow orange and blacken with soot around the edges.

Her eyelids drifted closed.

"Eyes on me, Lady," Killian commanded.

She opened her eyes and there he was, crouching over her, pinning her injured leg under his knee so she wouldn't be able to move it. One hand was flat against her chest, pressing her against the cliff wall, immobilizing her. The other hand held the steaming blade.

He gave her a look, waiting for her consent.

When she nodded, Killian pressed the burning-hot metal of her dagger against her thigh. A sizzling sound filled the air along with the scent of burning flesh. Her eyes watered, but she did not cry out at the agony. She gulped down the pain as he moved the blade across the edges of her wound, searing her skin.

She kept her gaze pinned on him; he only looked up from his task once to check on her. What he saw on her face made him press his mouth into a tight line. Her fingers clawed into the unrelenting stone ground with such force that a few of her fingernails cracked, and then she balled both hands into tight, shaking fists.

After what felt like an eternity, Killian withdrew the blade and set it aside. He softly wrapped a wide strip of linen around her thigh, over and over again until the cloth ran out. He must have noticed her shivering because he took off his coat and laid it over her. She was suddenly swimming in the warmth and the smell of him.

Her head felt like it was floating. Exhaustion finally overcame her. Neve let out a deep sigh, and everything went black.

26

Diving to the bottom of a frigid lake with a freshly cauterized wound was not exactly ideal. But they'd finally made it to Ula, and it was time.

The lake was a perfect circle, surrounded by a border of round, smooth rocks, so precise it looked as if they'd been hand-placed one by one. Its waters were crystal clear and glowing with a mythic blue light that came from somewhere in the deep. The night was dark and full of stars that reflected like glitter on the gentle waves of Ula's surface. The ground beneath their feet was fine white sand, a soft and sparkling powder. The air was cold and calm, their breath puffing like clouds.

It was truly beautiful.

"How deep is it?" Killian asked, leaning forward and peering into the lake.

Neve shrugged, her fingers working to unbutton her coat. "Not sure. Very few people have made it this far. You know how to swim, right?"

He smiled. "A bit late to be asking that question, don't you think?"

She felt his eyes on her as she dropped her coat into the sand and began peeling off the layers of wool. "I suppose," she said. "No going back now."

He tilted his head curiously. "Not that I'm complaining, but why are you taking your clothes off?"

Neve rolled her eyes and pulled down her pants, keeping her face neutral as her hands grazed her thigh, sending a fierce wave of pain through her nerves. She ran her fingers across the bandage to make sure it was still in place.

"We won't be able to swim as well in all these heavy clothes. And we'll need something to change into when we come back up so we don't freeze to death."

He nodded and started removing his clothes as well.

Soon, they stood before each other, shivering in their underclothes.

Neve raked her gaze over Killian's lethal body, clad only in a pair of cotton shorts. His broad chest and the trail of pebbled muscles down his stomach made the smallest smile lift her lips. Similarly, his hungry eyes were pinned on her breasts, barely contained beneath her thin camisole, and peaked from the cold night air.

He shook his head.

"You're going to lead me to my doom, Lady Nightmare. I know it."

She smirked. "You look good, too."

Tempting as it might be to reach out and touch him, she managed to keep her hands to herself. Neve turned and faced the lake, taking a moment to enjoy the serene beauty of it.

"Are you ready?" she asked quietly.

He was at her side, a solid wall of strength. "Yes."

"When we get down there, don't speak unless spoken to. The Oracle is...*particular*."

The lake seemed to glow brighter at the mention of its lone inhabitant. In warning or welcome, Neve did not know.

She looked at Killian, who gave her an understanding nod.

"Deep breath," she said.

One moment, they were locked in each other's gaze, filling their lungs with as much air as they could hold; the next, they were diving into the lake.

The shock of the cold was like a thousand needles driving into her skin. It threatened to knock the breath she'd fought so hard for straight out of her. She willed her body under her command and chanced a glance over her shoulder at Killian. The water was so clear, she could see him as easily as if they were on land. He gave her another nod and then, with all of their considerable strength, they propelled themselves down, down, down into the depths.

The lake seemed to go on forever, the glow at the bottom always just slightly out of reach. Neve's muscles burned as she pulled herself through water that seemed to grow thicker the further they dove. As they descended, the floating tendrils of lakeweed became more and more luminescent, beautiful colors dancing in the water's embrace.

With each stroke, the pressure increased, popping her ears. The lake stretched into an eternal, gorgeous abyss. The light at the bottom served as a guide, a vague assurance they were on the right path. Her lungs were screaming for air, and her limbs began to feel heavy. They were running out of time.

Determination had her clawing her way through the water, even as her body started rebelling against her. The glow at the bottom of the lake soon became a swirling vortex of color. A brilliant, prismatic radiance. They were almost there. Neve felt a surge of adrenaline burst through her veins, fueling their final descent.

For a moment, when they reached that stunning light, the world around them blurred and twisted. Neve wasn't sure if she was spinning or if the world itself was turning, but it made her dizzy. She fought against the vertigo. Colors spun and danced, time seemed to bend, and the very fabric of reality shifted. Then, as suddenly as it began, the whirlwind of magic came to a stop and spat them out onto a cold, marble floor.

The first breath of air was a ragged, sloppy gasp. The second gave her enough sense to look for Killian. There he was, on his hands and knees, taking great big gulps of air. Neve gave herself another few breaths to ground herself before standing and taking in their surroundings.

Behind them was a wall of water–the lake– and over it lay an iridescent, magical film. Neve turned. They were in a small antechamber. The floor, walls, and ceiling were all gleaming white marble. There were small black sconces on the walls filled with the same strange rainbow light they'd just swum through. The light caught the ripples of the lake, creating a glowing show on the surface of the marble. On the wall opposite the lake, there stood a huge crystal door.

Killian's hand was suddenly in hers, giving it a reassuring squeeze. She squeezed back and stepped forward. Anticipation bubbled up in her chest; the culmination of so many things was here, and the answers to her most important questions were just beyond this shining door.

She was ready.

Neve D'Aeth Lyra pushed open the crystal door and stepped into the room. The chamber smelled like garden mint and the sea. In the center of the room, there was a large glass cauldron with plumes of delicate smoke billowing out of it.

Behind it sat the Oracle of Ula.

She was dressed in silver gossamer that floated around her in phantom waves as if she were swimming. Her dark skin was smooth as porcelain, betraying not a single century of her ancient age. The Oracle's hair was a curly swath of onyx, and a circlet of opals sat across her brow. Her gaze was one of curiosity and slow amusement, with amber eyes that shone brightly.

"You. At last," the Oracle said, her voice like the slithering hiss of wind through grass.

"You know me?" Neve asked.

"Just as you know me."

"Then you know why I am here."

"You are here for many things."

"I am."

The Oracle gestured to the clouds puffing from the cauldron.

"Come closer," she said. "Lean in, take a breath of this smoke, and blow it back out at me. Let's see what the fates have to say about you."

Stepping forward, Neve leaned in close to the cauldron, sucking in a deep breath of the fragrant smoke. When she raised her chin, the Oracle's cool hands were cupping either side of her face. Neve felt Killian stiffen behind her and silently willed him to keep quiet.

"Now, my Queen," the Oracle whispered. "Blow."

Neve breathed the smoke into the Oracle's mouth. The ancient woman drank it all down before leaning back in her seat and raising her gaze to the ceiling.

When the Oracle's face lowered, her amber eyes were vacant and unseeing, devoid of all color. Neve felt Killian's fingers graze her wrist, in wordless question, asking if she was all right. She gave him a single nod and waited.

The Oracle's eyes flickered and returned to their ethereal amber shade. She furrowed her brow at Neve, confused.

"All I see is stars," she said. Something swirled in the still, dark pit of Neve's inner self. Something old and secret. The Oracle shook her head and beckoned Neve toward her. "Again."

Neve stepped forward, taking a greedy hit of the smoke. This time, she found the Oracle's lips against hers, soft and sweet, and she blew the great heft of clouds into the other woman's mouth.

She felt Killian's gaze burning on her, but didn't dare glance at him. Once again, the Oracle raised her face skyward, and when she looked back at Neve, her eyes were hauntingly colorless.

When the Oracle spoke, her voice was otherworldly; it seemed layered with many different voices, all twisting around each other. She spoke quickly, in one long train, without a breath:

"The crown now worn by a treacherous foe,
A kingdom's fate hanging in the balance, so
The truth unfolds, a warning clear,
The queen's great enemy is now in power here."

The Oracle gasped, a desperate ripping sound, as her eyes turned back to their amber shade. A furious tingle slammed through Neve's body, turning her fingers and toes momentarily numb. She knew it, she knew—

Before she could process the words, the Oracle reached across the cauldron and pulled Neve against it, strong fingers digging into her arms. "Again!" the Oracle rasped.

Neve did as she was told, sucking in more smoke and then the Oracle's mouth met hers, hungry and wanting, devouring the breath Neve released. The Oracle's hands let go of Neve with such sudden force that the Queen stumbled backward. Killian was there, an iron-strong arm at her waist. She could feel how rigid he was with worry and distrust, but Neve needed more - trust and safety be damned.

The Oracle was empty-eyed and frightening. The magical veil of her immortality seemed to be shifting and pulling away like a curtain. Her dark, beautiful skin began to crack like broken porcelain, the sockets around her eyes grew deeper, and her black curls started to fall from her head in clumps, landing on the pristine silver gossamer of her dress.

Neve pushed down every instinct, every emotion until there was nothing left on the surface but greed for the truth she'd spent her whole life seeking.

From a quickly aging mouth, the Oracle spoke again, in that same twisting, multi-layered voice as before:
"In shadows shrouded, the crown's heart ensnared,
A queen adrift, by her strength impaired.
Her brilliance veiled, 'neath a darkened plight,

To free her light, seek starry might.

To mend the path and own the key,
A starlit cry, for all to see.
Unite the moon, the sun, the skies,
To break the chains, let true light rise."

Some sleeping giant in Neve's chest stirred at the words, nearly choking her with its quiet awakening.

Gods, what is that? She thought.

It felt like cold fire, it felt like terrible gravity, it felt like it had *always* been there. Her mind could make no sense of the words the Oracle spoke, but that thing inside her understood all too well and stretched its arms wide to welcome the acknowledgment. Neve was vaguely aware that she'd doubled over with the power of it, clutching her chest as if to keep it from exploding out of her.

"Neve..." Killian's voice sounded far away, like they were underwater. But she knew they weren't, and she knew that he was right there, his arm still around her waist.

No. She belonged to no one but herself. And that included this beast, this power, this force uncurling inside her. With effort and a silent snarl, Neve unbent and stood tall. She squared her shoulders, planted her feet, and looked right into the Oracle's eyes, which were still unseeing as ghosts.

In the space of the few breaths that Neve looked away, the once-radiant Oracle had withered into an old crone.

"Neve, I think we need to leave," Killian said quietly.

"YOU," the Oracle roared, pointing her gnarled finger at Killian. Neve stiffened, and a wave of what could only be described as possession moved through her. Whether territorial of the Oracle's attention, Killian, or both, Neve did not know.

But it was another foreign feeling that had the unraveling force in her saying "*Mine.*"

The Oracle continued, her finger still pointed like a weapon. "You. You will face death twice, you will fail, you will lose her, you will lose everything again, you will find, you will fight, you will shield, you will bring death with you like luggage..."

Neve looked at Killian, his face was white as a sheet, his eyes bulging, and that muscle she liked so much ticked in his jaw.

"What—" he began..

The Oracle let loose a pained, frustrated shriek.

Neve forced her heart to beat steadily, even as she felt Killian nearly pulsating with panic next to her. The situation seemed to be blossoming into a tense state of chaos.

She took a deep breath and reached inside herself, reaching for that cold and terrible fire. She gave it a caress, and it seemed to purr at her as if to say "*hello*" and "*finally*."

In a voice she barely recognized as her own, Neve said firmly, "Enough."

At the very word, the Oracle's eyes faded back to amber, the veil of her youth returning as if she hadn't just been laid bare as a skeleton before them. The Oracle slumped forward onto the cauldron, which no longer puffed with smoke. Empty.

The Oracle looked at Neve sadly, gratefully.

"Go," the ancient one breathed. "You don't have much time."

Neve nodded in understanding.

"Thank you," she said. And meant it with her whole heart. She turned to Killian, who still looked haunted but ready for battle.

"Run," Neve commanded.

They sprinted through the chamber and the hall beyond, crashing through the wall of water. That same colorful whirlpool spun them around and around until they kicked free, and they were back in the lake.

Neve could see the vague dots of stars beyond the surface above. But it was far. So, so far. And the water was cold, much colder than it was on their descent. But Killian and Neve swam hard and fast, climbing one stroke at a time to the top.

Once they were nearly at the end, Neve's lungs were close to withering with need, and relief felt so close...

Until it wasn't.

Killian was two strokes ahead of her, and as he rose, he slammed into something hard. His eyes widened at her, the veins in his neck bulging with the frantic need for air.

Steeling herself, Neve reached up... ice. The surface of the lake was covered in a thick sheet of solid ice. Killian unleashed his fists upon it again and again and again, the water pulling strands of inky blood away from his knuckles. The ice didn't budge.

Neve flipped her body upside down, the lake's embrace squeezing her limbs, and she pelted the ice with furious, stomping kicks. The impact of the unyielding ice against her feet rang up her shins to her knees, but she kept kicking, right alongside Killian's fists battering against it.

She righted herself in the water and slammed her fists against it.

Neve and Killian's eyes met. No, there would be no surrender. They would not relent.

That much was clear from the wild and rageful look in Killian's stare. Despite it all, that powerful expression on his handsome face gave her the confidence she needed. To know that he was in this with her. That she was not alone in this fight.

Together, they released a barrage of blows onto the ice, channeling every bit of themselves into each strike. Cracks webbed across the surface, like intricate labyrinths leading them to freedom, but the ice still held firm. Desperation fueled their efforts as they pounded relentlessly, the sound of their battle echoing through the submerged realm.

Power, pure and complete, rolled off of them while they fought, even as their bodies began to lose strength.

Air, they needed air.

Neve glanced at Killian, whose punches were beginning to lose force, his feet falling out of the rhythm to keep him steadily afloat. His eyes looked like they were getting heavy. He was fading.

Truth be told, so was she.

But the sight of him slowing down set flame to her desperation, and she bared her teeth at the ice above them. Neve reached over with one hand and grabbed Killian by the back of the neck. She pressed her mouth to his, daring to release what little breath she had left into his mouth.

Fucking fight, she willed at him, clawing her fingernails into his skin. His eyes snapped open, and he gave her a nod as if he felt her will, as if he heard her.

They both looked up at the ice and, somehow reading each other's thoughts, they backed up, swimming down a little to give them enough space to gather speed and what remained of their strength. Darkness bloomed like spots of oil behind Neve's eyes, but she ignored it.

As one, together, they swam, ripping through the current. As one, together, they crashed against the ice and finally-

Finally...

Broke through.

Neve clawed her way across the slippery surface and pulled her body over the perfectly round pebble border and into the waiting sand. Her gasps for air sounded like screams in the night. She lay on her stomach and turned her head to see Killian doing the same, a mere arm's length away from her. They lay there, surviving, unable to do anything but look at each other and breathe.

Weakly, Killian reached his arm out toward her, and she reached for him. His fingers slid between hers and gave them a reassuring squeeze. They were alive. Both of them. And that was enough.

Interlude III

Above, the stars flared, one by one, and the skies cracked open with a glow of light. A great sigh of wind blew, like the clouds themselves were exhaling in joyful relief. Every living thing below stood up straight and beheld the light. Hope. Great and unending hope seemed to glitter down upon the kingdom of Eodia from the very heavens above.

The new gods roared.

The Queen had returned.

PART TWO

Woman on the Plains

27

"I don't like it," Killian remarked.

"There's no other way," Neve responded.

They needed to split up.

Killian understood the logic of it, but still couldn't stand the reality of moving in a different direction from Neve. All of his instincts, his unshakable sense of protection and duty, screamed at him to stay at her side. But she was right. There was no other way.

After the Oracle, they'd gone back to the Grey Stronghold to recuperate and plan their next steps. Neve decided the next steps would take her to the Capital, Sylvera, which was the hub of power in Eodia. It was where the Highborns lived and governed.

Neve believed she needed to get close to the Highborns, a belief that made Killian's blood turn cold in his veins.

He'd spent his whole life serving the Highborns, killing and torturing at their whim. Killian had intimate knowledge of what they did to people who crossed them. He'd been their instrument, after all, their weapon. The idea of Neve ending up beneath such a weapon made Killian nearly blind with concern.

But she insisted. The Oracle's words pointed in that direction as well.

The crown now worn by a treacherous foe.

It seemed Neve thought the Highborns were that foe, and he didn't disagree.

Killian knew there was more to the story that Neve wasn't telling him. Some other secret which may have been obvious to her but eluded him. What he understood was that the Highborns were a part of whatever would keep her from her throne, and for Neve, that would not stand.

Killian and his famous face were wanted for high treason. He would not be able to set foot in the Capital unless he wanted to be arrested or executed on the spot. He was willing to take that risk, but Neve was emphatically not.

So, they'd pored over the map of the kingdom and decided that Killian would hide out in a settlement a mile north of Sylvera. He and Neve would have to meet in secret; she would come to him when she could.

"Under no circumstances are you to come find me, Killian," she said in a voice that left no room for argument.

They were close to that settlement, Thornkeep, now. They would soon have to part ways and say goodbye.

It was December, and all of the trees were naked, their leaves covering the ground in a crisp, brown blanket. Snow would come soon, winter was near.

Neve sat straight-backed on Gisele wearing her heavy black cloak, the one that once bore the emblem of the Maere. Her dark hair fell around her shoulders, and she regarded him with cool, wary eyes.

The look on her face told him that she wasn't concerned about entering the Capital, but rather nervous that he'd succumb to his protective instincts and make a mess of her careful plans.

"That's too much to ask of me," he said. "There are absolutely circumstances that will have me running to you."

"Don't be difficult," she responded with an eye roll. "I can handle myself. You *know* that."

He pulled on Willow's reins, coming to a stop. He watched Neve's chest rise and fall with a deep, annoyed sigh as she came to a stop as well.

"*I* can't handle myself. Not if I think you're in danger."

Her face softened just a little. "Killian, I need you to trust me."

"I do. I know your strength, your power. But I also know theirs."

She trotted Gisele closer, so they were sidled up right next to each other and she reached out, taking the collar of his jacket in her fist.

"Then let me *break* them," she purred.

And damn if the sound of those words coming out of her mouth didn't ignite every single one of his nerves and set him ablaze.

She was so beautiful and terrible that he forgot what to do with his body and just sat there gaping at her.

"I will come to you as often as I can. I promise. But you need to stay in Thornkeep. No matter what."

He opened his mouth to protest again, but she stood in her saddle and crushed her lips against his, causing him to lose whatever thought he was about to express. Her kiss was deep, her tongue moving against his. It had his cock hardening in his pants, had him wanting to pull her off her horse and take her right there on the ground. He was dizzy with her scent and taste.

And she knew it.

She pulled away from him, and all of Killian's focus narrowed to the way she licked her lips, tasting him there. The faint blush that bloomed on her cheeks and chest invited him to drag his mouth over every rosy inch.

He leaned forward for more of her, but she held him at arm's length, her hands on his shoulders.

"I cannot risk this, and I cannot risk *you*," she said.

Killian's heart cracked. Knowing that he meant enough to her... it brought him back to himself, clearing the lustful fog from his brain and replacing it with the urge to do whatever he could to get her to say something like that to him again.

He took her hand and pressed his lips to her knuckles. "I swear. I'll stay in Thornkeep."

The wariness didn't leave her eyes, but she nodded. "Good."

They traveled the rest of the way in silence. When they reached the outskirts of Thornkeep, his gut twisted. This was it. Where they would have to part.

"I will find you soon," she promised. Killian knew she could see that his eyes were begging her to stay, that he was holding in a fiery stream of the word *no*. "Tonight, if I can. But soon, if not."

"Neve, I —"

She reached for him then.

"I know," she said and kissed him once more before digging her heels into Gisele's sides and riding off into a gallop.

He watched her go, and she did not look back.

~

Thornkeep looked just like every other run-down village in Eodia. Cottages in disrepair, dirty streets littered with garbage, and starving children begging along the roadway. The market stalls were meager; they were far from the growing season now, and the food looked scarce.

The settlement was quiet, sad, and gray. There were more taverns and courtesan houses than there were any other kind of business.

It was also crowded. Families set up camps in every free spot of land that was available. It seemed like there were two or three times as many people living in Thornkeep as there should have been.

Killian slid off of Willow and gave her a generous pat before leading her down the village's main byway. He had to watch where he walked, stepping over and around puddles of piss and worse. The stench was heavy. Too many unwashed bodies occupying the same space, and not a privy or fresh water source in sight for gentlefolk to care for their basic needs.

He stopped at two inns to try to find a room to rent, but they were both full, so he kept looking. Further into the village, the spaces opened up a little wider, feeling less like Thornkeep was pressing in on him. The air moved a little more freely, and Killian took his first clean breath since setting foot in the place.

There were more inns and taverns on the southern end of town, more camps, more shop carts, and more courtesans leaning against stalls, beckoning with bare skin despite the December wind.

Killian pulled into a clearing and took in his surroundings. His eyes moved to a cart selling smoked turkey legs, and his stomach growled at the scent. A lumbering man passed the proprietor a coin and was given a huge hunk of meat, the savory juices dripping down his outstretched hand.

And then, it suddenly felt like the ground fell out from under Killian.

The man turned, raising the turkey leg to his open mouth, when he froze and looked right at him.

There was no mistaking the long scar that raked down the left side of the man's face. No mistaking the weathered but kind look on him.

Arran.

The color leached from his former first General's face when he looked at Killian like he was seeing a ghost. The man crossed the space between them quickly and ferociously, with big stomping footsteps. Before Killian could think, Arran's arms were around him, yanking him into a rough embrace.

"Before you say anything, lad," Arran muttered quickly into Killian's ear, "Be careful. There are eyes everywhere here."

Killian stiffened. "Understood."

Arran pulled away, casting an anxious look at their surroundings and nodding behind Killian, further into the clearing behind a stretch of old, crumbling buildings. They found a rusting iron bench and sat.

"We thought you were dead, boy," Arran said, his gray eyes bloodshot and full of emotion. Killian swallowed the lump in his throat. "We were *told* you were dead."

"Who?"

"Everyone. The news came down from the Highborns and spread through the kingdom. You died in the Dark Forest, they said. Killed by the woman you followed, the Maere let the beasts of the Forest have what was left of you."

Interesting. Especially considering the battle he and Neve had fought against Rory and the Cavalry. The Highborns certainly knew he wasn't dead. Killian didn't say what he was thinking, though. He merely forced that old arrogance to light his face and shrugged with a smirk.

"It wounds me that you believed the woman could take me out."

Arran looked a little ashamed at that, as if he felt stupid and played. It hurt Killian to lie to his oldest friend, his father figure, but he got the feeling he wouldn't be able to trust anyone or anything in this town.

"It didn't seem so far off at the time. I saw how she fought. We all did. And the Maere..." Arran shook his head. "Where have you been?"

The lies flowed easily off his tongue.

"The Maere caught me following them. Took me prisoner, led me on a fruitless wild-goose chase around this whole gods-damned Island for months. They decided to head back to the southern continent before winter came. I guess they didn't want to be stuck here any longer than they had to be."

Arran took a hefty bite of the turkey leg and narrowed his eyes. Mouth full of meat, he asked, "They just let you go? Just like that?"

Killian shrugged. "I was of no use to them."

"And the woman? Neve. What happened to her?"

The sound of her name from between another man's teeth made Killian's skin prickle with violence.

But he swallowed it down and gave Arran a low, purely male chuckle and wink, letting his friend use his imagination.

Arran raised an eyebrow and grinned. "Good man, good man," he said.

Eager to change the subject, to get Arran to forget Neve's name, Killian asked, "What are you doing here?"

The mirth left Arran's face, and he gave another cautious look around them. "They razed Lowbarrow to the ground. Hythe, too. After you died- well, left, I guess. They wanted to punish you even in death, erase every trace of Killian Grey."

Anger began its slow, familiar crawl up Killian's bones. "*What?*"

Arran saw the change in him and lowered his voice even further.

"The last thing you want to do here is make a scene, lad. You need to keep quiet, don't bring attention to yourself."

Killian clenched his jaw. "Tell me *everything*." The timber of his voice rumbled in his chest, his fists tightening.

Looking around once more, Arran leaned in.

"It happened at night. The whole village was asleep. They sent in Mages, an army of them used magic to set the village on fire. We tried to get everyone out, but..."

The sorrow in Arran's eyes was enough to tell Killian that the Cadre hadn't been able to save the village.

"How many escaped?"

Arran couldn't meet his gaze. "Twenty."

Twenty.

The number was a burn against Killian's soul.

"Women and children screaming... It was a black night, lad. The Mages trapped people in their homes with magic and then set everything on fire. There was nothing left. Your cottage is ash. The whole village is ash."

Fury and grief skittered across Killian's bones like lightning. Bile rose in his throat, his gut rolling.

"I'll fucking kill them. All of them," he ground out.

It was taking every ounce of his self-control not to get up. Not to draw his sword and unleash himself on the Island until he found the Mages, the Cavalry, and the Highborns. Every last one.

Arran's hand was on his arm, gripping with bruising strength. "I do not doubt that you'll do just that. But you need to be smart. You *cannot* let your rage take you. Not this time."

Killian leaned forward, his elbows on his knees, and ran his hands through his hair. He forced himself to breathe around the swelling of hatred in his chest.

One breath, two.

"There's something else, Killian." There was dread in those words, so much dread that Killian knew whatever was coming next was bad. Very bad.

"What is it?" he managed to ask.

Tears lined Arran's eyes. "Logan and Fraser."

Killian's chest tightened. "What about Logan and Fraser?" he demanded, his voice nothing but quiet thunder.

A slow shake of Arran's head told Killian everything he needed to know. "Gone," his friend said.

Killian's body propelled him to his feet, turning his back to Arran. He wanted to throw something, hit something, kill someone, but there was nothing. Nothing but the crumbling wall of an old shack. He threw his fist into it, hard enough to make a hole in the rotting wood. He then pressed his forehead to the wall, and a scream released from the depths of him. A horrible, cracking sound that he felt from the bottom of his feet to the top of his head.

His friends. Dead.

Because he left. Because, on a whim, he followed a woman into a forest and left his brothers to clean up his mess. A whole village was burned alive as his *punishment*.

The Highborns may have told the world that Killian was dead, but they'd destroyed his home, his village, and his friends, *knowing* he would find out. It was a punishment worse than the dungeon or death. It was the killing of his very soul. Furthermore, it was a threat. A show of power.

They'd lay waste to everyone and everything he loved before the end.

He could never regret finding Neve, finding his path, his destiny at her side. But he would regret his recklessness. Thinking that his choice to defect wouldn't cause a ripple for anyone but himself.

Until the day he died, he would regret that.

Arran was at his side. "I am *begging* you to keep it together, Killian," he said in a quiet voice, full of warning.

With effort, Killian reined it in. Pulling and pulling at the tethers of his rage and grief until the storm of it was tucked back inside of him.

"Gillis and Rory?" he asked, his face still pressed against the cool, water-logged damp of the building.

"They're Cavalry now. On a mission to the west. Word of the fires in Lowbarrow and Hythe has spread to other villages. Small rebellions have begun to pop up across the kingdom."

"Why aren't you with them?"

"My mission is to make sure a rebellion doesn't break out here."

Rebellions were new. Before now, no one dared. Despite the relentless oppression the Highborns forced on the kingdom, despite the countless atrocities that were committed in their name and at their behest, there had never been a rebellion. Never even a whisper of one. But now...

It was as if Killian finally returned to civilization only to find it changing. Perhaps anger was finally making the gentlefolk of Eodia bold. Perhaps they were finally ready to fight, after all these years.

Perhaps, on some primal level, they could feel that someone was coming to deliver them from this hell.

And when she did, Killian would be there, his sword ready for blood.

28

Neve, in all her travels, had never seen a place so… *pristine.*

Just beyond the border of Sylvera, there was a public stable. Neve handed over a coin, renting a stall for Gisele so she could continue on foot.

She'd need to be able to move with the shadows here.

The streets of the capital were paved in clean, white sandstone. It looked as if they were swept and washed on an hourly basis, as not a single dirty footprint marred them. In contrast to the low, squat buildings found in most villages, here every building was a tower, tall and gray and perfectly symmetrical.

Instead of merchant carts, there were shops lining the streets, each with a large, gleaming glass window to showcase their wares for passersby. Bakeries with fresh bread and pastries glazed with sugar. Tea shops whose windows were stacked with jars and jars of different colored tea leaves. Dressmakers and clothiers with the finest fabrics and embellishments. Blacksmiths with the most ornate, shining steel she'd ever seen.

Neve trained her face to remain neutral as she observed each shop window, despite the awe gathering within her at all the beautiful things the people of Sylvera had at their fingertips. So many resources and riches that the rest of Eodia had no access to.

It was a strange feeling, the sudden urge to hand over a coin for things she didn't need while knowing the rest of the kingdom, *her* kingdom, languished in abject poverty.

The people here were different, too.

Women were trussed up like gifts waiting to be unwrapped: corseted and ribboned, in gowns that looked fit for royalty. So many pastel colors of silk, some that Neve had never seen outside of a sunrise. Each gown bore intricate embroidery and embellishments like beads and golden metalwork. The women were beautiful, but wan, as if that divine feminine spark inside each of them died long ago.

Ornaments. The women here were ornaments.

The men were sneering peacocks in belted jackets with the same colors and details as the women's gowns. Pastel greens and blues, ruffled shirt collars, stiff, shining fabric, and matching pants. They carried swords for decoration, thin blades that looked as if they'd easily snap upon impact, with hilts covered in jewels and fine metal.

Neve found herself wondering just how satisfying it might be to take one of those swords, break it over her knee, and watch the color drain from some preening man's face.

She realized within minutes that in her black leather, she stuck out like a sore thumb.

Neve swept into a dress shop with all the casual air she'd observed from the people of the Capital: entitled, confident, dead inside. As the door behind her closed, the dressmaker looked up from behind the counter. Her eyes widened at the sight of Neve. An older woman with graying red hair and a smattering of freckles across her face. She tensed as if sensing the danger that had just breezed into the establishment.

"Good morning," Neve said with a smile, making her voice go up an octave or two, bringing light into her eyes that told the shopkeeper she wasn't a threat. She gestured sheepishly to her leathers and gave the old woman an embarrassed look. "I've been traveling for some time, and I'll need some new clothes. I fear I might be rather hopeless."

The dressmaker softened, her eyes glittering, and a gentle smile showed off the dimples in her cheeks.

"Hopeless indeed, my dear. Let's get you into something suitable for a lady."

Neve dropped a palmful of coins on the counter, and the woman's eyes lit even brighter.

~

Mina, the dressmaker, insisted that Neve wash before even touching any of the finery in her shop. There was an inn in the tower above the clothier. Mina sweet-talked the landlord into renting a room to Neve.

The room was clean and spacious, with a large claw-foot bathtub behind a changing screen in the corner. It also had a closet where Neve stashed her belongings, all except her weapons and her book. She hid them in various spots throughout the room for easy access and tucked the book in between two pillows on the fluffy white bed.

Once clean, Neve padded down eight flights of spiral stairs and through a narrow hallway to the back entrance of the shoppe wearing a clean set of underclothes and a robe.

Mina took one look at her linen underclothes and scrunched her nose, insisting that there were far more fashionable items she should be wearing- items made of lace and creamy satin. The old woman bundled an armful of those lacy things together for Neve, wrapping them in brown paper and tying the package together with a strip of blue velvet.

If Mina noticed Neve's scars as she was undressing, measuring, and fussing over her, she did not show it. The Capital was sure to see plenty of strange people passing through. A bit of coin and a warm smile seemed to pay for a great many things: discretion included.

The dressmaker smelled of powdery vanilla and was kind. Neve paid close attention to her mannerisms so she could mimic them later, watching the way she dipped her head in a gentle bow each time a patron came in to browse or how she touched her fingers to her chin as she said *thank you.*

Neve also noticed the anxious way Mina would look up from her work every time someone passed the storefront window, on edge as if waiting to be caught doing something she wasn't supposed to.

"Do you own this place, Mina?" Neve asked. Mina was behind her, fitting laces through her corset, and she felt the woman tense.

"The Highborns own every shoppe, of course. But I manage mine."

Noted. "Of course, that's what I meant."

"Where did you say you were from?"

Neve let some of the fake honey melt away from her voice when she replied, "I didn't."

A tremor moved through Mina's hands, and Neve felt it against her back. But the woman just started tugging on the laces of the corset with skilled strength and said, "Right, then. Deep breath, dear."

After the hour-long ordeal of fitting and dressing, Mina finally took Neve's hand and brought her to a full-length, golden gilded mirror.

Her dark hair was pulled into a loose bun at the back of her neck so that the milky expanse of her throat and decolletage were exposed. The corset had certainly done its job. Her breasts were high and swelled over the square neckline of the sage green gown with every breath she took. The bodice of the gown was fitted precisely to her curves, and the skirt was wide and full, with sections of gathered fabric peppered with tiny silk rosettes of the same color as the rest of the gown. The sleeves were elbow-length, the shoulders ruched and slightly puffed.

As it was December, Mina gifted her a dark, muted green velvet cloak that matched and contrasted perfectly with her new dress. With the addition of a new pair of surprisingly weather-hardy boots and the package of lacy underclothes, Neve was an entirely different woman by the end of it.

Neve smiled. She would fit in here perfectly now.

"You're a vision, my dear. A true vision," Mina mused. The woman was glowing and very happy with her work.

"Thank you, Mina. This is exactly what I was looking for."

Neve D'aeth Lyra stepped back out onto the streets of Sylvera, beautiful and anonymous, and began her hunt.

29

There was no cure for the grief and guilt pressing down on Killian Grey. But he decided to look for it at the bottom of a whiskey glass just the same.

It was deep into the dark winter night. He sat at the bar in one of the countless taverns in Thornkeep, nursing his fourth drink and waiting for the burn of the whiskey to ease some of his pain. Or at the very least, mask it until he was numb enough to be able to sleep.

Arran was off on a patrol of the village, a task that seemed to happen hourly if not constantly, leaving Killian alone in a strange town with only his thoughts to keep him company.

Those thoughts were not friendly.

Five years ago, he'd failed his family. And then, almost immediately upon his release from the dungeon, he'd failed his Cadre and his village. His months traveling with Neve felt like a redemption, a reprieve. Now, finding out what happened when he left and the consequences of his choice to follow Neve, it was like the rug was pulled out from under his feet, and he was free-falling into the abyss of self-loathing.

It was his duty to protect his family, his Cadre, and his village. Killian had failed on all accounts.

You will fail... You will lose her... You will lose everything again...

The Oracle's venomous words slithered into his blood and made a home there.

You will bring death with you like luggage...

Killian drained his cup in one swallow and signaled to the barmaid for another. The whiskey went down his throat like acid and settled in his gut, roiling.

He should have been there for Logan and Fraser. They died as heroes, trying to save innocent people from the wrath of ruthless tyrants. If he'd been there, Killian could have helped, could have gotten more people out, could have stopped it, it may not have even happened at all... or he could very well have ended up as a pile of ash like the rest of them.

When he'd gone back to Lowbarrow after the dungeon, he hadn't dared stay at his cottage. Now that it was burned to the ground, all he could think about was what disappeared with it. All the memories of his family. Yes, the final memories of his wife and children were... unbearable. But all their good memories were gone too. Mornings at the breakfast table, his sons' first steps, quiet moments with his wife. Gone.

All gone.

He shot back another mouthful of whiskey.

A woman sidled up to him where he sat at the bar. She brushed her small breasts against his arm and leaned in close, reeking of ale.

"Hello, handsome," she slurred.

He shrugged his broad shoulder to gently move her off, but she didn't get the hint and pressed into him again.

"Not interested, love," he said in a low tone, staring into his glass.

"Oh come on," she said, boldly nuzzling her nose up the column of Killian's neck. "I could make you feel good."

He looked at her, the edges of his vision blurry with drink. She was bland. Thin and frail with skin so pale it was nearly gray and eyes that were muddied and without light. He was drunk enough that he was unable to think linearly, but aware enough to know that this woman was nothing compared to the one he'd spent the past few months with.

Not even close.

No one would ever be like Neve.

She was it for him.

The woman in front of him now reminded him of paper. Dull and fragile. Easily ripped apart. He didn't find that appealing. But still, he tried to be kind.

"No, thank you," he said, turning back to his drink, shrugging his shoulder again to brush her off.

Her hand dragged across his chest, groping the muscles beneath. Her touch was like the buzzing of blowflies. He tried not to cringe.

"Offer a girl some warmth on this cold night," she breathed. Her scent was a cloud around him: ale and dirt and loneliness.

"I said no," he replied, more firmly. His tenderness and patience had limits.

"I'll beg for it if that's what you like," she said. Her hand trailed down his stomach, aiming for the waistband of his pants.

"That's mine," a low voice purred from the other side of the woman.

The sound made something male and primal inside Killian stand at attention.

"What's yours?" the woman hissed, keeping her hand exactly where it was. She turned to reveal the unmistakable shape of Neve clad in her black leathers, her cloak pulled low over her face, only revealing her smirking mouth.

That fucking mouth.

Neve pulled her hood back just enough to show her eyes, which glanced down at where the woman's hand was resting on Killian's lap.

"*That's* mine," she replied.

Burning fucking gods.

Killian nearly choked.

The woman blinked at her and swayed drunkenly on her feet, but made no effort to move her hand.

Killian watched death sparkle in Neve's eyes, cold and complete. He liked her like this. Possessive, territorial. Of *him.*

Just like she'd been with the barmaid the night she shredded the hands of that warrior. Stepping into the maid's space with the promise of pain. A night that felt like years ago. He made the mental note to bring Neve to more taverns, just so he could see her growl at women on his behalf. Stake her claim publicly.

"It's true," he managed to say, having regained enough sense to try to diffuse the situation. He couldn't contain his grin as he glanced down at his crotch and said, "That belongs to her."

The temperature of the air around them dipped as if the ice filling Neve's blood was exhaling from her in a phantom breeze. And was she faintly... glowing? A warm, white light seemed to radiate from her eyes, her skin, and the ends of her gently curling hair. He shook his head.

Gods, this whiskey was strong. He blinked, and the light was gone, but the dangerous look on her face remained.

Killian knew Neve could make this poor woman kneel, make her crawl, end her just for touching him, and that knowledge was enough to nearly undo him completely.

But instead, Neve gently took the woman's hand off his lap and put a glass of water into it.

"Drink that and call it a night," she commanded.

The woman swallowed and nodded.

"You're right," she slurred, wandering off to the other side of the tavern.

Killian glanced over his shoulder, and sure enough, the woman was gulping down the water like it was her only lifeline.

Neve's scent, sweet clover and rain, made him dizzy. He couldn't help himself when he wrapped an arm around her waist and pulled her to him.

"My hero," he breathed against her neck, chuckling.

"You're drunk," she responded with quiet amusement and a hint of warning in her voice. "We should sit somewhere else. I don't want to make a scene. The last thing we need is gossip around the village about the famous Killian Grey nuzzling a mysterious woman."

He swayed a little as he stood, taking his refilled drink in hand. "You'll let me nuzzle you, though?"

She rolled her eyes and led him to a booth in a dark corner of the tavern where they sat next to each other, out of sight and earshot from the rest of the patrons.

Neve leveled her gaze on him, reading his drunkenness, perhaps even the pain beneath. Killian ran his long fingers up the side of his whiskey glass but didn't drink from it. Didn't want to drink in front of her, the need to numb didn't feel quite as important with her next to him, with the warmth of her thigh pressed against his.

"How was your day?" He asked, blinking, trying to appear less plastered than he was.

She leaned back, keeping to the shadows, pulling her hood so that he was the only one in the whole tavern who could see her face.

Damn, that face.

"I went shopping," she said.

His eyebrows raised. "Shopping?"

Neve smirked. "I bought a dress."

He hooked a finger in the collar of her cloak, peeking inside.

"No dress," he said, giving her a fake pout but unable to take his eyes off the cleavage bared beneath her leathers.

She swatted his hand away. "You're a mess. What happened today?"

Killian sighed and pushed a hand through his hair. "Arran is here."

Neve's eyes flickered. "From the Cadre?"

He nodded, feeling those dark thoughts take hold of his ankles to drag him under again. Neve showing up made him forget, just for a moment, the catastrophe that was handed to him today. Now it resurfaced with a vengeance. He swirled the whiskey in his glass, and then it all came tumbling out of his mouth.

"After I left to follow you, the Highborns sent an army of Mages to Lowbarrow. They burned it to the ground. Hythe as well. Almost everyone in the village was killed, including two of my men."

Neve grabbed his drink. Killian watched her throat work as she took it down in one swallow. He shifted in his seat. She flipped the cup upside down and set it on the table in front of them with a satisfying, crisp *clunk*, then pinned him to the spot with her eyes.

"Which men?"

"Logan and Fraser."

"Where is your brother? And the redhead?"

"Arran said Rory and Gillis were sent west with the Cavalry to curb some unrest. Small rebellions have been breaking out across the kingdom since Lowbarrow and Hythe were destroyed."

She sat back, shrouded in darkness. He knew her well by now. He knew that she was quietly absorbing the information and tasting it on her tongue, determining how she could use it for her benefit. Killian admired that about her, admired nearly everything. But right now, with the weight of sadness and the buzz of liquor upon him, he needed more from her. Gentle reassurance. Something kind and lovely. But he didn't know how to ask her for it without sounding weak and desperate. So, he turned inward on himself and said nothing.

"Why did they burn down your village?"

He ground his teeth and looked down at his hands, clamped together on the tabletop. "As punishment."

"Punishment for what?"

"My defection."

The shadows in their booth seemed to close in on him, sharp and cold.

"The Highborns slaughtered two towns to prove a point about your loyalty?"

Killian's stomach rolled, and nausea swept over him. He put his head in his hands.

"I shouldn't have left... I should have–"

"No," Neve said. There was a lethal edge to her voice that made him sit up and look at her. Lady Nightmare, death in her eyes. "You're not going to take this on."

"But, they were mine to protect–"

"I said *no*." The words rumbled like thunder and sparked like lightning.

She looked him in the eyes and leaned in; everything about her was quietly ferocious, dangerous, frightening. Neve took his face between his hands, and the gentle touch of her fingers was in contrast to her fearsome presence. It sobered him up in an instant.

"This blood is not on your hands. This wasn't your fault," she said.

His heart cracked. But she continued, and he listened, enraptured.

"We will make them pay for it. We will rip them apart one by one. The Mages, the Cavalry, the Highborns." He believed her. Truly believed her. "When we're done, there will be nothing left of them. Not even the marrow of their bones."

Before he could say a word, she slid closer to him and rested her head on his shoulder. Something so small. So ordinary. So generous. This beautiful, awful force of nature with her head on his shoulder... it nearly split him in two. In fear of breaking the moment, he just sat there, swallowed down his emotions, and rested his head on top of hers.

30

The Capital was huge. Neve had traveled across continents with The Maere and never once encountered a city so large. It took her two full days of exploring to get the basic scope of the territory, and even then, there was so much more to see.

Sylvera was mostly a city of affluence. It was clean and sparkled with wealth proudly on display. Citizens meandered around town with their noses in the air, not even looking at the servants and gentlefolk who cleaned up after them. The workers of the Capital edged out of the way when aristocrats marched in their direction as if they knew they'd be trampled if they didn't move.

Neve spent most of her time observing. She watched the way the aristocrats moved, the way their eyes shuttered against anyone or anything that didn't please them, the way they held their bodies tall with stiff entitlement. More than once, she'd seen a wealthy man raise his hand against someone going about their work, simply for existing.

Cruelty was a thick perfume in this place.

Some day, she would show them *her* brand of cruelty.

But, for now, she watched. She marked each one of their pinched faces.

Neve D'Aeth Lyra would remember each one and bring with her a reckoning when the throne was once again hers.

It was a cold day, and snow flurries gently drifted in the air. She walked the streets in her green dress and her velvet cape and kept out of the way. She was skilled in remaining unseen if she wanted to; therefore, even resplendent in her finery, very few people looked in her direction. In the few days she'd been in Sylvera, she hadn't glimpsed the Highborns yet. So she continued her hunt, waiting and watching.

Neve turned down an alley between two light gray towers, their high stone walls giving her a momentary break from the cold winter wind. When she turned the corner and out of the alley, she noticed she was in a part of the Capital she hadn't yet seen.

This area looked older. Much older. It was a twin of so many villages she'd visited in the past. Small homes, people wearing earth-toned cotton and wool. Dirty yet content hands worked the soil of family gardens, harvesting the last of the potatoes before the ground froze for the winter. It was a small and quiet settlement.

She recognized a few faces as people she'd seen along the main streets of the city, lighting lamps and sweeping the sidewalks, picking up trash. This must be where the workers all lived. Close enough to serve the Capital, but cut off from the luxury of it. A blight, hidden away so the wealthy wouldn't have to see them live lives that were so common.

There were about twenty or so small homes, all huddled together in a cul-de-sac. It was not as easy to blend in here. It looked like a close-knit community that was accustomed to living in fear of anyone dressed like her. Wary eyes followed Neve as she moved through the settlement. Backs straightened, folks whispered and pointed, and mothers brought their children inside as she passed. Fear and anxiety were palpable, and it was not the kind of fear she relished.

Neve walked quickly and gracefully, pulling the hood of her dark green velvet cloak down to hide her face. She found her way out of the cul-de-sac and onto a new street, this one paved with dark cobblestone that looked just about as old as the Island itself.

Moss and vines crawled up from between the cracks in the road. There were no houses here. Just three ancient stone buildings, each in various states of crumbling decay. Stone plaques jutted up from the ground around the buildings, and Neve soon realized that they weren't buildings at all, but tombs, and the plaques were age-faded death markers.

This was a graveyard.

"Take a wrong turn, love?" a smooth, feminine voice asked.

Neve turned her head to see a woman stepping out from behind one of the tombs. She was tall, lithe, and beautiful. Dressed in different shades of indigo and dark blue, she was like some ethereal mystic against the gray and dismal landscape of the ancient cemetery. She leaned against the tomb and crossed her arms, confidently awaiting Neve's explanation for stumbling into this part of the city. The woman had perfectly unblemished and unwrinkled brown skin. Her dark hair was cropped close to her head, showing off the sharp yet gentle angles of her cheekbones and jawline. Her big, tea-colored eyes were lined with kohl and glittered with amusement.

Neve herself often looked upon other people the way the woman was looking at her now. Self-assured in the knowledge that she knew something they didn't.

The kind of expression that made Neve strangely *want* to know this stranger's secrets.

Turning to face the woman, Neve shrugged off her hood and took a step forward. Her blue–clad counterpart took a step as well.

"This part of town could be dangerous for a lady like you," the stranger said. There was no malice in her expression, but rather an open curiosity.

Neve tilted her head. "It seems I've wandered a little far today. I appreciate the concern." She made no move to turn back, however.

The woman's gaze fluttered across Neve's face and then down her body. "That pretty dress will get dirty in a place like this."

Neve shrugged nonchalantly and decided to test the waters. "The main streets are just as filthy. Maybe in a different way. But filthy just the same."

The woman's eyes snapped back to Neve's face, suddenly filled with surprise and even more interest. "That's a dangerous thing to say."

"Perhaps," Neve responded, dropping a bit of her wall and letting the woman get the tiniest glimpse of who she was beneath the costume, beneath the silk and the smoke and mirrors.

The woman swallowed, her eyes bright, not with unease but excitement. "Are you new here?"

"To Sylvera, yes."

"But not to Eodia?"

That old and awakening spark deep inside Neve seemed to open up an eye and yawn. A flush of warmth moved up her spine, and the edges of her vision blurred with a sudden and fleeting glow of light. It was there and gone so fast that Neve could have imagined it. But she knew she hadn't.

"No. Not new to Eodia."

The woman considered her a moment longer before she said, "My name is Isolde."

Neve nodded. "It's good to meet you." Before Isolde could ask her name, Neve continued, gesturing to the graveyard. "Are you the groundskeeper here?" Knowing that was most certainly not the case, Neve offered her a sly smirk.

Isolde smiled. "No. I'm a bit of a librarian."

Neve arched an eyebrow. "There's a library in Sylvera?"

"Of sorts," Isolde replied cryptically. "Would you like to see it?"

"I would." Perhaps she agreed a bit too quickly, too eagerly, but Neve would never say no to seeing books, even if the circumstances were somewhat... questionable.

"Very well. Follow me, my lady," Isolde said, leading Neve into the shadowed doorway of the tomb she'd stepped out from behind.

Following, Neve wondered what Isolde saw in her that allowed her such unworried surety to turn her back. She could easily pull a weapon and end the woman right here against the cobweb-covered stone. Yet Isolde seemed certain she wouldn't.

At the same time, Neve was somehow sure there wouldn't be a blade in the other woman's hand for her.

Isolde fiddled with a heavy padlock, whose big iron key was on a powder blue ribbon around her neck. She slid the key into the rusted lock and turned it with a *thunk*, dropping the ribbon back down her shirt. She pushed the door open, stone scraping against stone, and stepped inside.

Neve followed.

The scent of age was a thick cloud. Dust, earth, the powder of crumbling stone. The smell of old bones.

Life-sized statues of people were carved into the walls of the tomb, and in the center of it sat a huge stone coffin. Curious, Neve walked along the perimeter of the space, and Isolde stepped to the side, watching.

Neve could feel her new companion's eyes boring into her back as she moved along the statues.

The stone-carved men and women were created with detail in a way that Neve could only describe as loving. The artist sculpted with great attention and dedication. Furthermore, their faces felt familiar to Neve, as if she'd seen them before but could not place where she knew them. Some distant and faded memories tickled the back of her mind, but it was just out of reach.

She walked along, looking at each statue in turn. Beautiful, regal people, all holding carved items in their outstretched hands. Some held ornate weapons, and some held depictions of plants, a cup, a small animal, a stone, a tree, a child, or a flame. A sun, a moon.

Neve came upon the final statue and stood before it. In one hand, it held a skull and in the other, it held a perfectly geometric eight-pointed star. Her eyes rose to its face, and her skin prickled with goosebumps. Large eyes, a delicately upturned nose, soft features, full lips. *Smirking* lips. For a moment, Neve forgot how to breathe.

Standing face-to-face with this statue was like looking in a mirror; its face was *her* face, nearly identical.

"Who are these people?" Neve asked, unable to tear her eyes from the statue.

"Don't you know?" Isolde asked quietly. Her voice sounded shaky, almost reverent.

Neve looked at her then, Isolde's light brown eyes were wide and lined with silver, glittering. Neve shook her head. "Should I know them?"

Isolde swallowed hard enough for Neve to hear, and blinked a few times before she said, "They're the old gods."

Warmth blossomed in Neve's belly, in her chest.

"I thought the Highborns destroyed everything belonging to the old gods on this Island."

"They don't know about this place."

"In their own city?"

"This part of the Capital is ... beneath them. Why should they dirty their boots in an old cemetery?"

Neve nodded and turned back to the statue in front of her. Reaching out, she ran her fingers down its arms, cupping its full hands in hers. "This must be..."

"Celesta. Goddess of life and death," Isolde replied, her voice once again full of emotion. "It's said that she could wield the power of starlight, that she was responsible for both the destruction of the world and its rebirth."

The terrible gravity of that sleeping giant in Neve's chest - the very thing she'd first felt at the Oracle, but somehow knew had always lived within her- gave a great yank on her insides and fizzled cold fire into her blood. She swayed, clutching the statue's hands to keep from falling to her knees.

Her head and her body suddenly felt *too full*. Like that strange power inside needed to be released, or it would keep building and growing until it destroyed her. Neve closed her eyes and focused on herself, her breathing, the feel of the stone-carved fingers against hers, the smell of dust, the sound of Isolde's breath.

It wasn't enough. Her skin itched. Her head throbbed, and her throat was full of icy burning. Neve pressed her lips together, focusing. She thought of a purple heather moor at sunrise, of crisp morning air, of vibrant autumn leaves falling from the trees above where she lay. Her thoughts moved on their own to the memory of Killian's mouth between her thighs, the feel of his shoulders beneath her hands, the woodsmoke and cedar smell of him, the way he made her morning tea, his hand in hers.

Somehow, her heart filled up with thoughts of him, and it grounded her. The thing in her sighed, and her shoulders lowered as the tension in them released. The memory of his smile and his hands and his shoulders and the way he held a sword moved through her body. The feel of his breath on her throat, his steady presence, the way he looked at her...

At last, she relaxed and opened her eyes, finding her forehead pressed to the brow of the statue, close enough to kiss. Her vision took time to adjust, as if she'd walked into someplace dark from someplace bright.

Isolde was at her side.

Neve expected her new companion's expression to be full of concern, or perhaps fear, but instead it was full of awe and wonder.

Isolde could have asked any number of prying questions at that moment. She could have asked what happened, or who Neve was, or why she had the face of the Goddess of life and death. Neve would not have been able to answer any of them, at least not with any certainty beyond a guess.

Instead, Isolde smiled. "So," she said. "How about I show you the library?"

~

A fist connected with the side of Killian's face, hard, and he staggered back. The crowd cheered. He certainly wouldn't let this asshole take him to his knees. He straightened, rolled his shoulders, and grinned, tasting the fresh sheen of blood across his teeth. The other man looked pleased with himself that he'd finally gotten a good hit.

Killian spat on the ground at the man's feet.

"Caught me napping, boy. Let's see if you have it in you to do it again," Killian taunted, his voice rough and eager.

He hadn't seen Neve again since she'd found him drowning his sorrows in whiskey. He'd dreamed of her that night but woke up the next morning hung over and alone, fisting his cock to the memory of her body.

It had only been a few days, but he missed her. He knew she was more than capable of taking care of herself, yet not knowing for certain that she was all right was driving him mad. Not to mention the thoughts of Lowbarrow and Hythe, Logan and Fraser, and his family… his obsessive thoughts were swirling around so much it made him dizzy.

Killian was not skilled at handling feelings of such profound failure and grief.

But he was skilled at violence.

He'd stumbled upon the fighting rings the day after he arrived in Thornkeep and had since spent nearly all his waking hours in this place. It was in the basement of a tavern called, unsurprisingly, The Bloody Fist. The space was large with three separate fighting rings. It was dark, musty, and smelled like old blood. The seedier populace of the village spent what money they had in this basement betting on the fights, drinking, and even darker pursuits.

The fighters, like the one before him now, were all untrained but vicious. They possessed a dirty and honorless way of battle that made for good sport. Killian often saw the same men being just as rough with the courtesans in the basement as they were with him.

It was satisfying to lay each of them out in front of a crowd, and he felt no qualms about leaving them bloody and limping at the end of it.

Killian always let them believe they were winning, allowing them to land bruising kicks and punches until their egos swelled and the crowds cheered for them. It was then that Killian would strike. One good blow was usually enough to take them out. For those he'd observed being particularly nasty with the courtesans and barmaids, he would make the pain last a little longer. Sometimes, until their faces were pulp and a group of men would have to pull him off of them.

There were a few fighters, though, young ones, that went toe to toe with him in the rings, and he'd let them win. They weren't much older than boys, clearly starving and willing for their bodies to be brutalized to earn a few coins. Their terror was palpable when they discovered he was their opponent, and the look of grateful relief they gave him when he let them take him down was good enough for Killian.

Truthfully, he didn't mind taking a beating. He relished the pain. Maybe it was a subconscious way to punish himself, maybe it just felt good to bleed. What was certain was that he was trained for violence, and his body was louder than his brain during a fight. His thoughts narrowed down only to movement, to fists and flesh and the triumphant pounding of his heart.

Covered in sweat, dressed in nothing but his low-slung pants, Killian knew that he looked formidable, dangerous. He knew that all eyes were on him. No one seemed to recognize him, despite what Neve called his "famous face". And if they did know who he was, they weren't bold or stupid enough to say anything. Here, he was not Killian Grey. Here, he was not the sworn knight of Eodia's lost Queen. Here, he was not a deserter or a failure.

Here, he was just a lethal body.

The fighter in front of him was more ogre than man. Big and burly, his bare shoulders covered in dark patches of coarse hair. Killian knew there was a woman in the crowd with bruises on her hips from this man's hands and that he'd given her a promise of more violence when he was finished in the ring.

Killian was going to make sure that never happened.

He let his opponent get another hit, this time right to the gut, and it sent the air *whooshing* out of him. Killian coughed, catching his breath, and bent forward with his hands on his knees. He watched the man's feet as he approached, and when he was right where Killian wanted him, he rose and delivered a catastrophic uppercut to the man's chin.

The fighter went sprawling to the ground, and Killian was on him in an instant. He pressed his knee down on his opponent's chest until he felt a rib crack, and the man opened his mouth in a scream. Then Killian went after his face and head, battering it with heavy fists until there wasn't much left except a mess of red.

It was over much faster than the bastard deserved.

Hands still dripping with someone else's blood, Killian strode up to the bar and took a seat. The barmaid, gray-haired with a face that hadn't hosted a single smile in at least a decade, handed him a towel and a mug of ale. He ran the towel over his sweat-drenched chest and stomach before wiping the blood from his hands with it.

The ale was dark and malty and felt cold going down his throat.

A velvet pouch full of coins was soon set in front of him on the bar with a heavy *clunk*. The man delivering it pulled up a seat next to Killian.

"Nice job out there. That guy was a piece of shit. You did us all a favor," he said.

Killian looked up from his ale to see a man about his age with long black hair pulled into a knot at the top of his head and a dark, well–shaped beard. Another fighter. He was also shirtless, with bruises and scars scattered on his olive skin. Upon a second glance, Killian remembered seeing this man fight, although he'd never faced him in the ring himself. A good fighter. Rough around the edges and lacking technique, but good.

Killian raised his cup, "Happy to be of service."

The man laughed, genuinely, and signaled the barmaid to bring him a drink of his own. "I'm Leo," he said, holding out his hand.

Killian shook it firmly. "Ewan," he lied.

"Everyone is talking about you."

"Are they?" Killian asked, lifting an eyebrow.

Leo nodded. "All the fighters are puffing up their chests, talking about how you aren't *that* good. That you'd be easy to beat." He said this with mirthful amusement.

"Not you?"

"Definitely not," Leo chuckled. "My wife would kill me if I came back to her in pieces."

Killian laughed and took a swig of his ale. "I know how that feels."

"Are you married?"

"No, but I have... someone who would kill me if she found a reason."

Leo nodded with a grin. He raised his glass.

"To the women who save us from our stupidity."

Killian couldn't help but smile, and he raised his glass as well, clinking it against Leo's. He swallowed down a gulp of ale. "Is that why you fight? For your wife?"

"And my two boys."

Killian's chest clenched.

Leo continued. "I was a blacksmith back home. Made a good living. But when we came here... there were already three other blacksmiths. Fighting's the only thing that pays enough to feed four mouths in this town."

"Where was home before Thornkeep?" Killian was certain he knew the answer, yet hoped against it all the same.

"Hythe. Bastards came in and sacked the village. Burned it to ash. I'm just glad we got out in time." Leo took a swig of his ale.

"I'm sorry," Killian said. More than Leo could ever know, Killian was sorry.

The dark-haired man shook his head. "The only ones that should be sorry are those fucking Highborns."

Killian stiffened, cutting a covert glance around them to make sure no one had heard. The last thing this man needed was to give the Highborns a reason to come for his family. Again.

Thankfully, no one paid any attention to them. Their conversation was drowned out by the sounds of fists against flesh and shouting.

Leo leaned in and lowered his voice. "There are rumors. That perhaps the Highborns aren't as powerful as everyone seems to think."

The hairs on the back of Killian's neck rose. He decided to play into it, cast a net, and see if he caught anything. "I've heard a few."

"You want to know the one I think about the most?" Leo asked.

Killian nodded.

"This one keeps me up at night. The story about the woman on the plains."

Killian's skin tingled.

"They say the Highborns sent the Cavalry after the man she loved. When they came upon the lovers traveling on the plains, the woman killed every single one of them. Some with her bare hands. They say she cut off the heads of the Mages that were there and laid them at the feet of the General. They say that the General was the only one she left alive so he could go back and tell the Highborns that she was coming for them."

Pride bloomed in Killian's chest and spread outward, into his bones and nerve endings until he was awash with the warmth of it. He knew, intimately, the glory of the woman he loved. But to hear someone else talk about her so reverently, with such respect, did something entirely new to him.

It gave Killian hope.

"I don't know about you, mate," Leo continued. "But that's a woman I'd follow into hell just to watch her make them bleed."

Killian knew.

He certainly knew.

31

Isolde placed her hands on the edge of the massive stone coffin in the center of the tomb and pushed. With effort, it began sliding open. Seeing that it was particularly heavy, Neve stepped forward and pushed the opposite corner.

A waft of air rushed up as it opened, lifting strands of her hair to swirl around her face. Neve expected it to smell of death, but the smoky scent of clove and incense hit her instead. Warm and inviting. She peered into the darkness. There were no bodies or skeletons eternally resting within.

Only a staircase leading down.

Neve looked at Isolde, whose eyes were sparkling with mischief and anticipation. "What's down there?"

"The library," Isolde responded. Then she laughed, a cheerful, vibrant sound, glancing down into the pitch black below. "I promise not to murder you."

The corner of Neve's mouth lifted in amusement. When was the last time someone joked with her? Someone other than Killian? Another woman? Perhaps it was Cara, just before the Maere entered the Dark Forest. A lifetime ago, it seemed, with all the living Neve had done since. It warmed something inside her that she hadn't known was so cold.

"Your turn," Isolde said.

"For what?"

"It's your turn to promise not to murder me. You're dressed like a puffed pastry, but I have a feeling you're not afraid of a little bloodshed."

Neve chuckled. "Fine. I promise not to murder you."

"Good enough for me," Isolde said with a nod. She climbed into the coffin and moved down a few steps so Neve could follow.

Puffed pastry, indeed. The voluminous sage green dress didn't make throwing her legs over the chest-high edge easy. But Neve managed it gracefully. She helped Isolde pull the lid shut above them. They were soon in utter darkness.

Isolde's hand found hers and held it, and Neve did not pull away. It was a touch that felt both friendly and necessary, given the fact that there was not a single speck of light, and Neve didn't know where she was going. They moved down the steps slowly, and Isolde walked with the confidence of a person who'd taken this dark staircase many times before, lacing her fingers between Neve's.

"This would be a perfect time to use your little trick," Isolde said.

Neve furrowed her brow. "My little trick?"

"You know, the glowing thing you do."

Ice trickled down Neve's spine, and she froze.

"What?" she demanded.

Isolde stopped moving but kept her hand in Neve's. "You don't know?" Her voice changed, the mirth faded slightly, and was replaced with something more serious.

Neve wished she could see Isolde's face, but the tone of her voice told her enough.

Since the Oracle, maybe even as early as arriving at the Grey's stronghold and revealing her true identity to Killian, Neve suspected something was... different.

She'd felt it only a handful of times, that strange *blooming* in her chest, the warmth, the change in the light around her. That feeling of a rising and ancient power coming from within her. The stirring. The suffocating fullness. She suspected something had changed, that something was growing, or more accurately, awakening.

But now a stranger had *seen* her glow, and that was worrisome. She couldn't control when the feeling came upon her, and therefore, she couldn't control who could witness it.

This could prove to be... inconvenient.

"What did it look like? The glowing?"

"Let's get to the library and I'll tell you." Isolde gently tugged on her hand, but Neve stood firm and unmovable.

"Now," she replied, her voice like a command. She felt a tremor skitter down Isolde's fingers at the sound.

"I first saw it outside when you said you were not new to Eodia. A small light, just in your eyes. A pulse. Then, when you faced the statue of Celesta. It again started in your eyes, but it spread. All over your skin, in your hair. This pulsing glow. I don't know what feeling came upon you, but it appeared... intense. Then, it faded."

Isolde's words felt true. It was why her eyes needed to readjust to the light when she opened them again. It was why she'd felt that cold burning spread through her. Neve didn't know what it meant, what exactly this *thing* was. For a woman so wholly self-possessed that very few things could surprise her, this development filled her with unease. She'd have to spend time learning about it, testing it. There was too much at risk, especially here in Sylvera. She was supposed to be anonymous here, forgettable, and she couldn't very well be a nobody if she started to glow.

"Thank you," Neve said. Isolde began walking again and continued to lead her down the stairs.

Neve counted fifty steps before the darkness broke and the walls around them became lined with gently flickering candles. Below, the stairs seemed endless, and above them was nothing but dark.

"There will be light the rest of the way down. We make sure none of these candles can be seen from the tomb above. No one has ever broken in, but the darkness is a precaution. Very few people know this place exists," Isolde explained, letting go of Neve's hand.

"How do you know you can trust me with this secret?"

Isolde paused and gave a gentle smile. "Because you're now trusting me with yours."

Neve said nothing.

They continued walking down the staircase, which seemed virtually endless. She could feel the pressure change as they descended, the walls felt just a little bit closer from one stair to the next, and the air felt cooler and cooler. That earthy incense scent grew until Neve could smell it in her hair and the fabric of her clothes.

She counted three hundred steps from where the candles appeared to the bottom.

Neve and Isolde stood before a huge stone door. The spark danced in Neve's chest as she beheld what was carved in the center. A crescent moon and stars above an ivory tower. The sigil of her house. She felt Isolde's eye on her as she reached up and traced the moon with two fingers.

"I should warn you," Isolde began. Neve looked at her then and tilted her head to the side in question. "A few of my friends are in the library right now, and they're a little...protective of what's in here. So just...be ready."

She rolled her light brown eyes and offered Neve a sheepish smirk before pulling the key out from under her shirt and sliding it into the lock.

Isolde led the way into a small antechamber. Neve felt movement so immediately that she didn't even have a chance to observe her surroundings. She vaguely heard Isolde shout as something big charged her. Neve struck blindly, turning and thrusting her arm out. The palm of her hand connected with the base of a man's throat and sent him to his back, choking. He was a big man, a wall of muscle that could certainly do some damage. But Neve was fast. And now he was lying in a heap on the ground, hands at his neck, struggling to find his breath. His deep brown eyes were wide with shock as he looked up at her.

Neve felt movement again and smelled metal. She twisted her body, dodging the arc of a sword, grabbing onto the arms that held it. She shoved and moved, slamming her opponent up against the wall with their hands pinned to the stone above their head. The sword clattered to the ground. Neve found herself chest-to-chest with a curvy woman who had hair so blonde it was nearly white. She sneered at Neve, who returned the expression with an easy smile.

"Who the fuck are you?" the blonde asked between grit teeth. Her eyes were light blue and filled with distrust.

"She's a guest, Sabrina," Isolde replied. "Play nice."

Sabrina's gaze flitted to Isolde briefly and then back to Neve. She nodded her head up to where Neve still had her arms pinned to the wall. "You can let go now."

Neve held her there a moment longer, just because she could, just to see a little uncertainty enter those blue eyes, and then let go. She stepped over the man on the ground and stood next to Isolde, who looked amused if not a little embarrassed.

"Sorry about that," Isolde said. "This is Sabrina, and that's Oliver. They're guards. Usually very good at their jobs, but they've never met someone like you before."

"Apparently," Neve replied. She looked down at Oliver, who was now managing to pull in a few wheezing breaths but was still sprawled on the ground.

"You ready?" Isolde asked. She gestured to a pair of deep indigo curtains that moved gently with a breeze from whatever lay behind them.

"Yes."

Isolde led the way, parting the curtains and walking through. Neve felt a tingling sensation in her scalp. Magic. But different from the kind the Mages used. This felt pure. Old. Sparkling. The curtains were velvet and felt soft as they brushed against the sides of her face. It seemed like there were many layers of curtains, and that those layers went on and on. She stepped slowly, following Isolde, parting fold after fold of blue velvet. Somehow, it didn't feel claustrophobic to be wandering through an endless and dark maze of fabric. It felt comforting, like a warm bath. Like how Neve imagined it might feel to come back to one's own home after a long journey. She wouldn't know exactly how that felt, of course, as she'd never had a home. But this soft velvet and the effervescent magic humming around her felt... right.

Finally, although almost inexplicably sadly, the final layer of curtains parted, and the room she found herself in...

Everything Neve had ever been released a deep, lifelong-held breath.

Her eyes filled with tears.

Above her was a concave, arched ceiling, and on it, seemingly lit from within, was a perfect depiction of the night sky. Stars. So many glittering stars. A glowing crescent moon hung from the center of it like a chandelier. The ceiling was painted a deep, fathomless blue–black. The stars and moon, their perfect glowing realness, there was no explanation besides magic, and she couldn't look away. Each star twinkled and pulsed with silvery gold light. It felt almost like seeing the real night sky for the first time. Except this one felt less infinite and more...intimate.

Tearing her gaze away, Neve took in the rest of the library. Or tried to. There was *so much* to see. The space was huge and round, curving in a wide, perfect circle. And the walls. The walls were high, stretching far up to that magical starry ceiling, and all except one dark section were fit with built-in shelves. The shelves were full of books. Each quadrant had a rolling ladder that a person could climb to reach the titles at the top. Neve had never seen so many books in her life. This place made the library at the Grey's Stronghold look like a broom closet.

The dark section of the wall, far on the north end of the library, appeared to be a door. It was obsidian black. There was no doorknob, but a burnished gold knocker in the shape of an eight-pointed star adorned the center of it.

Cozy and well-kept, the space seemed to nearly beg Neve to sit down and enjoy herself. The floors were covered in countless worn, yet colorful rugs. There was a big round table in the center of the library, large enough to fit at least 25 people around. The table was clean, with a few stacks of books in the center, along with a copper incense burner and a few candelabras. Chaises, overstuffed chairs, and benches, all upholstered in the same indigo velvet she'd just waded through, were arranged around the room, along with large scattered pillows and a few well-loved blankets.

One single, awestruck tear crept down Neve's cheek. A large presence was at her elbow, holding out a surprisingly dainty handkerchief in a giant hand.

"My lady," Oliver said. His voice was deep and raspy, and when she looked up at him, his brown eyes were warm, with no hint of resentment about the way she'd taken him to the ground. "I cried the first time I saw it, too," he said.

Neve took the handkerchief and dabbed her eye. "Thank you," she replied. She tried to give the handkerchief back to him, but he shook his head and gestured for her to keep it. "Sorry about the throat."

He chuckled, which resulted in a cough. It would take a little while for him to recover from that injury.

"I had it coming," Oliver said.

Isolde moved in front of her. She appeared to be quite literally beaming with pride as she spread her arms wide and motioned to the library.

"Well?" she asked. "What do you think?"

Neve looked up at the ceiling again and felt her muscles relax. "It's... It's everything."

Sabrina plopped down on a chaise and picked up a book. "You're not wrong," she said unenthusiastically, flipping through the pages until she found the one she was looking for and settling into the cushions.

Isolde pulled up a chair at the round table and slid a book from one of the stacks in the center towards her. It was a huge, heavy-looking tome. "Feel free to look around. I'm sure there are plenty of books here that you'd love."

Indeed, Neve thought, eyes panning the shelves. Her new companion was probably right.

She felt excitement as she approached the first shelf. So many books. Covers in all colors. Some new; some very, *very* old. Neve reached her hand out to touch one, but stopped short when her eyes caught movement.

A different book, one with golden embossed lettering on deep purple binding, seemed to push itself forward in the stack. Neve paused. Eyeing the purple book, she reached out again for a different one just to see what would happen. The purple book pushed out further, nearly off the edge of the mahogany shelf.

Sabrina chuckled from where she was sprawled on the velvet chaise. "That one likes you," she said.

Neve turned with a raised eyebrow and looked at the blonde. "*Likes* me? It's a book."

Sabrina rolled her eyes, annoyed, pointedly resting her book open-faced on her chest. "Izzy, do you want to explain how this works to our new friend?"

Isolde rested her chin on her hand, shaking her head at Sabrina's irritable countenance, then leveled her warm, kind gaze on Neve.

"The books here are... special. Enchanted as if they have minds of their own. As you browse, you'll notice that you don't necessarily pick the books, they sort of pick *you*."

"Interesting," Neve replied. She turned back to the shelf and gently removed the purple book. It vibrated in her hands, seemingly elated, and then was quiet. She read the title aloud, *"Court of the Empress."*

Isolde, Oliver, and Sabrina all laughed knowingly.

"That's a good one," Sabrina said.

"I still think about that one," Oliver replied, grinning. His cheeks were slightly pink- *blushing*? Strange to see such a big brute look so bashful.

"What is it?" Neve asked.

"It's a dirty book," Isolde said, giggling. Her eyes were bright and cheerful as she wagged her eyebrows suggestively.

Neve opened it and shuffled to a random page, reading the first line:

Exquisite, punishing thrusts slammed so deep into her that her eyes rolled back into her head with the sheer bliss of it.

Interest curled low in Neve's belly. Yes. Yes, she would like this book.

~

By the time Neve left the library and emerged back out into the cemetery, the dark cloak of night fell across the Capital. She looked up into the sky, no stars this evening. A stack of books was tucked under her arm, including *Court of the Empress,* and a key for the tomb tied to a blue ribbon was nestled safely between her breasts under her dress. Isolde told her she was welcome in the library any time, despite still not even knowing Neve's name. The invitation was genuine, as was Isolde's insistence that she wanted Neve to come back as often as she could.

Neve couldn't help but wonder what other secrets the library held. Isolde, Sabrina, and Oliver were militant about its protection, and while there were plenty of priceless books down there, Neve got the feeling there was something else as well. Something deeper, something more, something that was tied to her. She felt it when she saw the statues of the gods in the tomb, and she felt it when she first laid her eyes on the library.

This secret place was theirs to protect.

And yet, somehow, it was also hers.

32

The way his veins pulsed under his skin when his muscles tensed made Neve feel hungry. She sat silently in the shadows of Killian's room, watching him toss and turn in his sleep.

His room was on the top floor of some dingy inn in Thornkeep. It was sparsely decorated and small. It smelled of him. Woodsmoke, pine, skin, sweat.

It was late, crawling closer to dawn than midnight. She'd been reading *Court of the Empress* in her bed in Sylvera, and it left her restless and aching in a way her hand could not remedy. She'd tried. She couldn't stop thinking of Killian, a craving for him sank deep into her core. So, she'd come to him.

He was dreaming anxiously, gripping the sheets with his fists, muttering her name. Each time he groaned, "Neve", she smiled, and that delicious, hot tightening clenched inside of her. He slept naked, and he was all sharp lines and rolling muscles.

Neve quietly shrugged off her cloak and pulled off her leathers until she stood at the end of his bed in nothing but the lace and creamy satin underthings Mina sold her. They felt good on her skin, and she imagined they'd feel good under Killian's hands, too.

Knowing exactly what would happen the moment he sensed the presence of someone else in his room, she leaned forward and pressed her hands to the mattress. At the slightest movement beneath him, Killian shot into action.

And Neve let it happen.

His big hand snatched around her throat, pulling and lifting her as he slammed her down onto the mattress beneath him. Half-feral from being yanked from his dreams, a growl rumbled in his chest as he bore down on her.

He was kneeling over her, one of his knees was beside her hip, the other was between her legs; his hand still squeezing her throat, she moved to grind herself against his thigh.

Her blood heated as she watched his face change. Killian blinked and looked at her, really saw her. His eyes first widened in shock, and he pulled his hand from her neck, looking down at it momentarily as if he wasn't quite sure who it belonged to.

"Neve, I nearly killed you," he said, his voice rough.

"No, you didn't," she purred, dragging her core against his leg again. This time, she did it slowly so he could feel it.

A muscle ticked in his jaw, and he looked down at her body, at the lace and satin chemise barely containing her breasts, riding up around her hips, baring her to him.

He blew out a shaky breath and ran his knuckles over the fabric skating above her soft stomach.

"Gods, am I still dreaming?"

She stretched out beneath him, raising her arms above her head. Her fingers found the wooden slats of his bedpost, and she curled her hands around them.

Killian went wholly still, tracking her every movement.

Neve wasn't entirely certain he was even breathing. She moved her hips again, and his eyes darkened.

"Touch me and find out," she said.

A low moan released from his mouth as he leaned down and kissed her. His hands were greedy and palmed her breasts, thumbs circling her nipples. She sighed and moved her tongue against his. All of her nerve endings burst into flame when he rolled her nipples between his thumbs and forefingers.

Her hands moved to his shoulders, but he caught them and pushed them back onto his headboard.

"Keep them there. I want you at my mercy," he whispered. The shiver that moved through her body nearly cracked her spine.

Biting back a smirk, she wrapped her hands around the headboard slats again.

"Good girl," he murmured, urging her body to grind against him, this time harder, searching for the friction that could bring her to the release she nearly desperately needed.

Killian pulled down the top of her chemise, and his ravenous mouth latched onto her nipple. He sucked deeply, causing Neve to moan and arch her back off the bed. His hand moved between her legs, one finger running up her slit with tortuous gentleness. He growled at what he felt there.

"It feels like you've missed me," he groaned, moving his expert mouth to her other nipple and dragging his finger slowly against her again.

"Yes," she breathed.

She felt him grin against her breast, then he was moving down her body, prowling down every inch of her. He spread her legs with his hands and pushed the backs of her knees up onto his shoulders, where he settled comfortably between her thighs. He dragged his tongue up her wetness and groaned.

"*Fuck*," he said. "You taste so good."

Her body began to shake with need as he feasted on her. She couldn't control the whimpering pleas that rolled out of her mouth. Her head became dizzy and light, his tongue delivering the perfect sucking, swirling pressure against her clit. Her skin broke out in goosebumps as the agonizing tension kept building and building.

She looked down her body at him and found his gaze pinned on her face, watching her, waiting for her to break for him. Looking into her eyes, never taking his mouth from her, he slid one long finger inside of her. She cried out and arched into the tingling, growing pleasure he was giving her.

She was close. He knew she was close.

He thrust his finger in and out, adding a second one as he worked his tongue against her with steady, punishing pressure.

"Come for me, love," he commanded, curling the tips of his fingers up inside of her, wrenching a sound from her throat that she'd never heard before. "That's it, come for me."

The orgasm hit her like standing on the ledge of a tower with a strong wind battering at her back until it pushed her off. More and more, and then it was too much, and too much again; then suddenly she was free-falling and all cognition was lost, and it was just her body and the atmosphere colliding.

Waves upon crashing waves of pleasure ripped through her as she came harder than she ever had before. When Neve finally found her way back to herself, she was shaking, and she was sure she'd screamed out Killian's name at some point, but now she was just panting and boneless. He was above her again, and her face was in his hands.

When she opened her eyes, she saw him there, and the expression on his face nearly crushed her beneath its weight. His eyes were soft and full of wonder. His fingers gently pushed the hair from her face and caressed her cheeks. They were breathing in the same rhythm as if they shared the same lungs. Killian gave a small shake of his head.

"So beautiful," he whispered.

She reached up and ran her fingers through his hair, then settled one hand at the nape of his neck and the other against his chest. His heart hammered against her touch.

She tenderly wrapped her legs around his waist, urging him closer, and she felt his hard tip nudging at her entrance. His eyes rolled for a moment and then settled back on her face with that same devoted expression.

"I want you," she said. "Only you."

He moved his hips and pushed into her. They both drew in a gasp at the exquisite sensation of their joining. He rolled his hips, slow and deep. So deep. New waves of pleasure bloomed inside of her, but she didn't dare close her eyes; she couldn't tear her gaze from Killian's beautiful face and the worshipful yearning she found there.

Neve's skin was ablaze, her nerves sparkling like sunlight on water, and a new feeling pressed down on her heart. The same feeling that had come upon her the day Killian bent the knee to her. When they cared for each other after the lycanthrope attack. When he cauterized her wound. When they went to the Oracle, they lay gasping on the bank of Ula after nearly drowning together. When he held her hand for the first time. When he made her tea. When he made her laugh.

Her body was so full of him. And now... and now her heart was filling with him as well. He shifted so that his pelvis ground against her clit as he thrust into her, deeper and deeper. His breath was becoming ragged, and she knew he was getting close. Her pleasure was climbing higher and higher. His eyes searched her face, and Neve knew he was feeling exactly what she was, maybe more.

"Neve... I –" he stopped himself.

"Say it," she urged, her toes curling and her legs beginning to shake. "Say it at last."

"I love you." The words were a gasp that turned into a rough moan as he reached his climax.

His declaration. His moan. His final thrust. All sent her blasting into an ecstasy that had tears spilling from the corners of her eyes.

Killian laid his head on her chest, cupping her breast with one hand. Her hands combed his sweaty hair and held him there as they both recovered in a mess of breath and trembling.

"I love you," she said.

She expected to lose some of herself the first time she said those words to another person, to him. She expected to feel as if she was betraying herself, her destiny, her independence.

But the words were true. And when she said them, all she felt was a weightless relief. As if keeping the words inside her was a chain, and saying them set her free.

He stilled.

After a moment, he raised himself on his elbow and looked down at her, throat bobbing.

"Say it again," he requested quietly, almost timidly.

"I love you."

The corner of his mouth curled up in a smile. "You're not only saying it because I just made you come so hard the whole village could hear you scream my name?"

She laughed and rolled her eyes. "I wasn't that loud."

"Yes, you were," he chuckled. "Now answer my question, Lady Nightmare. Do you mean it?"

"I mean it, Killian. I love you."

There was a fluttering in her chest like thousands of soft moth wings taking flight.

He kissed her then. Deep and sweet and true.

33

Muted morning light dappled in through the dusty window. The world outside was white with snow. It floated down from the sky in fat, fluffy flakes. Killian only halfway registered the beauty of it with his focus pulled toward the beauty asleep in his bed. She was on her side, facing him, her hair a silky, curling dark froth against the pillows beneath her head. Her bare shoulders peeked above the woolen blankets, and there was a rosy blush to her cheeks. He liked the thought that perhaps that blush was just for him.

"*I want you, only you,*" she'd said to him.

He felt the same for her and had since the moment she swept into his world in that blue gossamer gown. He'd loved her soon after and now... Now she loved him.

When those three words came out of her sweet, breathless mouth, he thought for sure that he would up and die right then and there. The way his chest filled up in that moment was almost too much to bear.

He would do anything for this woman. He would die and come back for her. He would lay all her enemies at her feet and build their grave with his bare hands. If there was no wood, he'd fuel the pyre with his own body, and when he was burned away from the memory of history, he'd *still* come back for her.

Killian reached out a hand and caressed her full lips with his thumb. Her green-gold eyes opened with a few drowsy blinks, and his breath caught in his throat. Gods, he was a lucky man.

"Hi," he said, and brushed a tendril of hair away from her face.

Her lips curled up into the smirk that drove him mad.

"Hi," she replied. She stretched and the blankets slipped down just enough to bare the swell of her cleavage for him. He stroked his fingers along her collarbone and leaned forward to nuzzle his nose against hers.

Killian didn't want to think about the fact that as long as she was spying in Sylvera, their time together was limited. Having her so close, especially after confessing their love, he wanted nothing more than to spend every moment with her.

She lifted her chin and kissed him. The warmth of her lips immediately ignited him. He slipped his hand under the blanket and around her waist, pulling her closer. She was naked under the covers, and her bare skin pressed against him made his chest fill up with a deep sigh.

"The more I have you, the more I want you. I can't seem to get enough," he murmured against her mouth. He kissed down her chin and into the inviting crook between her neck and shoulder, tasting her.

"So greedy," she said with a chuckle, arching closer to him.

He pulled her leg over his hip and pressed against her.

"Oh, I'll show you just how greedy I am for you." He moved his hand up her waist and over her breast, drawing torturously slow and soft circles around her nipple. It hardened under his touch, and he felt her pulse quicken against his tongue.

She was utterly magnificent always, but especially like this.

The way she melted for him, the way her body reacted to his touch...

He was lost in her and barely noticed when she shifted her position and nudged him onto his back until she was crawling on top of him. And then he was more than acutely aware of every single one of her movements against him.

Her hair was a curtain around her face, and there was a mischievous light in her eyes. In the space of a breath, she was sliding down his body, and his heart was slamming against his ribcage.

His eyes went wide.

"Neve," he breathed, watching as she pulled the blankets down and moved her body between his legs. Her eyes were pinned on his face as she brushed her soft lips up the length of his hard cock. His legs trembled, and all the breath squeezed out of his lungs.

"Do you want this?" she asked, dragging her mouth across the head this time.

His hips bucked. He grabbed two fistfuls of the sheets beneath him to keep himself from completely losing his mind.

"Oh fuck," he said. "*Please.*"

She grinned, and then her tongue was swirling on him. He let out a deep moan.

Chest heaving, he watched as Neve sucked his tip into her mouth and grazed her tongue along the underside. She licked him once more before sliding him between her lips. He watched as she hollowed out her cheeks and sucked him and he hissed between his teeth.

She looked up at him with his cock in her mouth and if that alone wasn't enough to undo him, it almost certainly was when she took his hands and placed them on her head, giving him a small nod.

"Neve," he ground out. His fingers speared into her hair, and she swallowed him deeper down her throat. She added a hand and pumped and squeezed him in rhythm with her mouth.

It was torture and heaven all at the same time.

She looked up at him again through her long, dark lashes, and he could take it no longer. He gripped her hair and thrust into her mouth.

She moaned.

He thrust again.

And she gave him another moan. Encouraging him. Asking for it. Wanting it, wanting him.

He kept thrusting, and she met him with each stroke. All he knew was the heat of her mouth and the sounds of her moans around him. All he wanted was her. He watched the length of himself disappear into her mouth as he moved his hips. It had him wild with desire. He thrust harder and deeper, and her fingernails raked down his stomach.

Killian's whole body was hard and tight with need, from his grinding jaw all the way down to his toes. The pleasure she was delivering to him was like a thunderstorm, catastrophic and complete.

No one had ever swallowed him down with such wickedness.

Suddenly, he was overcome with such a desperate urge to be inside of her that he thought his heart might explode from it.

"I need you, Neve," he managed to say, although how he remembered how to speak was beyond him.

She raised a naughty eyebrow and continued to suck.

"I need to feel you," he pleaded. "I need to be inside of you."

Neve took him in her mouth again, this time right down to the hilt, and he growled as she pulled back up.

Panting, he fisted her hair and yanked her head up roughly. She gasped, her lips swollen and wet, eyes heavy-lidded with lust.

"*Now*," he commanded through his teeth.

Losing what was left of his control, he sat up, circled her waist with his arm, and threw her onto her back. Without any warning or preamble, he slammed into her. A cry tore through her throat as he did it again and again.

She reached up and grabbed his jaw, pulling him into a hot kiss. She opened her mouth for him, and he swirled his tongue against hers. The moan she gave him did him in. With one final thrust, he unleashed himself inside her.

When his vision finally unclouded and his brain solidified once again in his skull, he lay down next to her and pulled her against him so they were face to face. He ran his hands down her back and held her close.

"I want you like this, every day," he said.

"I feel the same way."

"How long do you have to be in Sylvera?"

Her eyes shuttered just slightly. "I don't know, Killian. I have a lot to learn there."

"I know. And I support you. But...I can't stand being away from you so much. I want to fall asleep next to you every night and wake up to your beautiful face every morning."

"I want that too. But everything I'm doing now in the Capital is so that this kingdom has a future," she said gently. Neve pressed her hands against his chest, right above his heart. "So that *we* have a future."

He nodded. "I'll fight for that future with you. I've just...never been a patient man."

She widened her eyes playfully in mock surprise. "I'm shocked."

He laughed and slapped her ass, then gripped it in his palm. "Promise to come back to me, all right?"

Her smile faded, and her eyes were sincere when she said, "I promise."

34

For the first time in Neve's life, duty and desire were at war within her. What she *wanted* to do was lock herself in a room with Killian and only emerge for food and water. What she *wanted* to do was go explore the library and lose herself in the books there.

What she *needed* to do was hunt the Highborns.

So, trussed up in her green Capital gown and cloak, she walked in slow circles around the perimeter of the tower she now knew belonged to them. Neve spent her first few days in Sylvera listening and observing, and while she hadn't yet laid eyes on the Highborns, she did find out where they lived and ruled. Now all she needed to do was stay in the shadows and wait.

It was snowing, the flakes were as fluffy as pillow feathers as they came down around her and landed on her eyelashes and the tip of her nose.

There was an ache between her thighs that, with every step, reminded her of Killian and the way he'd moved inside of her. It also reminded her of what they'd said to each other and the promise she'd made to come back to him.

Neve would not fail to keep that promise.

Despite the snow, there were still plenty of people walking the streets. It was as if there just wasn't much else for the wealthy citizens of Sylvera to do than shop and parade themselves around in front of each other. Very few of them paid any attention to her, and those who did were men whose gaze lingered on her breasts and didn't make it to her face.

Neve kept her focus locked on the entrances and the gate around the tower. There were three doors to the building, one on each of the north, south, and east sides. The west wing of the building was strange in that it had no windows and no doors; it was just a great gray block of nothing. She imagined that whatever happened in the west wing of this massive tower had never seen the light of day. There was a white iron gate all along the perimeter of the building, its pickets looked as sharp and deadly as spears. The gate was too tall for any person to scale or climb; there were no rails to use as footholds. There was one door in the gate, secured with three heavy padlocks and two Cavalry guards posted inside.

The guards were big, broad, and looked bored. Neve steered clear of their sightlines as she stalked the tower, but even if she hadn't, they likely wouldn't have noticed her. They weren't particularly alert, which told Neve that no one in the Highborns' inner sphere believed that someone would even *think* about crossing them.

Good.

Let them be shocked when she came for them.

Neve heard the clatter of metal on metal, and she moved across the street from the tower and slipped into the shadows. Someone was unlocking the gate. One of the guards seemed to be the keeper of the gate key and used it on each of the three locks. Then, both guards stepped aside with a shallow bow.

Cold violence spread like ice through Neve's blood, and she pulled the hood of her cloak down low over her forehead, casting her face further into darkness.

The first person who walked out of the gate was a woman. Young, pretty, afraid. She had wide eyes and a visible hand-shaped bruise on her neck. The woman's gaze was downcast, submissive, and full of terror. Neve could see from where she stood across the street that the poor girl was shaking, and not from the cold.

Behind her...

Quiet rage filled Neve's ears with roaring silence.

Behind the woman walked two men. Both were tall with golden hair and dark, dead eyes. Their skin was pale and sallow. They were slim and incredibly tall. One had his hand on the nape of the woman's neck, and he had a light dusting of beard along his sharp jaw. The other walked a step behind, leering at the woman with an expression that looked hungry. He moved closer to her and leaned down, sniffing her hair.

The woman cringed.

The men were much, much older than they appeared, and they weren't exactly twins, but at first glance, they looked like they could be. Certainly brothers.

Certainly, who she was looking for.

The Highborns.

Neve's instincts told her to move, told her to strike them down and wade in their blood until she knew for sure they were dead. She took a deep breath, forcing her body into stillness. She could feel the evil rolling off of them in great, stinking waves.

In response, the power inside her opened both eyes. It didn't yawn and stretch and lazily awaken, the way she'd felt to come alive before. No. It woke with a snap. It was snarling.

It demanded death.

Cold fire began to sink into her.

She knew she needed to get out of there.

As much as she wanted to watch them, to hunt them, she didn't trust the power inside her not to flare and make her skin light up like a candle. If *they* saw that happen, she was sure everything, her entire plan, perhaps the entire future, would be destroyed.

She hid in her cloak and moved swiftly along the edges of the boulevard, keeping her senses open for danger while pushing down the damper on the thing inside her. Her heart raced, pounding against her sternum. The pressure inside began building so much that it was nearly painful.

It wanted to be released.

No.

It wanted to be *unleashed*.

Faster and faster she walked, stealing a few glances behind her every so often to make sure she wasn't being followed, that she hadn't been sniffed out. Her skin was humming, her stomach was clenching, and it was taking everything she had to keep herself in one piece.

Finally, she made it to her building. She went through the back entrance and sprinted up the stairs. Once she was in her apartment, she shut and locked the door, then dragged the vanity chair in front of it, angling it under the doorknob.

She felt like she was suffocating and overfilling all at once.

Frantic, she pulled off her cloak and reached behind herself to tear at the laces on her gown. Chest heaving with ragged breaths, fueled by both fury and adrenaline, she loosened the corset enough to slip out of the dress and leave it in a heap on the floor.

Wearing just a silk and lace chemise (a new one, because Killian had insisted on keeping the one she wore to Thornkeep), she stood in front of the gilded full-length mirror in her room and looked at herself. The skin on her chest was flushed with exertion, but nothing else was out of the ordinary. No shimmer, no glow, no otherworldly light shone from her. Thinking perhaps the mirror wouldn't register it, she looked down at herself. Nothing.

She stopped, forced herself to slow down. To breathe. Neve no longer felt the power stirring in her. It felt as if, somehow, between seeing the Highborns and making it back to her apartment, it had once again gone dormant. Everything inside her was quiet, except for her slowly fading fervor.

This wouldn't do at all.

Not being able to control the power was one thing. But not even being able to predict when it manifested was another thing altogether.

She needed to learn more.

~

This time, when she entered the library, Neve didn't have to fend off any overzealous attacks from Oliver and Sabrina. She just walked right in.

The two guards sat in conversation with Isolde at the round table, and they all turned to look at her when she strode through the curtains. Their eyes lit up when they saw her. Well, Isolde's and Oliver's at least. Sabrina just gave her a cursory wave and a once-over glance at Neve's clothes.

"I like this better than the puffy thing," Sabrina said, gesturing to Neve's leathers and black cloak. "I feel like I can respect you in this outfit."

"Gods, Sabrina, would it kill you to try to be nice?" Oliver remarked, blushing again with embarrassment.

"That *was* me trying to be nice," Sabrina replied.

Oliver clenched his jaw and shook his head, glaring at Sabrina. "Why are you the way that you are?"

Neve couldn't help but laugh. She liked their dynamic; she liked *them*.

"No offense taken, I assure you. I respect myself more in this outfit, too."

"We're glad you're back. I was hoping you'd come tonight," Isolde said.

Sitting down at the table, Neve looked at what they'd been discussing. A map of Eodia was spread out in front of them, marked up with different symbols.

Lowbarrow and Hythe were crossed out with thick, black lines. Stars marked Sylvera, Thornkeep, and at least twenty other towns across the Island. Even more interesting was the placement of a symbol that looked like a crown. The Dark Forest was marked with a crown. As was the town beyond the heather moor, the plains, Mourner's Pass, Ula Lake.

Neve did not think it was a coincidence that the places she'd been, the places she'd caused a scene, were marked. They were tracking her movements.

Killian mentioned that people were talking about "the woman on the plains". Some man he'd met told the story of their encounter with the Cavalry as if it were a legend already. The man claimed he'd follow such a woman into hell, into war.

Neve leaned back in her chair casually, relaxed and the picture of perfect ease. She looked over the markings on the map again and understood who her new friends were and what those carefully drawn stars on the paper before them signified.

Rebels.

Isolde was eyeing her curiously, but it was Sabrina who spoke up first. "You're not going to ask about the map?"

Neve shrugged. "It's not my business." Her response must have surprised Sabrina because the blonde opened her mouth to reply and then closed it, furrowing her brow. It felt like Sabrina *wanted* Neve to ask about it, but she wasn't about to play games. She knew enough for now, and if they wanted to offer her more, she'd wait for them to make that move.

"Well," Oliver said, leaning forward and pointing at the star drawn on Sylvera with a grin. "This is us."

"Oliver!" Sabrina shouted.

Oliver flinched back and put his hands in his lap. Neve smiled. He reminded her of a big dog. Handsome and huge, courteous and protective, but a bit dumb. She fought the urge to give him a little head pat.

"Sorry, I thought we agreed that she was–"

Isolde interrupted this time and gave Oliver a gentle smile.

"I have a feeling the Lady has a pretty good idea what the markings on the map mean." Her brown eyes slid to Neve with warmth and a strange, sparkling awareness.

Neve relaxed further into her chair and leveled her gaze at Isolde. She searched the other woman's face for any hint of deception but found none.

She let the look linger a little too long, long enough so that Isolde shifted in her seat, and she blinked away the tiniest itch of unease. Neve meant the look as a warning, letting a hint of her dark nature touch her new friend, just enough to keep Isolde from becoming too comfortable with her too fast.

Finally, Neve broke her gaze and turned her attention to the bookshelves, to the thousands and thousands of books crammed together with seemingly no system of organization. It was time to change the subject and get back to the reason that she came to the library tonight in the first place.

"If I'm looking for something specific in here, how do I find it?"

Isolde's face brightened, and she stood, tall and graceful, stepping away from the table to the stacks. She looked up at the shelves lovingly, then back at Neve. Isolde gestured with a hand for Neve to join her. The youthful excitement Isolde had about the library was infectious, so Neve moved next to her.

"Ask the library," Isolde said.

"I don't understand."

"Ask the library for what you're looking for and it will find it for you."

"I just... say it?"

"Say it or think it."

Neve had seen enough marvels in her life to believe that nothing was impossible. So, she took a deep breath and closed her eyes.

I want to learn about my power, she thought. She was met with silence at first, and then –

A sound like thunder rolled and echoed through the library. But, a thunderclap had a beginning and an end, and this... this sound just went on and on.

"Holy shit," Sabrina said.

Neve opened her eyes, and the thing inside her *grinned.*

The books, all of them, were vibrating against the shelves, moving on their own. It was like applause. There wasn't a single book that sat still.

"Whatever you asked for made the books very excited," Isolde whispered. "I've never seen them do this before, at least not all at once."

As flattered as she was that the books seemed to like her, Neve still needed to find *actual* answers. She tried again.

Thank you for your enthusiasm. But I need to learn about it, what it is, how to control it. Can you help me?

The books reluctantly quieted down. All except one on the curve of the northern wall, near the black door. Neve spotted the way it rattled and pushed itself out of the stack with a dusty groan. She moved to it on swift, eager feet.

When she reached the shelf, the book pushed itself a little further out. Instead of reaching for it, she held her hands out, palms up, just underneath it.

"To me," she said quietly.

It did.

It shimmied to the edge of the shelf and then dropped gently into her hands. The binding was covered in black silk, the title embroidered on the front in gold thread.

Queen of Death.

A shiver trickled down her spine. Neve opened the cover, and the book moved on its own again, its pages flipping on a phantom wind until it lay open in her hands to a drawing of a woman holding a skull in one hand and an eight-pointed star in the other.

A woman with a face eerily like her own.

Celesta, goddess of life and death.

35

The smell of her on his sheets was a blessing and a curse. It made Killian wild with desire and mad with longing. He couldn't bear to wash Neve's scent away, but he also couldn't stand to roll around in his bed, reminded of what he could not have.

So, back to the rings it was.

Killian spent long hours throwing his fists for coins over the next few days, attempting to work out the ever-rising storm of tension inside him. The heaviness of guilt and self-loathing, the loneliness, the gut-wrenching yearning that accompanied being apart from the woman he loved. The violence was certainly a distraction, but it did not bring him relief.

His knuckles were split open and bleeding as he sat at the bar. It was early in the evening, and the crowds hadn't yet started to ramp up, but he'd been in the basement since the morning and had seven fights under his belt for the day already. He'd won them all, of course.

Killian looked around the tavern, quietly taking it all in. Women sliding into men's laps, men fighting in the rings, people drinking heavily, and smoking pipes.

This place was filthy, roiling with the odor of desperation, but it was better than hiding out in his room doing nothing. He spied Leo sitting in a booth in the corner, speaking to someone in a deep blue cloak. From his vantage point, the stranger's back was to him, but Killian could see Leo's face clearly. He was speaking low to his companion, alternating between grave seriousness and something that looked close to excitement.

The more time he spent with Leo, the more Killian suspected he might be a part of the rebellion network. The dark-haired man often spoke candidly with him late into the night over many drinks at the bar. He was a dreamer, envisioning a better future for his children. One where there was no Cadre or Cavalry, no Highborn rule. It was treason to say such things, but Leo didn't seem to have any fear of being overheard, and no fear that Killian himself would report the blasphemy.

Hearing an outsider's perspective on his Cadre was a humbling experience. According to Leo, it was a band of brutes who delighted in punishment and torture. Brainless and spineless killing machines with no respect for life.

Killian wondered what Leo would think if he found out who Killian truly was.

He also wondered, often, how he had never known about the gentlefolk of Eodia's disdain for him and his brothers. Would it matter to them if they knew that he and the Cadre were only trying to survive, like the rest of the population? Would it matter to them at all if they knew the Cadre's brutality was how they protected their own families from the Highborns?

Killian wondered what Leo would have done in his position. Leo loved his family and would die for them, but would he commit the same atrocities that Killian had to protect them? Something told him that Leo would not, that Leo would find a different way to protect this family without torturing and executing on the Highborns' whim.

Leo, then, was a better man than he was.

Killian hadn't seen much of Arran since arriving in Thornkeep. It was probably for the best. According to Arran, the Highborns were concerned that Thornkeep would become the next hotbed of rebellion. Most of the survivors from Lowbarrow and Hythe had come as refugees to Thornkeep. So, Arran was in charge of enforcing the town. He patrolled night and day, acting as the Highborns' watchful eye. The presence of the Cadre member in the village was meant to send a warning that anyone who stepped out of line would be dealt with swiftly and without mercy. Arran was a loyal man, perhaps the most loyal person Killian had ever known. Fiercely dedicated to both friendship and duty.

But what Arran did with that sense of duty, what Killian had once done in the name of loyalty, left a bitter taste like ash in his mouth.

Things had changed since he followed Neve into the Dark Forest.

He had changed.

If he was truly honest with himself, it probably happened long before he met Neve. Killian was never the same after his family was killed. The why of it all had haunted him for years. He'd been told, through a Cavalry messenger, that the Highborns believed his family was slain for retribution against him. That the Mages were hired by someone whose family member was the victim of Killian's executioner's blow. When Killian asked who it was, he'd been told it did not matter and not to question the gift of knowledge the Highborns were giving him.

But now he wondered.

What if...what if his family hadn't been slain in the name of revenge?

What if it was for some other reason entirely?

Knuckles stinging, he flexed his fists a few times. Killian watched as Leo and his companion stood and came up next to him at the bar. Beneath the hood of the blue cloak, Killian saw that Leo's friend was a woman.

She was tall and willowy with pretty dark skin and light brown, mirthful eyes. She offered him a smile as she passed, smelling of incense and clove, as she swept towards the exit and disappeared beyond the doors. Killian watched her go with a furrowed brow. Something felt...familiar about that woman, although he knew for certain he'd never seen her before in his life.

"Was that your wife?" Killian asked.

Leo straddled a stool and took a deep drink of his ale with a shake of his head. "No, just a friend."

"A friend who meets you for a quiet chat in a place like this?"

"There are precious few places on the Island these days where a man can have a quiet chat without prying ears or eyes. I'm sure you know that."

"I was prying," Killian said with a smirk.

"I know, but you don't count." Leo gave him a snarky wink.

"Why's that?"

"Because I trust you."

Killian swallowed down the last of his ale and rested his arms on the bar in front of him, looking sidelong at his friend. "Not sure I've earned that quite yet."

Leo just shrugged, regarding Killian with his dark eyes. "Are you fighting any more this evening?"

Killian rolled his neck, cracking it and feeling a temporary relief in his coiled muscles. "Not sure. I've been here since morning, but–"

"Come over for supper," Leo said.

Killian wasn't sure he'd ever been invited to someone's home for supper. He also wasn't sure he'd ever had a friend like Leo, someone who didn't know him or his past. Someone who hadn't grown up in the warrior barracks with him. A friend who didn't want to spend time with him because of his famous name or the stories told about him, but rather because they got along well. He understood the offer likely meant very little to Leo, but to Killian, it felt like an honor he wasn't worthy of.

"I couldn't. Times are tough, I don't want to impose."

Leo rolled his eyes and clapped Killian on the back, standing. "You need a good meal, and my wife will have my balls if I don't show up with you tonight. She insisted that I bring you home to meet her."

~

Leo's house was small and cozy. Somehow tidy and messy at the same time, and it smelled like the food simmering on the hearth. There was the sound of children giggling and shrieking with joy coming from a corner room. It was truly a home. And it broke Killian's heart.

He watched from the doorway as Leo strode inside and to the right, straight into the kitchen, to greet his wife. She was short and curvy, in a dirty lavender dress, and her chestnut brown hair was pinned up messily on the top of her head.

When Leo leaned down and kissed her, Killian looked away, his heart clenched with longing and jealousy at the simplicity of their domestic life together. Something he'd once had and lost. Something he'd likely never have with Neve.

Leo's wife turned, and Killian saw that her belly was round with pregnancy, her hands curving around it on instinct. She looked at him with incredibly intelligent violet-hued eyes.

"Don't just stand in the doorway. Come in, sit down," she commanded.

Killian smiled and gave her a little bow of his head.

"Of course. Thank you." He moved to the table, where there were five place settings. She really had expected Leo to ask him over.

She held out her hand, and Killian made to shake it gently, but her grip was firm and demanding.

"I'm Kat," she said.

"Ewan," he lied.

Her eyes narrowed just slightly at that, and she tilted her head to the side. She opened her mouth to speak, and Killian thought she was perhaps going to even question the name he'd given her. But instead, she shouted, "Boys! Supper!" in his face so loud and suddenly that Killian flinched.

Leo was bringing the roasted chicken to the table, laughing, when the unmistakable whirlwind of two raucous boys came barreling around the corner and into the kitchen.

Killian's heart plummeted into his gut.

Pink-cheeked and wild-eyed, Leo and Kat's sons were adorable little beasts. They both had mops of dark hair atop their heads and their mother's eyes. They ran toward Killian and looked right up at him with curious, excited expressions.

"Who are you?" the older one asked.

"Did you bring us any toys?" said the younger.

"This is Daddy's friend from work," Leo said. Kat snorted at the word "work," and Leo gave her a lovingly annoyed look. "He's called Ewan, and no, he did not bring you any toys."

Both boys pouted up at him. Killian raised his hands in surrender.

"My apologies, gentlemen. Next time, I'll know better."

They seemed satisfied with that answer and took their seats at the table. Leo dished up chicken, potatoes, and vegetables onto their plates and then gestured at the seat in front of Killian with the fork in his hand.

"Please, have a seat."

Killian pulled the chair out, wincing as he scraped the legs along the floor, and sat down. Leo served his wife first, then Killian, then himself. Only when everyone else began to eat did Killian start eating as well. It had been a long time since he'd enjoyed a truly home-cooked meal, especially sitting at the table with a family.

It mended and broke something inside of him at the same time.

"Leo tells me that you're not married, but you have a lady. Where is she?" Kat asked.

"She's in a different village right now, while I'm trying to find work," Killian lied, shoveling a hefty bite of chicken into his mouth. It was well-cooked, tender, and tasted like it had been roasted in garlic and butter.

"I'm sure she doesn't like to be away from you this much," she replied.

Killian smiled at her. "I'm not sure about that. But I certainly don't like it. I much prefer it when she's around."

For the first time since meeting her, Kat's eyes softened. She reached over for Leo's hand and squeezed it. "You love her, don't you?"

"Yes," Killian responded, blowing out a breath. "She's all I can think about."

A blush crept onto Kat's cheeks, and she looked like she was trying to hold back a smile. Her gaze cut to Leo. "Why don't you talk about me like that when I'm not around?"

Leo laughed and brought her hand to his mouth, pressing his lips to her knuckles. "I do."

"He does," Killian added. "All the time."

The smile that broke on Kat's face could have lit up the whole village. She positively beamed at Leo. "Good," she said.

After supper, Leo offered to get the boys, Henry and Jasper, washed up. But Kat insisted that she'd take care of it so he and Killian could talk. Leo cleaned the dishes, then pulled a piece of paper from a small bookshelf on the other side of the hearth, setting it in front of Killian on the table.

It appeared to be a map of Eodia, with strange markings throughout. Stars and crowns, and two X marks.

"What's this?" Killian asked.

Leo sat down in the chair across the table from Killian and gave him a long look. He seemed a little nervous, like he wasn't sure he wanted to take the conversation further, but he squared his shoulders and took a breath.

"We could use a man like you," Leo said. "A man who can fight."

The hairs on Killian's arms stood at attention. He leaned forward. "Who's 'we', Leo?"

Leo pointed to a star marking on the map, on Thornkeep. "That's us."

Killian swallowed. "You gonna make me ask again? Who, exactly?"

"People who want a better world for our children. People who believe the woman on the plains is real."

"Rebels," Killian said, his voice low. He wasn't sure he wanted to have this conversation. Life was dangerous enough for families like Leo's, but being a rebel was as good as a death wish.

The Highborns were already suspicious of Thornkeep harboring rebels, which was why Arran was here after all. If they found out Leo was part of the network...they'd kill him.

Leo nodded. "We're rallying," he pointed at the twenty-or-so stars marked across the map. "And we're growing, every day."

Killian placed his palm over the map.

"Leo, listen to me," he said. "You have no idea what they'll do to you, to your family, if they find out you're a rebel."

Leo clenched his jaw, and Killian saw the ferocity his friend often unleashed in the rings.

"Kill me?" he asked. "Or, worse? Send Mages to my home to murder my wife and children in their sleep?"

Hot, violent fury filled Killian's veins like lava. "What did you just say to me?" his voice was sharp as knives, and he was almost certain he was baring his teeth.

"I know who you are," Leo said. "Killian Grey."

36

Neve stumbled over her own feet, falling forward into a hard, unyielding chest and a pair of arms that didn't move to save her from the collision. Off balance, she went to her knees on the cold, icy sidewalk. She raised her voice an octave, softened it, and let out a little whimper when her legs made contact with the sandstone.

She looked up slowly, at the impeccable white clothing, the tall frame, and the face of pure evil that loomed over her. Two faces. She'd run into the bearded one, and his brother now stood, equally unimpressed, at his side.

The Highborns looked down at her, on her knees before them.

"Clumsy girl," the clean-shaven one sneered. The bearded brother just stared at her, with nothing in his eyes besides malice and the glimmer of pleasure at seeing a woman at his feet.

"I–I'm so sorry. My shoes... they slipped on the ice." Neve made herself seem delicate and afraid; she filled her eyes with terror, and added a little tremble to her body for good measure.

She'd stalked the Highborns for days. Watching them, following them. In the week Neve hunted them, she'd seen them with three different women. Each was timid, innocent, and afraid.

They were prey.

She only watched them from afar, with no way to see what went on behind the closed doors of their tower, but she had a pretty good idea that the women who fell into the Highborns' path did not come out of it alive. Each one was as good as dead the moment she ended up in their clutches.

The only way to get close to them, to unravel them from the inside, was to become one of those women herself.

It wasn't hard to transform. She wore her green dress but no cloak despite the winter air. She'd made her cheeks pink with just a little extra rouge and braided her hair into two plaits that dripped over her shoulders. She walked demurely, as if unsure of herself and her own body. She spoke quietly, softly.

And now she knelt before them, the picture of perfect, innocent submission.

The bearded one reached out and took her face in his cold hand. His skin felt like paper, and beneath the plume of cologne on his wrist, he smelled old. Like dead leaves floating in a stagnant pond. Everything about him felt rotten.

He gripped her jaw with long, bony fingers and forced her to look up at him. She did, beneath bashful lashes. She forced her eyes to water and her bottom lip to quiver. His focus landed on that trembling lip, and he pulled a waxy thumb across it. Killian had done something similar to her the morning they woke in Thornkeep together. But this... this was altogether different. This was a possessive, lecherous move.

And Neve would remember it.

There was nothing in the eyes of the man who stared down at her. Devoid of color, black as soot and dead as bones. Her gaze flicked to his brother. The same flat reptile eyes. The same nothingness. The same bitter hate.

She lowered her gaze as the thumb made another pass across her mouth, this time dipping in just slightly, grazing her teeth.

"I'm so sorry, my lords. If there is a way I can make it up to you..." Neve looked at them again. "I'm yours to command, of course."

She let the innuendo sit there. She'd meant it to sound exactly like it did. But her facial expression, her body language, and her voice betrayed none of her cunning. For them, for all the world to see, she was a pretty young thing who didn't know what she was saying, what such words could mean to men like these.

Neve watched, her face still held in the bearded one's hand, as he looked to his brother. Some wordless conversation passed between them, and when it was finished, the clean-shaven brother moved behind her. She felt his hands on her arms, pulling her to her feet. His fingers felt like twigs wrapped in dead skin.

"My dear, you must be so cold. Out here in only your dress," he said in her ear. She felt his chest at her back, his hands flexing and unflexing on her arms. It reminded her of the wraiths in the Dark Forest. He towered over her, they both did, and the one behind her peeked his head around her. She felt his gaze burning down the bodice of her dress.

"We should get her warmed up," the one in front of her, the bearded one, said. "Would you like that?"

She made her eyes go wide, swallowed audibly, and nodded. "Yes, sir. Yes, please."

They shepherded her past the high iron gate, through the east door, and into the tower. The bearded one led the way, and the other walked close behind her. Too close.

Neve memorized each step she took into the manor. She eyed where every one of the windows was, and the damage they'd cause if she needed to jump out of one to escape. She etched the shape of each doorway into her brain. She counted her steps and how many dimly lit wall sconces they passed as they moved from one hallway to the next. She took in every detail, every speck of dust, and every floating cobweb as they moved.

The floors were bare, with no carpet or rug to cover them and warm them up. The walls were also empty, not even the dusty outline of where a piece of art may have once hung. Just blank, gray stone. The tower was as dark and empty as the eyes of her hosts.

The Highborns brought her into a formal sitting room. Propped in the corner was a narrow credenza with various glass bottles of liquid crowded on top. There was one threadbare, sagging sofa in the middle of the chamber, a piece of furniture she was sure was at one time ornate and expensive but now was nothing more than a faded relic. In front of the sofa sat a large, low table whose surface was covered in dust. An enormous fireplace took up a good portion of the wall on the other side of the table. The fire was merely embers.

The room smelled of ash and decay.

She knew she was in the west wing, both by paying attention to the path they'd taken from the east door where they'd entered and by the fact that there were no windows in the room. In her mind, Neve calculated how fast she'd have to run to find the nearest exit.

"Please, have a seat," the clean-shaven brother said, moving toward the bottles on the credenza while the bearded man tossed a few hefty logs onto the dying fire, causing it to cough up a cloud of sparks and crackle back to life.

"Thank you," Neve said, making her body move stiffly to the sofa. She chose the middle and feigned nervousness as she sat straight-backed at the very edge of the cushion. "Your graciousness is...well, I'm very grateful."

The bearded brother sat down to her left, draped his arm across the back of the couch, and pressed his thigh against hers. "What's your name, dear?" he asked.

She folded her hands in her lap and looked down at them, feeling his gaze rolling over her like worms on her skin. "Cora," she lied, with a fake shaking breath. "And yours, my lords? What may I call you?"

"I'm Balor," said the bearded one. "And my brother is Cael."

Neve felt the power inside of her blink and rumble at that, but she forced it down and ignored it.

She knew what those names meant.

Cael sat down to her right, just as close to her as his brother was. He handed a drink to Balor and then one to her, his fingers dipping below the rim of the glass and into the liquid as he awkwardly handed it to her. Deep inside, Neve cringed, but she didn't let it show, and she brought the glass to her nose and sniffed.

Absinthe. And something else.

"This smells strong, I... I've never really drunk alcohol before," she said.

Balor chuckled darkly. "It will warm you up."

She pretended to take a sip. Then pretended to cough.

The Highborns laughed.

"Oh my," she said, letting just the hint of a smile grace her mouth.

"Lean back, relax," Cael said. She looked over at him as sweetly as she could, and he demonstrated by moving back and settling deeper into the sofa.

"I'm sorry. I'm just nervous. To be in your presence, to be invited into your home, is a great honor, my lords."

Cael grunted an arrogant laugh, but Balor's hands went to Neve's hips. His fingers curled around her curves as he pulled her back into the sofa. He left one arm settled behind her, hand resting on her waist. *Gripping.*

"The honor is ours, indeed. It gets lonely in here, with just the two of us," Balor replied. It sounded scripted, like he'd said it before. Perhaps hundreds of times. Perhaps more.

"I'm sure it does. But for someone like me... I've admired you from afar for so long. And now to be here, with you... It's surreal," she said gently. Not all of it was a lie. But certainly she meant it differently than they received it.

"Admired us, have you?" Balor asked in a low voice.

Cael's hand was on Neve's leg, slowly gathering the fabric of her dress as if he meant to lift her skirt.

As Neve stalked them in the previous days, she'd watched closely as each of the three women they'd been with entered and exited the tower a handful of times. Sometimes the Highborns would accompany the women in and out. Sometimes the women would arrive and leave on their own. Until they each eventually went in and never came out again. She'd watched the way the Highborns would touch the women in their company. Intimately, possessively, fiercely. There was violence in every grasp of flesh.

So, she'd had time to prepare, to focus on the greater good over the violation of her skin. She was a skilled warrior and knew how to use every weapon in her arsenal. This was not the first time she'd used her body against an enemy. She'd done it plenty of times with The Maere. She'd even done it to Killian before he proved himself to her. Neve reminded herself this was no different.

Except that it was.

There was more at stake.

The Highborns were not just *an* enemy; they were *the* enemy.

But Neve would not win this game if she allowed herself to think of them as anything other than men. Especially when she was utterly alone in the windowless west wing. Especially when their hands were on her.

"What is it?" Cael murmured, his dusty breath blowing along her neck, into her ear. "You've admired so much about us?" He bunched more of her skirt in his fist, and the hem was rising slowly up her shins.

Balor's hand crawled up her back until it was on the nape of her neck.

The greater good, the greater good, the greater good.

"I have heard stories of what Eodia was like before your family line was in charge," she said. Both brothers stopped moving, as if frozen. "I don't like those stories. I much prefer things as they are now."

Neve didn't have to turn her head to know that they were looking at each other, sharing another silent conversation. Then Balor's hand tightened on the back of her neck, and Cael's was on the bare skin of her knee, having pushed her skirt up to her lap.

"Why is that, dear?" Balor asked, inching closer.

Neve knew they were both poised to strike. If she said the wrong thing, if they caught a lie in her inflection, or if she stumbled over her answer, they'd kill her. Or, at least, try.

But she would not say the wrong thing.

She would say the exact right thing.

Neve deliberately relaxed into their hands, into their touch. She let them feel her muscles uncoil. She leaned back against the sofa and looked them both in their dead eyes, one after the other.

"Because this kingdom has *always* belonged to you. And the Lyra bloodline got what it deserved."

37

Killian was about to lunge across the table and rip out Leo's throat, but suddenly Kat was there at her husband's side, leveling a fearsome look at Killian.

"My children are in the other room. There will be no violence in my home, do you understand?" she said in a quiet, commanding voice.

Reeling yet admonished, Killian nodded.

"Say it. Say you understand," she hissed, her eyes bright and merciless.

He nodded again. "I swear."

Holding her pregnant belly, Kat lowered herself into the chair between Killian and Leo. She pulled the map out from under Killian's palm and set it in front of herself instead.

"Leo assured me that we could trust you. That you would be, at the very least, sympathetic to the cause. So, either he misjudged you, or you are just really terrible at adapting to surprises. Which one is it?"

It felt like being scolded. Shamefully. But he felt like he'd been exposed. He couldn't help but think he'd made a mistake along the way, that he'd shared something he shouldn't have that could compromise his anonymity here, or worse, Neve's mission in the Capital.

"I'm not a fan of surprises."

He took a deep breath and forced himself to calm down. His mind raced back to all the conversations he'd shared with Leo, and he couldn't think of anything he'd said or done that would have given him away. Knowing the future of the kingdom,

Neve's future, and her safety were in the balance, he'd been careful.

Killian looked across the table at his friend. "How?"

Leo looked sympathetic. "We're...very well connected. The rebels, that is. We have a lot of information available to us."

"What kind of information?"

"Verified information," Kat added. "About the Cadre, the Cavalry, the Highborns. You."

Killian's head felt like it was being crushed between two giant hands. He couldn't risk this. Leo, Kat, the rebels... they could be dangerous to everything Neve was trying to do. If they knew about him, could they know about her? Had they put two and two together and discovered that the woman Killian loved was actually their famed Woman on the Plains?

He took another deep breath and leaned back in his chair. "Yeah?" he asked, allowing a slice of deadly warning to edge into his voice, onto his face. "What exactly do you know?"

Kat and Leo exchanged a look, and it was clear at that moment that he was seeking cues from her. That she was in charge of this initiative, and within this household at least, she was leading the rebellion actions. Kat sighed and gave Killian a look that was equal parts warning and apology.

"We know what *really* happened to your family...and why."

His stomach crashed to the floor, and there was a roaring so loud in his ears he was certain he'd gone deaf.

"*What.*" It wasn't a question. It was a demand. Bile rose in the back of his throat, and he was struck with a sudden vertigo that sent his world spinning.

"Careful," Leo said quietly, looking at his wife and taking her hand. He was worried. Worried about what Killian would do, to them, to her. Killian wanted to reassure them both that he wasn't a threat, but at that moment, he wasn't sure. All he could do was try to keep breathing.

Kat spoke softly. Her words were gentle yet measured and full of strength. "The rebel network has been around for a long time, Killian. Five years ago, it was much smaller. Just a few handfuls of people scattered around the Island. These people were watching you closely. They were watching everyone in the Cadre closely, so they could report on where you might be going and who you might be bringing to... what I'm sure, at the time, you considered justice. When the Cadre made a move, the rebels would try to alert the village that you were coming. It was rarely successful. But it was a start."

Killian said nothing. He could barely move.

"There was a lot of...interest amongst the rebels when you were arrested. Many were angry that you were merely thrown in the dungeon rather than executed. It seemed like a double standard, considering the executions you'd committed for crimes far less severe than murdering a dozen Mages," Kat said.

Nausea hit Killian. The way she spoke about who he was when he led the Cadre, the things he'd done, the use of the word *murder*... it made him sound like a monster. Maybe he was.

"But there were those of us who were more interested in what happened to your family and why."

Killian swallowed and peered down at his clenched fists on the table before him. He couldn't look at her. "And?" he asked, his voice rough and gravelly.

Leo and Kat looked at each other again. This time, Leo spoke. "We had a spy within the Cavalry at that time. It didn't last long; he's dead now. He spread the news that the Mages you killed were indeed responsible for the deaths of your family."

Something broke inside Killian. Some sick relief mixed with a flood of grief.

"But..." Leo continued.

Killian looked up at him then, sure that he could take no more.

"They were paid to do it."

Rage, depthless and dark, pooled into Killian. "Who paid them?"

Wrath and disgust rose in Leo's brown eyes.

"The Highborns. They felt that your family was distracting you from your duties. That you weren't as focused as you'd been before you... became a father."

Lightning quick, Killian was on his feet. His body moved on its own, sending the chair skidding back and crashing to the floor. Hot tears pricked at his eyes, and he covered his face with his hands.

"Mama! What was that noise?" a bell-chime voice called out, followed by the sound of little feet scampering out to the kitchen.

He couldn't bear it. He simply could not. His heart broke with every pounding beat. Killian moved to the front door and stumbled outside into the cold night air. Snow crunched under his boots. He shuffled to the side of the house and put his back to the wall, sliding down until he was crouching like some hunched, broken thing. His cheeks were wet with tears, his whole body shook with the force of his pain and fury.

For so long, he'd been desperate for answers. For truth. This *felt* like the truth. Some thought that had been whispering in the back of his mind for five years, some missing puzzle piece, had finally been found. Despite having the truth now, it still felt like the whole weight of the world was crashing into him, pressing down on him, crushing him.

His memory flashed to his children. The way they would run to him when he came home. They'd jump on him, and Killian would pretend to fall, toppled over by their might. "Such strong boys," he'd say. And they'd crawl all over him, pawing at him with their sticky hands. Such small hands touching his face and reaching into his pockets for the trinkets he'd brought home for them. Screaming with delight in his ears until they were ringing with the noise of it all. Their round cheeks were pink and warm with exertion and elation. Daddy was their favorite person, their favorite plaything.

And then, overnight, Killian wasn't Daddy anymore.

He wasn't a Husband.

He wasn't anything.

And now, on this cold winter night, he finally knew for certain why.

Perhaps if he'd been more focused on his duties. Answered commands from the Cavalry faster, been more diligent, been more brutal... perhaps they'd be alive now. Perhaps he never should have entertained the idea that a man like him could have a family, because if he hadn't, he wouldn't have been the reason three innocent, *such innocent*, people met their ends.

His wife, of course, knew who he was when she married him. But did she know the risks? Truly? Had she known the brute that she'd married, the depth of Killian's violence?

He could have spared her. He could have walked away when she needed help. He could have left long before they married, long before they brought two sweet babies into the world just to be snuffed out a few short years later.

He could have done so many things to spare his family from their doom.

The sound of feet on snow drew Killian's attention upward and his face out of his hands. Leo and Kat's youngest, Jasper, stood in front of him with an open and curious look on his face. The boy was so small that they were face-to-face, despite Killian crouching.

"Are you crying?" he asked. The little man couldn't quite say his "R" sounds yet, so they came out sounding like "W's".

Killian swallowed down a sob at the sweet earnestness of the question and nodded.

"Yes.. I am," Killian replied gently. From the corner of his eye, he saw Leo in the doorway, leaning there with his arms crossed.

Jasper nodded. "Mama was right, then."

"About what?" Killian sniffed and then wiped his eyes and nose across his sleeve.

"Sometimes I cry when I get hurt, and Mama says even big, strong warriors cry." Jasper's eyes were as big as two moons and just as bright.

Killian nodded. "Your Mama is right."

The boy nodded and stuffed his fingers into the pocket of his pants. He pulled something from inside and held it out in his little hand for Killian. The gesture tugged at his heart. Killian opened his palm to accept the offering. Jasper dropped a pebble into it. Grey stone with red speckles and curving gradients. Bloodstone. It was smooth and round as if it'd spent years underwater, and it was warm from being in the boy's pocket.

"What's this for?" Killian asked.

Jasper tilted his head to the side as if to tell Killian that the question was seven ways of being stupid. "Presents always make me feel better."

A great rush of emotion swelled up in Killian's throat, but he managed to swallow it back. "How kind of you. But I don't want to take something that belongs to you."

Jasper rolled his eyes. "It's just a rock." With that, he scurried back into the house.

Killian rolled the pebble between his fingers, feeling a sense of overwhelming gratitude and grief.

"He's a good boy, Leo."

"I know," Leo replied from the doorway.

"You were going to ask me to join the rebellion. Before you told me everything else."

"I was."

"Did you tell me the rest to convince me to join?"

"That was Kat's choice. She thought you deserved to know."

"And if I don't take up the cause? What then?"

Leo was silent for a moment. Then he heaved a deep sigh. "I'd hate to see you stay on the wrong side of history, my friend."

"Does your plan include killing them? The Cavalry, the Highborns?" Killian asked. He almost included the Cadre but couldn't. He wasn't there. Yet.

"Yes," Leo said. "Every last one."

Killian looked up into the night sky where the stars were spilling like seeds across rich, black soil. He knew in his bones that this was the right choice. He knew he couldn't protect Leo and his family, and others like them, if he wasn't part of it. And he knew that the fate of the rebels must somehow be tied to Neve, their rightful Queen, the Woman on the Plains.

So, he made his choice and said, "You have my sword."

38

When Neve crept into Killian's room, she expected him to be asleep.

As soon as she was out of earshot of the Highborns' tower, she found an alley to duck into where she stuck her fingers down her throat and purged her stomach of the absinthe and the barely dissolved white poppy seeds Cael slipped into her glass. An often deadly sedative.

As it was, Neve had grown a tolerance to most toxins after being forced to ingest them starting at a young age. It was part of her training for the Maere. Poison identification through taste, learning what each one does to a person's body by experiencing it firsthand. It was a brutal thing to put a child through, but look at her now. Nearly immune. Much like magic, it would take *a lot* of poison to put her down. If she'd been anyone else, though, she wouldn't have been able to walk out of that manor on her own.

She'd gone to her room above the dressmaker's shop. It was when she undressed that she noticed the marks on her neck and shoulders, left there by Balor's zealous mouth. Neve stared at those marks in the mirror for a long time. The silence in her room was so complete. She'd touched the marks with her fingers as if she could wipe them off.

But she couldn't.

A strange, cold feeling oozed into her. One she'd rarely felt in all her life. Shame. And guilt. A slimy sense that she'd somehow betrayed everything she held true, who she was, her kingdom, the man who loved her.

Yes, it was for the greater good. Yes, what happened in the tower put her exactly where she needed to be. This would bring her close. This would make her succeed.

But.

If she were honest, the cost felt almost too high to pay.

She knew she owed it to Killian to tell him what happened, what she'd done. Neve bathed in scalding water, then dressed in a loose tunic and leggings before slinking out into the darkness. All she could think about as she moved through the winter trees and snow was how sick she felt with their hands on her, their mouths on her. She almost hadn't been able to keep herself together despite her expertise and training. How angry, violated tears threatened to prick the backs of her eyes the whole time.

Perhaps she wasn't as mighty and brave as she thought. Perhaps her courage had limits.

By the time she made it to Thornkeep, it was deep into the night. Her mind was a torrent of uncomfortable emotions that seemed to choke out all of her logic and leave her floating in unease.

She'd endured much worse, and yet ... somehow not.

Neve was a highly skilled assassin, possibly the best that ever lived. She'd been stabbed and sliced, shot through with arrows, strangled and tortured. She'd fought a wyvern and won.

And yet... somehow this felt like it was closing in on too much.

Neve was silent as she opened Killian's door, expecting a beautifully slumbering man, and to wake him by crawling into bed next to him. Letting him hold her. Deeply and desperately hoping he would give her the space to tell him, praying he would ask her what was wrong so she wouldn't have to be the one to start the conversation.

She needed nothing more in the world than his tenderness that night.

But she found him sitting on the edge of the bed with his head in his hands. Killian looked up at her, and the raw emotion in his expression stopped her in her tracks. Something happened. The look on his face was the same one he'd given her after the wolves, after the wyvern, when she told them they had to separate.

He looked devastated.

It broke her heart, the look on his face. She wanted to comfort him, turn his sadness to dust, and blow it away. Lay waste to whomever or whatever made him feel so low.

But it also meant something else.

It meant he would not be able to hold space for her the way she needed right now.

Neve shut and locked the door behind her, already weary. She steeled herself and did her best to push her thoughts, her feelings, down, down, down.

"What happened?" she asked.

With haunted eyes and needful arms, he reached out to her from where he sat.

"Come here," he said. His voice was rough and vulnerable.

Neve moved towards him, and when she was within the grasp of his fingers, Killian circled her waist and pulled her to him. He pressed his face into the crook between her neck and shoulder, on the right side, the side that was devoid of the stains left by Balor's mouth.

Neve kissed the top of Killian's head, taking a deep drag of his scent. Cedar, smoke, sweat. It centered her. So she buried her face in his hair and closed her eyes, breathing him in. She wrapped her arms around his broad shoulders, feeling his tension ease against her touch. His long fingers snuck under her tunic and lazily stroked the soft skin of her lower back.

"What happened, Killian?" she repeated.

"I went to supper at Leo's house tonight. I met his family."

Neve furrowed her brows, resting her cheek on the top of Killian's head. "And?"

"They showed me a map. It was of Eodia. Covered in markings; stars and crowns."

Neve knew exactly what came next.

"They're rebels, Neve."

"I'm not all that surprised."

"I'm not either."

"So, what's the problem?"

He kissed across her collarbone, then pulled back slightly to look at her face. His eyes, his beautiful eyes, were so sad.

"They know who I am. And they know what happened to my family— what *really* happened."

Neve massaged his scalp with the tips of her fingers and listened. He told her that the Mages he slaughtered that night did kill his family, but they'd been paid by the Highborns to do it. At that moment, hearing the rageful way he spoke about them, Neve knew she couldn't tell him what happened to her tonight, what she'd done. Not after this. Not when he just found out the ugly truth that the people who'd been passing her between them tonight like a shared snack were the very same people who'd paid for the deaths of Killian's wife and children.

She couldn't do that to him. She could bear her own pain, but she couldn't bear adding to his.

"I'm going to rip them apart," he swore.

Neve offered him a raised eyebrow and a ghost of her normal smirk. It was all she could muster. "Get in line, handsome. I get the first crack at them."

The sadness in his eyes faded just slightly, and he laughed. He pushed the hair back from around her shoulders and cupped her face in his hands.

"As you wish, my lady." Killian's eyes moved across her face and down her neck.

His gaze stopped, then he went utterly still.

His focus was frozen and fixed on the left side of her throat.

On the mouth-shaped bruise.

Gently, he touched her chin and used his fingers to urge her face to turn to the side. He moved his thumb over the mark and then pulled his hand back as if the touch burned.

"Neve?" he asked quietly.

She said nothing.

She couldn't.

His eyes met hers, and his brow furrowed.

"Neve?" he asked again. A muscle feathered in his jaw. Her heart squeezed in her chest. "What's this, love?"

She shook her head.

"You don't want to know," she said.

He huffed a breath out of his nose, and she heard his teeth grinding behind his lips. His hands dropped to his lap, where he clenched them into tight fists. Neve stepped away from him and pressed her back to the wall.

He stood. "Tell me. Please." His eyes searched her face with increasing panic.

Neve took a deep breath and released it slowly. She'd wanted him to ask. Hoped for it. Perhaps she imagined it a different way, more tenderly, but this is what she'd wanted after all.

"I was with them tonight," she said. Her voice came out soft and steady.

Killian passed a hand over his face and looked at the floor. "Who?"

She lifted her chin. "The Highborns, Killian. I was with the Highborns."

His eyes widened and *blazed* at her.

"What did you...What happened?" His voice was strained, barely a whisper. Killian's face was a mask of hardly contained emotion: fury, fear, and the sharp lines of jealousy.

It was that last feeling she could sense from him, the jealousy, that made her heart fog over with ice. The same heart that Killian himself had helped warm, as he'd taught her how to love and be loved. The way he looked at her now, the way his molten eyes kept glancing toward the mark on her neck. Something about it gave her a feeling of being *owned*.

But here was a man who'd thrown his whole world away to bend the knee and follow her, who'd risked everything, including his life on multiple occasions, for her mission, for her. This sweet brute of a man loved her and was hurting. So, she would offer him kindness at this moment.

Neve was gentle when she spoke.

"I've been following them for days. Learning their movement. They always had a woman with them, in their arms. So I placed myself in their path and became one of those women."

He crossed his arms and dragged his teeth over his bottom lip. They were only standing a few feet apart. The distance suddenly felt infinite.

"I need to know what that means, Neve."

He was asking for honesty, not asking her to protect his feelings, so she would give it.

"They brought me into their manor and sat with me. They gave me a drink spiked with white poppy- a sedative."

A hiss came out of his mouth, and he moved to her quickly, taking her face in his hands. His touch was trembling, his face contorted with concern.

"They *poisoned* you?"

She moved her hands to his wrists, taking his hands from her face and placing his palms against her chest so that he could feel her steady heart, so he could know that she was safe.

"I'm fine, Killian. I promise. The sedative didn't affect me."

The air *whooshed* out of his lungs as he leaned down, resting his forehead against hers. "They could have killed you, Neve."

She shook her head. "No."

He pulled back and looked at her. The desperate expression in his eyes told her exactly what he was about to ask.

"Did they..." he swallowed and glanced at the mark on her neck again. "Did they touch you?"

Neve lifted her chin and didn't hesitate when she looked him in the eyes and said, "Yes."

A quiet grunt came out of his mouth as if he'd been punched in the gut. He took a staggering step back from her. And another. Then his whole face and body went hard and tight, like a bowstring pulled taut, ready to loose an arrow. He was combusting, and Neve was watching it happen before her eyes. She could almost smell the rage on him.

"You let them put their hands on you?" he growled.

Neve's breath caught. The power inside her blinked awake. There was something in his tone, something she was sure he didn't intend, but it was there nonetheless.

An accusation.

She leveled her gaze at him. "Yes. I need to get close–"

He cut her off. "Their mouths, too?" he pointed at her neck. "You let them put their mouths on you?" His voice was rising, getting louder, more frantic.

Neve did not like the direction this was going.

She knew he was raw. He'd been dealt so many blows since arriving in Thornkeep. Finding out what was done to Lowbarrow and Hythe because he left, that two of his friends perished in the aftermath, and discovering what truly happened to his family. She knew he was devastated, and his emotions were on a hair-trigger.

She gave him grace for that.

She gave him sympathy.

But what she would not do is give him space to take it all out on her.

He turned his back on her before she could answer his question. His shoulders were rising and falling with his shallow, angry breaths.

"Did you fuck them?" he gritted out, unable to turn around and look at her when he said it.

Everything inside her went cold. Her power seemed to uncurl and spread out, stretching.

"What did you just say to me?" she asked, forcing a bit of warmth into her voice, just in case, *just in case* she'd heard him wrong.

Killian turned then, slowly. He still couldn't look at her. "Did you fuck them?"

The ice in her veins straightened her spine.

"No," she said. Her voice was low and steady, final.

Briefly, his shoulders sagged with some hint of relief. But rageful worry found him now and would not let go.

"But they could have. If the white poppy they gave you worked, they could have."

"I was in control–"

He cut her off again. "The risk you took today... the danger you put yourself in..."

"Killian, this was part of the plan. To get close to them–"

"It was reckless," he spat.

Neve went still. All she could feel now was a familiar cold fire. Icy, invisible smoke plumed within her. No. Not just within her. Out of her. The room grew colder as the power inside pushed outward.

"I have never been reckless."

Killian was so deep in his head, so drenched in his storm of emotion, he wasn't even aware of the temperature change around them. He didn't notice the command in her voice. It was as if he wasn't even listening to her.

"I cannot bear the thought of them touching you, Neve. They're monsters."

"I know they are. That's why-"

"They murdered my family, my *children*, and you let them get close to you."

Her power was writhing against her bones. "Killian-"

"I am sworn to you. I am supposed to be your line of defense. And you did this alone, without even telling me."

"I'm telling you now-"

He was on a roll. He wasn't listening. He didn't want to hear any of her explanations. It was as if he just *wanted* to be outraged. Just wanted to give in to his emotions rather than entertain reason.

"You should have told me *before*."

Something inside her snarled, and the room became colder, frost blooming on the window. He'd never made her feel ignored before. No one had. He'd always paid attention and watched her cues. And now, in this state, he seemed to be lost in a blur of feeling, unable to see beyond himself.

"I do not need your permission," she said.

His jaw clenched. "You risked your life today. And with your life, you risked the future of this kingdom."

Neve's anger crashed into her, and she took one dangerously slow step forward.

"What I did today, what I put myself through, was *for* the future of this kingdom."

"You did it because you think you're invincible. But you're not. I've watched you bleed," his gaze was wild. "I've already watched you bleed too many times. I can't bear the thought of your blood on *their* hands."

"You're not listening-"

"Being apart from you has been driving me mad. And now, to know that you're actively putting yourself in danger... you're breaking me."

Neve was reaching the edge of her patience. But the sorrow in him held her back.

"Breaking you? I–"

"Like you said, you don't need my permission. But you do owe me some consideration," he said, with a sneer on his lips.

Inside her, there was an *expansion.*

Her power was alive.

And while she wasn't glowing, some other facet of this thing was rising. Something regal. Something royal. It reared.

And whatever it was breathed cold fire.

You do not yield, it seemed to say, *even to him.*

"It's as if you don't even think of me when you make decisions," he continued, pacing back and forth. "Meanwhile, I think of you with every choice I make. I *consider* you. Because you're my–"

"I am your Queen," she said. Her voice was deep and lethal.

He stopped moving, stopped breathing. Everything stopped.

A weighty and absolute silence settled over the room. Hurt flickered across Killian's eyes, but Neve was out of sympathy. Her capacity for gentle coddling was full, and now she found herself somewhere beyond human feeling. Someplace that saw the world as it was, the big picture. Someplace where she understood his pain, but was somehow above it. A place that had no room for this conversation because the kingdom, the world, was so much bigger than one person's hurt.

Even if it was the person she loved.

Killian looked at her as if he was seeing her for the first time, as if with those four words she'd stripped him bare and taken him to his knees.

As if he'd forgotten that, beneath everything else about their relationship, she was his Queen and he was her knight.

Eyes wide, he sat on the bed and lowered his gaze.

"You speak to me as if you have *forgotten who I am*. To forget who I am is a weakness. *Your* weakness," she said.

He remained silent.

The silence stretched.

Neither she nor he moved to apologize.

Neither she nor he moved to attempt a resolution.

She'd pulled rank and drawn a line in the sand, and now here they were.

Neve wanted to reach for him. But he wouldn't even look at her.

It was time for her to go.

Opening the door, she looked over her shoulder at him one more time.

"I meant it when I said I love you. That hasn't changed."

He didn't turn toward her. Instead, he simply bowed his head and said, "Your Majesty."

39

"She seems quiet," Sabrina said.

"She's always quiet," replied Oliver.

"Too quiet."

"What does that even mean?"

"She's freaking me out."

"*You're* freaking *me* out."

Despite her sullen mood, Neve was amused listening to Sabrina and Oliver bicker about her.

She'd been too restless to sit when she arrived at the library, so she stood at the stacks, gently paging through *Queen of Death.* Sabrina and Oliver were sitting at the table, halfway through playing a game of cards, and Neve looked over her shoulder at them. Their eyes widened, as if surprised that she'd heard them talking about her with her back turned. She gave them a raised eyebrow, and they quickly turned back to their card game.

She liked them.

What she didn't like, however, was the muddled feeling in her mind. It had been four days since her fight with Killian. She still couldn't shake her sense of unease. She was no stranger to conflict or confrontation; in fact, she was excellent at it. But with Killian, conflict felt different. Everything felt different with him. Guilt felt different. Frustration felt different. Anger felt different.

Before him, emotion was nothing more than an itch in the back of her skull that passed as quickly as it arose. And now...now she felt like she had an open, festering wound that she couldn't stitch up.

To make matters worse, this was the very first time in her life that she'd ever found herself caring what someone else thought of her. Somehow, her thoughts kept wandering back to the same question: *Will he still love me?*

She had no doubt he'd still follow her. He'd bent the knee and sworn himself to her. That wasn't about to change. She did not question his loyalty to her crown, not even for an instant. But the way he'd bowed his head, unable to look at her...the way he'd heard her tell him she loved him and refused to respond in kind...*Your Majesty...*

Perhaps Killian Grey was no exception to the fickleness that plagued the hearts of most men. Perhaps she'd been wrong about him, thinking he was different, thinking his devotion to be unconditional. The thoughts were barbed thorns stuck in her veins. A weight pressed down on her chest from the inside. Neve knew, even having never felt it before, that it was the weight of heartbreak. Heavy and sharp, it left desolation in its wake.

Beneath the desolation, though, something else rose.

The thing within her. The power. It felt electric, alive, and like it was *prowling* for a fight. It was wicked, cruel, and yet somehow righteous. It seemed to feed on her heartbreak, growing fatter as each sliver of sorrow slashed through her. It rolled and widened like some great tentacled beast from the deep seas. *Stretching.*

Neve welcomed it.

When sadness and her questioning mind became loud, the power in her would answer it with an uncoiling of itself. Instead of trying to suppress it, of fearing it, Neve began to give it space to become the shore against which her mourning and worry would crash, breaking those feelings apart and sending them back to the dark ocean of her heart.

Neve lay sleepless in her bed the night after the argument, and she was overcome with the desire to run to Killian, to find a resolution. A rush of anguish crept in, and Neve felt the hackles of her power rise. Her first instinct was to push it down, but she didn't. She breathed into it and opened herself up to it.

She'd risen from bed and stood in front of the mirror in her room. She watched herself as she let the pressure build and build. Her skin tingled. Her insides felt like crackling, cold fire. Her head felt like it was being crushed between two mountains and then... then there was a release. In the mirror, she saw it happen.

It started in her eyes, faintly. A glow. Somehow warm and cold at the same time. It spread like freckles across her cheeks, down her face and neck, into her hair. Illuminating her from the inside out until her whole body was awash with sparkling light.

Starlight.

Beautiful silvery gold starlight all over her, within her, surrounding her.

The power seemed to know she was watching, seemed to understand how much she liked what she saw. Neve smiled at her reflection. The glow brightened with a gentle pulse. But that pulse was not quite as gentle externally as it had felt internally.

The pulse of power found resistance against the mirror and shattered it in an explosion of a thousand sharply dancing shards.

In shock, Neve stepped back and looked down at herself. The glow was gone. Even more curiously, despite how suddenly and violently the mirror burst apart, she didn't have a single cut on her. The shards were everywhere, all over the room. Stabbed into the walls and floorboards, and stuck in the curtains. But there were no pieces of glass anywhere near her. Looking down at the floor, there seemed to be a perfect circle around where she stood, absent of glass. The power had acted as both a sword and a shield. It was a weapon and protection.

It was then that Neve decided to give the power a space within her.

To give it a home.

The ancient book in her hands now, as she stood surrounded by the comforting quiet and incense scent of the library, held a great deal of lore about Celesta, Goddess of Life and Death. Celesta drew her power from the night sky itself. She would raise her voice and call the stars to arms, like sworn knights. Then she would pull their lethal fire down, down, down into herself and unleash it upon her enemies.

Another story told of a time when she was displeased with the world. The people had become evil with greed, the natural resources were depleted, leaving the most marginalized to starve and die, and the seas began to warm and rise, covering more and more of the land. So Celesta called upon the sky and pulled so much power down that when she released it, she destroyed the whole world. Turned it to ash and dust. Sent it back to the ether.

Celesta then gathered up a few fistfuls of that dust and rolled it between her hands until it became round. Rolling and rolling and pouring her power into it until she created a new world from the ashes of the old one.

Supposedly, that was the world they lived in now.

Goddess of Life and Death.

Wielder of Starlight.

Destroyer of the Old World.

Mother of the New World.

And, somehow, someway, all of this was connected back to Neve.

She knew it was not a coincidence that every depiction of the Goddess' likeness looked like her. Neve and Celesta shared the same face, almost exactly. It also didn't seem to be a coincidence that Neve's power felt like starlight. Unlike the goddess, Neve didn't have to pull it from the sky into herself. It was already *in* her, a part of her. And it likely always had been.

Isolde drifted through the velvet curtains and into the library. Her usual relaxed, mirthful countenance seemed oddly dimmed. Neve watched Sabrina and Oliver stiffen in their seats, both setting their cards down on the table, the game entirely forgotten.

"What happened?" Oliver asked gently.

Isolde's eyes cut to Neve for a brief second, then went back to her friends at the table. "It appears the Cavalry and what's left of the Cadre are beginning to become rather... aggressive in their pursuit of rebels."

Ice crackled up Neve's back from the base of her spine at the mention of the Cadre.

Anger bloomed in Sabrina's eyes. "Burning towns down again?"

Isolde nodded solemnly. "To the west," she hovered over the map spread out on the far end of the table and pointed to a town. Neve moved close to see just as Oliver and Sabrina crowded around them. "Corcoran. Two members of the Cadre and a handful of Mages sacked the village and burned it to the ground."

Neve knew exactly which Cadre members they were. The redhead, Gillis, and Killian's brother, Rory. Former Cadre, now Cavalry, she supposed.

Rory was the worst kind of man. Entitled, without honor, cruel for the sake of making himself feel bigger than he was.

She'd brought him an apple the day they met, away from the rest of the group, and then told him that if she saw him again someday, alone, she'd kill him. That he would go to his grave unremembered. His face had gone pale, and she'd felt his fear at the truth in her words.

Those words were still true today.

"How many survivors?" Oliver asked.

Isolde sank into a chair and released a sigh. "None."

The library went silent and cold.

The power inside Neve stretched.

"They came in the night," Isolde continued quietly, "The Mages shut the town down. Locked families in homes and people in taverns. The Cadre ravaged the village and then set everything on fire. A few people tried to escape, and the Cadre cut them down."

"Bastards," Sabrina snarled.

"Women? Children?" Oliver asked, his eyes wide and his mouth set in a tight line.

Neve knew the answer before it came.

Isolde shook her head. "I'm told..." She cleared her throat. "I'm told there was no mercy shown."

Oliver buried his face in his big hands, and Sabrina placed her hand on his shoulder and squeezed, her eyes bright. Neve could see that Sabrina was trying not to cry; she was shaking with the effort against it. Isolde's face was awash with the most sincere empathy Neve thought she'd ever seen.

Neve committed some dark killings in her time, but she'd never slaughtered innocents. *Children.* The depth of cowardice in those Mages, in Rory, in the Highborns who'd ordered it was unfathomable.

Before the end, Neve would spill their blood with a grin on her lips.

Isolde reached over and took Neve's hand in hers. She looked up at her with gentle, sad eyes. "We need your help," she said.

Something, some little firework, burst inside Neve so suddenly that she nearly stumbled. Oliver and Sabrina's heads lifted, and they looked from Isolde to Neve with surprised yet eager expressions. The way they looked at her, all three of them, the hope suddenly kindling in the sparkle of their eyes, spoke volumes.

They knew.

They knew who she was, what she was.

They knew she was the Woman on the Plains.

They knew she was more than that.

Neve felt her back straighten, her chin lifted, and she brushed her thumb across the soft skin of Isolde's hand, still resting in her own.

"What do you need?" she asked, her voice low and steady.

Isolde's gaze drifted over to the black door in the wall, the one place in the whole library absent of books.

"That door hasn't been opened in... I don't know, maybe centuries. Based on our research, it's supposed to lead to a room that holds important books, artifacts, and weapons. From the time of the gods. Before Nyx was killed. Things that could... help you." That last part was pointed straight at Neve. "And what helps you, will help us."

Neve understood.

"Why hasn't the door been opened?" she asked.

"It will only open for someone worthy. Someone with royal blood," Isolde squeezed Neve's hand. "With gods-blood."

The power inside Neve grinned and sent a sizzle of recognition through her veins.

Isolde smiled softly. "Are you ready to tell us your name?"

Everything in her warmed with something akin to joy and purpose. And she found herself wishing Killian was with her, to see this, to exist in this moment with her, so that one day they could look back on it together and remember the turning point of this whole story. But he wasn't with her. So she took a deep breath and took in this moment for herself.

With a smile, she said, "My name is Neve. Neve D'Aeth Lyra."

40

Neve stood before the black door and felt a deep humming coming from the other side. The door itself was old and heavy, made of ancient wood so dark it looked like it had been burned black. In the center of the door, there was a burnished gold knocker in the shape of a star. The metal looked worn as if it had been touched by many hands over many years.

"This door has never opened for anyone," Isolde said, standing at Neve's side.

"And you think it will open for me?" Neve asked.

Isolde smiled. "I think you can do a great many things that others can't."

Neve would never be able to get used to the sincere kindness Isolde offered her. And she was grateful for it.

She reached out and put her hand on the knocker. It was warm to the touch, and the power inside her purred. She rapped the knocker against the door once. A deep, resounding noise. Out of the corner of her eye, she saw both Sabrina and Oliver flinch at the sound. It was followed by a rustling. Turning her head, Neve saw the books on the shelves vibrating gently, almost dancing in their spots.

But the door didn't open.

She knocked again. The sound was louder this time, and the books on their shelves shook harder. Next to her, Isolde was bouncing slightly on her toes, excited.

"Try once more. Third time's a charm, they say," Isolde mused, unable to hide the joyful grin spreading on her face.

Neve took a breath and knocked one more time.

There came a great *sigh*. Inside her, around her, from her friends, and behind the door. The books went silent. Neve heard Oliver let out a shaking breath while Sabrina whispered: "*Holy shit.*"

The door creaked and groaned.

And it opened.

The scents of old leather and seawater wafted out of the room behind the door. It somehow smelled like home. Neve's skin was buzzing, and her heart was a steady, hard thump behind her ribs. She took a step inside, and when she saw what was there, she could have fallen to her knees in awe.

The ceiling was high, domed marble, and the walls and floors shone with the same stone. Similar to the library, the walls were built-in shelves, but instead of books, the shelves displayed artifacts, weapons, and scrolls. Ancient things. In the center of the room was a pool filled with gently rolling, crystal clear water. The pool floor, stairs, and sides were covered in beautiful dark blue and gold mosaic tiles that came together as a picture of the night sky.

"Isolde?" Neve asked. "Tell me about this place."

"Of course, my Queen," Isolde replied. Neve paused, but Isolde said it so naturally and casually as if she'd always been saying it. As if it wasn't new information. Perhaps it wasn't, perhaps she'd always known. Isolde led the way into the room, and Neve followed.

"This place is known as the Chamber of the Gods. It's a place reserved only for those who share your bloodline. It holds history, legacy, maybe even magic."

"And the pool?"

"It's said to hold healing waters. Gifted to your forebears by the god of the sea."

Neve crouched down near the edge of the pool and dipped her fingers in the water. It was warm, hot even, and fizzed around her hand as she dragged it through the bubbles. It made her skin tingle in a way that felt like comfort. She imagined that if she had a wound, these waters could indeed help to heal it. She stood. Instead of wiping her hand dry, she spread the water up her arms like a salve. It left her skin feeling silky and warm.

"You keep speaking of the gods and gods-blood," Neve stated.

"There is a reason the Lyras have always been favored by the gods, why Eodia itself was favored by the gods before Nyx was killed. It's because the Lyras *are* gods. Well, part gods, at least." Isolde explained.

The information was a lot to take in, but at the same time, Neve was not shocked. It felt true, it felt right. As if this was the missing piece to the puzzle all along. The forgotten chapter in all of the stories she'd spent her life reading.

Isolde touched her shoulder tenderly and smiled. "You are descended from Celesta herself. It is the reason the women in your family have been so powerful and such effective rulers. It's also what led to the inevitable demise of your family line. The half-brothers were also part-god. But not as significantly as Nyx. They had no true power, only the gift of long life. They could not stand that Nyx was the one who was blessed with the power and favor of the gods and that they were left virtually impotent. That's why they killed her. They assumed, wrongly, that with her death, her power would be given to them. Instead, the opposite happened. The entire kingdom was cut off from the gods' favor."

Neve nodded, listening, while her eyes roamed the shelves around her, taking it all in. Shiny weapons gleamed in the dim light and were displayed uncluttered and with reverence. As she scanned the items in the chamber, her attention was pulled to an alcove where a blue velvet pillow sat. Atop the pillow was a golden crown adorned with a scattering of diamonds and eight spikes topped with the shape of stars.

Isolde followed Neve's gaze to the crown, then looked back at her. "Everything in this room belongs to you. Including that."

Without a thought, Neve drifted over to the alcove and stood before the crown. She ran her fingers across the velvet of the pillow it sat on; there wasn't a speck of dust on the soft fabric, despite having sat in this room for centuries at the very least. She moved her hands up, gently brushing the gold, feeling the diamonds against her palms, the sharpness of the stars atop the spikes against her fingertips. The moment felt intimate and pure, and within it, Neve knew without a shadow of a doubt that it was hers.

"Would you like to wear it?" Isolde asked quietly.

Neve shook her head. "No. Not yet."

As she turned, her eyes fell on something in the back corner of the chamber, something shiny and silver leaning up against the wall. Neve moved closer and felt her heart stutter in her chest. A beautiful shield, in its center was a familiar knotwork, the sigil of House Grey. A strange sense of both pride and mourning filled her as she knelt and traced the knotwork with her fingers.

"You said that everything in this room belongs to me. But this doesn't. This belongs to someone else," Neve said quietly.

Isolde knelt beside her. "Yes. But who it belongs to is your choice."

Neve nodded. "I know who I choose."

~

Killian Grey was drunk. He sat at the bar in the basement of The Bloody Fist, wallowing and slugging back glasses of whiskey like they were water and he was dying of thirst.

Anything to make his mind stop racing. Days. It had been days since Neve came to his room and told him what happened with the Highborns. Killian regretted every moment of that conversation. But he particularly regretted the way it ended. She'd told him she loved him. And he'd been too stupid and stubborn and hurt to say it back.

Gods, he was an asshole.

Of course, he loved her. He'd loved her the moment he first saw her, and he would go to his grave loving her. Longer. Forever. Yet he'd let her leave him that night without any reassurance.

And now...

Now he had no idea if she would ever come back to him.

His mind kept going back to the mark on her neck. How *they'd* touched her. He knew that it hadn't been easy for her, that she hadn't *wanted* their hands and mouths on her. But she'd done it to get close to them. Allowing them to violate her body in ways that made Killian's blood boil with rage. And instead of being there for her, supporting her, being the man she needed in that moment, he'd been selfish. Selfish and stupid, and he'd ruined it all.

Twice now, he'd run towards the Capital to go hunt her down, drop to his knees, and beg forgiveness. Twice now, he'd made it halfway before remembering that he couldn't. She'd told him explicitly to never come to the Capital to find her. For his own sake and the sake of her mission. He couldn't do that to her.

So, here he was. Wallowing and whiskey.

A large presence slid into the seat next to him. Turning his head, Killian expected to see Leo, but gray hair and a grizzled, scarred face met him instead.

Arran.

"What are you doing here?" Killian asked, taking a blurry glance around the basement to make sure no one was paying attention to them.

"I could ask you the same thing, lad," Arran replied, eyeing the drink in front of Killian and the row of empty glasses on the other side of him.

"Laying low."

Arran leaned in. "You should lie a little lower."

"Why's that?"

"Thornkeep is of particular interest right now. To the Cavalry and Highborns."

Even through the haze, Killian knew what that meant. His stomach lurched. "Rebels?"

Arran nodded. "Things are moving quickly. There are rumors of some... woman." Killian's spine stiffened. "Some woman that's got the rebels all excited. They seem to think she's important, the key to gaining traction. It's as if they forget who they're fighting against. There is no traction to gain against the Highborns. There is only obedience or death."

"Perhaps these rebels would prefer death over blind obedience," Killian said, knowing full well that he should keep his mouth shut, but his tongue was loose and his patience for bullshit was thin.

"Dangerous words, lad," Arran said through clenched teeth, his eyes wide, not with shock, Killian realized, but with fear. His old friend, this man with a body covered in battle scars, was afraid.

"You can't tell me that you sleep well at night, knowing all the things we've done. In their name. Out of fear of what they'd do."

"Killian," Arran said in a whisper, leaning close. "You can't talk like this. Not to anyone. Not even to me. You know why I'm here in Thornkeep. It's my job to take down any threats to the regime."

Killian leveled his gaze at his friend and raised an eyebrow. "Do you think I'm a threat?"

Arran searched Killian's face like he'd never seen him before, like the man who'd once been his commander, his brother in arms, was now a stranger. Truthfully, if Arran felt that way, he wouldn't be wrong. Killian wasn't the same man anymore. His family's death changed him, and prison changed him. Neve had changed him. He *was* a stranger to his friend.

Something cold crossed Arran's features. A look that Killian was deeply intimate with. The calm calculation of a seasoned warrior. A killer's consideration.

"Are you?" he asked.

Killian turned toward his old friend and looked him right in the eyes. "Not to you."

A breath huffed out of Arran's nose, and he shook his head. "What are you playing at?"

"Not playing," Killian said, swallowing down the last of his whiskey.

"Listen to me," Arran urged, looking around the basement again with increasing concern. "You need to be careful. The Highborns are sweeping across the Island, destroying whole villages over just *whispers* of rebellion."

"See, that's the thing, Arran," Killian interrupted, rage crackling in his chest. "It's not the Highborns destroying these towns. Killing innocents for the sins of one or two people. It's not the Highborns getting their hands bloody, is it?"

Arran faltered and looked down at the bar.

"No," Killian continued. "No, it's men like you. Like Gillis. Like my godsdamned brother."

Without looking up, Arran said, "This used to be your life, too. You're no better."

"You're right. I'm no better." And he wasn't. Killian knew the wretchedness of his soul, the dark deeds he'd committed. He knew the blame for what happened to his family rested as much on his shoulders as it did on the shoulders of the Mages and Cavalry who'd killed them. But not as much as the Highborns.

Never as much as them.

The only thing he could do to atone would be to work against them now.

For the rest of his life.

Even if it killed him.

Arran stood. He hesitated and then seemed to think better of himself and clapped his hand down on Killian's shoulder.

"Be careful, Killian," he said. "Please."

The light was low, but Killian was almost certain he saw the gleam of tears in Arran's eyes. His friend squeezed his shoulder, then turned on his heel and made his way through the crowd.

A heavy stone of grief and unease settled in Killian's stomach. As he watched Arran leave, he got the sick feeling that this would be the last time they would meet as friends. The next time they saw each other, they could very well be enemies.

41

Balor's teeth grazed Neve's collarbone as he slipped the sleeve of her dress off her shoulder. His breath smelled of old, dried rose petals. Stale and musky like a tomb. She wanted to cringe, she wanted to reach into his chest and yank out his still-beating heart and sink her teeth into it. But she forced her face and body to relax, feigning ecstasy while she screamed inside.

Cael stood near the fireplace, watching.

He leaned an elbow on the mantle as his other hand crept closer and closer to the waistband of his pants.

Neve tracked the movement and, as Balor's tongue swept up the side of her neck, she gave Cael a sultry smile. As if she wanted it. As if she wanted them.

"How does she taste, brother?" Cael asked, his voice rough.

Balor just moaned.

Neve closed her eyes and imagined all the ways she would hurt them. How she might like to sever their spines so that when she brought her wrath down upon them, they'd be paralyzed, unable to do anything but watch as she flayed the skin from their bones. How she might like to slit their throats and watch their blood stain the carpet. How she might like to unleash her power on them, just to see what damage it could do.

This was her third experience spending time with them. It was always the same. It was always, "My dear, my dear, come in from the cold." Then they'd bring her to the great room, start a fire, offer her a drink laced with poison, wait a few minutes while she played-acted the effects of the white opium, and then they'd have their fun.

It never went further than the use of their greedy hands and mouths. Which made Neve wonder if they could even perform with their cocks. They were old, after all. Very old. Much older than they appeared. The idea of their impotence was a comfort and a weapon she could use later.

But.

Their hands and mouths were enough.

When they touched her, it felt like spiders crawling across her skin.

So, she spent the time pretending to be half-asleep and dumb with lust while she daydreamed about their demise. Each time her mind wandered to Killian and the look on his face when he saw the mark on her neck, she'd shut it down so fast it nearly made her dizzy.

She couldn't think about that.

She couldn't think about him.

Not while the Highborns touched her.

Not when she was so close.

Because, as it turned out, when they believed Neve to be swimming under the effect of the poison they gave her, they talked. And what they revealed made all of this worth it.

Just as she knew it would.

At length, they spoke of their deep-seated hatred of the Lyra bloodline. They didn't seem to like the idea of women in power all that much. They talked of Nyx in particular, as if they knew her, laughing about the feeble way she met her end. The way they described it... It was as if they'd been there and committed to memory how her blood had flowed.

They spoke of the rebellion, the scourge as they called it, and their plan to burn down every village in Eodia until they snuffed them out. They were accustomed to total dominance, and that sovereignty was being threatened. The Highborns seemed to take offense that anyone would dare challenge the way they ruled. Supposedly, they planted spies amongst some rebel factions, which is how they decided where to send the Cavalry and what was left of the Cadre.

Above it all, they were planning something. Something big. Something they seemed to think would break the rebellion in half and end it all in one fell swoop.

"You seem a little tired, my dear," Balor murmured, clumsily shoving his hand down the bodice of her dress. *Groping.* Cael chuckled darkly across the room.

Neve imagined herself pulling out each one of Balor's teeth with her bare hands, one after the other after the other, until there was nothing left but a useless, bloody maw.

Instead, she lolled her head as if she were nodding off. "Yes," she mumbled. "I think I should go home."

"So soon?" Cael asked.

"If that's all right?" she responded, slurring her words.

"Of course, of course," Balor said. Kneading her flesh with his clammy fingers.

"But–" Cael protested.

Everything inside Neve stilled.

They'd let her leave without question twice now. Would tonight be different?

"...I haven't gotten my turn with her tonight."

"You chose to watch, brother," Balor replied nonchalantly. "Besides, the ball is tomorrow night."

Interesting.

"What ball?" Neve asked sleepily.

"Oh, silly us," Balor said, kissing her cheek. "Have we forgotten to invite you?"

"I'd like to be invited." She forced a giddy smile, forced excitement to sparkle in her heavy-lidded eyes.

"All of the most important people in the Capital will be there. Of course, we'd love for you to come," Cael replied, the jealous impertinence in his voice from a moment ago was gone, replaced with playful arrogance.

The wheels in Neve's head were turning. This could be her chance. To get the confirmation she needed to move ahead with the next part of her plan. To weaken their defenses.

To finish it.

To end them.

"Wear something pretty," Balor said with a grin.

42

There was the scent of fire and ash. Of blood. The sound of screaming and swords.

Killian woke with a jolt. It was deep into the dark middle of the night. He'd taken too much to drink again and passed out in his bed. He hadn't even taken off his boots. For a moment, a sweet, precious moment, he thought the smell of death and the wailing had come from his restless dreams.

And then he opened his eyes.

A wild orange glow lit his room from outside the dirty window. Woozy, he stood and stumbled over to look outside.

Thornkeep was on fire.

Killian braced his hand on the wall and blinked a few times to be sure he wasn't seeing things.

Then he moved.

He grabbed hold of his rucksack and began throwing his meager belongings into it. A dirty shirt. A book. A heavy pouch of the coins he'd saved from his fights. As he tore through the room, his hand landed on a scrap of silk and lace. Neve's slip. The one she'd let him keep. The one he kept under his pillow. Killian paused long enough to bring the cool fabric to his face and inhale. It still smelled like her. His heart lurched as he stuffed it into his bag.

He threw on his jacket and armed himself with all the weapons he had, strapping his longsword to his back. He knew what this was. Arran had come to warn him the night before.

Thornkeep is of particular interest, he'd said.

Fuck.

With a knife in hand, Killian opened his door and moved out into the hall. It was quiet. But he could still hear the muffled screaming coming from outside. Keeping his eyes open and his wits about him, he moved quickly down the staircase and into the tavern on the first floor of the inn.

His feet nearly slipped out from under him. When he looked down, he could see why. Blood. Thick, warm blood pooled across the tavern floor, under his boots. Looking up, he took in the state of the tavern.

Death. Nothing but death.

Bodies were strewn everywhere. Sliced and ripped apart. Patrons and barmaids, young and old, men and women. All dead, nothing left but meat. It was so, so quiet. The dead were all citizens of Thornkeep; there wasn't a Cavalryman among them. Someone had come into the bar and laid waste to everyone in it before a single person could make a move against the slaughter. There had to be at least twenty or thirty bodies. It seemed like heavy odds against a handful of soldiers.

Unless...Unless they'd brought Mages.

Kilian's shock was fading, leaving frothing anguish and rising rage in its stead. He moved toward the tavern entrance, carefully stepping over body after body. He pushed at the door. It didn't budge. As he pressed his hands against the wood, flames erupted along the walls of the pub, all along the perimeter.

Just like every town before this, they were going to burn it to the ground.

Great black plumes of smoke rose from the growing fire, and it climbed up his nostrils and down his throat. It burned his eyes. He shoved at the door again. Nothing. The door was either blocked from the outside or sealed by magic.

He turned back toward the staircase, thinking maybe he could jump out the window of his room upstairs. But fire roared to life as if fueled by an accelerant, engulfing the stairs instantly.

He took a breath, and smoke filled his lungs. A violent cough ripped through his chest, choking him. The heat of the fire licked his skin, making him sweat. He had a feeling the smoke would suffocate him before the blaze burned him alive.

No.

No, he would not die.

Not today.

The staircase collapsed and splintered in a rain of sparks, folding in on itself and sinking. This had to be magic. No natural fire could move this quickly or this completely.

Killian faced the door again. He thought of all the people, the families, on the other side of the door that needed his help. He thought about Neve and how if he died, he'd never have a chance to beg forgiveness and tell her he loved her over and over again.

He thought of Leo and his pregnant wife and their little boys.

His blood went cold.

Good gods, that's why they were here. They knew about Leo and Kat. The Cavalry, the Mages, Arran. They were coming for Leo and Kat. The rest of the village was just collateral damage.

His throat felt like it was lined with broken glass. He couldn't take a breath. But the righteous fury that filled him was stronger. *He* was stronger.

Killian steeled himself and reared back, throwing his foot into the door with a mighty kick. The force ricocheted up this leg, banging through his knee. It did not open. But it shuddered. Gritting his teeth, baring them like an animal, he kicked again, feeling the wood groan between the force that kept it shut and the force of him. With a growl, he kicked one more time, and it moved.

Blessed fresh air flooded into his lungs as the door exploded from its hinges and launched out into the town square.

Killian took a wheezing breath and then another. Without thinking, his hand reached back and drew his sword.

And then Killian Grey, having broken the Mage's magic with strength alone, walked out into the night.

Cavalrymen in pristine white were dragging screaming citizens through the square. Mages, hidden in their brown cloaks off in the shadows, worked their magic quietly, like cowardly little snakes. Buildings spontaneously burst into flame. Women and children were banging on second-floor windows, weeping and wailing, as fire took their homes while they were trapped inside.

The wind outside was cold. It was snowing.

Soot clung to the drying sweat on Killian's skin. With his sword in one hand and a knife in the other, he moved as smoothly and quietly as death through the chaos of the town. A flash of white sped toward him. His body moved instinctively. His sword arced through the air until his blade met flesh and bone and tore through it. He was so fast that he didn't even see the face of the Cavalry soldier he killed until the man's head separated from his body and rolled to a stop against Killian's feet.

There was a shout, and another soldier came for him. Killian's sword moved as an extension of his arm and easily slid into the man's chest. He pushed it through the other side and stood nose-to-nose with the soldier as the light in his eyes went dim and then out completely.

This is what he was made for.

Killing.

He knew he needed to get to Leo's house, and fast. But looking around at the crowded and burning town square, his conscience was screaming at him. To do something. He couldn't put out the fires. He couldn't save everyone. But his mind flashed to the battle he and Neve fought on the plains. When he'd been rendered useless by the Mages, leaving her to fight the Cavalry alone. Neve, in her brilliance, had known the only way to win was to take out the Mages first, to make the magic stop.

Men were easier to kill when they didn't have magic to hide behind.

Killian slunk into the shadows and smoke of a smoldering building, his eyes on the four brown-cloaked figures near the tree line. His attention was focused and locked on every movement they made. The muttering of their mouths, the grasping of their fingers in the empty air. He was silent as he prowled toward them.

It was over before they even knew he'd come for them.

He moved with strength and grace, one arm brandishing the sword and the other slicing with the knife. The four bodies were left in a pile at his feet. There would be no more fires, at least not from the spells crafted by these Mages.

But he knew there were more throughout the village.

He'd find them all.

But first, he had to find his friend.

Killian broke into a sprint and tore through the village, putting down any white-clad soldier that stood in his way. He left a trail of death in his wake. His body felt strong, and his mind was clear. Any traces of the night's binge drinking were long gone, replaced with determination and the instinct to fight. And the sharp, acrid bite of panic.

His heart pounded heavily.

He hoped he wasn't too late.

Skidding to a halt, he paused behind a vacant storefront near Leo's house and peered around the corner. The cottage wasn't on fire. Yet. But it was surrounded by a handful of Mages and the Cavalry. And...

Killian's heart stopped.

Arran.

Three Cavalry soldiers held Leo back, and Arran stood before him with the point of his longsword digging into his friend's chest. Even from a distance, Killian could see the terror and desperation painted across Leo's sharp features.

There was no sign of Kat or the children.

Mages stood at the threshold of the cottage facing the closed door, moving their hands and muttering their incantations. Leo was struggling against the men who held him, face wet with tears.

"Take me! Take me! Let them go!" his friend screamed.

The man was begging. Begging for death in exchange for his family. But where were they? Had the Cavalry taken them? Killian's eyes searched the surroundings, but he could find no trace of them.

"We're going to make you watch. So you can see how the choices you made caused this. That their blood is on your hands," the soldier behind Leo sneered.

"Let me finish this," Arran said through clenched teeth. "The orders were to take him out, not torture him."

The Cavalryman seemed to glare at Arran. "You follow *my* orders."

Arran said nothing.

Killian's blood heated, and a frantic sense of fear rose in his throat. Flames came alive in front of the cottage, and Leo let out a strangled roar, thrashing against the men holding him back. The Cavalry soldier, the one seemingly in charge, threw a foot into the back of Leo's legs, sending him to his knees. Without effort, Arran shifted his grip on his weapon, the blade still pinned to Leo's heaving, screaming chest.

That's when Killian saw it.

The small hand on the kitchen window. The mop of dark hair atop a head barely tall enough to look out the glass. Leo's youngest was in the house. Horror clenched Killian's guts. He watched as a hand pulled the boy back from the window. It was Kat, her pretty face set in a hard line, eyes wild with fury and fear. She had an ax in her hands and, with a sneer on her lips, she thrust the weapon into the window with strong, capable arms.

Magic sparked at the contact. Glass that should have shattered remained whole. Even from where he stood, Killian could see the color drain from her face with the realization that she and her children were trapped.

Leo saw his wife in the window. He was weeping, thrashing, his face was a red mess of tears and spit, and terror.

If Killian went to Leo first, the Mages would kill the family trapped in the house. If he went to the house first, Arran and the Cavalry would kill Leo. He couldn't do both, not at the same time.

There was only one thing he could do.

Killian Grey sauntered out of the shadows with as much swagger as he could muster and loudly tutted his tongue in dramatic disapproval.

"Tsk, I thought the Cavalry was supposed to be tough. And here you are, using Mages to do your dirty work."

Everyone stopped. Even the Mages. The fire at the edges of the cottage banked and slowed. Recognition sparked in the eyes of the Cavalry soldiers. Arran looked like he'd seen a ghost. Leo's shoulders sagged with what looked like tentative relief.

"Killian, please. My family–" Leo rasped. The soldier in charge sank the tip of his boot into Leo's stomach, doubling him over.

"The great Killian Grey," the soldier snarled with sarcasm.

Killian sketched a mocking bow. "In the flesh."

"The Highborns would *love* to have a word with you."

"Well, sounds like you'd certainly be a hero if you brought me to them, wouldn't you?" Killian stretched his neck, popping the muscles.

Something akin to greed lit up the soldier's eyes. "Perhaps."

Sheathing his weapons, Killian smirked, then held his arms out to his sides, an offering. "Why don't you let this nice man and his family go? And I'll come with you willingly."

"No," Leo protested.

Arran shook his head, eyes wide.

At this moment, Killian didn't care what Arran thought. Or what Leo said. All he cared about was getting this catastrophe to stop before the cottage truly went up in flames.

The soldier raised his eyebrows. "It would be that easy? I have a hard time believing you'd turn yourself in so willingly. You know what awaits you if you come with us to the Highborns. You're wanted for high treason."

Killian glanced at the Mages, who seemed frozen, waiting for a command. "You have Mages. I know you can have them weave a spell to keep me docile as a kitten. I'm all yours if you let this family go."

"And if I don't?"

Lethal calm flooded into his voice, into his eyes.

"Then you'd have to go up against me," Killian gave the soldier a once-over from head to toe and chuckled cruelly. "And you'd be dead before you drew your weapon."

Anger flushed the soldier's cheeks.

Good.

Killian made a show of looking around. "Everyone is waiting for you to make a choice here, boy. What's it gonna be?"

"I think I want both. I want you *and* I want them," the soldier said.

"You want death, then."

The soldier smirked. "I'm not a fool. I know I'm not a match for you," he drew his sword and pointed it at Arran. "But he is."

Killian's heart jumped to his throat. He worked to make sure his anxiety didn't show on his face when he looked at Arran.

The soldier took a step around Leo, grabbed a handful of hair from behind, and rested his blade against his throat. "I'll hang on to *Daddy* here, make him watch his family turn to ash. Arran can deal with you."

And, with that witless command, his oldest friend advanced on him.

Bile rose to his throat as Killian drew his sword. They circled each other. Prowling with the grace of bodies that were meant for this, bodies that had fought beside each other for years. Killian knew that even Arran was no match for him. But what the Cavalry soldier was hedging his bets on was how hard it would be for Killian to make the first move, to draw first blood against his friend's flesh.

And in that assumption, the soldier was right.

"Walk away," Arran said in a quiet voice that only Killian could hear. "Run, and don't look back."

Killian shook his head.

"No," he replied with a commanding finality that brought a wet sheen to Arran's pleading eyes.

Shifting his sword in his weathered hand, balancing and re-balancing the weight, Arran clenched his teeth.

"I don't want to do this," he whispered.

Killian squared his shoulders and lifted his chin. "Then don't."

"I don't have a choice."

Rage and impatience began to blacken the edges of Killian's vision. He swung his sword at Arran's head, arcing it in a lazy way that he knew his friend would be able to block. The move brought them closer together. Killian searched his friend's eyes, searching for honor and integrity. Searching for the love between men who were not born as a family but had become brothers through the chaos and mournful horror of the lives they'd lived together.

"You have a choice," Killian whispered. "I was once your commander. Not too long ago. Whose commands are you going to follow tonight, Arran? His?" Killian cut a glance at the Cavalry soldier before pinning his heavy gaze back on Arran's face. "Or mine?"

"They'll kill me," Arran bargained softly, shamefully.

Killian's lip curled over his teeth, and he knew how he looked, like rage and fire and blood. Like a killer. "You think I'm going to leave a single witness?"

The night brightened with a burst of new flame.

The Mages were back to work.

Killian was out of time.

Panic fueled his next words. "I need you *now*. I need your answer *now*. Or I swear to all the gods above I will empty your throat onto the fucking ground, friend or no."

Realization settled into Arran's features, his eyes went cold, and his jaw tensed. Killian had made his choice. And he was choosing someone, something else, above the blooded bond that forged their friendship long ago.

"I'll follow you. Tonight. One last time," Arran said.

The implication in those words was clear.

They were friends tonight, but this was the end of it.

There was screaming coming from inside the cottage. Kat and the children. It elicited new roars from Leo.

The greater good.

It was worth it.

It had to be.

Killian and Arran moved as one, sliding through the snowy winter night like a furious wind. The Cavalry was not expecting, nor were they prepared for two Cadre warriors to rain violence down upon them. But that's exactly what happened.

Killian went for the one in charge first. He moved too quickly for the soldier to track his movements. In the space of a breath, Killian was behind him, fisting his hair much like the Cavalryman was doing to Leo.

"Nice try. You almost had me," Killian hissed in his ear before dragging his sword across the tender skin of the man's neck. The soldier made a desperate gurgling sound before the life left him, and he dropped to the ground, coming to his final resting place in a puddle of his own blood.

Arran thrust his sword into the gut of the second soldier, digging it in deep and twisting the blade. The third soldier dropped his hold on Leo, drew his weapon, and slashed out toward Killian. The blade skimmed across Killian's forearm, but it was no more than a scratch. Growling, Killian moved and sliced his sword down with one hand, cutting into the soldier's chest and down into his abdomen.

Killian, covered in hot blood that didn't belong to him, looked down on Leo, who was still on his knees. He offered his friend his hand. Gratitude was raw on Leo's face as he took Killian's hand and rose to his feet. Leo took a sword from the pile of dead Cavalry and, with a snarl, stalked toward the fire-wielding Mages.

Killian and Arran followed.

Unlike the soldiers, the Mages knew they were coming.

43

Killian felt a tingle that started at his toes. Immediately, he knew what was about to happen. The three Mages were going to paralyze them, make them stand and watch as the cottage burned down. Killian kept walking toward the Mages. Each step became heavier, like trudging through molasses or quicksand.

"What is this?" Arran asked.

"Keep moving, keep moving until you can't," Killian said, the heaviness spreading up his shins, making his knees suddenly feel like rusted metal, his thighs like boulders.

"Fuck," Leo ground out.

Killian managed to turn his head to see that Leo was stuck; his whole body had gone immobile. The man's eyes were wild and desperate. The veins in his neck bulged with the strain of his effort against the magic. They were so close. Within spitting distance of the Mages and the cottage. The screaming inside the house went on and on.

Quietly, Killian was thankful for that. When the screaming stopped... that's when he'd know he failed.

He just had to reach the Mages. If Killian could do that, he could end this. But each step forward was tiny and took every ounce of strength he had. He was sweating, shaking.

"I can't," Arran groaned. Killian looked over, and sure enough, the huge warrior was frozen in place. "I'm so sorry." Arran's eyes were filled with the tragedy of failure.

Right, then.

Just him.

Grunting, Killian took another step, barely able to lift his foot. He felt his hips locking up, the rippling muscles of his torso tightening and trembling. Every bit of him was fighting against the magic. Straining and pushing. It was painful.

The Mages stood there, working their spells beneath the shadows of their brown cloaks. The cottage was engulfed in a blaze that now raged so violently that the clearing was bright as daylight. Killian took another step, his ears fixed on the screaming coming from inside the house. It fueled him.

He would not let that woman and her sons die. He couldn't.

His memory flashed to his cottage.

His wife and children.

Not again.

The pain of fighting the magic was all-consuming, but Killian Grey did not relent.

He thought back to the mantra he'd repeated when he was released from prison, when he'd confronted his empty home for the first time.

I am Killian Grey. I yield to nothing. I will not be afraid.

He took a step.

I will not be afraid.

I yield to nothing.

I am Killian Grey.

Another step.

Gods, he was so *close*.

"Please don't stop," this came from behind him. A plea from Leo. "Please."

Killian clenched his teeth so hard he thought he would crack a molar. Sweat poured down his brow, washing other people's blood into his eyes. He blinked and took another minuscule step. The pain was immense. It felt like his body was tearing apart, tendon by tendon.

But he did not yield.

He took a breath and closed his eyes. Strength. He needed more strength. And with that thought, Neve's image blossomed to life in his mind. Neve, whispering "shhh" as she gutted a thief in Hythe. Neve, washing in the river of the Dark Forest. Neve, walking across the battlefield like the queen of death, heads of the Cavalry in her hands. Neve, crushing her mouth to his that first time.

Killian opened his eyes. The magic weighed down his arms and climbed up the column of his neck, making it harder to breathe.

"I will not be afraid," he said out loud.

The Mage in the center of the group gave a rotted-tooth grin.

His whole body was betraying him; tears of pain and exertion stung the corners of his eyes. Behind him, Leo was sobbing. The screams in the cottage were becoming quieter.

This was it. There wasn't any time left. Fighting a scream, he moved, one foot and then the other.

"I yield to nothing," he cursed, throat locking up halfway through the words. He was almost there, almost.

There was a loud crack as the flames licked up to the roof of the cottage, sinking the corner of it in on itself. The roof would soon completely cave in. Leo's family would be crushed to death instead of burned alive.

He knew he would die for this. He would lay his life down for this family if it meant getting them out.

He had to.

He hadn't been able to save his own family.

He had to save this one.

The pain alone was enough to nearly kill him, magic coursing like poison in his stiff bones. The Mages were just out of reach...

And then they weren't.

Somehow, Killian managed to take that final excruciating step. Somehow, he raised his arm. Somehow, his fingers grasped.

The center Mage's pulsing throat was in his hand, dewy eyes going wide with shock, wide with the knowledge that death had come at last. Shaking, Killian squeezed. Suddenly, it was easier to move. So, Killian bared his teeth and lifted the Mage off his feet by the throat.

"I am Killian *fucking* Grey," he growled and snapped the Mage's neck.

With his other hand, the hand that brandished the sword, he made a sweeping and lethal thrust, cutting through the other two Mages. They slumped to the ground in a messy death.

The magic was gone, and his body felt brutalized, yet Killian could move freely again. A sweet and welcome mercy.

But, he didn't have time to revel in it. Didn't have time to think about how he'd done the impossible. He needed to get Kat and the children out of the smoldering house.

He laid down his weapons and shrugged off his rucksack.

Without thinking, without looking behind him to see where Leo and Arran were, Killian kicked down the front door of the cottage. It turned to cinder as it fell, but Killian didn't have time to pay it any mind.

He launched himself into the fiercely burning home.

Smoke assaulted his mouth like a lover's tongue, eager and relentless. The cottage was so hot, he could feel the leather he wore shrink against his body. Killian moved to where he remembered the kitchen was, to where he could hear Kat screaming her children's names over and over.

"Henry! Jasper!" Her voice was hoarse and wrecked.

Through the orange haze, Killian found her. She stood holding onto the kitchen counter with one hand and her pregnant belly with the other. She saw his shadow amidst the smoke and squinted until he came into view, and then her watering eyes widened.

"My boys! Find my boys!" she begged.

Wordlessly, Killian scooped Kat up into his arms and carried her toward the empty maw that was once their front door. She cursed and screamed at him, clawed at his neck and arms, and fought against him.

"Not me! Find them! Find *them*!" she roared. Killian took it all, let her pummel him with fists and fingernails, and moved as fast as he could out of the cottage and into the clearing.

Killian's heart was a hammer against his ribs, his lungs were full of soot. Leo ran at them, screaming words Killian couldn't hear. He could hear nothing save for the pounding in his head and the quieting screams of the two little boys still in the house. He pushed Kat into Leo's waiting arms, and Leo clutched his wife with the aggression of a man possessed.

Kat didn't notice. She turned in Leo's arms and lunged for Killian, rage and a mother's violent love twisting her soft face into something deadly and terrifying. She was wild with it. Feral with fear. Growling words at Killian that he didn't have time for.

He took her face in his dirty hands and looked her in the eyes. She must have seen it on his face- the honesty, the determination, the truth that he'd die to make this better- because she stopped, chest heaving for breath.

"I will find them. Do you understand?" Killian rasped. "I promise."

Killian filled his lungs with as much clean air as he could and ran back into the cottage. The heat of the fire was a brutal wall that he had to move past. The house was a cacophony of crackling flame, groaning wood, and tiny screams. His focus narrowed to the sound of those screams. He followed them. Past the kitchen, to the right, down a short hall. He could see nothing but fire and smoke.

There was a sound like a falling tree in the forest, and then a ceiling beam came crashing down above him. He moved out of the way as fast as he could, but not fast enough. Some edge of the beam collided with his back and sent him to his knees. His spine was burning. Killian opened his mouth to cry out in pain, but no sound came. Instead, his mouth filled with smoke, and his lungs withered against it. It was choking him.

He crawled toward the sound of the children.

Crawled across the burning floorboards on his hands and knees.

Killian turned into a small room where the sounds of crying were louder. And there they were. Henry and Jasper, red-faced and huddled together. Holding each other and wailing. Killian's heart faltered. He dug his hands into the wall and pulled himself to his feet. Despite not being able to breathe, despite the pain, he stood.

"Come here," he managed to say, his voice a ghost in his throat.

He held his arms out to the boys, gesturing madly with his hands for them to come to him. They did, without a moment's hesitation. Killian crouched down, and they ran into his arms. He held them close and picked them up, one in each arm, pressed against his chest.

"Don't let go of me, no matter what. Okay?" He said. Killian felt both of them nod, then he drew in all the strength he had left and ran.

He put all his trust in his legs to carry him. He could hear and feel the cottage crumbling to ash around him. He could feel his body burning. But most of all, he could feel the two small boys in his arms, shuddering and clinging to him, burying their faces in his neck.

So, Killian moved. Killian ran.

He leapt over fallen beams and trails of flame.

He moved.

He kept moving until the threshold of the doorway was beneath the melting leather of his boots. He kept moving until the cold night air sliced like knives across his too-hot skin. He kept moving until he collapsed in front of Leo and Kat, with their children, alive, in his arms.

Kat fell to her knees, and Leo followed. They put their arms around their boys, around Killian. The words coming out of their mouths were wet with weeping.

All Killian could do was sit there, trying to find his breath, trying not to pass out from pain and exhaustion and smoke suffocation. Distantly, he felt Kat pawing at his face.

"You saved us," she sobbed. That brought him out of his survival-focused daze. He looked at her. "You saved us," she said again.

Emotion overcame him like a mighty tidal wave. He looked at Kat's face, at Leo's. Their wordless and absolute gratitude was plain to see. He looked down at the boys who'd crawled from his arms into their parents' laps. Then he looked back at the cottage as it became nothing but a heap of blackness collapsing in on itself.

He'd done it.

He'd done it just in time.

This time, for this family, he wasn't too late.

44

Neve hadn't danced in many years. The beat of the music in the ballroom made her want to sway her hips. But she had work to do.

There was a mirror on the wall behind a table holding a bowl filled with dark red punch. She caught a glimpse of herself in the semi-frosted glass. Her hair was pinned up in a braid that coiled around her head like a garland. Her lips and cheeks were pink with a virginal blush.

She looked young, innocent, and trustworthy. Neve wore a dress of cream silk that covered most of her skin but clung to her ample curves like oil. The skirt of the gown had just enough flow and volume to hide the daggers strapped to her thighs beneath.

A lion dressed as a lamb.

Neve found a seat among the line of chairs against the far wall of the ballroom. She made herself into a wallflower and raked her attentive gaze across the space. It was decorated beautifully with expensive-looking candelabras and swaths of sweeping white fabric. Crystals hung from low-burning sconces, casting rainbows across the walls. The ballroom was bare of flowers; it was December after all, and instead was accented with boughs and garlands of blue spruce and juniper, filling the hall with the scent of evergreen. Tables covered in white lace were laden with food and drink, fine china, and gleaming flatware. A twelve-piece orchestra was set up at the far end of the room, playing song after sumptuous song on well-tuned strings, brass, and percussion.

The dance floor was large and full. Giggling ladies drank sparkling wine and eager men spun them around, their pastel skirts twirling like flower petals on the wind.

The only thing that surprised her was the number of men in attendance. In her experience, people who hosted balls tended to invite more women, so the gentlemen at the event could have their pick. Not here. For every three men cavorting around the hall, there seemed to be one woman. But none of the guests appeared to mind. The ladies seemed thrilled to be passed along from one gentleman to the next, reveling in the attention.

Neve looked down at herself, smoothing the wrinkles out of the silk on her bodice and fluffing out her skirt just slightly so it wouldn't cling to her thighs and show the outlines of her weapons. She folded her hands in her lap and went over her plan in her mind once again. She would dance, she would drink, and she would become a giggling lady spinning around the floor.

Then, she planned to surprise the Highborns and tell them that she knew who they were. Who they *really* were. She knew they wouldn't risk her making a scene. Not with all these people around. *The most important people in the Capital*, they'd said. So, she expected they wouldn't protest when she offered to have the conversation in a quieter, more private room.

And when they went to that quiet, private room, she would show them who *she* was.

Neve would end their wretched existence and their wretched reign in one fell swoop.

She was so close to victory, she could taste it.

It tasted like blood.

"May I have this dance?" A white-gloved hand appeared in front of her, pulling Neve out of the strategy puzzle in her mind. He was tall and lean in a way that screamed wealth, with hair the color of copper. Looking at his soft, clean-shaven face and confident brown eyes, Neve could guess that this man had never done a day's worth of hard labor in his life.

Neve knew that she could ruin this boy with the flick of her thumb. It would be so easy to empty him of that easy confidence and shake him until he was a shell of the person he'd walked into the manor as.

But the character she was playing, *Cora*, was a different story. Cora would be flattered and bashful and blushing with dewy anticipation.

So, that's what Neve became. She gave a shy look down to the floor, then back up at the hopeful suitor. She gazed at him beneath her dark lashes and smiled demurely.

"I'd love to," she heard herself say, sliding her hand into his. His glove was warm and slightly clammy from his palm sweat. But he led her to the dance floor with a practiced flourish.

He gave her a controlled turn and then rested his free hand on her waist. It was chaste; she felt no tightening of his fingers or hungry grasping. He stood straight and smiled at her.

"What's your name?" he asked, beginning to move. She followed his lead and started to sway with him.

"Cora. And you?"

"Dominic Chambers, at your service," he replied with a little bow of his head.

Neve forced a blush to her cheeks. "It's nice to meet you."

He smiled again. "Shall we?"

She nodded, then he began to spin her around the dancefloor in earnest. Dominic was a good dancer, excellent. The kind of skill that came from good breeding and etiquette classes that started from birth. He moved her across the ballroom smoothly and with a grace that was easy to get lost in. A touch of joy crept up inside her.

Soon, a different man tapped Dominic on the shoulder and said, "May I cut in?" and, of course, Dominic said yes, handing Neve off to another pair of arms.

This continued for the rest of the night. Over and over again, she was passed into the hands of the next would-be suitor who expertly danced her in circles that, despite herself, left her a little dizzy and a little excited for more. It was hard to keep an eye on the ball, on who was coming or going, while being dipped and spun around and around. Each time she thought she might have a moment to catch her breath, another pair of arms scooped her up and brought her flying through the music.

Neve found herself closing her eyes, feeling the weeping violin and the sensual cello and the gut-punch beat of the drum. The giggling flute and regal horn. Then she would catch how deeply she'd begun to swim in the melodies. She remembered herself long enough to cast her eyes around the room, searching for the Highborns, scoping out any changes to the party, before a new song and a new man swept her into the next wave of rhythm.

Neve was having *fun*.

Her skin was warming, and small tendrils of her hair fell away from her tightly coiled braid. The men who danced with her all became faceless. There was nothing but the music and the movement of her body.

"May we cut in?" a voice asked, finally breaking her from her trance.

Her spine stiffened.

They had arrived.

The current dance partner spun her one last time, into Balor's waiting arms. He caught her hand and slid his arm around her waist, pulling her close. The musty dried flower scent of his breath skated across her face. Neve felt a presence at her back and knew that Cael was behind her. She looked up, and Balor's face was utterly cold. There was nothing in his eyes. Not lust, not greed, absolutely nothing.

Something felt different.

"Look at you," Cael murmured from behind her, running his knuckles down the nape of her neck.

"I was hoping to see you both tonight," she demurred with a gentle smile.

"Well, here we are," Cael chuckled.

Balor did not smile. Didn't so much as raise a blonde eyebrow. "Are you enjoying yourself?" he asked, his voice flat.

The orchestra started playing a slow song. Mournful. A dirge. Balor pressed Neve tighter against his chest and swayed. Behind her, Cael followed the movements, his hands cupping her shoulders.

"Yes," Neve replied sweetly, betraying none of the unease that was flooding into her bloodstream. "I think this is the best party I've ever been invited to."

"Good," Cael said, his voice low.

Neve heard the tell-tale snick of a door being shut. Then another.

And another.

She took a chance and looked beyond Balor's stone-cold face, past the emptying dance floor. Three of the four ballroom doors were closed. Men, dressed in their finery, stood in front of each one.

Stood like soldiers.

"This party is all for you, my dear," Balor whispered in her ear.

Everything inside of her went still.

Neve glanced at the final open door. Hooded figures pooled in, one after another, their faces hidden beneath their brown cloaks. Mages. There had to be at least twenty of them, filing into the ballroom and surrounding the perimeter.

The last door closed.

Locked.

Fuck.

The dance floor was empty. Just her and the Highborns. The other guests all moved to take up posts near the doors, around the edges of the room, with the Mages. A few men pulled back the lace covering the food tables and retrieved weapons that were hidden in the shadows underneath.

This was a set-up.

And now she was surrounded.

Alone.

Alone against the Highborns and an army of men and Mages.

Neve's heart somersaulted against her ribs. The power inside her was silent, cold. But she took a breath and lifted her chin.

"All this for me?" she asked. Not with Cora's voice, but with Neve's. The charade was over. A lethal smirk played on the corner of her mouth.

If she was going to go down, she'd take them with her.

If this was the end, Neve would end it well.

"Of course, all for you," Cael said. "This is a family reunion of sorts, isn't it?"

And there it was.

The confirmation she'd been seeking.

It was true.

"Did you think that a descendant of our sister—"

"Half-sister," Balor corrected.

"Did you think that a descendant of our *half-sister* could come to our kingdom, our city, and that we wouldn't know?" Cael sneered.

Balor traced his nose along her hairline. "We could smell the Lyra on you from miles away, girl."

Neve did not let them see how twisted her guts became. She didn't even tremble despite everything in her screaming to make a run for it. That she was in danger.

She was not afraid of them.

She was not afraid of death.

She was afraid of not *finishing*.

She was afraid of failing.

But that's what was happening. One big, epic failure. For a woman who always outsmarted her opponents, she'd made the deadly mistake of underestimating the Highborns, the Half-Brothers.

She knew who they were.

She knew they killed Queen Nyx centuries ago. Somehow, somewhere along the way, Neve convinced herself that she was different. Smarter, stronger, better than her predecessor.

She'd been wrong.

Neve swallowed it all down.

"Did it frighten you?" she asked, leaning her head back and turning her neck to look into Cael's empty eyes. "I'm sure you heard stories about me."

Balor gripped her chin and pulled her face back toward his. He bared his teeth at her. Good. Let him get angry. Anger made people sloppy. Even if they were hundreds of years old and half-gods.

"It did, didn't it?" she continued. Get under their skin. It was her only chance at getting them to slip. "It scared you to know I was coming for you."

Cael gripped her shoulders. Hard.

All she needed was for them to make one mistake.

Just one, and she could put them down. She knew she was dead either way. But she could at least die with Highborn blood on her hands.

Neve laughed. "I bet it made you feel so *small*," she purred.

"May I have the next dance?" a voice asked. It came from behind Cael. Neve stiffened. The voice was vaguely familiar, but she couldn't place it.

She did, however, note the change to Balor's expression. Something like malignant humor crept into his eyes. His gaze flicked behind Neve, and his mouth spread into a wide grin.

"Of course, of course. I believe you've met before."

Before she could move, Balor and Cael spun her around and shifted their position, becoming a wall at her back. Arms slid around her body. She looked up into one of the last faces she expected to ever see again.

Not after the massacre on the plains.

Command Sergeant of the Cavalry.

Rory *fucking* Grey.

His face, a lackluster version of the face belonging to the man Neve loved, was a mask of cruel satisfaction. He leaned down, pressed his mouth to her ear, and said: "You should have killed me when you had the chance."

PART THREE

Queen of Death

45

The Capital was quiet. Eerily so.

Perhaps it was the winter cold, but there was no one walking in the streets. Many of the shops seemed closed despite it being in the middle of the day.

Killian spent two days helping the survivors of Thornkeep try to salvage what was left of their village. Luckily, only about half the town was reduced to ash, and there were more survivors than he expected there to be. It was a small mercy; it meant that Killian had finally done something right. But it also meant the already meager resources and shelter available in Thornkeep were no longer enough to sustain the population.

Leo's cottage was rubble, as was the inn where Killian spent his nights. They were homeless. Leo said he had a friend in the Capital who could take them in, Killian included. Neve's warnings about Killian showing his "famous face" in the Sylvera rang through his head, but he didn't have much of a choice. He was utterly exhausted and needed time to regroup. Killian didn't think he'd ever been this bone-tired in his life. He could barely move or think, so when Leo and Kat offered him a place at their side, he agreed.

The ride to Sylvera was short and somewhat loud. Henry and Jasper were excited to be visiting a new place. Kat turned it into a game to keep them occupied, to keep their spirits up after the trauma they'd endured, telling them stories about the "big city". But when they rolled across the border into the Capital, the boys deflated a little. And Killian could understand why. Instead of the promised excitement and change of scenery, they were met with emptiness and silence.

Kat led the way down a main Capital street that should have been bustling with activity but was simply dusty with leftover snow. The wind was sharp and howled between the tall buildings. Henry and Jasper grumbled and pouted as they sat cuddled in front of Leo on his horse. They turned a corner down a narrow alley between two gray towers, and it suddenly looked like they'd entered an entirely different city.

Older, dirtier.

Killian's brow was knit as he followed Kat and Leo. It looked like they were heading into an ancient cemetery. Three huge stone tombs stood stalwartly in the clearing, the ground covered in a scattering of crumbling grave markers. He opened his mouth to say something when a figure clad in blue stepped out from behind one of the mausoleums. Killian reached for his sword, nerves frazzled, mind and body drained, and stopped.

The person pushed back the hood of their cloak, and Killian vaguely recognized the pretty face. Smooth dark skin, kind eyes. He watched as Kat and Leo waved at the woman and then dismounted their horses. They moved stiffly, probably just as exhausted as he was.

The woman crouched down and grinned, opening her arms, and the boys ran to her, shouting, "Izzy! Izzy!" They crowded into her outstretched arms and smothered her with love.

Killian couldn't help the smile that tugged at his mouth.

The woman, Kat whispered that her name was Isolde, and the boys were amongst the very few people who called her Izzy. She opened the door of the tomb she'd stepped out from behind and led their rag-tag group inside. Killian gave Willow a loving pat when he left her tied to a tree next to the other horses and followed.

Instead of death, it smelled like cloves in the stone crypt.

There was a series of strange maneuvers that, in a normal situation, Killian would not follow blindly. First, it was Isolde opening a coffin and climbing inside, the rest of them behind her. Then it was the dark staircase that made his anxiety spike and his heart race until there was light again. Then the door with the sigil of House Lyra etched into it. Then a hollow antechamber. Followed by velvet curtains, Killian nearly had to swim through.

And then.

Then Killian Grey stepped into the most beautiful library he'd ever seen.

Henry and Jasper ran into the chamber as if they'd been there dozens of times. Kat and Leo approached a surly-looking blonde woman and a man with dark hair shorn close to his head. The man's size was impressive, taller and broader than Killian, but his eyes were gentle, and the way he moved was clunky but unimposing. Kat and Leo embraced the two, and they exchanged hushed greetings amongst themselves.

Killian turned his head to see Isolde regarding him calmly, with a shine in her eyes. It was a look of recognition steeped in secrets, and it gave Killian the distinct feeling that this woman knew him, or at the very least, knew *of* him.

"You're a Grey," she said simply.

He felt, rather than saw, the blonde and the big man turn their attention in his direction. Killian gave her a slight nod. "And you're clever."

Isolde smiled, bright and sparkling. "So I've been told," she offered him her hand. "Welcome to the right side of history."

A chill skittered up his spine at the truth in that statement. He shook her hand, and it was warm in his palm. "Better late than never, eh?"

A nod and another smile. She gestured at the room, at the books and chairs, and overall coziness of the place. "We heard about what happened in Thornkeep. Thank you for what you did."

He said nothing.

"You must be exhausted," she continued. "Please, make yourself comfortable. There's plenty of space to lay out your bedroll if you need to sleep. It's safe here."

Everything in him sagged with relief at the thought of sleeping. Even if it was just a few minutes. He'd been awake for nearly two days at this point. He thanked Isolde and walked along the bookshelves, his eyes and body too heavy to read any of the titles he scanned. He found a spot to spread out his bedroll, on the far end of the library, in front of a black door with a gold star-shaped knocker in the center.

Killian lay down and fell into a deep slumber almost instantly.

~

"Do you think she'll come to the library today?"

Familiar voices were a low hum to his ears as Killian slowly stirred awake.

"I'd like to meet her."

"We haven't seen her in a few days. Before this, she was here every day."

"You don't think...something happened to her?"

A laugh. "You obviously haven't met her."

Killian opened his eyes and sat up. There was no way to tell how long he'd been out, but Leo, Kat, and the library companions were sitting around a large table talking. A hefty cutting board covered with meat, cheese, and fruit sat in front of them, along with a few bottles of wine, one of them empty. Killian moved his gaze around the room and found Henry and

Jasper curled up in a chair together, fast asleep and covered with blankets.

Stretching his tight muscles as he stood, Killian took the first deep breath he'd taken in days. The sleep had done its job; he felt rested, if not a little groggy. He sauntered over to the table and took a seat next to Leo, who passed the board in Killian's direction. Grateful, he piled a handful of meat and cheese into his mouth as the conversation continued.

"I haven't seen her around the Capital for a few days, either," Isolde said. Her face was still warm with kindness, but there was a furrow between her brows as she spoke.

"You're worried," the big man stated, noting the look on Isolde's face.

"I'm not sure."

"Do you think she'd just leave? Without telling anyone?" Kat asked.

Isolde shook her head, the crease on her forehead deepening. "No. There are things here that belong to her. She wouldn't leave without them, even if she decided to move on without telling us."

"Who are you talking about?" Killian interjected, tossing grapes into his mouth.

Everyone paused, looked at him, then looked at each other. Killian had a feeling that they were weighing whether or not they could trust him with the information. Which, after everything that happened recently, felt like a bit of an insult.

Isolde rested her attention on Killian's face and looked him in the eye. "The Queen."

Killian nearly choked on the grapes in his mouth, his skin flushed with heat.

"*Who?*" he asked again, certain that he'd heard wrong. Certain that he was imagining things.

Isolde's gaze did not leave his face, Killian's didn't leave hers.

"The Queen," the blonde woman said. "All those rumors? The Woman on the Plains? The flares in the night sky a while back? It was her. She's come back to take the throne."

It felt like a boulder was being lowered onto Killian's chest.

Neve.

They were talking about Neve.

Stars glittered in Isolde's eyes. "You know," she stated.

Killian swallowed. "I know."

"What does he know?" the big man whispered to the blonde woman.

"Gods, Oliver, pay attention," the blonde whispered back. "He knows *her*."

"You know her?" Leo asked.

Killian tore his eyes away from Isolde and looked at Leo, and at Kat, who was peeking around her husband, and nodded.

"Holy shit," Kat said, her eyes widening into saucers.

That boulder was pressing down on Killian in earnest now.

"What is *happening*?" Oliver whispered.

"Shhhh!" the blonde hissed.

"She's the one you talked about. She's yours," Kat murmured as the color drained from Leo's face.

Killian looked down and shook his head.

"She's... she..." he couldn't get the words out, so he paused and took a breath, started again. "I'm hers."

When he looked back up, there were tears in Kat's eyes, and she was clutching Leo's arm, digging her fingers into his skin. He didn't seem to notice.

Turning his attention back to Isolde, Killian just tried to keep upright. "She's been here? You've met her?"

Isolde nodded. "Many times." She tilted her head. "When did you see her last?"

Killian thought of their fight. The shame of it felt like a wet blanket wrapped around his ankles. "A week ago, I think."

"It feels strange that no one has seen her lately," Isolde said, chewing her lower lip. "News of what happened to Thornkeep is everywhere. She would have heard by now. And, if she knew you were staying there, she would have gone to you."

Killian wasn't so sure she would, not after what happened between them the night she'd gone to the Highborns..

Oh, gods.

"Did she tell you about meeting with the Highborns?" Killian asked, and everyone stiffened. For the first time, Isolde lost complete control of her face, and her eyes went round, haunted.

"No," she said in a quiet voice.

Killian pushed back his chair, stood, and started pacing. "The last time I saw her, she came to visit me in Thornkeep. She told me she'd met with the Highborns, that she was getting information out of them. It was part of her plan."

"That's not good," the blonde said.

"No. It's not," Isolde confirmed.

She stood and leaned over the table, spreading out a map. It seemed to be a larger version of the map Kat and Leo showed him the night Killian had supper at their cottage. Isolde pointed to Thornkeep, which was now crossed out with two thick intersecting lines.

"The Cavalry went to Thornkeep two nights ago," she moved a trembling finger over the map to Sylvera. "But there was also a heavy Cavalry presence in the Capital that night. More than usual, enough to be noticed. And they were all at the Highborn's manor."

The library was filled with knowing silence.

Something in Killian's soul tore open, leaving a black hole that threatened to suck him into the abyss. "They have her."

46

Neve D'Aeth Lyra always knew she'd meet a violent end. But not like this.

Not without her active participation. Not without her consent or agency. Not paralyzed and useless, just watching as *he* brutalized her body.

Somewhere in the dripping, dank cellar, Mages worked their magic on her. Day and night, whatever that meant. All sense of time was lost in these conditions. She could hear them muttering, the coarse friction of their robes shifting. Neve thought perhaps all twenty Mages that came to the ball were now down here in the darkness with her. That must be it. There would be no way they could keep her so utterly under their spell, not unless all of them shoved their magic into her at once. Hour after hour.

They did not sleep.

Neve was constantly pressing her awareness against the pressure of the magic, searching for a weakness, a gap. Some small sliver she could use to pry apart its hold on her. She wouldn't stop trying until she found a way out.

She would keep trying until she was bled dry.

Sometimes the magic took her under so completely that she couldn't move, see, hear, or use her voice. She could only *feel*. Nothing but pain.

When that happened, Neve found that she had a hard time understanding if she was alive or dead. It felt so much like what she'd imagined death to feel like. Cold, final, half-aware. Other times, the magic allowed her to open her eyes, to speak, to hear, but not move. *Never* letting her move.

When they let her see, there was only one face. One set of hands, stained red with her blood.

Rory Grey.

She could see him now. She was prone on top of some sort of stone slab or table. Chains dug into her wrists and ankles, presumably in case the magic faltered. He leaned down into her face and smiled. He was sweating. His white Cavalry uniform was a ruin of red. Neve imagined that what was left of her cream silk dress looked worse. Rory dragged the flat side of a knife down the center of her body, between her breasts, down her stomach, and back up again.

"You're a mess, *your highness*," he sneered.

Neve just blinked at him.

She knew what he wanted from her. He wanted her fear, he wanted her pain. His manic eyes were nearly begging her to scream or cry. He wanted to see her lowered.

Rory Grey wanted to *break* her.

She would never give him what he wanted.

"They want me to put your body on display on the King's Road. Nail what's left of you to a tree so all the rebels can see with their own eyes that you're not coming to take the kingdom for them."

Rory Grey liked issuing threats.

He leaned in close, his nose touching hers, a bead of sweat falling from his forehead onto her cheek. All she could smell was his unwashed body and her drying blood.

"When I'm finished with you, all that's left will be your bones," he whispered.

Pulling back to look at her face, she was certain he was hoping to see terror. She gave him a smirk instead. Spit flew from his mouth as he cursed at her.

Then he pressed the knife to her skin and went to work.

~

The icy blade of worry stabbed Killian over and over again. In his throat, in his back, deep into his pounding heart. It was an acute torture, knowing Neve was in danger and no one, not a single person, knew where she was. Killian was a lightning storm of anxiety, crackling through the library, lost and looking for something, anything, to strike and burn.

"I'm going out into the city to seek answers," Isolde stated blandly, pulling her cloak tighter around her shoulders and moving toward the curtains at the entrance.

Killian launched himself forward. "I'm coming with you."

She stopped and turned on her heel. Killian was in such a frenzy that he nearly collided with her, and would have if she hadn't extended her arm and placed a pitying hand on his chest.

"No," she said.

Nostrils flaring, he growled, "I wasn't asking permission."

Isolde's face was kind, but there was something underneath, something commanding that tightened her mouth. "And I wasn't asking for a debate."

"Just try to stop me. I *dare* you." He side-stepped to move around her, but Isolde easily shifted with him.

It was a dangerous choice to place herself between him and the exit, between him and finding Neve. But there was no fear in her eyes.

"We have the same goal, Killian. I have sources in the city. Secret ones. They will talk to me, but make no mistake, they will *not* talk if you're with me."

"I'll hide, they won't see me."

Isolde took a step closer to Killian. "I will not risk my credibility for your impatience. This is our best chance at finding her. I doubt you're willing to risk that, either."

Heart racing, he opened his mouth to argue, but somehow her words found a way through the clouds muddling his brain and reached him. He took a step back, took a breath, and realized he was trembling.

"Please," he said. It was the only word he was suddenly capable of choking out. "Please."

Isolde's eyes softened, filling with feeling. "I promise. I will return with answers."

And then she was gone.

Killian couldn't breathe. His mind raced with all the things that could have happened to Neve. Captured, injured. Missing. Hurt. Killed. Stinging bile rose in his throat, and his chest heaved. Panic filled his lungs, leaving no room for air. It had been two, nearly three days. So much could have happened, and Killian couldn't imagine that any of it could be good.

He wished he could believe that she was fine, that this was an overreaction. He wished he could believe she was holed up in her room, cozy with a book. He wished he could believe that she'd stride in through the curtains, smirking and rolling her eyes at their concern.

But he couldn't.

Where she could be, what could be happening to her...the thoughts destroyed him. Worse, their last conversation was playing on a loop in his mind.

Did they touch you?

Yes.

Then it was all white noise.

I meant it when I said I loved you.

Your Majesty.

He hadn't said it back. He'd been too proud, too hurt, too stupid to say it back. And now... Now she was gone. Gone, likely thinking that he no longer loved her.

If that was the last conversation they'd ever have...

If she'd gone to her death thinking that he didn't love her...

It would kill him.

Killian suddenly didn't know what to do with his body, so he just started walking around the library in circles, feet stomping against the thin rugs and the stone floor beneath. He felt utterly helpless. All he wanted to do was run after Isolde and hunt down answers with her.

He felt a hand on his shoulder. He was so on edge that he startled and spun around, fists clenched. It was Kat, holding sleeping little Jasper in her arms.

"Can you help me?" she asked.

Killian blinked, coming out of his panicked daze, just a little bit. He managed a nod.

There was a knowing light in Kat's eyes. She looked down at Jasper and then back up at Killian.

"This one has been having nightmares - about houses on fire, of course- and my arms are getting tired from holding him. Can you take him for a bit?"

Before Killian could respond, Kat handed over her son to him. Jasper was warm in his arms, that specific warmth of restlessly sleeping children. It radiated from the boy and straight into Killian's chest, instantly soothing a fraction of his fear.

He found that he could breathe again.

Kat must have seen the way Killian relaxed because that knowing look spread across her whole face, and she winked at him before walking away. Gratitude filled him. He would never understand how women, specifically mothers, always knew the exact right thing to do for someone in crisis.

Jasper was a grounding weight against him, and Killian moved to the big table, joining the rest of the group, and took a seat.

He tucked Jasper's head under his chin and closed his eyes. He breathed. In and out. In and out. When he opened his eyes, he expected everyone to be staring at him, in pity or judgment, but they weren't. Kat and Sabrina were quietly strategizing over the map. Leo and Oliver were arm-wrestling. Henry was sleeping, mouth wide open, in the same chair he'd been passed out in for hours.

Leo cut him a glance, his face tense with exertion as he tried to pin Oliver's arm. Oliver hadn't even broken a sweat.

"We'll find her," Leo said.

"I know," Killian replied quietly. He knew they would find her. But in what condition?

"There's a reason Isolde is in charge of the rebellion," Oliver added, voice steady and arm unmoving while Leo's forearm pulsed and trembled with effort. "You can trust her. Neve did." The man's eyes went wide and his skin went pale when he looked at Killian. "Does. I mean Neve does."

Isolde leading the rebellion was new information, but it didn't shock him. It made sense.

With a grunt, Leo pinned Oliver's arm. Killian was certain the bigger man let his friend win, as penance for placing a past-tense on Neve's name. Despite himself, Killian thought he might like the big man. He was simple but good, and he'd be a hell of an ally in a fight.

Jasper shifted in Killian's arms, relaxing a little, sighing.

"How did she seem?" Killian asked, his voice barely above a whisper. "When she was here with you, how did she seem?"

"Bitchy," Sabrina remarked without looking up.

A laugh barked out from the back of Killian's throat. He couldn't help it. He certainly hadn't expected that response, but he liked it. He might like Sabrina a little bit too.

Oliver blanched again and cut her with a glare. "Gods, Sabrina. Do you even think before you open your mouth?"

Without missing a beat, she said, "Do you?"

Oliver blushed. "Well, at least I try. She's our Queen, you can't just say things like that about her. Especially around him."

"What? Am I wrong?" Sabrina looked up at Oliver. "She *is* bitchy. And I'm sure, more than anyone else, he knows that." She pointed at Killian. "Listen, I like her. I'll follow her to the ends of the earth. I just wouldn't want to be alone with her, you know?"

Killian held back another laugh.

Oliver shook his head and angled toward Killian, trying to block his friend from the rest of the conversation. "Don't listen to her. Sabrina's still bitter that Neve tried to kill her." Killian raised an eyebrow. Oliver shook his head again and shrugged. "It's not important."

"I am *not* bitter," Sabrina muttered.

Oliver ignored her. "When Neve was here, she was lovely. She liked the books. And they liked her. She was always a little quiet, but nice to be around. She just had -has- this thing where you sort of always want to be around her. You know?"

Killian smiled. "I know." This was helping. The toddler in his arms. The banter. "Did she seem like she was... happy?"

Oliver nodded. "I think so. She was never whistling and skipping around in here, but she seemed content. Some days more than others. The last time she was here, she seemed a little... I don't know... sad? But not in any kind of obvious way. Just quiet and in her own head."

The last time she was in the library.

After their fight.

Killian tried not to think about it. Tried to focus on the conversation, the sleeping child drooling on his shirt. He knew that his emotions would work against him if he gave in to them. He needed to stay grounded and stable. His tendency to fly into a rage was always reckless. Killian couldn't afford to be reckless now, not when Neve's life was hanging in the balance. Not when his strong emotions were the reason they'd fought, the reason she hadn't felt comfortable coming to him to explain her plan.

Killian knew he hadn't made their relationship a safe place for uncomfortable conversations.

He vowed to change that.

For now, Killian needed to stockpile his rage and fear so that when it came time to find her and deal with the people who'd taken her, he would have a mountain of fury within him.

Then, he would be an avalanche and bury them all.

47

There was blood in her mouth.

Neve thought for sure it was coming up from her lungs. Her arms were tied and suspended by a rope above her head, and her toes grazed the cold floor. Rory Grey had her magic-paralyzed body hanging from a hook on the ceiling. He was beating her. His fists were dripping with red, whether from his shredded knuckles or her split skin, she did not know.

It was hard to breathe. Neve could feel her body begging for death. But her mind and her voice would never. She'd already lost a lot of blood to his knife, and now this. He kept hitting her and hitting her. She'd heard her ribs crack at some point, and that was when breathing became painful and blood had bubbled up on her lips.

Neve was not in good shape.

And Rory Grey was ecstatic.

She watched as he circled her, over and over again. There was a sinister light in his eyes as they raked over her body, deciding where to hit her next. His sallow skin was shining with sweat, and he looked sickly in the dim light. Sickly but nearly vibrating with excitement.

Unable to move a single muscle aside from those in her face, she swayed limply from the rope. Rory's ruined hands slid to her hips and gripped her to keep her still.

"Enjoying yourself?" he asked. His breath stank, as if old slivers of meat were stuck between his teeth. "I know I am."

She gave him a slow blink.

"Come on," Rory drawled. "From the looks of it, you'll be dead soon. We don't have much time left together."

Neve knew what he wanted. She wasn't being tortured for information. It was clear his orders were to kill her, not question her. Perhaps the Highborns thought she was already dead; perhaps she was supposed to be. But he was dragging it out. Because he could. Because he had twenty Mages keeping her still. He could have asked her any number of things about who she was, the rebels, the secret library in the graveyard. But no. He didn't seem to care about that. What he wanted was for her to break.

Neve hadn't made a sound.

Not while he dragged a blade across her skin over and over. She stayed silent and stoic as he made her bleed until the edges of her vision went black. She hadn't grunted when his fists railed into her back, sides, stomach, her chest. Didn't offer him so much as a gasp, even when she felt her ribs break and impale into her lung.

Neve wanted to give him nothing. Not her pain. Certainly not her death.

Not today.

She felt his thumbs lazily caressing her hips as he held her still. He thought he was taunting her with the occasional gentle touch. He thought he *knew* her. But he did not.

She was stone, and before this was over, he'd break against her.

He would break against her, even if it was the very last thing she did.

Neve reached inside herself and searched for her power, for the sleeping giant. It was silent. Cold. Of all the times for this new, strange power to elude her, this was the least convenient. She could use a little help. But, she'd have to do this on her own.

It was clear at this point that no one was coming to save her.

She pressed her awareness against the Mage magic, seeking just one tiny foothold, just one tiny crack. The Mages must be getting tired by now. Neve wasn't sure how long she'd been in the cellar, but she was certain it had been at least a few days, if not more. Neither the Mages nor Rory had stopped. No one had eaten or slept. So, Neve waited. She would keep waiting until someone slipped.

Then she'd rally up whatever strength remained in her to save herself, before ripping the world apart in vengeance.

"Come on, girl, you don't have to pretend to be so tough," he sneered. "I know this hurts."

"How small..." Neve croaked, her voice barely audible. The words felt like glass in her throat. The breath it took to speak had her swaying again with effort.

His eyes brightened, probably because he hadn't heard her, probably because he thought she was asking for mercy.

"What's that? A little louder, love."

Neve cleared her throat, drawing another wet and raspy breath. "How small you must feel, unable to bring me down on your own."

He snarled and wrapped his fist around her hair, yanking her head back at a sudden and sharp angle. "I have you now, don't I?"

"Only because you have an army of Mages keeping me still," she responded. Gods, it hurt to talk. Each breath was a stab to her chest.

The hot spray of his spittle landed on her face as he cursed at her. "Before the end, I'm going to make you *beg*."

Neve forced a bloody-mouthed smile to rise on her lips. "Before the end, I'm going to cut out your heart and wear it as a necklace."

Growling, the sound more animal than man, Rory ripped the ropes from Neve's wrists and let her body slam in a heap to the cold floor. She landed on her side, the same side with the broken ribs and mangled lung. It took everything she had not to let loose an agonized scream.

More blood spilled from her mouth. Not good. Not good at all.

Neve felt Rory's arms scoop her up and carry her to the stone table, where he dropped her on her back. Her head cracked against the granite, and a sick, dizzy spinning invaded her head. Rory climbed on top of the table, one leg on either side of her waist. He pulled the knife from his belt and held it over her with a rage-trembling hand.

"Black her out!" he commanded. He'd said this a few times before. It meant he wanted the Mages to take away the rest of her senses. Except for her sense of sound and touch.

Darkness crept over her vision slowly until she could see nothing at all.

But she could feel.

Oh gods, she could feel it all.

48

Noise erupted. But strangely muffled, as if Neve were underwater. She heard voices but couldn't understand the words. Along with the echoes of shouting, she heard sharp sounds and wet sounds. She tried to open her mouth to speak, but her lips wouldn't move. Her eyes wouldn't either. Was she still under the Mage's magic? Hours, days, maybe years later? Or was she dead? Finally dead.

Everything hurt. She never imagined death would hurt so much. Her whole world was pain.

She could smell fresh blood. Was it hers? Had Rory opened another one of her veins? Surely she was dead. The things he'd done to her... There was no way she could have survived. And yet...

And yet.

Neve was aware of the weight of her body pressing against the unforgivable stone table. She was aware of movement in the cellar, movement like a battle. Neve was aware that there was breath moving from her mouth and into her chest. Her breath. She was breathing. Alive.

She heard a gruff shout, something that sounded very close to "*Where the fuck is she?!*" Dimly, she knew that voice. It kindled a warmth in the space beneath her ruined lungs.

Oh, please, she thought.

Please, please, please. Let it be him.

She dared to hope that Killian had found her. Neve tried to speak again, tried to move, to see. But she was frozen. When he finally found her...

He would think she was dead.

For the first time since she was captured, panic sluiced through her blood.

More voices. She recognized three of them. *What an occasion*, Neve thought grimly. Her rescue managed to pull Isolde, Oliver, and Sabrina out of the library for once. She felt her heart tripping over itself, with both gratitude and fear. Was there anything left of her to rescue?

She wanted to scream, *was* screaming in her head.

The Mages. Take the Mages out first.

So they can release me.

Please.

I'm not dead.

I'm alive, I'm alive, I'm...

~

The guards were fodder and never stood a chance.

Isolde's sources, including an undercover member of the Cavalry, revealed that when Neve was captured, she was taken to a west-wing cellar in the manor. The Highborns fled, along with most of the Cavalry, heading eastward. A handful of guards stayed behind to protect the home and keep up appearances that the Highborns were still in the Capital.

Kat stayed back in the library with the children, but everyone else followed Killian. He'd fully intended to rain hell on the manor by himself, but Leo and his new companions wouldn't hear it.

"She's my Queen," Oliver said. "I go where she is."

Even surly Sabrina insisted on her devotion to Neve and armed herself with as many deadly objects as could fit on her person.

So, Killian and the rag-tag group of rebels stormed the tower.

Finding the cellar was easy. Once inside, they were met by a line of burly guards who appeared shocked to see them. They put up a good fight, but they were no match for Killian or the fighters with him.

And then, in a corner like a spider hiding from the light, Killian found someone he never wanted to see again.

His brother.

Rory was filthy. His once white Cavalry uniform was now a mottled mess of brown and red. There were circles under his eyes, and he looked gaunt and ill. Even from a distance, Killian could tell his brother was exhausted and weakened. His hands were wrecked and looked like he'd been punching something over and over.

Killian's stomach dropped to his knees.

Whose blood was Rory wearing?

Killian was vaguely aware of sound and movement further into the cellar behind a makeshift partition, but his focus was on the dirty bastard leaning against the wall in the corner.

"Where is she?" Killian growled, covering the space between them with two long strides. His hands gripped Rory's collar.

His brother didn't bother fighting back, but instead, he smiled. A cruel, grotesque thing. Yellowed teeth, the corners of his dead eyes crinkled, pushing dirt and dried blood deeper into his skin.

"You're too late," he rasped.

The rage and grief that roiled through Killian had no space for mercy. He pulled his knife and nestled it firmly against the base of Rory's bobbing throat. He would not believe he was too late. He could not.

"*Where.*" It wasn't a question, but a demand.

Across the cellar, he heard an ominous series of gasps and exclamations. A gagging curse from Sabrina. A sob from Oliver. Then Killian's name. But it wasn't a shout. Isolde said his name in a way that felt like a death sentence.

Killian went cold.

He turned and was met by Leo and Oliver, a wall of muscle between him and whatever was on the other side of the cellar. Their faces were stricken and pale. Oliver wasn't even trying to hide his tears; the big man was openly weeping.

"What–" Killian began.

Leo shook his head. "Killian, you don't want to see this."

He stilled. "No."

"You don't want to see *her* like this," Leo said, voice cracking.

Time seemed to slow down.

"Hold him," Killian said, gesturing numbly at his brother and pushing past his companions.

Each step he took was heavy and became more and more impossible as what was on the other side of the cellar came into view. A stone table, an altar. Isolde and Sabrina stood at the foot of it, heads bent like funeral mourners. When he saw what was on top of the table, everything stopped. His heart stopped. His mind.

At that moment, the very world ended.

~

At first, Neve felt the gentle and trembling caress of Killian's fingers on her face. It filled her with a comfort she could not name. If she could move, she would have smiled, beamed, and danced with joy.

But then Killian was wailing.

His mouth crushed against hers, and she ached to kiss him back. But she couldn't.

"No, no, no," he wept. There was a terrible and frantic edge to his voice that she'd never heard before. She hoped she never would again.

The Mages, my love, she willed. *Mages are hiding here.*

Of course, he couldn't hear. Because she couldn't speak.

He was screaming now. Words like *please* and *I'm sorry* over and over again. His hands were rougher. Neve felt them gripping her, shaking her. It hurt. Everything hurt.

I'm alive, I'm alive.

Please, the Mages. Behind the partition. The Mages.

He shook her again, and agony lanced through every single one of her nerves. More than anything in the world, she wanted to scream. She wanted to roar. Killian's pleading mouth pressed against hers again. Then his head was on her chest. His stubble scratched against her open wounds, and the weight of him pressed against her ribs. Too much pressure. He'd crush what was left of the breath from her lungs, and then she'd truly be dead.

The Mages, Killian. The fucking Mages.

Neve felt him slow down, heard the noises from his mouth quiet.

His ear was pressed to her chest, and he was listening.

"Her heart," he choked out. He pressed his head against her harder. Her lungs buckled. "Her heart is beating."

He stood up straight, and Neve felt both relief and despair at the loss of his touch. Every touch was painful, but it meant that she was alive and he was here. Killian's hands brushed her face again, gently, full of love and longing.

"Neve, open your eyes, love. Wake up."

There was a whisper in the dark.

"Did you hear that?" This came from Sabrina.

Neve could feel Killian shift as he followed the sound. From what she could tell, Isolde and Sabrina went with him.

Yes, yes. Find them.

A hatch creaked loudly, like a crow's caw in the din.

"Mages," Sabrina grunted.

"You're all dead," Killian said, in a voice so lethal and final it could have ended life on its own.

The screaming started then. As did the slow loosening of the magic keeping her still. First, she could move her toes, then her fingers. As Killian's blade ran through every Mage, more and more of Neve's body came back under her control. Legs, hips, arms, neck.

At the moment the last Mage gave up the ghost, Neve's eyes opened, and the greatest sense of freedom she'd ever felt poured into her, rushed over her, overcame her in every way possible.

She sat up, ignoring the pain. Ignoring how close to death she still lingered. She needed healing. But she needed something else first. Neve scooted to the edge of the stone table and placed her feet on the ground. She knew she had mere moments before the adrenaline of being released left her. Mere moments before, she would surely collapse.

She would make those moments count.

Neve straightened her back and walked.

But where she expected to see Rory, she found Oliver and another man slumped over and nursing fresh wounds.

Rory Grey was gone.

49

Killian had seen battle and death many times throughout his life. But he'd never seen someone as brutalized as Neve survive. He was astounded that she could move at all, let alone stride across the cellar. But she did. And, awestruck, he watched it happen.

When she found that Rory was missing, Killian saw the way Neve swayed on her feet. He was at her side in an instant, catching her in his arms. He scooped her up and held her close.

"I've got you," he murmured. He looked down at her, and her eyes met his. Those beautiful eyes. Some sadistic mercy must have urged Rory not to mangle her face because it was the only part of her body that was unmarked and unbroken.

Killian barely noticed the sheepish way Oliver and Leo tried to apologize for letting Rory slip away; he didn't even bother listening to their story of how his brother managed to escape. His attention was fixed on the woman in his arms, his Queen, his everything. Her muscles were going limp against him, and he could hear how her breath labored.

"How can I help?" he asked quietly, forcing his alarm down, putting a calm facade in front of his rampant fear.

Something was wrong.

Neve opened her mouth to speak, but a cough came out instead, a cough that sprayed deep red mist. Blood. A trail of it seeped down her chin from the corner of her lips. Killian wanted to scream, cry, burn the world down. Instead, he held her, smiled at her.

"You're all right. I've got you. Try again, Neve, tell me how to help you." It took gargantuan effort to keep his voice level, and yet he felt a tremble move through his words.

She nodded, closed her eyes, swallowed, and tried again.

"The library," she managed. "Take me to the library."

Killian wanted to argue. She needed a medic or a healer, not books. He wondered for a moment if she was simply seeking a pretty place to die, instead of this dank, offal, and blood-polluted cellar.

But the way she fought to keep her eyes open, the way the breath went in and out of her like a saw cutting through lumber, brooked no space for debate. He would do as she asked, whatever it was.

The others rushed to Neve's side, crowding around. Oliver shrugged off his cloak and tucked it around her, and Isolde pushed a strand of hair back from Neve's face.

"There's a healing pool in the library. That's where she wants to go," Isolde explained quietly.

Killian kept his eyes on Neve, and Isolde kept hers on him. She nodded.

"Hurry," she rasped. "I don't think I have much time."

Choking down the swell of fear in his chest, he pulled Oliver's cloak tightly around Neve, held her close, and ran. He was in a daze, his focus was solely on the sound of his feet beating against the snowy cobblestones, and counting Neve's breaths as he sprinted.

Whatever strength remained in her seemed to fade. With each step Killian took, he felt Neve becoming more and more limp in his arms.

"I've got you," he said over and over again, burying his nose in her hair. His heart was thundering behind his ribs. He didn't think he'd ever run so fast in his life, yet he feared he wasn't fast enough.

Time was not on their side.

His memory kept sneaking back to the sight of her on that stone table. She'd been utterly destroyed. In that wicked moment, he thought she was dead, he was ready to tear apart the world to avenge her, and then follow her into the end.

And, if instead this was the end, if they ran out of time, he would follow her still.

There was no him without her.

Killian was vaguely aware that his companions were with him, following closely. Barely noticed when they reached the graveyard, entered the tomb, or started down the dark staircase. Isolde and Oliver led the way down, Sabrina and Leo behind.

Relief edged him as he moved through the blue velvet curtains and into the library. She was still breathing, but there was no rhythm now; her breaths came at strange and terrifying intervals.

Isolde led him to the black door at the far end of the chamber. She took Neve's hand.

"Touch the door, Neve, you're almost there."

Killian's brow furrowed, and he moved closer to the door so Neve could reach. Isolde guided her near-limp hand to the gold star knocker in the center. Neve's fingers twitched and stretched outward until her hand was on it. She knocked weakly three times. The door groaned open.

By the feel of it alone, Killian knew this room was special, that it contained power. But he didn't care. All he cared about was getting Neve into the glittering pool.

Isolde was at his side and reached out for Neve. "Let me help you lower her in."

Shaking his head, Killian kicked off his boots.

"No," was all he said. He gently removed the cloak from around Neve's struggling body. Kissed the top of her head as he stepped into the pool, fully clothed and with one singular goal.

The water sputtered and fizzed around his legs. Killian sat down with his back against the side of the pool. As gently as possible, he shifted Neve in his arms so that she was sitting in front of him, her back resting against his chest.

The water, reaching up to Neve's chin, started to bubble and swirl excitedly and turned from a clean, iridescent blue to a cloudy pink as it lapped at her wounds.

He had one arm curled around her upper chest and could feel her heart beating against it. Slow, too slow.

He cupped his free hand and dipped it into the water, taking some and tenderly trickling it into her hair, then caressing her face with it. He bent his head, leaning forward and pressing his cheek against hers.

"I've never met anyone as brave as you," he said. He felt her nod.

Killian knew she was trying so hard to be all right. To survive this.

The pool began to warm and whirl, sending bubbling waves against them in a rhythmic rush. The motion quietly lulled him. Killian could feel the magic. It was pure, so fundamentally different from Mage magic. It felt clean and holy. He'd never cared for the gods, but here, in this place, he closed his eyes and wished. Prayed.

Please, please, please, he begged.

~

Sudden movement thrust Killian awake. He hadn't even realized he'd fallen asleep, yet here he was, startled and instantly frantic. He was still in the pool, the water now just gently fizzing and back to that shimmering light blue color it was when he first saw it.

But that's not what caught his attention.

Neve.

She shifted lithely and stood with her back to him. All traces of her ruined dress were gone. She was naked before him, wet skin glistening in the subdued light. Killian tried to speak but found he had no words. He watched a bead of water trail lazily down the small of her back, over the curve of her ass. Her skin bore no wounds, no new scars.

Killian couldn't move, couldn't make a sound as Neve walked to the other side of the pool and up a set of tiled steps. She stood tall and strong and reached into an alcove.

His breath caught in his chest and he stood.

In her hands, she held a crown.

She turned toward him, magnificent. There was a glow to her skin, a light that seemed to come from within her. It shimmered around her naked curves like moonlight. Killian had never seen anything so beautiful in all his life. Until she looked at him, her gaze caught his and held.

And then she placed the crown on top of her head.

Without thought, Killian walked through the pool towards her and stepped out, his wet clothes clung heavily to his skin. Briefly, he wondered if perhaps he should kneel before her. This felt like a moment that warranted a show of fealty, of devotion. But instead, he slowly and gently took her face in his hands.

"I love you," he said.

Her eyes warmed, just a little. They were full of the same coolness they'd always had, the same mischievous ferocity. But there was something new in her regard. Something sad, haunted. And something else that Killian could not name. But that warmth, that small warmth, was all for him.

"I know," she replied.

Neve turned and reached for something that was leaning against a shelf. Light glinted off the metal. When she lifted it,

Killian saw what it was, and his soul shifted. It was like seeing an old friend or the feeling of finding something once thought lost.

A shield. His shield.

Neve's eyes met his, and she held it out to him.

"This belongs to you," she said.

Killian accepted it from her, feeling the weight of it in his hands and sensing the *rightness* of it.

"It's time, Killian." Neve's voice caused a shiver to go down his spine. "It's time for us to take what's ours. It's time for us to rule."

50

Later, she would have time to process how it felt to look death in the face and then turn her back on it.

Later, she would have time to reflect on how, if she'd just told someone, if she hadn't been so arrogant to go alone, she could have avoided getting caught.

Later, she would have time to dip her hands into the deep, dark well of her wrath and soak the world with it.

But now, Neve just needed to feel human.

Alive.

Killian's iron-blue eyes were full of feeling. There was love in there for her, tenderness, admiration. But there was also anguish, harrowing desperation.

Neve took a step closer to him, aware of the visual. She stood before him naked, all regal glory with shining wet hair and skin, the crown atop her head. She watched his gaze move down the length of her body, the roundness of her curves. His throat bobbed when he made it back up to her face. He must have seen the want in her eyes, the way she dragged her teeth over her plump bottom lip.

She stepped into him, pressing herself against his chest. The sodden clothes he wore were cold against her skin. Neve looked up at him, and her gaze didn't leave him as her hands unbuckled his belt. There was a rasp around the edges of the breath that came out of his mouth, the sound made warm desire curl in her lower belly.

"Are you sure?" he asked.

Neve let his belt drop to the floor and cupped his hard length from outside his pants. It twitched against her fingers as she squeezed, and a low moan sizzled in Killian's throat.

"Yes," she said. He set down the shield, reached to the back of his neck, and peeled off his wet shirt. Neve tracked each drop of water, then trailed down the grooves between his muscles. Her stomach was seized with a hunger that had nothing to do with food.

He leaned down and brushed his lips against hers, then took her face in his hands and kissed her. Neve could have melted against the heat that bloomed between them. She had missed him, gods, she'd missed him.

Her bottom lip was between his teeth then he soothed the bite by sucking on it. Neve's hands deftly undid his pants. She was distantly aware that they slid to the floor, and he stepped out of them. His breaths quickened, and she could feel all the strong emotions she'd seen in his eyes pouring into her from his kiss.

Wrapping her arms around his neck, she pressed herself against him, as if she could crawl into his skin and live there. His hands moved down her back, over the curve of her ass, they gripped her thighs and lifted her and she hooked her legs around his waist. Neve could feel him against her, hard and teasing. She ground her hips, and he groaned, breaking the kiss.

He looked at her with a mix of worry and worship.

"Are you sure?" he asked again, his voice rough. "After what happened... I don't want to hurt you."

She loved him for asking, she loved him for caring. But she *needed* him. So, she ran her fingers through his hair and grabbed a handful of it, gently jerking his head back. A feral light sparked in his eyes.

"Make me feel something other than pain, Killian. Please."

Briefly, he went utterly still. And then he was nothing but movement.

His mouth was on her neck; kissing, sucking, biting. Neve lost herself to it. Gravity shifted, and she found herself lying down, an age-soft rug beneath her back and Killian above her. The crown dug into the back of her head just slightly, and she reached up to take it off, but Killian caught her hand.

"No. Leave it on," he said, the desire in his voice was the only command she'd ever bow to, and she would bow to it now.

He trailed his hand down her stomach and between her legs, where he began stroking her with a menacingly slow rhythm that made her muscles tremble. Neve's eyes rolled back, and Killian made a tsk noise with his mouth.

"Look at me, Lady Nightmare."

So, she watched and his tongue twirled around one of her nipples before taking it into his mouth and sucking. A low, purring moan rolled out of her from deep in her chest.

After so much pain, her body was suddenly wild with pleasure. Every nerve and synapse was wide awake. Even her bones seemed to vibrate. Killian's mouth moved to her other breast, and her back arched off the floor. His hand was still caressing between her legs, so gently and slowly, it was maddening. Neve writhed beneath him.

"Your mouth," she breathed. "I want your mouth."

A low chuckle rumbled from his lips around her nipple, it made everything inside of her clench so tightly she thought she might explode from that alone. He moved down her body and with unbearably strong hands, he spread her thighs and lowered himself between them.

He flattened his tongue and dragged it up her cunt and Neve's back arched again just as his mouth closed around her clit and he sucked.

She rocked against his mouth greedily, looking down at him as he worked. The pressure and ecstasy within her built at an alarming rate. Maybe it was the way he watched her as he licked and sucked, maybe it was the expertise of a mouth that truly understood her, maybe it was finally being free of the horror in that cellar. Whatever it was, she felt her heart hammering in her chest, and her whole body shook as he brought her higher and higher.

"More," she heard herself say. More of what, she didn't know.

But he seemed to know.

He grinned and slipped a long finger inside of her, curling it up slightly then thrusting it in and out with the same rhythm he used as he sucked her clit. Neve cried out at the divine melody he was making with her body. Before she could breathe, he was coaxing her to a violent climax. Everything in her and around her began to stretch and sing and fill up to overflowing. And as she plummeted over the very edge of the world, she let out a scream that might have been his name but might also not have been a real word at all.

Neve was in a daze, and Killian's mouth was on hers. She would taste herself on his tongue.

"You're so beautiful when you come for me like that," he breathed.

She met his eyes as he notched himself at her entrance. She could feel how hard he was, how his body was vibrating with need. It took her a moment to realize he was waiting for her to consent, so she nodded and gripped his hips, digging her fingernails into his skin.

At the first nudge of him, she forgot her own name. He sank into her to the hilt, and they both groaned, eyes locking on each other. He began to move, and she moved with him. Soon, they only shared breath and movement and hearts that beat in the same rhythm.

The expression on his face was nothing short of reverent, as if she were the most beautiful and precious thing he'd ever seen in his whole life. Perhaps she was. Perhaps she was even looking at him the same way.

This man, this tortured and complicated man with big feelings who was, on paper, the exact opposite of her, somehow seemed to fit perfectly. In her body, in her life, in her kingdom. She'd once believed she didn't need this, what he was offering her, a partner, love. But then she met Killian. And he'd taken the time to get to know her. And he'd made her tea. He'd made her laugh. He'd made her come. He'd devoted himself to her before he'd even known who she was.

As he moved inside her and as she met him thrust for thrust, she understood that having a partner wasn't a liability. It simply made her stronger. She was never so powerful as she was with him at her side.

"I love you," she said, her voice no louder than a sigh.

His eyes filled with such intensity that it was almost hard to watch, but she didn't look away.

"I love you," he replied.

She kissed him, and then another orgasm slammed into her. It had her tightening around him, and soon he followed her over the edge, and they swirled into the abyss of ecstasy together.

~

"Well, that sounded fun," Sabrina remarked as Neve and Killian emerged from the gods' chamber and into the library. She even whistled.

Oliver, for his part, turned a shade of red usually reserved for apples and tomatoes.

"*Sabrina!*" he scolded, swatting her with the scroll he'd been pretending to read. She just laughed, put her feet up on the table, and tucked back into her book.

In the afterglow, Neve went snooping through the closets and chests in the gods' chamber and managed to find several pairs of linen pants and tunics in a cedar box. She and Killian slipped into them so they wouldn't further scandalize their companions with their nudity after what they'd undoubtedly heard. However, Sabrina was the only person with enough gall to say anything, and Oliver seemed to be the only one scandalized, judging by the blush on his cheeks.

Neve scanned the rest of the library. Two little boys sat on the floor in the corner with the dark-haired man Neve recognized from the cellar. They were playing with little wooden horses and knights. The man looked up at her, offered a subdued smile, and a bow of his head. The boys paid her no mind. Isolde sat at the opposite end of the table from Sabrina and Oliver. A pretty brunette with a heart-shaped face and a pregnant belly sat next to her, meticulously looking over the rebellion map that was spread before them.

Admittedly, Neve still felt a little out-of-body, a little like a ghost. She wasn't sure how long she'd been imprisoned and tortured, but it had certainly been enough time to make her entirely lose her bearings.

The world felt changed, different. Or, perhaps, it was she who was now altered.

Her mind flashed to Rory's knife, the smell of his sweat. She swallowed hard and shook her head.

Killian, at her side, discreetly leaned in a little closer. The feel of his strong presence helped to anchor her.

"You all right?" he asked quietly.

Her heart acknowledged not only how in-tune he was with her, but how he understood that she didn't want the others to know that it would possibly take her a long time to feel normal.

Neve nodded and squeezed Killian's hand.

"I will be," she whispered. She felt him squeeze her hand back, and then she moved to take a seat at the head of the table.

Everyone in the room sat up a little straighter; their attention was drawn to her with a near-magnetic pull. Killian took the seat to her right. Even the dark-haired man and the little boys quietly moved to the table and sat down. No one spoke. They all waited.

It occurred to her, in some muddled way, that whatever she said now would be her first official act as Queen and that these people in the library were the very beginnings of her court.

"Thank you," she said. She looked around the table, and her gaze met each person's eyes. "Thank you for coming for me. You found me. You saved me. I am forever in your debt."

"There is no debt–" Isolde began, but Neve lifted her hand, and her friend went quiet.

"What you did today will never be forgotten," Neve said. Before anyone could demure or offer more humility, she continued. "The night I was captured, I was at a ball. I thought it was for the citizens of the city, but, as it turned out, it was all for me. Somehow, the Highborns discovered my identity." Neve gave a breathy, mirthless laugh and shook her head. "I imagine it's because I don't look quite as anonymous as I thought I did. I think I resemble the women of my house a little too much, and I learned here in this library that I share a face with the goddess Celesta. It was my mistake, thinking they wouldn't notice, thinking I could outsmart them."

"You're very smart, my Queen," Oliver said quietly.

Little flowers bloomed in her heart at his sincerity. She smiled at him.

"It's a mistake I won't make again," she assured. "Nearly everyone in attendance at the ball was Cavalry, in disguise. The women, too, I suppose. I danced with most of them. They spun me around the ball like I was any normal woman on any normal night."

Beneath the table, she felt Killian's hand on her thigh, his thumb moving in a gentle, reassuring caress.

"Then the Highborns arrived. And the doors locked. All but one. Twenty Mages filed in. I was outnumbered, entirely outmatched. Another mistake I won't make again." She felt Killian's hand clench on her leg as if to temper the rage that undoubtedly was rising at the thought of what was done to her.

Around the table, her companions leaned in close. Even the children sat open-mouthed like she was telling the most exciting faerie tale they'd heard in a long time. Reliving the worst blunder of her life was not easy, and it didn't feel like a very interesting story to her, but she needed to tell it just the same.

"'This party is all for you,' they said, 'A family reunion'." Their words tasted like ash in her mouth.

"Family reunion?" the pretty brunette asked.

Neve looked around. Killian's brows furrowed in confusion. The rest all waited for her to continue. Only Isolde showed any sign of understanding. She gave Neve a gentle, kind smile. A nod.

"They said, 'Did you think that a descendant of our half-sister could come to our kingdom and that we wouldn't know?'"

Sabrina's mouth dropped open. "Holy shit."

"What?" Oliver asked. "What does that mean?"

"It means," Neve went on, "That the Highborns are the half-brothers of Queen Nyx. They're half god, which seems to have blessed them with long life."

"How is it that, in 300 years, no one has noticed that the governors haven't changed?" the dark-haired man asked.

Neve lifted her shoulder in a shrug. "Very few people in Eodia have come face-to-face with them. Those that have are either Cavalry, Mages, or people who spend their whole lives in the Capital and are conditioned not to notice or ask questions."

"It's true," Killian added. "Even the Cadre never saw the Highborns in person. We were always given orders by proxy through the Cavalry."

"So the Highborns are not only responsible for the oppression of this kingdom's people, they are also responsible for Eodia being cut off from the old gods, for the curse on the Island, and everything that has happened since?" Sabrina asked. There was a dangerous edge to her voice that Neve quite liked.

"Yes. And that is what I need the rebels across the kingdom to know. This information needs to spread quickly," Neve said.

"I can make that happen," Isolde responded with a confidence so deep that Neve knew it would be done.

"Good." Neve stood and raised her chin. "I want every last person on this Island to understand. I want them to know."

Her companions around the table all stood, ready for her command.

Neve's chest filled up with so many things at once that she thought it all might overflow from her. Pride, gratitude, love. Truth. Hope. And the most righteous rage she had ever known.

"Tell them their Queen has returned and she wants vengeance."

51

Snow floated gently down from the clouds. Just a scattering of flakes, a reminder that it was still winter and would be for quite some time. Neve's breath was a puff of fog in the cold air. She sat straight-backed and steady in Gisele's saddle, wearing her fitted leather armor with the sharp crystal epaulets glinting on her strong shoulders. She'd braided her hair in a thick plait that rolled down her spine, and on top of her head was the glinting crown of House Lyra. She was in stark contrast to the snow, the grey buildings, and the pastel-clad citizens of the Capital.

She was a dark smudge coming to blot out their light.

At Neve's request, Oliver and Sabrina warned the gentlefolk of Sylvera to stay at home today. Those who worked to clean up the messes of the aristocrats, who lived in the humble cottages near the library in the old part of town. They were told to lock their doors, take the day off, and above all, stay away from the main streets.

The rest of the city was given no such courtesy.

Women and men dressed in watercolor garments lined the sidewalks and watched with wide eyes and creased brows as Neve rode Gisele at a slow gait down the center of the street. She looked at each one of them as she passed.

Killian rode behind her on Willow, and Neve could feel his eyes on her. She had the sense that he wouldn't let her out of his sight for a long time. She didn't mind.

She knew they made a wicked-looking pair, a fact that gave her no small amount of joy.

They made their way to the center of the city, toward the Highborns' manor. Isolde had spoken to her spies, and, upon Neve's capture, the brothers left town, heading east - presumably to Lyra Castle. They thought she was dead and assumed that her death could be the key to freeing the palace. After all these years, they wanted to rule from the only seat of power in Eodia that the people and the gods would truly bow before.

Neve planned to follow them, greet their disappointment, and end them once and for all.

But first, she had business in the Capital.

As she neared the manor, she could see a stalwart line of Cavalry in front of the gates. They stood shoulder-to-shoulder, armed with swords that shone in the dimly overcast light of the midwinter day. Left behind to protect and defend the city while their commanders and comrades went in search of glory. They'd been alerted to Neve's approach, likely by a scout. It didn't matter.

They would all be ash in the end.

Neve brought Gisele to a halt, Killian and Willow moving beside her. She looked over at him, and he nodded, his eyes glittering with pride and the promise of violence. Neve loved him for it. She lifted her chin and turned back to the Cavalry guarding the gate.

She ran her gaze over each of their faces and saw the same thing. Arrogance, a warped sense of self-reverential duty, and the edge of fear. The kind of fear one might have when seeing a ghost. Or a hungry predator in the woods.

Both were correct.

Many of the men standing before her spent the evening of the ball dressed in finery and spinning her around the dance floor. Neve remembered the scent of their colognes, the touch of their hands, and the melody of the music. She remembered everything. Including the sound of doors locking, of weapons being drawn, the stink of cowardice as they watched the Mages put her down and Rory Grey scoop her up in his arms like a bridegroom. They'd watched him carry her over the threshold and into her waiting doom.

Hate was too bland a word for what she felt for them.

"The Highborns are not here," a soldier said.

Neve lazily turned her attention to him. She knew his face. *Dominic Chambers, at your service.* The first to ask her to dance that night.

"I know," she replied, then spread her lips in a villainous smile. "But *you* are."

"We are to execute traitors and disruptors on sight," Dominic said. There was a catch in his voice. A stumble.

"It seems like you tried that already with me," Neve looked down at her body, then back up at him. "I don't think it worked."

"Stand down and come with us willingly," another soldier chimed in.

Neve held up her hand. "No interruptions."

An uneasy shuffle rumbled through the group. They were unsure, unorganized. If Neve had to guess, they were all of the same rank. The Highborns hadn't left any generals or captains behind. And why would they? If they thought she was dead, Rory would be here to lead, and there would be no threat beyond the rebels. They would need all the trained muscle they had to make it through the bramble maze at Lyra Castle.

All disposable soldiers were left behind in the Capital and scattered amongst the kingdom's towns. Where they no longer perceived any risk.

"Justice is important to me," Neve said. "So I'll offer you a chance to right your wrongs-"

Someone laughed. "You can see you're outnumbered. You're not in a position to offer anything."

The power inside her stiffened, stretched, and yawned. *Hello, old friend.*

Faster than any pair of eyes could track, Neve slipped a dagger from her boot and sent it flying through the air. It hit its mark, lodging in the soldier's throat and sending him as a bloody mess to the ground.

"I'm fairly certain I said no interruptions," Neve stated.

Fear was sharp in the air, but no one else moved. No one checked on the fallen soldier, no one even looked at him. That told Neve all she needed to know about the value these soldiers placed on one another's lives, on life in general.

Killian dismounted his horse, drew his sword, and began a slow and dangerous stroll along the ranks of the Cavalry. The soldiers stiffened, the grips on their weapons tightened and wavered. They knew who Killian was. They knew the next person to speak or move would most certainly die at his hands.

The Cavalry outnumbered them, but they were no match for Neve and Killian.

"I will offer you one chance to lay down your weapons and kneel to me," Neve said. She watched the wrinkles deepen around the soldiers' mouths, and a few of them rolled their eyes. A few had the sense to look like they were smart enough to consider her words carefully. "Kneel to your Queen and you'll be spared."

That sleeping giant in her, the power, the light, sat up and started expanding. Neve wasn't sure why it slept when she was captured and tortured. Perhaps it was a test. But it was awake now. Writhing and awake.

No one moved to kneel. She didn't expect them to, but offering the choice was important to her. Neve opened herself up, letting the power have more and more space as it plumed like clouds within her. She felt it first in her chest, in her gut, her head. It moved through her blood, into her bones. When it first came to her all those weeks ago, it felt like an unbearable pressure. When it first came to her, it felt like a foreigner.

But now Neve understood. It was a part of her; it was her lineage, her legacy, her blood. God's blood. And, as she gave it space, acknowledged it, called it by name, she found that she could almost bend it to her will. Almost.

Neve let the power build and build until she could feel that now-familiar crackling, the sparks. The quality of light changed around her, the eyes of the Cavalrymen widened, and she knew what they were seeing. What she'd seen when she tested the power in front of the mirror. Glowing. Starlight. She remembered what happened when she'd let the power pulse, when the mirror shattered around her.

Let's see what you can do, she told the power.

Neve sent out a pulse of that power. She recognized the sound before she realized what she'd done. A mammoth and sharp crashing sound cut through the winter silence of the Capital. All the many windows adorning the Highborns' tower exploded and blew out, raining glass down upon the Cavalry. Most of the men ducked and covered their heads. A particularly large shard fell and stabbed through the back of one of the men, killing him instantly.

Killian looked at her with equal parts awe and excitement.

Her power purred with satisfaction, but began to build again. It wasn't done. *She* wasn't done. Neve sent out another pulse, and this time something sparked and caught fire. The small flame grew quickly, and in the space of a blink, half the manor was engulfed in a star-powered blaze. A fitting punishment, considering the way the Highborns had turned so many villages of the kingdom - *her* kingdom- to cinders.

The Cavalrymen were shouting now, but Neve barely heard it. She dismounted and slid to the ground, stalking forward. The power crackled through her as she approached Dominic Chambers. She could see her light reflected in his terrified eyes.

She knew she was both magnificent and awful all at once.

"You spoke of traitors," Neve said. "What do you call it, Dominic, when you ask your Queen to dance and lead her to her death instead?"

Neve felt no remorse when she saw the tears in his eyes, when he shook his head and opened his mouth to speak. She drew a dagger from her hip and held him close as she sank the blade between his ribs.

"It's called treason, soldier," she whispered.

As Dominic slumped against her and crumpled to the cold ground, Neve looked over at Killian and nodded. Then the Queen and her Knight unleashed themselves upon the Cavalry.

The soldiers were trapped between a burning tower and the molten fury of Neve D'Aeth Lyra and Killian Grey. They had nowhere to go, and no aid was coming for them. So they did what men do when they are desperate and without hope: they fought. They bared their teeth like animals, they hurled insults, they swung their swords. As if it would do any good. As if their effort would make any difference.

But Neve saw the look in their eyes. They knew they were dead men. Dead men who wanted to go out fighting. Neve obliged.

She and Killian moved like ink spilled in water: smooth and graceful, a spreading stain of death. One by one, the Cavalry soldiers fell. Neve and Killian's blades were sharp and unerring. Blood spilled hot and steady until all that was left was a tower engulfed in flame and a pile of dead men on the ground.

Her eyes met Killian's. The blade of his sword was dripping red, and his blue eyes were bright with victory. Seeing him like this, lethally triumphant, she understood that they belonged together, that he was meant for her.

They moved toward each other. With the burning fire at their back and the bodies of their enemies at their feet, Killian wrapped an arm around Neve's waist and yanked her against him.

She gripped his sharp jaw in her bloody hand and crushed her mouth against his. Neve felt wild for him, the way she'd felt after their first battle against the Cavalry on the plains. The bloodlust adrenaline, the power still swirling in her chest, the love for him. It was a heady, chaotic feeling, and Neve had never felt more alive than she did in that moment.

Killian pulled back and looked at her, his chest heaving and his eyes foggy with the same feeling that rushed through Neve's body.

"You were incredible," he breathed.

Neve smirked. "I know."

With a grin, Killian kissed her again, then said: "What now, my lady?"

"Now we are going to take back my castle."

They turned and began walking back toward the library, down the main street, leading Gisele and Willow. The crowd on the sidewalks was larger now, it seemed as if every citizen in the city- aristocrats and gentlefolk alike - left the warmth of their homes to come and watch. Neve wasn't sure what she'd expected from the people of Sylvera when they looked upon her. Fear? Hate? Anger? But she saw none of that. Nothing could have prepared her for what she saw.

As she passed, the people knelt.

They bowed. They lifted their eyes to her, and Neve's breath caught in her lungs at what shone there. Hope. Gratitude. Despite having just witnessed her destroy a building with some otherworldly power and mercilessly slaughter a dozen men right in front of them, they beheld her like they'd been waiting for her their entire lives. Neve understood at that moment just how deeply oppressed the people of her kingdom were under the watchful eyes of the Highborns and the quick-to-punish weapons of the Cavalry and Cadre. She understood that even the wealthy in their perfect pastel bubble spent their lives in fear of one misstep that could lead them to the executioner's block.

Neve also understood that she'd vastly underestimated the deep-seated hope for the return of someone they could call Queen. The hope of House Lyra. The hope of *her* return to Eodia.

Beside her, Killian took her hand and squeezed. She looked at him, saw the pride in his eyes, and suddenly felt so overcome with feeling, with humility, that she thought she might go boneless and fall to her knees with the rest of them. But she remained on her feet, she continued to walk, she continued to look each person she passed in the eyes as if she could reassure them that she would succeed. That she would end the Highborns once and for all, take back the castle, and spend the rest of her days working to be worthy of the reverence and hope that was on their faces.

And she would.

She would, or she would die trying.

That was her silent promise to them. Her people.

Interlude IV

The news spread like warmth across the cold Island.
News, this time, not rumors.
The Queen has returned.
She glowed like the night sky.
She's coming for the castle.
She's coming for the kingdom.
A week's ride away.
Behind the vast and deadly bramble maze, Lyra Castle waited.
There was a quiet rumble deep in the earth beneath its foundation.
The skies above were full of dark clouds, so dense they could be stone.
The Highborns were close.
The Half-Brothers approached.
The wind howled.
It would be over soon.

52

"I go where you go," Isolde stated.

"The library?" Neve countered.

"Is in good hands." A smile brightened Isolde's face as she gave a pointed look to where Kat, Leo, and the children sat at the table in the center of the library.

"Leo will want to be at Killian's side."

Isolde shook her head. "Leo wants to be with his family. Besides, I outrank him. He doesn't have a choice."

"Oliver and Sabrina?" Neve smiled as she watched her friend roll her eyes.

"I'm afraid you're stuck with them," Isolde replied. "They also go where you go."

The answer filled Neve with warmth. She glanced toward the library's curtained entrance, where Sabrina and Oliver stood, rucksacks on their backs and bouncing on their toes with excitement. Isolde moved to join them, and Neve watched as her companions took in the sight of the library one last time, committing the details to memory.

Killian emerged from the secret room, fully armed and so rugged that a sizzle of desire curled low in Neve's belly. He had a bag of weapons over each shoulder, his shield in one hand and a stack of books in the other. The corner of his lips tipped up on a smirk when he noticed her watching him.

"The way you're looking at me, Lady Nightmare," Killian said in a low voice when he reached her. His eyes raked down her body playfully, then back up to her face. "It's almost as if you like me."

Neve raised an eyebrow. "I might be a little fond of you."

He leaned forward and brushed his lips against the shell of her ear, sending a shiver skittering up the back of her neck.

"Keep looking at me like that and I'll order everyone out so I can bend you over that table and give the books a good show."

Neve turned her head and nipped at the sensitive skin just beneath his jaw. A low groan vibrated in his throat, she felt it against her mouth, and into her core.

"Don't make promises you can't keep, Killian Grey."

"We're literally right here. We can hear everything you're saying," Sabrina interrupted from behind them, the annoyance in her voice was sharp.

"I'm so uncomfortable right now," Oliver whispered.

A laugh, a real one for the first time in… gods, Neve couldn't even remember the last time she truly laughed, bubbled up in her chest and spilled out of her mouth. The smile on Killian's face as a result was nothing short of magnificent.

"I like that sound," he said, the heat in his gaze fading to a gentle sweetness that reminded her of the comfort of a warm bed. "The things I would do to hear you laugh like that every day…"

"Let's make it through this next part. Then I'll let you try to make me laugh for the rest of our lives," she replied. Pink splotches of color bloomed on his cheekbones. The great Killian Grey, bashful and blushing for her. Indeed, she wanted nothing more than to spend her life on Eodia's throne with this man at her side.

But first, of course, they had to survive taking the Castle.

Isolde's rebel spies revealed that, in the single day since Neve burned down the tower and liberated the Capital, riots were breaking out in nearly every village on the Island. Some towns were more prepared for battle against the stationed Cavalry than others. But they fought nonetheless, even as they looked their executioners in the face.

Every town they needed to move through to get to the Castle was rife with conflict. The Queen and her Court were ready. Neve intended to remove the Cavalry threat from each village as they traveled. Her retribution for slain citizens would be swift and without mercy.

The Highborns brought a considerable amount of Cavalry with them to the Castle. An army. Rebel spies reported seeing upwards of three hundred troops escorting the Highborns to Lyra.

Neve's rag-tag group of five fighters against the rumored three hundred Cavalry were not good odds.

Terrible odds.

Catastrophic.

However, the Cavalry and Highborns would have the bramble maze to contend with before even coming close to the doors of the Castle. It was miles and miles deep. It would take hours, if not days, to move through, if they could move at all. The cursed brambles were so mighty that no weapon was strong enough to cut them down. It was a true death trap, a graveyard full of the bleached bones of the people who'd tried to conquer it. No man had ever managed to make it through the maze to the palace doors.

Neve was holding onto the legends of the bramble maze as her source of truth. Hanging her hopes on the idea that the maze would do the killing for her when it came to the Cavalry.

And then, of course, she and her Court would have to find a way through themselves.

The journey before them would be bloody, with odds stacked high against them. Death was jealous, hungry, and waiting.

But Neve had to believe she could do this. For the kingdom. For the man she loved. For the people willing to fight and die in her name.

For the hope she'd seen in the eyes of those who knelt for her in the Capital.

For children like Henry and Jasper, who deserved to live a quiet life without fear of evil in the night and burning alive in their bedrooms.

For herself. To finally have a place to call home.

Killian handed her the stack of books he held. Neve examined their spines to see their titles and smiled. *Queen of Death. The Family History of House Lyra. Court of the Empress.* And two other titles Neve knew to be along the same lines as *Court of the Empress*: smut.

"Two are for glory. The rest are for... inspiration." He said with a wink.

Neve rolled her eyes but slid all five books into the saddlebag on her shoulder.

"Are you ready for this?" Killian asked. Good humor still lingered in his expression, but his eyes met hers now with no playfulness, only care. She would never get used to the way he checked in on her, but she would forever be grateful for it.

Neve gave Killian a nod and turned to her other companions, head high and back straight.

"It's time," she said.

~

Night fell as they reached the first village outside the Capital. The sky was full of dimly blinking stars, and the air was so cold that it stung Neve's cheeks, and she pulled the hood of her cloak close around her face. Her breath plumed in thick clouds in front of her.

Midwinter was unforgiving, full of frost and ice.

She hoped they'd find an inn to spend the night, but mostly she hoped that the town itself would still be standing. She wondered how many of the villages across the kingdom, *her* kingdom, were decimated either by unrest or the careless injustice of the Cavalry and Cadre. How many villages would need to be rebuilt?

The weight of the crown, nestled safely in one of her saddlebags, was heavy and uncertain.

As they slowed on the King's Road and angled into the town, they were greeted by the sounds of shouting. Neve's hand drifted to the dagger on her hip, and she rested her gloved fingers on the hilt. She watched Killian's hand do the same on his sword.

Her senses opened up, searching for the sounds of battle and strife. But instead of the clang of weapons, she could hear the gentle lilt of music, and instead of the sharp tang of blood, Neve could smell the warming spices of mulled wine.

A central square of the village was transformed into a wonderland of flickering light and laughter. Enormous bonfires crackled at each corner, their warmth inviting the townspeople to huddle around. Flames danced and leaped, casting intricate shadows on the snow-covered ground. The scent of burning wood mingled with the sweet aroma of roasted chestnuts.

Winter solstice.

Time was a whirlwind, and Neve had lost track of the month completely. The surprise was a welcome one.

In the center of the festivities, an ancient oak tree stood tall and proud, adorned with shimmering strands of silver and gold. Villagers draped colorful ribbons and wreaths around its branches. Beneath its majestic boughs, a group of musicians played lively tunes on fiddles, flutes, and drums, their melodies echoing through the village.

Around the tree, couples twirled and spun, their laughter filling the air as their footprints created patterns in the snow. The village children, bundled in layers of clothing, giggled and chased one another, their rosy cheeks bright and shining.

Killian was the first to dismount. Isolde, Oliver, and Sabrina followed suit, tying their horses to nearby trees. There was a look of anticipation on her companions' faces as they looked at her, silently asking permission to join the party. Neve couldn't hold back a small, pleased smile as she nodded. Snapping sparks of some sort of melancholy joy kindled in her chest. She watched as, despite being strangers, the villagers welcomed her friends with enthusiasm. An older woman with braided silver hair and a smile on her face placed a garland of evergreen and holly on each of her companions' heads as they entered the square.

Killian waited for Neve, his eyes glittering as he watched her take it all in. There was a knowing look on his face, like he understood what she was thinking without saying a word out loud. Perhaps he was thinking the same thing. That everything had been so bloody and violent for so long, it was almost surreal to come upon a pocket of the kingdom that was fertile with joy and celebration. Neve's heart hurt from the perfect beauty of this village, its festivity. If this town had been touched by trauma recently, the gentlefolk showed no sign of it tonight. This place was lucky and rare in such dark times.

Neve slid off of Gisele, and Killian took care of tying her up with the other horses and then returned to Neve's side. He took her hand. She slipped the hood of her cloak off her head and looked at him for a long moment. The dark circles under his eyes and the newly deepened worry lines between his brows were evidence of what recent events had done to him, to them. But there, in his blue eyes, was the swirling sweet love reserved for her. Despite it all, that part of their story remained without wavering.

He glanced over at the revelry, then back at her. Something about the set of his mouth felt like a plea, like he wanted nothing more than to see her join the party, to find some speck of happiness here. She remembered the look on his face when he'd made her laugh earlier, and Neve knew she could give him the solstice gift of seeing her find ease, if only for this night.

"Tonight," she said quietly. "I'm just Neve, and you're just Killian, and we don't have a war to fight or a kingdom to win."

His shoulders relaxed, and she could see the coiled tension leave his body. He pressed his lips to her temple.

"Tonight, then," he said.

She tugged his hand and led him to the square. Neve bent her head before the old woman and let her set a wreath of spruce on her head. She turned in time to watch as the crone set one atop Killian's head as well, before grabbing him by the face and smacking a big, closed-mouth kiss on his lips. Killian's eyes went wide, and Neve laughed as the woman let him go with a big grin.

She winked at Neve. "Hope you don't mind, lass."

"Not at all," she replied.

Killian raised a playful eyebrow at her as they walked further into the square. "Not at all?"

"If you haven't noticed, I'm not exactly a jealous lover."

He rolled his eyes and caught her around the waist, pulling her close.

"No? Do I need to remind you of the time you came to my rescue at the tavern when some woman was trying to climb me like a tree?"

Neve feigned ignorance and fought back a smile.

"I don't know what you're talking about."

Killian gripped her waist tightly and leaned in. "Let me remind you, then. I recall that you pointed at my cock and said 'that's mine.'"

"A simple statement of fact," she replied with a shrug.

He took her chin between his thumb and forefinger and lifted her face, brushing his lips against hers. "You're not wrong."

His laugh was a breath that she could taste, and it drew her closer to him until she parted his lips with the gentle swipe of her tongue and kissed him. One of his arms circled her waist, pulling her hips against his while his other hand found the nape of her neck. He gripped her there, deepening the kiss, and Neve could feel the pounding of his heart against the hands she pressed to his chest.

Neve was acutely aware, especially in this moment with his mouth on hers and his heart thundering against her palms, how close they'd come to losing each other. First, their fight and the interminable silence that followed. Then, when Killian faced down Mages and Cavalry in Thornkeep. Then her capture and torture, very nearly her death.

Wild thorns of anxiety prickled behind her sternum.

She'd never in her life had as much to lose as she did now.

But, she'd promised Killian tonight. She was not a Queen at war; he was not her knight. They were just two people, as they may have been if the world they lived in were gentler and kinder.

As his mouth moved with hers and his fingers lost themselves in her hair, Neve had a vision of a different life. A quiet one. One with a cottage and a garden, and a marriage. A library full of books. A crackling hearth.

That could never be their life. But here, on winter solstice with the sound of music and the smell of pine and the warmth of Killian's body against hers, it was a pretty thought.

Killian's mouth moved down to her neck and fluttered lazily over her steady pulse. Neve felt his lips curl up in a smile as the music changed from a classic lowlands ballad to something a little more raucous with a heavy drum beat. Before she took her next breath, Killian was dancing her through the crowd, spinning and spinning. A laugh sprang from her as she followed his footsteps and let him swing her around with him, snow crunching beneath their dancing feet.

The pace was quick, but Killian was sure, pressing her against him with one hand on her lower back, unless he was twirling her away only to snap her back into his arms with a grin. Cold air nipped at Neve's cheeks, and her hair loosened from her braid, but she barely felt any of it. The world around them became a blur of snowflakes and firelight, clouds of breath and rhythm.

He leaned back a little to look at her face, and what he saw there made his expression open up with an explosion of joy. Neve had never seen him so happy. It was simple and pure and complete.

It made her want to wreck the world and rebuild it anew if only to see him look at her like that every single day. She wanted to erase the past and change the future for the sake of that smile alone.

And she *could* do it.

Would do it.

She would win the war and change the world to guarantee he'd find joy like this again.

As the music reached its crescendo, Killian pulled her closer and laughed against her ear, and they continued spinning and twirling beneath the dark solstice sky. Faster and faster, they were a whirlwind of celebration until Killian dipped her low and held her there.

The song came to an end. Neve could vaguely hear laughter and cheers from the townsfolk, but all she could focus on was the dizzy sight of Killian leaning over her and the strength in his arms. Their chests heaved as one, puffs of breath plumed in the winter air. Neve's heart thrummed in her ears, and she was certain she could hear Killian's there too, in her head, in her body. His eyes were bright and shiny, the tip of his nose pink with cold.

"I didn't know you could dance like that," Neve said in a breathless voice, unable to hide the grin still plastered to her face.

Killian's gaze dropped to her lips, then back up to her eyes.

"Glad I could surprise you."

He captured her mouth with a hot kiss that sucked the air right out of her lungs and made her fingertips dig into the muscles of his shoulders. He pulled away and pressed his forehead to hers, closing his eyes.

"Gods, I love you," he whispered.

"I love you, Killian Grey," she replied.

The moment was interrupted when Oliver came striding up to them with mugs of steaming mulled wine in his hands. Killian pulled Neve back upright from the dip but kept one arm around her waist and tucked her in close. Oliver's cheeks were pink, and his smile was genuine and warm. He handed the mugs of wine to Neve and Killian. Neve took a deep sip and let the spices warm her blood.

"Isolde got us rooms at the inn for the night," Oliver said, raising his voice just enough that it made Neve wonder exactly how many mugs of wine the guard had already downed. "There's a huge feast in the dining room that the innkeeper invited us to."

The promise of a hot and hearty meal had Neve and Killian immediately following Oliver to the inn. And, just as he'd explained, there was a huge feast laid out on a long table in the main dining room. Half a dozen roast chickens were steaming on platters across the table, along with baked potatoes swimming in dark yellow butter, good hard cheese, apples, charred cabbage, and crusty bread. The savory scents alone were enough to make Neve's mouth water.

Isolde waved to them from the end of the table where she sat, enjoying the meal. Neve slipped into the chair next to her. Killian leaned over the table and piled food onto a plate that he set in front of Neve before making quick work of taking a heaping helping for himself and digging in. Oliver plopped down next to Isolde and brought a chicken leg to his eager mouth, the juices dripping down his hand.

The first mouthful of food Neve took nearly made her eyes roll back in her head with pleasure. It had been a while since she'd had food this good, and she was certain it would be a while until they were all able to eat this well again. She was intent on savoring it. She scanned the dining room. At the other end of the table sat a group of gentlefolk, laughing loudly and eating their fill, sloshing their mugs of wine as they spoke.

The door opened, bringing in a dusting of snowflakes and two women draped over each other, giggling. Neve needed to take a second glance before she realized one of the women was Sabrina, her face flushed and happy with no trace of her usual surly countenance. Her arms were wrapped around the waist of a pretty redhead whose lips were nuzzling into Sabrina's neck. Neve watched with a smirk as Sabrina whispered to the woman and slipped a room key into her hand before separating from her and joining the group at the table.

"You didn't want to invite her to eat with us?" Oliver asked, taking another bite from his chicken leg.

Sabrina sat down and scrunched her nose at him. "I figured she might lose interest in me if she had to sit and watch you have your way with that roast chicken."

Oliver shrugged. "It's good chicken."

Beneath the table, Killian's hand slid across Neve's lap and gripped her thigh. The touch made a fist of heat clench in her belly. She gave him a sidelong look that seemed to communicate the rush of desire to him because his hand flexed again and moved a little higher. She watched as he pressed his lips together as if to hold back yet another grin, this one purely male and full of promise.

The look on his face made Neve want to end the meal and drag him up to her room, but she held back. She ate well and watched her friends poke fun at each other and laugh, and drink. It wasn't lost on her that friendship like this was a rare thing in her life. These people were with her because they wanted to be with her. After all, they *liked* her because her presence somehow made perfect sense in their close-knit group. This was no small thing, and Neve felt grateful.

"Thank you," she said to them. Their laughter faded, and each of them looked at her with just a shred of confusion. "Thank you for being here. For coming with me."

Neve met their gaze, noticing the fresh spark of emotion on their faces, the suspiciously wet sheen in Oliver's eyes, and offered them her sincerity. She bent her head in a slight bow, silently acknowledging all they'd given up to be here with her, the risk of following. Isolde reached over and took her hand, giving it a firm squeeze.

Sabrina smiled gently, then cleared her throat. "Well, I've been waiting for an apology for the time you tried to kill me, but I suppose this will do."

53

It was late by the time Neve and Killian made it up to their rented room. They feasted and drank and laughed with their friends and the townsfolk for hours. The big meal and mulled wine made Neve's body feel warm and sluggish in the most delicious and unfamiliar way; she couldn't recall a time that she'd ever been able to let herself loosen up so much. She was thankful for it.

Killian entered the room first, and when she turned to shut the door, she felt him close behind her, his chest against her back. Desire turned the warmth in her belly to full flames as he towered over her and pressed her into the door. Neve turned the lock and tilted her head.

"Need something?" she purred with a smile.

"Mmhmm," he murmured in response. Killian's breath was hot on her neck, and it sent a shiver down her skin. Neve felt the graze of his teeth and arched her back to bring him closer.

"What do you need, Killian?"

He didn't answer but his mouth continued to kiss and suck on the delicate skin of her neck, sending her eyes rolling back in her head. The pace of his breathing in her ear kicked up, and he started pulling open the ties and buckles of her leathers with expert fingers. There was nothing gentle about him as he yanked her armor off and tossed it aside, and then began undoing the laces of her corset with increasing desperation.

"Remember the first inn we stayed at?" He asked, his voice rough and husky.

"You slept outside my room," Neve replied with a smile.

Killian moved his hips and shoved her against the door, hard, and her whole body clenched with wicked anticipation.

"You asked me to lace up your corset the next morning," he said through clenched teeth.

Neve let out a rough laugh, feeling his cock pressing against her ass as he pulled and pulled on her laces.

"I remember," she said.

Her corset came undone, and Killian quickly flung it to the floor, wrapping his arms around her and palming her bare breasts with both hands. Neve's knees went a little weak with the hungry way he groped her and the low sound that rumbled in his throat.

"Do you have any idea what that did to me? Wanting you so badly but not being able to touch you?"

"I knew exactly what it did to you," she said, her voice barely more than a strained whisper.

"I bet you did." He turned her around, pushing her back against the door, and leaned in to kiss her. Neve tilted her chin up to meet him, but he pulled away quickly with a grin, denying her.

A thrill burned through her. She loved him like this, commanding and arrogant.

Killian took a step back from her, his gaze tracking each move she made, every breath she took, devouring her naked breasts with his eyes as he pulled off his armor and the tunic underneath. His taut skin gleamed in the low firelight of the room, stretched over his big, deadly body.

Neve's mouth watered, and she squeezed her thighs together at the sight of him: his heaving chest, the muscles rolling down his stomach, the wild look in his eyes.

And he was all hers.

She reached for him, wanting nothing more than to feel him on her fingers, but he blocked her with a devilish smirk and advanced on her, pinning her wrists above her head with one hand. The scent of him enveloped her, the sweat and cedar on his skin and the mulled wine on his lips. He laid the open palm of his free hand on her chest and leaned his forehead on hers.

"Why's your heart beating so fast, Lady Nightmare?"

"I think you know," she replied. There was a growing pressure low in her belly and between her legs that had her feeling starved and lightheaded.

He smirked again. "Say it."

"I want you."

"*Where* do you want me?"

The sound of his growling voice, his dirty mouth, the feel of him so close... it was all nearly enough to make her feral. And then his hand started moving. He slowly brushed down her body, touching her skin with just his fingertips. She started shivering and couldn't stop, her body reacting to the build-up of need and no release.

"Inside me," she said. "I want you inside me."

Neve watched the muscle in his jaw clench, the smile on his lips. He nodded and slipped his hand beneath the waistband of her leggings, moving lower until he cupped her pussy. He let out a low growl and leaned closer, giving her cheek a tender kiss.

"Fuck," he said in her ear and flexed his fingers. Neve had to hold back the whimper that threatened to explode from her mouth. "So wet for me and I've barely even started."

She ground her hips against his hand and turned her head to nip at his throat.

"Then *start*," she demanded.

He chuckled but did as she asked and moved his fingers in slow circles against her clit. She moaned with pleasure and leaned her head back, her body relaxing into the friction of his hand. His eyes were intent on her face, watching every reaction, full of heat and mischief and the curious wonder of a man wanting to see exactly what he was doing to a woman. The way he watched her, the way he paid attention and moved with her responses, was something she'd never experienced before him, and it made everything so much more intense.

"You're so beautiful like this," he whispered and kissed her. Neve gasped against his lips, kissing him back hard as he increased the speed and the perfect, perfect pressure of his fingers.

"Right there," she moaned.

"Right there? What's going to happen right there, love?" he asked, his voice rough but teasing. "Tell me what's going to happen right there."

Her pleasure built, like waves in the sea at high tide, more and more, bigger and bigger, crashing into her.

"I'm going to come for you," she breathed.

His hand moved faster, and she moaned, all thought falling right out of her brain. Everything was him and his fingers and his mouth on hers.

She was close. So close. Tremors moved through her body, and she sagged a little against Killian. She was about to absolutely explode... when he stopped. She opened her eyes and stared at him with fury as frustration blasted through her.

"Don't stop," she commanded, but the sound of it came out as a plea.

He was grinning again. In her wild state, Neve had only two thoughts: to either throw him down and take her pleasure from him or rip out his throat.

"I've got you, I promise," he whispered, moving his mouth down to her tits and sucking a nipple into his mouth. She cried out, a violent sensation flared through her, and she bucked her hips against him. "I'm just going to make you wait for it."

His mouth moved to her other nipple, and she felt him scrape his teeth across it. She sucked in a sharp breath.

"You're a villain," she said.

Killian chuckled and dropped to his knees. He lifted her foot and slipped off her boot, then did the same to the other. He ran his hands up her calves, then her thighs, massaging her muscles as he did. It felt so good, and she relaxed a little again. His hands gripped her hips and hooked into the waistband of her leggings before he pulled them down.

She was utterly bare for him. He shifted closer and pulled her left leg over his shoulder.

"Would a villain kneel before his Queen like this?" he asked.

The sight of him on his knees for her, looking up at her with those eyes and that handsome face, nearly undid her. She reached down and ran a hand through his hair. He closed his eyes at her touch, then buried his face in her.

He feasted on her, licking and sucking and *groaning* against her. Her mind was a frenzy of light and color and love and need. She sank both hands into his hair, and he moaned, sending a vibration deep into her core.

"More," she breathed in a voice that wasn't entirely her own.

Killian slid a finger inside of her, and when she moved her hips and cried out, he added a second finger and curled them, stroking that sensitive spot inside her. Her legs began to shake, and she looked down at him. His eyes were on her, and she felt like her heart could explode, followed by the rest of her body.

Neve's pleasure built again, but this time, because she'd come so close once already, it was cataclysmic. It felt as if, should she just let go, the world would turn upside down and implode. There was a small, desperate part of her that wanted to beg him for release, but when she looked in his eyes, she knew she wouldn't have to. She saw it there. His own need for her pleasure.

So, she let go. The orgasm hit her like dragon fire, hot and all-consuming. It kept going, wave after wave of tingling, crushing ecstasy. Neve was vaguely aware that she let out a scream, vaguely aware that her body failed her and she went limp in Killian's arms. He caught her, and she clung to him, head reeling and dizzy, body buzzing.

Killian lifted her and carried her to the bed, where he gently laid her down beneath him. He kissed her jaw and cheeks, brushing the hair from her face.

"Still whole?" he asked.

She finally opened her eyes and smiled at him, somehow spent and needing him more than ever. "Still whole."

"Good. Because you have no idea how much I need you right now," he said.

He undid his belt and kicked off his pants, and then there was nothing between them. His cock was hard and throbbing against her entrance. Neve wrapped her legs around his waist and her arms around his shoulders and pulled him into her.

They locked eyes as he sank deep, both letting out a shaky breath. She felt it then. The string that connected them in some fated, cosmic way.

They were always meant to find each other, to belong to each other, to be *this*.

Earlier, she'd had the thought that she'd never in her life had so much to lose. But she'd also never had *so much*. There was a long period of her life when she assumed love was a liability. She'd been wrong.

No. Love was a weapon. It was power. It made her stronger. *He* made her stronger.

Killian's eyes were full of love, wild and infinite. He moved his hips with deep, steady strokes until he could feel her tightening around him as she once again began to crescendo.

"You feel so good," he said quietly and picked up his pace, driving into her over and over, never taking his gaze from hers.

There was nothing beyond them. No kingdom. No world. Only them. Only movement and breath, and the race to release.

Neve found hers first, and as she shook and clenched around him, Killian followed, spilling into her and pressing his mouth to hers in a needy kiss. She moved to unwrap her legs from around him, but he gripped her hip to stop her.

"No, not yet. I want to stay like this," he panted.

She nodded and caressed his cheek. "We have time."

54

The winter sunrise cast a rosy lilac glow through the window, and Killian lay in bed, watching the dawn wash across Neve's skin as she slept. He felt honored to see her like this, utterly bare and unguarded. He felt honored that she trusted him with her body, her heart, and her protection in the night. Most of all, he simply felt honored to be hers.

He slipped from the warm covers and pulled on his pants, keeping as quiet as he could. He crept over to the table on which their rucksacks sat and he rummaged through her bag, looking for the tea she loved, the peppermint kind he'd made her every morning as they'd traveled to Ula. Killian found the small pale green tin it was kept in, but when he opened it, he found it empty with only a scattering of still-fragrant tea leaves littering the bottom. This would not do.

Hastily, he pulled on his shirt and a thick woolen sweater and stepped into his boots. He didn't bother with his sword; he was only going out to the market he'd noted around the corner from the inn, but he did strap his knife to his belt.

Killian leaned down and brushed his lips against Neve's temple, taking a deep breath of the clean, clover scent of her wild, dark hair. She stirred slightly, and he pulled the quilt up over her naked shoulders to keep her warm.

"I'll be right back," he said quietly.

The village was quiet, most of the townspeople still asleep in their homes after a night of solstice revelry. As Killian passed the square, he noticed it had been cleaned up, with only the tree still decorated, festive ribbons fluttering in the cold wind. Thinking back on the previous night, he smiled to himself.

Dancing with Neve, watching her laugh and move to the music, feasting with her and their new friends... and then everything that happened between them behind the locked door of their room. He could easily say that it had been the best winter solstice he'd experienced in all his life. Perhaps even the best night of his life.

Killian was lost in his thoughts, in a daze of sleepy mirth, as he browsed the market. The shopkeeper, a stout old man, smiled at him and pointed him toward the shelf of teas and provisions. He found a pretty peppermint tea that, when he smelled it, brought him back to those mornings in the wild with Neve, after nights of sleeping under the stars in each other's arms. His heart was warm.

He paid for the tea and strode back out into the village, snow crunching loudly beneath his boots. It was the only sound in the whole town this early.

Until it wasn't.

Perhaps if he weren't so sated with love, he would have been more alert.

Perhaps if he hadn't felt so safe in this sweet little village, he would have been smart enough to bring his sword.

Perhaps if he hadn't been daydreaming about the soft body of a beautiful, dark-haired woman, he would have heard the other footsteps in the snow behind him before it was too late.

But it was too late.

Something hard and cold slammed against the back of his head with so much force that his vision went spiraling and black, and he crashed to his knees on the cold ground.

Nausea came over him in a hot wave, and he smelled the coppery tang of his blood. The tea he'd bought for Neve tumbled from his hand into the snow as he lurched forward onto his elbows, unable to stay upright. The pain and pressure in his head were immense.

"Hello, brother," an all too-familiar voice said.

Killian's blood went cold with rage at the sound. He managed to turn his body just enough to see who was behind him.

A tall, lean body and a face he knew almost as well as his own.

Rory.

Behind him stood Gillis and Arran, as well as a sea of white-clad Cavalry. He might have been able to count how many were there if his head wasn't swimming and his vision wasn't blurry. But he knew there were many, and every sword was drawn.

He caught Arran's gaze, but his old friend looked away from him quickly.

Killian was outnumbered and on his own.

"Been waiting my whole life for this," Rory said with a smirk. Then his face changed to something twisted and full of fury before he reared back and threw a kick into Killian's jaw that nearly rattled the brains from his head.

Killian's vision clouded again, but this time it didn't clear and instead sent him into a deep, dark hole from which there would be no return.

~

Neve woke to the sounds of breakfast being served downstairs in the dining room. Muffled laughter and the clanging of flatware against plates made its way up to her room through the floorboards and thin walls. It made her wonder if the whole inn had heard her and Killian last night, the sounds he'd brought out of her. She smirked and rolled over, reaching out for him, but her hand only found a cold, empty pillow.

Sitting up, the memory of Killian's gentle kiss against her head came back to her, along with his tenderly spoken words: *I'll be right back.*

Neve's brow furrowed as she recalled opening her eyes in the moment he departed, just long enough to take in the quality of light. Amber and purple. Warm dawn on a cold winter morning. She looked out the window now. A gentle snow fell from a light gray sky, the halo of the sun visible through foggy clouds.

I'll be right back.

The position of the sun told her that dawn had passed at least half an hour ago, if not a full hour. She glanced around the room, taking in their armor still strewn across the floor where they'd left it last night. Their weapons were in a pile in the corner, Killian's sword propped up against the wall.

Ice filled Neve's veins, and power flared in her chest.

Something was wrong.

She could feel it, the *wrongness*, in her bones. She slid her into her clothes and strapped on her leather armor. The power inside her felt different now, in a frenzy, a desperate sensation that hadn't come to her when she was captured or when she shook hands with death.

But here it was, now, in the absence of the man she loved.

Run, it seemed to scream at her. *Run and rage.*

Neve noticed the glow on her skin as she tied the laces on her boots with quick fingers, but she didn't have time to overthink it. She strapped four daggers to her body and then paused in front of Killian's sword.

He would need it.

She gripped the handle and pulled it free of its sheath; the metal gleamed in the dreary light. It felt good in her hand, and her power surged forward at its weight.

She caught sight of herself in the mirror as she moved through the hallway to the staircase of the inn.

She cut a wicked figure, and there was a look on her face that she'd never seen before.

She looked like Death incarnate.

The only brightness to her was the shimmering star-glow on her skin. Everything else was as black as doom. She was thunderclouds and lightning rolled into one lethal body.

An uneasy hush settled over the dining room as she passed through. The townsfolk hesitated, bringing forks to their mouths, eyes widening at the sight of her. Neve could smell their fear. But she didn't care. She had one singular need.

Find Killian.

With her Knight's sword in one hand, she stormed out into the village.

All of her senses honed in on the faint noises east of the inn. The sound of men and metal. In her mind, she cursed Killian for leaving alone, for feeling confident enough to go without his sword.

She knew he was hurt; she could feel it inside of her, tightening that string that bound them together. And part of her hated him for it, for being reckless with his safety, for making her feel the unfamiliar sharp bite of fear. No. It was more than fear. *Terror.* She was terrified for him.

Her power burst out from her, melting the snow on the ground in her path as she moved. Somewhere deep down, she was aware of how dangerous she was. Her skills were unmatched when she was controlled and unemotional. She had no idea what she was capable of now that she was, for the first time, unable to find her deadly composure.

If he was injured... if he was *dead*...

She would end the world with her wrath.

The fear wiped away any sense of honor or nobility in her.

The Queen demanded death.

Thrumming with power from the top of her head to her toes, she turned the corner at the village square and halted. Everything within her and around her went still, even the wind stopped blowing, and the snow stopped falling. The world went quiet and perhaps even stopped turning.

More than a dozen Cavalry soldiers.

And…

And Killian on the ground at their feet.

Blood upon the snow.

She stalked forward without thought.

Pressure built inside of her. *Let me out.*

So, Neve released the breath she'd been holding and blinding light exploded from her, shoving the Cavalry, sending them all on their backs a yard or so from where Killian lay.

Confused shouts rang through the quiet morning as they looked around to see what had happened. Neve felt it when their baffled eyes found her. She felt their disbelief, their momentary wavering.

She took a bare second to glance down at Killian. Unconscious, covered in blood and bruises. But breathing. She knew then what they'd done to him. An ambush.

She'd walked in on them beating him to death.

Her rage had teeth and claws. It was *hungry*.

She stepped over Killian, putting herself between him and the cowards who were now scrambling back to their feet. Neve lowered the sharp tip of Killian's sword to the ground, drawing a line in the snow in front of her, then raised her chin and leveled her gaze first on the Cavalry, then on each of the three familiar faces in the crowd.

Gillis, a follower without a mind of his own.

Arran, Killian's oldest and dearest friend, a traitor.

And *Rory*…

She would watch them all die today.

"You," Rory sneered. The look on his face was one of pure hatred, but she could see the fear underneath like an illness waiting to take hold.

Neve grinned. "Me."

Behind her, she heard Killian mutter her name. "Neve?" His voice was weak and hoarse.

"I'm here," she replied, keeping her eyes on the warriors in front of her, readying themselves to attack.

The first Cavalryman moved.

Power rolled out from her chest in a warm wave, down her arms, and Neve watched as it spread beyond her body and bathed Killian's sword in her deadly, white light. She raised an eyebrow at it, curious, then lifted the sword and arced it through the air. The blade sliced, no... *burned* through the soldier's flesh and split him in half. His torso and head lay to her left, and his legs to the right. The surprise she felt was thrilling.

Then they all came for her at once.

The burning starlight on the blade left a trail of radiant sparks in its wake, illuminating the air with each swing. The clash of steel rang out as the Cavalry came for the Queen. Each of her movements was swift and precise, searing light burned with each true strike as she laid the men to rest one after another.

She shoved the sword through a waiting belly and turned just in time to block a blow from someone coming up on her side. It was Gillis. He thrust his sword at her again, but she moved quickly and pressed the flat of her burning sword to the side of his face. His mouth opened in a scream, spittle flying as her power cooked his skin.

She grabbed him by the collar and looked him in the eye.

"Traitor," she hissed and shifted her grip, turning the sword and dragging it across Gillis' throat. His blood spilled down his front in a hot, steaming rush.

As much as she wanted to savor every life she took, Neve kept moving. She became less of a woman and more of a force of nature as the power flowed from her and the rage for what they'd done to Killian swallowed everything else.

She was insurmountable.

Neve carved through the Cavalry like they were nothing but meat on a platter until there was no one left besides Arran and Rory. They both towered over her, huge men and just as skilled in death as Killian was. But she knew for certain that they were not as skilled as her. The look on Arran's face told her that he knew it; there was a sadness in his watery eyes that, in a different circumstance, in a different life, might have made her feel pity for him.

But there would be no mercy today.

Rory came for her, but she had other plans. She thought of her power and what she wanted, and somehow, by her will, her starlight pooled out and wrapped around him like chains. His eyes went wide.

"What–" he managed, but Neve sent another pulse of her power into him and slammed him against the wall of the nearby storefront and held him there.

It was the same for Arran. A sharp pulse of her power shot straight into the man's chest, sending him flying backwards and plastering him against the wall right next to his Commander.

"I never wanted it to end like this," Arran grunted, face going pale at the way her magic wrapped around him like vines.

"You made your choice," she replied.

Finally, she turned to Killian, and her eyes scanned him for injury. He was in bad shape, but there were no fatal wounds that she could see. His handsome face was bruised and swollen, and the hair at the back of his head was matted with blood. His sweater was torn, baring his chest and the bruises blossoming there. They'd had their fun with him. But it didn't matter anymore; they were all dead.

All except two.

Neve glanced over at Rory and Arran. Her power still held strong, keeping them captive and pressed against the wall. A touch of malice curled Rory's features, but he was stiff and pale with something else: horror.

Next to him, Arran was quiet and somber.

Turning back to Killian, she bent down and took the sword. It was no longer glowing, but it was warm to the touch despite lying on the cold ground.

"Get up," she said to Killian, quietly but not gently.

He looked up at her, his blue eyes clear and knowing. He took a deep breath and ground his teeth hard enough that the muscle in his jaw popped so sharply she thought it might break the skin.

Neve watched as Killian put himself back together and slowly, painfully, rose to his feet. His chest heaved with exertion, but he glued his eyes to her, as if the sight of her and the authority she commanded were the only thing keeping him upright. He straightened his back and lifted his chin. Neve had never been more proud of him.

Killian swayed a little, and from the sideline, Rory let loose a snide, mocking laugh.

"Fuck," Killian growled.

But Neve set her hand on his waist and steadied him. He reached for her and ran his trembling, bloody knuckles along her cheekbone. She put his sword in his hand, and he gripped it hard.

"For what he did to you.. He's yours," Killian managed, setting a pointed glance at Rory. "Bring him death and make it hurt. But... Arran is mine."

She nodded and strode oh-so-slowly toward Rory Grey.

He knew.

He knew death was coming for him.

As Neve neared, Rory began to thrash against the magic holding him, but it was of no use. He was outmatched. One more step and Neve stood before him, nearly nose-to-nose. She looked him in the eyes as she drew her dagger.

"What did I tell you would happen before the end of this?" She asked, her voice smooth as caramel.

"Fuck you," he seethed.

Neve clicked her tongue and caressed the blade of the dagger over his chest. She made a small, shallow cut that brought a hiss from between his teeth.

"Try again."

"I *had* you," he growled.

Neve thrust the dagger into his gut and yanked it out, a move so brutal and fast he didn't even know what happened until it was done.

"Try again," she repeated, ignoring his shriek of pain.

"Bitch," he said, but the word sounded more like weeping than an insult.

She pressed the blade against his groin and watched his face contort with terror.

"One more time. What did I tell you would happen before the end?"

"Fine, fine!" He breathed desperately. "You said you'd cut out my heart and wear it as a necklace."

Neve smiled and leaned in close to him. She put her free hand over his mouth and dragged the dagger back up to his chest.

"Good boy," she purred.

Then, she cut out Rory Grey's heart.

55

Each step forward was heavy and difficult. Killian's head was an aching, awful mess that made it difficult to keep his eyes open, let alone move. Every time he shifted, even with just a breath, his left shoulder screamed in agony. Dislocated. The same injury that happened to him in the Dark Forest after fighting the Magham, which made the pain twice as bad.

Killian stuck his sword in the ground and grabbed his left wrist with his right hand. He took a breath and *pulled*. There was a sickeningly loud pop as the ball of his shoulder clunked back into the socket. Tingling pain radiated down to the tips of his fingers as nausea rolled through him. He clenched his teeth to fight a grunt.

Rory's and Arran's bodies were wrapped in warm white light. Neve's light. Bands of it bound them against the brick wall, swirling around them in a sparkling glow.

His brother sagged lifelessly against the magic. As satisfying as it would have been to end Rory himself, Killian knew that his death belonged to Neve and Neve alone.

There she stood: a stunning dark storm in the white winter morning. Her black leathers clung to her curves like oil, her hair was wild and untamed in the gentle breeze. She watched him with a cool expression, her full, wicked mouth was plump and relaxed. Blood speckled her cheeks like freckles. There was a faint light still emanating from her skin, but when he'd been half-dead on the ground, he could have sworn she'd been glowing as bright as the stars themselves.

His Queen had gone to battle for him, laid waste to them all.

All except his best friend.

The red mess of his brother's heart sat in her upturned palm, dripping blood down her wrist and into the snow at her feet. The corner of her mouth lifted cruelly when she tipped her hand and let the heart slide from her fingers, discarded like trash. It landed with a gruesomely wet plop on the frozen ground.

A violent chill spilled down Killian's spine.

For his part, Arran was still, and there was nothing on his face besides exhaustion and maybe a twinge of sadness at the corners of his eyes. Killian understood that sadness because it permeated through all the other emotions, heating his blood.

He knew what had to happen now.

There was no other way.

"You can release him," Killian said.

Neve tilted her head to the side. To anyone else, she would have looked impassive. Lethally indifferent. But Killian saw it. The nearly hidden flare in her eyes, just for him. She was worried for him, and the thought warmed something very cold in his chest.

He was utterly unworthy of her.

For a moment, he thought she would decline, but she was a warrior herself, after all. She understood.

Neve's gaze slid to Arran, and Killian was reminded of the serpentine predator she truly was beneath that extraordinary surface. She didn't make any other moves, but the chains of light around his friend began to fade as if that otherworldly power manifested purely from Neve's will alone.

Arran stumbled forward as the power let him loose, and as he found his balance, he once again became the fine-tuned warrior he was.

Arran shook his head, taking one hesitant step toward Killian, then another. "Never thought I'd see this day."

Killian's arm moved so fast that it was nothing but a blur. He slammed his fist into his best friend's jaw with such force that it took him to the ground.

A wave of dizziness made Killian sway. He was sure that he had a concussion. But he bore down through the haze.

"Should have thought of that before you and the rest came for me with my back turned. I never imagined you'd become such a coward, Arran."

Arran recovered more quickly than Killian anticipated and moved quicker, too. He swiped Killian's legs out from under him with a low kick, sending him down. Arran stood tall and unfaltering.

"I was following orders," he said, rubbing his jaw.

Killian's whole body was on fire with pain, the ache seeping deep into his bones. His head swam so violently that he was seeing double. But he rose to his feet and pointed his sword at his friend's chest.

"Let's finish it."

Arran eyed the blade, likely remembering the way it *burned* through flesh when Neve wielded it. He shook his head.

"No magic weapons. Fight fair."

Killian snarled, sliding the blade up and resting it under Arran's chin, nicking the skin at his Adam's apple.

"Fair? That's bold, all things considered."

Arran didn't back down, but there was no hate in his eyes. "It was an opportunity the Command General decided to take."

Killian thrust the sword forward a little more. "And if I cut your throat now. Would that be an *opportunity?*"

A sad smile played on his friend's lips. "But you wouldn't. I know you, lad."

"No. Not any more." Killian said.

The older man's sadness deepened. "No. I suppose you're right."

Arran's hand went to the sword at his belt, but he hesitated, eyes moving to Neve. Fury was a firework in Killian's chest. His hand lashed out and grabbed Arran by the collar.

"Don't even look at her. She is beyond you, do you understand me?"

With a deep swallow, Arran nodded and rested his eyes on Killian's face. So many years passed between them at that moment. From the early days of Arran teaching Killian to fight in the barracks, when Arran was a young man and Killian was a child. To the days when Killian surpassed his mentor and became his leader.

"I can't believe we're doing this," Arran said, voice faltering.

Killian shook his head. "Neither can I."

They separated just enough to size each other up. The edges of Killian's torn sweater flapped against him. The unraveling yarn would be a liability, so he reached behind his neck and pulled it off over his head, along with the tunic underneath. The wintry air was icy cold on his skin, but it helped to push back the dizziness and nausea crowding his head.

Arran came for him. Arcing his sword through the air with precision but no fury. Killian met the blow with his weapon, the sound of metal clanging through the silence between them. There wasn't much power behind it. Almost like Arran struck first simply because he wanted Killian to respond.

Almost like Arran wanted to die fighting, but didn't want to spill Killian's blood.

A lump formed in Killian's throat.

"I gave you a chance to fight for the right side," he said, pushing his sword up and shoving Arran back.

They circled each other slowly, feet moving in near unison.

Teacher and student.

Father and son.

Lifelong friends.

Now, this.

Arran rushed Killian again. Another half-hearted slice that Killian easily blocked and countered.

"I spent my life doing awful things because I thought there was no other choice," Arran said. His eyes were watery in a way that made Killian's chest seize up.

Emotion rushed in, and Killian's body responded with an unleashing of strength. He went after Arran hard and fast. His friend blocked each of his moves, but with less and less precision of his own. Killian could taste the heartbreak between them.

"I *gave* you a different choice," he growled between clenched teeth.

The first tears spilled down Arran's wrinkled cheek as he nodded. "I know, lad. I know you did."

Memories flashed in Killian's mind.

Arran, wrapping Killian's split knuckles with linen in the barracks after his first real fist fight.

Arran, training Killian how to use a sword.

The look of pride on Arran's face when he watched Killian win for the first time. The look that stayed on his face through the years when Killian kept winning.

Laughter over pints of ale in far-away taverns.

But then came other memories. Arran, standing by as the Cavalry burned Thornkeep to the ground. As Kat and the children were trapped in their cottage. Arran, standing by as Rory and a dozen Cavalrymen ambushed him while he was shopping for tea for the woman he loved.

No. There was no going back.

"You know I can't let you go, right?" Killian said.

Their swords were almost an afterthought, both of them moving on muscle memory alone, attacking and blocking in practiced motions. As if they were sparring for fun like they'd done for so many years.

Arran didn't answer. Killian snatched the older man's collar and turned them both toward Neve. She leaned casually against the wall next to Rory's wilted corpse, hand still dripping with blood.

Lady Nightmare, indeed.

Killian's heart thrashed in his chest with the knowledge of what he was about to do. He brought Arran close and said in his ear, low and clear:

"If I don't kill you, she will... and it will be so much worse for you."

Arran's shoulders slumped. Killian could feel his friend's surrender. He turned and met Killian's eyes. Decades of brotherhood were written in his sorrowful gaze. But there was something else, too. A plea.

"Then have mercy on me and do it yourself," Arran said quietly, steadily.

Killian knew this was the right thing. The only thing.

He swallowed hard and pressed his lips to Arran's forehead in a harsh kiss. A farewell.

In the end, Killian gave Arran mercy. He made it quick.

56

There was a string in Neve's chest. Pulled tight and tangled around itself. The very same string that seemed to connect her heart to Killian's. She'd seen battle more times than she could count, all the horrors and atrocities that went hand-in-hand with violence. But seeing Killian broken on the ground surrounded by men with his blood on their shoes... it changed something in her.

As an instrument of death herself, she'd made her peace with it long ago. *His* death, on the other hand, while logically inevitable, felt like the one thing in the world she wouldn't come back from as herself.

A healer in the village took good care of Killian's wounds, gave him a few different foul-smelling tonics to heal any internal bruising, and a kindly pat on the cheek, before reassuring Neve that he was fine.

All the same, Neve felt uncharacteristically...clingy and wanted him near her, touching her, the warmth of him, the sound of his breath.

So she insisted that he ride with her on Gisele as they left the village. He liked that, liked being needed and wanted by her, so he just raised his eyebrows and smirked before climbing up behind her and bracketing her hips with his strong thighs. She rested her back against his hard chest, feeling the faint beat of his heart beneath the layers of their winter clothes.

He leaned forward and wrapped his arms around her waist, resting his chin on her shoulder.

"I could get used to traveling with you like this," he said into her ear.

She huffed a laugh. "Don't get used to it. I'm just not convinced you're well enough to ride on your own."

Neve felt the vibration of his chuckle in her spine.

"You think I'm too weak to ride a horse?"

"Maybe," she replied with a shrug.

He moved his hands down her hips and gripped them, pulling her tighter into him. She felt it then. He was hard.

"Does this feel weak to you?"

Wiggling her hips just enough to pull a quiet groan from him, she shook her head. "That happened fast."

Killian's lips brushed the side of her neck. "With you, always."

The King's Road was blanketed in fresh, white snow. It clung to the naked tree branches, making them laden and heavy. The kind of heaviness that blocked out all sound save for the ones they made, the crunching beneath hooves, and the quiet chatter amongst Isolde, Sabrina, and Oliver, who rode behind.

It was late afternoon by the time their group got moving, so the sun was low and dim in the sky, casting a muted pink hue and just enough light to lend a little sparkle to the top icy layer of the snow.

"Are you all right?" Killian asked quietly.

"I should be asking you."

"You have. A few times. Now it's my turn."

Neve took a breath and let it out slowly, releasing the tension that bunched her shoulders.

"I was worried about you."

Moving his hands from her hips, he wrapped them around her waist again and brushed her temple with his lips.

"I know."

"I woke up and you were gone. You left your weapons behind. I didn't like that."

"I know," he said again.

"Where did you go?"

He paused, and Neve could hear his throat working as he swallowed.

"I wanted to make you your tea. But you were out. So I went to the market to find some for you."

That space inside her, the one big enough for the love he offered, shifted painfully, and it was suddenly a little harder to breathe.

"You nearly died for tea."

He clicked his tongue playfully. "I wasn't even remotely close to death."

Ignoring that, she continued. "When I found you...When I saw that you were hurt, I became something else. Something new."

"I noticed."

"I have never felt...out of control before. But when I saw you like that, it changed everything."

"What I remember feels like a fever dream, but I know what I felt. So much *power*."

She nodded. "So much."

"And it was as if you weren't using the power, but rather that you *were* the power. It was you."

Memories of the feeling flashed through her mind, cold fire bending to her will, massive and infinite. But untethered, untested.

"That's how it felt on the inside, too."

"Which bears the question again: are you all right?"

She shifted Gisele's reins into one hand and used the other to lace her fingers through Killian's, where they drummed lazily against her lower stomach.

"I wish I had more time. The power is new, evolving. It seems to only come alive when *it* wants to. I didn't feel an ounce

of it when I was captured. I can't trust it to rise when I need it to.
I need more time to figure it out. But..."

"We're very nearly out of time," Killian finished for her.

Neve swallowed past the lump in her throat and nodded.
"We are."

"I've had the pleasure of getting to know you and
watching the way you fight. You've taken out armies with your
bare hands and a couple of daggers. You fought a wyvern, and it
simply had to look in your eyes to understand the force you are,
and it walked away. I've seen people bow to you- living and dead.
You have never once doubted yourself. Don't you dare start now."

She shook her head. He misunderstood. It wasn't doubt,
but rather risk evaluation. There was so much at stake now, and
the power was a loose cannon that she couldn't control. All the
same, the way he evangelized her brought a warmth into Neve's
blood and a sweet taste to her tongue. Her greatest supporter.
The one who taught her how to let herself feel.

So, instead of an explanation, she just said: "I love you."

Killian relaxed a little, pulled her closer.

"If things went sideways today and you hadn't shown
up... I would have gone to my death a happy man knowing I was
loved by you."

A strange mixture of catastrophic joy and sorrow moved
through her from her head to her feet in a wave that nearly made
her dizzy. She thought that maybe that's what love was. It was
the choice to toe the edge of two worlds: the all-consuming bliss
of possibility with someone and the cold agony of knowing that
someday, either by death or design, there would be a parting.

"I'm afraid," she said, so quietly that she wasn't sure he'd
even hear her.

But he did.

"Lady Nightmare, afraid? Of what?" His words and tone
were light, teasing even, but his fingers made gentle circles along
her knuckles, against her waist. She knew that he was

reassuring her with his touch, reminding her that he was there, he was listening.

"It seems that the only thing I've ever been truly afraid of... is losing you."

There it was. She'd said it. Let it out in a breath of frost that puffed in the air and slowly disappeared against the fading daylight. She'd given voice to it, the thing that hurt most, the thing that *changed* her this morning, turned her into something *other*.

Contrary to what she may have once guessed, the admission didn't weaken her; instead, it made her feel brave, strong. Saying it out loud was a powerful truth that loosened the tension in her muscles, in her gut. Even the power within her let out a quiet sigh and curled up like a cat in the sun.

It was small and miraculous: a study in letting go.

Killian shifted in the saddle and leaned forward so he could see her face. His eyes were bright and full of love. He cupped her jaw in his hand and pressed his lips to hers. The kiss was gentle, almost chaste, yet filled with feelings that couldn't be named with words. Neve softly sucked his bottom lip and opened her mouth for him. A desperate little noise cracked in his throat, and he deepened the kiss, sliding his tongue along the edges of her teeth and against the warmth of hers. His hand moved from the side of her face to the nape of her neck, where it squeezed once, then held, pulling her deeper.

With a shaking breath, Killian broke the kiss and pressed his forehead to hers. He stayed like that for a moment, and Neve could sense that he was working something through in his head, breaking something apart and putting it back together. She waited, tasting his breath, feeling it warm her cheeks. Finally, he pulled back just enough to look at her, to search her eyes.

"I want to be yours until we are old, until my hands are so frail and gnarled they can no longer pick up a sword. I can't promise you that nothing will happen to me, but I can promise you that I will do what I do best."

"And what is it that you do best?"

"Fight," he said with a wry smile. "I will fight for you, for us. For a long life together. A life they can write stories about when our bones are dust. Many, many years from now."

Neve smiled back at him.

"That's a good promise." She tilted her chin, offering his lips to him again, but a voice called out from behind them.

"Hate to break up this pretty moment," Isolde said.

Neve turned her head and looked back at her companions. Oliver and Sabrina were squinting into the distance. Isolde's face was devoid of her usual mirth. The warmth of her intimate conversation with Killian faded, and a chill broke through her heavy layers, making a shiver skitter across her skin.

"There's something in the trees ahead."

Neve shifted in the saddle and Killian straightened behind her. There, some ways up the King's Road, Neve could see a series of what looked like black flags hanging from trees on both sides of the road.

But the way they swayed, the way the branches sank...Neve knew they were not flags.

"Hold on," she said in a quiet, steady voice.

Killian settled against her, hands holding her hips. She gave Gisele a practiced squeeze with her thighs, and they took off at a gallop. A thick dusting of snow flew up around them as they sped down the road, closer and closer to something ominous, something dreadful.

When they were close enough to see, Neve pulled back on their reins and brought Gisele to a stop.

"Oh, gods," Killian cursed in her ear. She felt a thin tremor roll through him. But for Neve, everything went still. Still and quiet.

Six on one side. Six on the other. Dangling feet in dirty black boots. Ropes creaked against the tree branches, ropes noosed around twelve necks. Black cloaks, a garment as familiar to her as her own skin. A sigil on the chest: a white crescent moon held by a black, raised hand.

It was an emblem she remembered tearing from her cloak and letting fly away on the breeze in the purple moor. It felt like ages ago now.

She slid off her horse and walked slowly down the center of the road. Killian and her friends were utterly silent, a world away, it seemed.

Neve looked up at each face. Faces she'd grown up with. Now empty, pale, blue-lipped. She found herself pausing at the feet of one of them. A cascade of scarlet hair pooled from the hood of the dark cloak. Cara. *The closest thing to the friendship she had.* Back then, at least.

"Gods, is that–" Oliver began.

"The Maere," Neve finished, her voice deep and steady but with an edge.

Killian was at her side, not touching her, not speaking, but he was there. His presence was enough. Neve's life had been spent with these bodies that now hung lifeless from the winter trees. Adventures to the farthest corners of the world. Battles against the gods of other continents. Undefeated. Untouchable. Until now.

She touched her palm to her chest, where the emblem would be if she still wore it.

This was a message. A brutal love letter from the Highborns to her. To show their power. If they could end the Maere in one fell swoop, imagine what they could do to Neve and her four warriors. She felt it then. The way she'd underestimated them, their age, their strength.

Turning her head, she looked at Kilian. She saw it there, too. In the dark smudges under his eyes, in the set of his jaw, and in the muscle that feathered there.

He knew what the Maere were capable of, and to see them, a legend, end so easily...understanding fell over both of them. What they were up against, truly, was much, much worse than they thought.

"How?" Killian asked. "You're...they're god-hunters. This is what they do."

Neve shook her head.

"How did they kill Nyx? How did they spend three centuries gaining influence while remaining undetected? They're powerful...much more powerful than we thought."

The magic in her chest sizzled with a mixture of rage and unease. And soft, sad mourning. These deaths belonged to her, and she knew there would be more before the end.

She turned her gaze down the King's Road, in the direction that she knew Lyra Castle waited.

It was time.

57

A giant ghost, an ancient haunting titan, fashioned from the purest cream limestone. Lyra Castle. Dressed in the regalia of nature's reclamation, muted sage-green moss and sinuous vines coiled gracefully around curving ivory walls. Turrets spiraled upwards, their tips adorned with glistening crystals that refracted the starlight, casting a dazzling display across the snowy landscape below.

Towers soared skyward, their ascent seemingly unending as they pierced through the very fabric of the heavens, daring the clouds to obscure their reach. Each tower was crowned with delicate spires that glowed softly in hues of silver and gold. The windows of the palace felt like eyes to a new realm, framed in intricate scrollwork and adorned with stained glass that depicted stories of Eodia's Queens, glowing outward from some phantom light within.

Cradling the castle in its thorny embrace, a hedge maze of brambles unfolded like a tapestry. Stretching for miles, the maze sprawled in every direction, in shades of dark green and dry brown, its edges painted with snow. Barely visible in the distance beyond the maze were the castle gates, forged from pure gold that sparkled under the night sky.

This moment was the stuff of dreams for Neve.

She'd made it home.

It took them half a week to make it to the Castle after the winter solstice. Neve was tired. Her body was sore, and her skin was tender from days out in the cold.

But now... now her power was awake, stretching, warming her from the inside out. Now she was seeing Lyra Castle, a place she'd only read about, *dreamed* about since she was a child. All those books and stories...none of them offered any justice to the real thing. No, the beauty of it was beyond even her wildest imagination.

It was a clear night, the crescent moon was high and glowing bright enough to light the way. The sky was a riot of shimmering stars, more than anyone could count, more than could be measured. There were so many stars that the dark blue–black of the sky barely had any space to nudge contrast.

Killian took her hand in his and squeezed it.

He felt it too. The perfection of this moment, the importance of it.

"We're here," Neve said with a sigh that contained only a fraction of her awe.

"Home," he replied, voice catching.

"Home."

"Wow," Oliver said from behind them. He, Isolde, and Sabrina all pressed in close against Neve and Killian's backs, looking out from their vantage point on the hill where the King's Road came to an end.

Sabrina let out a low whistle, her breath a puff of smoke in the wind. "I honestly never thought I'd see this place. It's..."

"Magical," Isolde mused.

Neve heard a sniffle, then another one. She turned to see Oliver wiping tears from his eyes with the backs of his big hands. She loved him a little for it. She gave him a pat on the arm, and he moved his hands to look at her, cheeks wet and eyes shining.

"Thank you," he said. "For letting me come here. With you."

Neve nodded, smiling.

Sabrina made a show of rolling her eyes but nestled a little closer to Oliver and put her hand on his shoulder. Isolde hugged his waist, barely able to reach around his thick, muscled torso.

Neve wanted to stamp this moment on her memory: the three of them embracing, starlight and tears in their eyes.

She started to turn back toward the castle, but Killian caught her by the chin. A tender smile played on his lips, revealing a vulnerability that only Neve had the power to unveil. His hand, calloused from countless battles, traced her jaw like it was the most priceless thing he'd ever touched. His piercing blue eyes, usually as fierce as the stormy sea, softened with an intensity that made Neve feel a little like she was drowning. The flickering light played on the chiseled contours of his face, highlighting the strong jawline and the hint of beard that adorned it.

The look in Killian's eyes spoke volumes—love, longing, and a promise of forever, the promise he'd made to her to fight. Silvery strands of moonlight painted the space between them until he pulled her close, and there was no space at all.

"Everything has been worth it. All of it. Just to see you here. To see that look on your face." His words were a rush of breath against her mouth. Then he kissed her, and Neve could think of nothing else.

A sound cut through the night. A particular twang and swish overhead. Neve felt it move strands of her hair. There was a second, a third. A cacophony of them. And then she was on the ground, pressed into the snow with Killian holding her there and covering her body with his own as a shield.

Arrows.

The sound was arrows.

In the dark, and in their awe, they'd failed to see what lay in wait for them down the hill and in the shadows of the bramble maze.

The enemy.

"Are you hurt?" Killian whispered above her.

"No. You?" Neve asked, and he shook his head. She didn't love being pinned beneath the protective arch of Killian's body, so she slipped out from under him and twisted into a low crouch.

"Everyone whole?" Killian asked the others.

"Just a scratch," Sabrina replied, dabbing her hand against the thin tear in her clothes and the line of blood on her bicep. Her face was pale, with no sign of her usually annoyed bluster. She wasn't happy with this surprise either.

Oliver ripped off a piece of fabric from his tunic and absent-mindedly wrapped it around Sabrina's wounded arm without being asked. "Whole," he confirmed.

"Me too," said Isolde.

Neve peered down the hill into the shadows. She could see movement along the perimeter of the hedges. No torches, no campfires. They'd been waiting in the darkness. She saw the glint of dull metal in the moonlight.

"There's more. Cover."

Arrows were shot into the night with a well-practiced unison thrum. Killian dove over Neve again, covering her. He pulled his shield free and held it above them with one long arm. The arrows sounded like rainfall until they thunked into the trees, and the icy ground, and pinged off the metal of Killian's shield.

Silence once again pressed in on them.

"Good?" Killian asked the group.

No injuries this time.

"We're a target up here," Neve said. "We need to move."

A sword, taken from the room in the library, was strapped to Neve's back. She pulled it from its sheath and rolled her shoulders. A familiar feeling washed over her, into her. The walls of iron locking tight within her, the cold readiness of battle, the dark and deadly calm.

There would be blood tonight.

Her eyes moved over the shapes in the shadows, counting them, tracking each shift in motion, each barely-there puff of breath. Cavalry would be easy to cut down. But somewhere, down in that maze, the Highborns waited. She remembered the way the Maere hung lifeless from those trees on the road. She would not join them in death today.

Her power hummed.

"Stay low. Move fast," Neve commanded. Then she took a breath and ran.

The temperatures had dropped, turning the recent snowfall into ice on the ground. Neve's boots slid like skates as she raced down the hill, body in a half-crouch as she moved. Killian was right next to her at each step, reacting to the ice with a little less grace than she was, but he kept upright, his eyes darting back and forth between her and the figures in the looming darkness. Neve kept one ear trained behind her for Isolde, Oliver, and Sabrina. So far, they were still with her, cursing as their feet slipped and stumbled.

The air above them shifted, and she knew more arrows were coming for them.

"Careful!" she called to the companions behind her, but she did not slow. A little ember of rage kindled in her blood for the relentless pursuit they were given, the cowardice of the Cavalry using arrows in the night. For the fact that she hadn't noticed them hiding out there. She wanted nothing more than to get up close and personal with them, make them look her in the eye.

At the bottom of the hill, they slid into a clearing, now utterly exposed. Killian raised his shield above her. It wasn't big enough for both of them, let alone their whole group. She could feel the arrows coming, the pressure of at least a hundred of them moving downward from their climax in the sky above.

Hundreds. The odds weren't in their favor.

It was dark, and there was nowhere to hide. She weighed the options. If they ducked and covered, they'd be struck down. If they kept running, she wasn't confident that they'd all be quick and attentive enough to dodge the arrows. Someone was going to die.

Then, Neve recalled the way she'd *willed* her power to hold Rory captive.

Maybe...

With a shift in focus, she tapped into that ember of rage, let it grow, let it claw at her power. She thought of the Cavalry, clustered together and warm, planning their assault. The soldiers likely chuckled and congratulated each other on their cleverness. The way they *hid*.

Cold fire answered. It was a living, crackling thing. It grew and pulsed with the beat of her heart. It moved through her veins, welded to her bones. Her feet moved beneath her with speed and grace, but above her... her *will* blossomed. As soon as she felt it, the way it thrummed outward, a faint glow lit her hands, glittering across her winter-frigid skin.

She stopped and looked up.

"No! Neve!" Killian screamed, skidding to a halt, eyes wide with panic. It took him a moment to understand, to see. His wild gaze ricocheted around her body, her face. He seemed to be caught in some desperate space between horror and awe. Neve saw it in his expression when he realized what was happening, what she was doing. She gave him a knowing look and pointed up.

A gasp released from his heaving chest.

Above them, there was a shimmer of warm white light. Thin as a gossamer curtain and undulating in the air like waves in water. The first arrow hit, and with a spark, it bounced. Then another. And another. Neve watched as one by one, the rest did just the same. Not a single arrowhead pierced the veil of the power suspended over them. The light did not fracture. It did not bend beneath the force of the colliding weapons. It remained unmoved and unbothered, like the night sky itself. Ancient and never-ending.

"Holy shit," Sabrina mused, breathless.

Neve could hear shouting. Cavalry commanders attempted to regroup after watching every single arrow miss its target. They'd expected this to be easy. They'd thought they had the upper hand. Good. Their frustration was a balm.

"Will it hold if we keep running?" Killian asked. He took her hand and stared at it, marveling at the starlight on her skin. He brought her wrist to his mouth and pressed his warm lips to her pulse.

Neve nodded.

"It goes where I go," she said. It was true, at its core, the power was her. It bent to her will the same way her words did, her body. At least it seemed to. But she knew for certain it would keep them safe.

She had a brief moment to catch the grin on Oliver's face, the pride in Isolde's eyes, the awe still keeping Sabrina's mouth open in an "O" shape. And Killian. The look on his face could have set the winter on fire. Then Neve turned back to the rushing and shouting along the perimeter of the brambles, the massive Castle looming like a promise beyond.

They were so close.

Launching forward, Neve led her friends toward battle. Sure enough, the power moved with them. The Cavalry sent another wave of arrows as if they couldn't believe they'd failed the last time. She could hear the twang of their bowstrings now, the *whoosh* of their release. Every arrow dropped against Neve's power and then fell useless into the snow.

It didn't take long to make it to the mouth of the maze. Neve slowed as they approached. She left a few yards distance between her group and the perimeter, enough space to react to whatever other tricks they had waiting. The moon was bright, and now that she was close, she could see the pink-cheeked faces of Cavalry soldiers peering out at her from the dark. For once, they weren't clad in all white. Over their uniforms, they wore dark-colored hooded cloaks, the better to stay hidden in the night.

She wondered how long they'd waited and when they'd first seen her on the hill. Had they watched her friends embrace? Had they watched the way Killian kissed her? Had they seen the way she looked at the Castle like it was a dream, and it was hers?

No matter. Let that scene be the last they witnessed before their deaths.

But then the faces began to multiply.

More soldiers stepped into the light of the glowing moon. They poured out of the entrance to the maze. Their ranks seemed to bloat and expand. More and more marched out until they formed lines of defense to block the way in. They kept coming. An avalanche of them.

The number of arrows shot at her in the clearing did not reflect how many soldiers were gathered there. No. There were more than a hundred. So many more. The rumors were true, then. As the defense lines finished forming and the last soldiers stepped out, Neve counted nearly three hundred.

Three hundred Cavalry against five warriors.

And beyond the massive numbers, the Highborns remained hidden.

Neve glanced over her shoulder and looked at her friends. For the first time since she'd met them deep beneath the ground in the library, their expressions opened, and she saw fear. Naked, raw fear. All three of them, her stalwart companions.

Swallowing past the sudden tightening in her throat, she moved her gaze to Killian. Her breath eased. There was no fear there. Not even a whisper of it. His resolute eyes watched the Cavalry, counting, calculating. Then he looked at her. His face was hard with the promise of violence, and, despite the circumstances, her warm need for him danced through her. It was the look she'd seen when he faced her after she lured him to Hythe and took the killing of those thieves for her own. It was the look he'd given her when he realized she'd tested him in the Dark Forest. When they fought Rory on the plains. When he'd taken on the lycanthropes in the Vale. She knew that look and the menace of it gave her more comfort than anything she'd ever known.

"Remember," he said. "I'm going to do what I do best."

Fight.

"And you," he continued, gaze roaming over her face, her body, into her very soul. "You're going to show them who you *really* are."

The corner of her lips twitched up. "And who's that?"

His grin was awful and beautiful all at once.

"Lady Nightmare. Queen of Death. Heir of Nyx. And the scariest fucking woman I've ever met."

58

The apparent Command General stepped forward. Well, the new Command General, Neve supposed, considering she'd cut out the heart of the last one. He was tall and grim with sharp cheekbones and a long, pointed nose. His eyes were dark and bored. He held his hands out to his sides, gesturing at his army, and a smile absent of any hint of bliss spread across his thin lips.

"I think we're beyond negotiations at this point, don't you, my lady?" He said. There was a rattle in his voice that spoke of ill health, perhaps too much time spent out in the cold.

Neve said nothing. Her hands were loose at her sides, fingertips drumming on her thighs. She tilted her head and moved her gaze across the ranks. She read the faces, marked the ones that looked afraid, the ones that looked too arrogant for their own good. She counted them, and then counted again, no amount of mental calculations had five against three hundred making any sense. They needed to get around, to get through, into the maze. The numbers would only work to their advantage in the maze because the Cavalry couldn't pass through it unless they went single-file, or they'd all risk being impaled on the thick-as-ax-blade brambles. It was their only chance. But there were three hundred bodies between her and the entrance. She and the others would have to thin the herd significantly to even get close.

They had no choice but to fight their way through and take out as many soldiers as they could as they went.

Peeling back the veil of her power above them, pulling it into herself, it settled back in her chest with an anticipatory rumble. The feeling was welcome, somehow comforting. Neve raised her face to the night sky, to the moon that glowed bright, and to the stars scattered across it like spilled sand. A memory came to her then, of lying under the same sky on her birthday with Killian. Glitter in his blue eyes. The star shower.

As if in answer to her thoughts, a star fell across the sky. Then another. And another. Until every single star above jumped and danced and streaked across that celestial dark blue canvas. They cascaded and dimmed, only to blink back awake and do it again and again. Millions of them. The sky was listening to her. The sky was alive.

A puff of air, full of awe, exhaled from her mouth. She forced her gaze to the Cavalry, nearly all three hundred now peering skyward with creased brows and open mouths.

"Now," Neve whispered to Killian and the others. She drew the sword at her back, and watched it glow in the grip of her hand as her power answered the surge of adrenaline in her blood.

Killian drew his as well and gave her a final, resolute nod, his eyes serious and bright. "Now."

The moment she moved, the ground rumbled with the thunder of three hundred pairs of boots charging directly for them. All at once, the entire army launched forward, like they'd simply been waiting for her to take one step, just one. And when she did, every line of defense responded, the sound of unsheathing steel rang like a bell in the night, the roars of men like falling rock. A rush of air moved toward her, the vibration of collective movement, collective violence.

Neve gave one last look to Killian and to her friends, then braced her body for impact and threw herself into the fray.

Blood misted into the cold air as her blade met flesh. Neve thrust her glowing sword into the first chest she found and watched steam rise from the gaping wound. She twisted to find another soldier at her heels and moved like rushing water to dodge his weapon and slice hers through his middle. She fisted the hilt of her dagger with her other hand, yanking it from the holster at her hip and shoving it into the grimacing face of another assailant. Neve barely registered his scream. She knew she had to keep moving. If she stopped, she'd be dead. So she didn't stop, not even to try to find Killian or the others in the crushing mass, not even to breathe.

Forward. Forward was the goal. Every death she delivered brought her one step closer to the maze, to fickle safety, an even killing field. She hoped the people she cared for would meet her there. Her heart stuttered. She had no idea where Killian was, but she had to trust that he'd fight, that he'd live. Neve pushed his pretty face out of her mind. She locked it all down: the love, the emotions, the concern. She slipped into her most primal self, where all that mattered was winning the fight, surviving the bloodshed while delivering her own. She spilled throats into the snow. The body count left in her wake was a trail marking the ground she gained.

A huge soldier stepped in front of her and gave her a lopsided grin. Bigger than Killian, bigger than even Oliver, he towered over her and was nearly as broad as two men put together. Where the Cavalry found a behemoth like this... she would never know. He didn't carry a sword, not a single knife. Instead, he wielded a warhammer: massive and stained with old blood. The other soldiers gave him a wide berth as if they didn't trust him not to swing that heavy metal in the direction of their heads.

"Pretty, pretty," he said, spittle forming at the corner of his mouth. He gave his big hammer a swing for show, twisting his wrist, letting the head woosh through the air.

She waited. No one came near them, and a few soldiers stopped to watch. Neve wondered how many times they'd witnessed this brute flatten someone, how many rebels, villagers...how many women. It seemed to be interesting enough to stop them in their tracks, so it must have promised to be quite the show. There was a lustful gleam in the onlookers' eyes. The same look, even more heated, was plastered on the gargantuan man's face.

It made her want to split him open.

Split them all open.

The veins and muscles in his thick neck strained as he made the first move. He swung the hammer at her with incredible force but very little aim. She easily sidestepped the blow, squared her shoulders, and waited again. The onlookers all jeered. Neve was vaguely aware that they were forming a circle around her. She'd have to be smart. One wrong move and not only would her body break, but the crowd would fall on her like vultures and pick her apart piece by piece.

The giant bared his teeth at her like an animal and swung again. Neve dodged it, twisted, and sliced out with her dagger. It dragged across his hip, opening him up but not hitting anything vital. A rough grunt came from his mouth, and he went a little unsteady on his feet. For only a second.

The hammer was moving through the air again, aimed at her neck, so she dropped into a squat and let it sing through the wind above her. Her sword arm moved, arcing the glowing blade through the meat of his thigh. She could smell the burning flesh, the heavy blood.

It didn't stop him.

He used two hands to bring the hammer down toward the top of her head, a roar tearing through his throat. Still in a crouch, she jumped backward. Something caught her ankle- another soldier's outstretched foot- and she was suddenly on her back, face aimed at the star-shower sky. The hammer slammed against the ground, mere inches from her cheek, dangerously close. So close that her teeth rattled in her jaw with the force of that thick metal hitting the ice.

Neve heard laughter, cheering, and the giant raised the hammer again, bringing it down with all his might toward her chest.

~

Somewhere in the clamor of battle, Isolde heard a raucous cheer rise up. There were too many voices, and they didn't belong to her friends. A chill went down her spine. But she had to keep moving.

The librarian was good with a sword, but she was even better at dodging danger. Isolde had a keen sense of space and an uncanny ability to anticipate what another person might do. Some might have said she was clairvoyant if they paid enough attention. So she moved through the crowd like a vapor, quick and anonymous. Hands grabbed for her and found nothing but air. Weapons sliced for her but ended up lodging in the bodies of other Cavalry instead.

Her heart pounded wildly in her chest, her lungs fluttered like birds behind twin ribcages. She missed the books. She missed the warmth of the library's hearth. But now...now she was living through what could be one of the greatest stories of their time. She was fighting alongside her Queen.

All the work Isolde had done to organize the rebellion, to help people hope, to help them believe in a different world, to lead...it was all coming to a head now.

However, she could admit that she never expected to be on the frontlines with Lyra Castle looming like a great ivory myth above her. She wouldn't change it, though. No. This was where she belonged.

Isolde could very nearly read the thoughts on the faces of the men she passed as she slipped beyond their reach. They were greedy. Greedy for blood. For glory. Each of them wanted to be the one: the hero who brought the heads of her and her friends to the Highborns.

But they especially wanted to be the one to bring the Queen's head to them.

A sword thrust out for her. Isolde spun like a dancer away from its edge and watched as it sank into a soldier's gut. There were blades everywhere, everything was dark and sharp and cold. The further she moved into the throng, the more dense the crowd of soldiers became. But she knew they needed to get to the maze. There would be no respite, no moment's peace until they were amongst the brambles. The whole army couldn't follow them at once. Not in there.

There was a grungy musk smell of too many unwashed men in one space. A smell that no amount of fresh air could clear from Isolde's nostrils. She pressed on. Dancing through the grasping arms and stabbing swords. She used her blade to cut the knees out from under a soldier who came too close, then again as she ran another through. The deeper she moved into the Cavalry's ranks, the more she had to use her weapon, and she did so with a practiced flourish.

Isolde Markham had always been graceful.

Some of her favorite memories were of early mornings and late nights and pretty afternoons, dancing with her mother.

Her childhood was filled with flowers and quiet music. Their home was a sanctum of perpetual spring. She often held her mother's hands and asked to be spun in circles until she was too dizzy to see straight. Her mother held her and laughed with her nose pressed into the top of Isolde's head.

Until one day, men came to her village.

She couldn't remember much from that day, but she remembered they were dirty. She remembered what they called themselves: the Cadre. She remembered the way her mother cried when a man with a scar on his face put the noose around her neck.

"Look away, Izzy," said her mother. And then the man strung her up until she stopped crying and her eyes closed. The flowers in her mother's hair fell to the ground.

The thought of her mother's execution had Isolde driving her sword through a soldier's throat. She felt his blood spray her cheeks. She breathed through the trauma, the rage of the memory, until she found her center again. She thought of the books. Of seeing Neve in the graveyard for the first time and *knowing*. She thought of the way she felt when they crested the hill and Lyra Castle came into view.

Isolde looked up into the night sky with a grateful sigh.

Those stars. Shooting across the sky in a dance of their own. She knew the Island was cut off from the gods; she knew it wasn't possible...But still, this close to the Castle with the heir of Nyx in her midst, Isolde had never felt so sure that something, someone *other* was there.

Celesta herself, ushering the daughter of her blood home.

Books would be written about this night. Isolde only hoped she'd live long enough to find them in the library.

It was becoming harder and harder to slip through the crowd. Soldiers were stomping forward, shoulder-to-shoulder, leaving very little room for Isolde to continue moving the way she'd done until this point.

She looked into the crushing mass of people and met the eyes of a man holding a bow and arrow, the bolt aimed straight for her. Isolde had time to swallow and take a breath, but she did not have time to dance out of the way. There was no room to move.

She heard it before she felt it. A wet *thunk*.

Time seemed to slow.

Suddenly, it was just her and the falling stars and the arrow jutting out from her chest, in that delicate space between her shoulder and collarbone. Isolde had the distant thought about how she liked that place on her chest. Because it was the place lovers always kissed to make her feel cherished. And now, there was metal there. Foreign. Painful. Her stomach roiled, everything went quiet, and Isolde's knees gave out.

She sank to the ground.

It was cold. She could feel the snow melting against her warmth, seeping into the fabric of her pants. Then... then there were legs everywhere. Feet. Soldiers marching past her, over her, *on* her. Isolde felt the weight of them. Her right arm was useless. She used her left to try to protect her head as they kept coming, kept stomping, kept *crushing*. She could not breathe against the stench of them, their closeness, or the pain now radiating through her body and turning into an acute agony.

Isolde felt a boot collide with her temple, and the last real thought she had was of those flowers in her mother's hair. Lilacs. And then there was only darkness.

~

With his sword, Killian slit a soldier's throat. With his other hand, he brought his shield down on the head of a man with such force that he could feel the crunch of a skull on the other side of the metal. Killian was covered in sweat despite the cold. Covered in blood. The odor of death rose all around him. He had to keep going.

He'd heard a brutish cheer from the other side of the battlefield a moment ago. It sent an eerie slice of unease through his whole body. His only thought was of Neve. That they'd killed her. But surely, he'd know if she was dead. Surely he'd feel it. He had to believe that to keep from sinking to his knees, to keep breathing.

There were so many of them. Killian was in a constant state of motion just to keep from getting killed himself. He hadn't stopped moving. Not once. Not even to peer through the fray to try to find Neve, the others. They were all on their own, the Cavalry having quickly mowed through and separated their whole group. He had no sense of where the Queen and their friends could be, if they were even still alive.

Above, the stars still fell like snow.

That had to mean something, right?

It had to mean that Neve was still out there somewhere, alive.

So, Killian pushed his way forward and ended lives. Some of the soldiers who met his sword were older, experienced. Some were young, barely older than boys. There was a small part of him, deep inside, that rankled with guilt. He knew most of these soldiers didn't have a choice but to join the Cavalry, and didn't know any better than to follow orders blindly. He could see it in their eyes, the fear, the pleading look as if to say, "There was no other path for me."

There'd never been any other path for Killian, either.

He was born and raised to kill. If he hadn't been so good at it, he'd likely have ended up in the Cavalry himself rather than leading the Cadre. But he was good at it. Very good. It took him over thirty years, a long story indeed, to find his way out. And he'd made it out just barely by the skin of his teeth. If Neve hadn't chosen him, sought him out, tested him, asked him to follow...he'd be fighting against her with the Cavalry in this battle. On the wrong side.

He imagined he'd have gone up against her himself.

Maybe killed her.

Maybe found death in her beautiful hands.

But now... now all he could think about was finding her. He thrust his sword through the chest of a soldier who came at him from the front, then turned and brought his blade down through someone's shoulder, twisting it into his spine. It was chaos. The soldiers were unorganized and frenzied, so on edge that he'd seen them turn on each other more than once- reaction and instinct ruled, there was no strategy.

Perhaps the Highborns believed that with such unbalanced odds, they did not need a strategy. Perhaps they just didn't care and were hungry for blood. They'd miscalculated the value of Killian Grey's skill, then. He understood war far better than any of the soldiers on this field. He knew what to do when presented with a bit of chaos and a little luck.

A soldier came for him, big and grimacing. Instead of lifting his sword, Killian just grinned. With a shove of his powerful body, he used the soldier's momentum against him, turning him toward his comrade. Killian hid behind the soldier's back as Cavalry steel sank into a fellow Cavalryman's stomach. A few men nearby saw what happened, but did not see Killian or his part in it. One shouted "Traitor!" and pointed with a shaking fist. The group of soldiers turned on each other, swords and knives, and fists. The group grew to about a dozen men, moments ago allies, perhaps even brothers-in-arms, suddenly ripping into one another like animals.

Killian understood, perhaps more than most, how effective betrayal could be.

He moved with wicked stealth. Killian shoved one soldier into another, shouted a muffled "Long live the Queen!" and slipped out of sight as another snarling group converged on each other, rabid and incensed at what could only be assumed was blatant treason.

Perhaps it was the days out in the cold together, inner turmoil amongst the ranks, terror, and confusion over the battle at hand... whatever it was, it caused the Cavalry to turn against itself with marvelous ease. Distantly, probably near the mouth of the maze, a Commander must have noticed the infighting. His ill-timed bellows of "Enough!" and "Stand down!' only served to add to the sharp paranoia and confusion of the melee that grew suddenly and monstrously. Another group turned on the men next to them. And then another.

Soldiers stumbled, clamored over one another. They fell and rolled in piles, fists flying, heads slamming against ice. They barreled into each other, hands greedily grasping for throats. Swords swung and stabbed. There was screaming, loud and ripping through the night. They were grunting and growling, showing who they truly were beneath the pristine white garments they so proudly wore under their cloaks.

There would be no regaining control of the ranks. At least not the ones swarming around Killian in the aftermath of his maneuvering. The men were dissolving into bloodlust and bafflement, and it spread like a disease, thick and heady. Killian shoved through the teeming crowd, killing as he went, as he grappled against the chaos and moved closer and closer to the looming dark of the bramble maze beyond.

59

If the hammer fell, it would crush her. Her lungs and heart would impale on the shards of her shattered bones, and she'd be done, sent off to whatever abyss waited beyond death.

But Neve was not done.

Her fingers released their grip on her weapons, and she followed her instincts, pressing her bare hands to the ice-packed soil. This time, when her power released, it didn't pulse, but it *flowed*. Everything inside her was suddenly warm and buzzing. The very ground beneath her seemed to lurch, like a heavy puzzle piece coming undone. Neve felt the foundation shift.

The Cavalry had encircled her and the hammer-wielder. Now, within that circle, the snow was awash with her glow. It shoved the soldiers back a step, their eyes wide with shock. Neve locked her gaze on the man above her, pressed her hands to the ground once more, and smiled. Another lurch in the earth took him off balance. The hammer tumbled from his hands as his feet failed him. He went down with a heavy thud. He landed on his back just as she'd done, but from the pinched look on his face, it seemed like the impact was much more painful for him.

Neve stood.

Her power spread out, it curled around the big man's prostrate form, binding him to the ground. It bled beneath the feet of the immediate crowd around her, and it latched onto their boots, clawed into the leather like celestial traps. She looked over her shoulder to see their panic, the way they shimmied and pinwheeled their arms as they tried to get loose. She would come for them soon, but first...

She bent down and wrapped her hands around the smooth handle of the hammer. It was heavy, but she lifted it and took it with her. She stood over the giant soldier and straddled his hips with her feet. As he fruitlessly struggled against the chains of her power, she rested the head of the hammer at the base of his throat. She watched his eyes. There was a moment where he looked a little incredulous, like he might even laugh at her. But then he understood what she was doing, and his dark eyes glazed over with fear. She leaned forward on her arms, on the hands that held the hammer to his neck, and pressed her weight into it. His mouth opened, gaping like a fish, but no sound came out. His eyes bulged. Neve pressed down harder and waited. His limbs thrashed beneath her, but she held him there until, strangling against the weight of his weapon, he let out a final rasp and went limp.

Neve let the hammer slip from her hands and clunk to the ice. She turned in a slow circle, her power was a rabid thing, gnawing at her for more release. The pressure of it was filling her head, her lungs. She felt like she had the morning she'd unleashed on the men that attacked Killian.

She felt outside of herself; she felt *other*. Many thoughts swirled through her mind, but only the loudest broke out from the din.

Show them who you really are.

First, there was wild, crackling heat. It rushed from her body, from her mind, in an almost painful wave. Neve let herself feel it. She did not brace herself against the cold burning, but instead she became the power, the agony.

Then there was screaming.

She watched as her magic rippled across the ground beneath her feet and pushed out from her skin. Her body became the anchor of this great and terrible essence. Snapping white flames licked up the legs of the soldiers in the circle, bursting and devouring as they continued up their bodies. It swallowed them whole, snuffing them out.

It.. no, not it. *She.* She only released her fiery hold on them when there was nothing left but ash. Then Neve let herself expand, her power reaching and seeking more. More death.

Show them who you really are.

So, Neve D'Aeth Lyra did.

~

Truth be told, Sabrina had never been in a battle before. Not a real one. Not one that mattered. There was nothing special about her skills. She knew how to fight and kill just as well as any of the Cavalry on this field, but she had nothing in her arsenal that would help her be *better* than them.

Except for her rage.

She would always have that.

Something was on fire at the eastern edge of the battlefield. The smoke was heavy and rich; it smelled like grilled meat. The flames made the night glow with an eerie white light. She didn't have time to think about it, though. She was just trying to stay alive.

Sabrina took an elbow to the chin and tasted blood in her mouth. It kindled her fury. With a growl, she thrust her sword forward and sank it into the belly of the nearest soldier, the one she assumed had hit her, but she didn't know for certain. There was no way to know. The crowd was thick, and everything was chaotic.

She'd grown up with five brothers. All of them were dead now. Or, at least, she thought they must be. Once they were of age, they'd all joined the Cavalry. It was simply what was expected of them. Their father was once a high-ranking Command General. He'd died young, as most Cavalrymen did. As most men did in Eodia. Women, too. No one was long for this life on the Island.

Sabrina only ever wanted to be a soldier. Just like her brothers, her father. But women weren't allowed. Since she was a little girl, she'd trained and trained. She was good. Not great, but good. She thought maybe they'd make an exception, because her father had been respected, because all of her brothers were amongst the ranks. But when she went to plead her case, to beg, the Commanders laughed in her face.

Then they'd beaten her unconscious and tossed her in an alley like garbage.

It was Isolde who found her. She still remembered the sound of her voice in the dark. The gentle caress of her hands. The feeling in her gut when Isolde whispered, "It's all right, you're safe with me."

Sabrina loved Isolde from that moment on.

Loved her and expected nothing in return.

Isolde saved her and showed her the first kindness she'd ever known. She gave Sabrina a home, a mission, and a family. And while she would never love Sabrina the same... It was enough.

To be in Isolde's presence, to live this life by her side, to be her friend... that was enough for Sabrina.

She swung her sword, finding flesh and muscle. Gods, there were so many of them. Her body felt tender and bruised beneath her second-hand armor. Her muscles ached. But she pressed on. The Queen was somewhere in the fray. Sabrina knew that Neve should be her priority. She knew she was here to protect and defend the Queen, the only person who could deliver her and the rest of the Island from this brutal life under Highborn rule.

But, honestly, all she cared about was finding Isolde.

Beyond the crowd, Sabrina could see glimpses of the bramble maze. She was getting closer. Above her, the stars shot through the sky, illuminating the ivory towers of Lyra Castle with flickering speckles. Sabrina was somehow hot and cold at the same time. Her heart hammered in her chest, and the adrenaline boiled in her blood to the point of pain.

Still, she barreled forward.

Her feet caught on something. Sabrina could not find her balance, and she fell, feeling the impact vibrate up her hips. Her pants tore, and she could already feel the blood blooming on her knees.

"Fucking bullshit," she cursed through clenched teeth.

When she saw what she'd tripped over, Sabrina's entire world ended.

Isolde.

Her friend was curled up in a ball on her side, one arm covering her head. There was an arrow through her chest. Blood blotting the ice beneath her.

No.

A scream ripped through Sabrina's throat, cutting into the night like a blade through cake. She covered Isolde's body with her own, hands searching, feeling for life, for anything.

"No, no, no, Isolde," she wept.

Her eyes were blurry with hot tears that froze on her cheeks. Her shaking fingers found the side of Isolde's throat. Sabrina forced herself to shut up for a moment, just long enough to pay attention, to feel Isolde's pulse fluttering against her fingertips.

Relief was like a warm blanket.

Sabrina turned to Isolde and pulled her into her arms. Isolde opened her eyes, squinting and blinking like it hurt.

"You're here," she said, and despite being injured, she still smiled at Sabrina, whose heart simply cracked right down the middle at the sight.

"I'm here," Sabrina said. "Do you think you can walk?"

Isolde seemed to pause, taking stock of the way her body felt. Then she nodded. "I think so."

"We have to get out of here. We have to get off the ground."

They'd be crushed if they stayed where they were.

It was a wonder that Isolde hadn't been utterly trampled.

Sabrina pulled her gaze from Isolde's face and looked up. A group of soldiers stood above them, their swords pointed and ready to strike. Six. Seven. Eight. Maybe ten. Against two.

The edges of Sabrina's vision clouded with rage.

"I know you're in pain," Sabrina said. "But I need you to do something for me."

Isolde's brow furrowed, and she shifted, straightening up with a wince. "What?"

Sabrina's heart jumped into her throat, knowing what was waiting for her. "I need you to run."

There was fear in Isolde's eyes now. "Sabrina..."

"Shut up and listen," she hissed. "You need to get into the maze. I'm going to clear a path for you. And I need you to run."

"Together. We can make it there together."

Sabrina was still crying. She didn't think she could stop if she tried. "Please," she said, her voice breaking. She didn't wait for a response.

She stood, placing her body and her sword between the army and Isolde.

Widening her stance, her skinned knees stung as they scraped against the rough fabric of her torn pants. She tilted her head to one side, then the other, popping the joints. Her lips curled in a sneer. Sabrina took a deep breath to steady herself, then she let her rage rise and rise.

Sabrina pointed her sword at the group of men slowly advancing on her and said, "Let's go."

~

It was always assumed, because he was big and strong, that Oliver was a born fighter. That couldn't have been further from the truth. He'd grown up in a gentle home, his parents were gardeners and farmers. Oliver believed in good earth that could grow lovely and nourishing things.

That's why he'd learned to fight. He wanted a future in which the people he loved could just live in simple joy. Grow carrots, read books, and sleep soundly in their beds at night. The Highborns made a life like that impossible. But, despite never having lived in that kind of peace, Oliver believed that it existed somewhere, and that it could exist here in Eodia.

He just had to help the Queen take the Castle.

They were so close.

So close to that beautiful future that if he closed his eyes, he could almost smell the freshly tilled spring soil.

With his eyes open, all he could smell was flesh.

Bloody flesh. Sweaty flesh. And somewhere to the east of where he stood, burning flesh.

He stood taller than most of the men on the battlefield; he could see farther, wider. The ranks had thinned, but there were still so many soldiers. As he'd moved through the crowd, he'd seen fights break out amongst the Cavalry. Huge brawls that ended with dozens of dead men littering the ground. He'd even seen groups of men escaping into the night, deserting. Those who didn't run and avoided the infighting but found Oliver...they found death. He cut through them easily, and his sword was dripping red.

A few yards ahead of him, there was a gap in the crowd. In the center of that gap, he saw blond hair lifting into the wind. He'd know that hair anywhere. He squinted. It was Sabrina. Fighting off a growing group of soldiers. And behind her... a dark-haired woman in blue was crouched on the ground. Isolde.

Oliver's heart fell into the pit of his stomach, and his guts seized. His friends. His *best* friends. His fellow dreamers. No. This would not do.

He made easy work of cutting through the crowd; his only focus was on Sabrina and Isolde. He wouldn't let anything happen to them. He couldn't. Oliver barely noticed the men he killed. He didn't take his eyes off that gap in the crowd, the blonde hair.

Finally, he made it through. He slid into the clearing and sidled up to Sabrina. She was bleeding. She looked tired and rough. But she was alive. Her eyes were wild when they met his. Her gaze was frantic. Her panic was a living, breathing thing.

He offered her a smile. A real one. "Hi," he said.

Sabrina's gaze softened. Just a little. Oliver noticed that way her tense shoulders lowered from her ears. He noticed the deep breath she released, as if she'd been holding it for a long time.

"Hi," she said, the corner of her mouth ticking up just slightly.

Oliver glanced back at Isolde. There was an arrow sticking out of her chest, the sight of which made a nasty shiver skitter down his spine. But she seemed alright, shakily rising to her feet. She grinned at him, wavered, reached out, and placed her hand on his strong shoulder to steady herself. "Hi," Isolde said.

He couldn't help the dumb chuckle that bubbled out of his chest. He absent-mindedly swung his sword at a soldier who came for him, catching the man with a slice across the chest.

He turned to the army. Oliver pressed in close to Sabrina, and with Isolde's hand still on his shoulder, he and Sabrina went to work. This time, as he stabbed and sliced, he advanced, bringing his friends with him. They were a little army of their own. They always had been, the three of them.

Oliver and Sabrina were the front line. Isolde, behind them, managed to thwart attacks from the rear. How she was standing, let alone fighting, in her condition, made Oliver thunderstruck with admiration. The flowing blood of Cavalry soldiers made the ice slick beneath their feet, but still, they gained more and more ground.

Finally, they reached the front, to the mouth of the maze. The three of them, together. Elation filled Oliver's chest. The entrance to the brambles had been abandoned at some point during the battle. Now, all they had to do was slip inside and wait for Killian and Neve to join them.

Oliver was nearly giddy with relief, with the knowledge that they'd made it, that they were so much closer to the end. He pulled Sabrina and Isolde into a hug that was more instinct than anything else. He felt their arms squeeze him back. He kissed the tops of their heads, one then the other.

"Let me go in quick to scope it out. We can find a place to lie low until Neve and Killian make it here," Oliver said.

Sinking deeper into the shadows of the entrance, Isolde nodded and leaned against Sabrina, who seemed content enough for a quiet pause and the embrace of Isolde's warmth at her side. Oliver smiled.

He crept through the entrance and turned a corner. He was careful to stay in the very center of the narrow path. It was dark, but glinting in the muted starlight, Oliver could see the brambles, jutting out like thick spikes from the hedges. He turned another corner, making sure to remember which way he went- it wouldn't do them any good if he got lost already. The dark of night would be their enemy in the maze. The paths were overgrown with roots. There was barely space between hedges to move single-file, especially for a man his size. He and Killian would need to be extra cautious as they moved through this death trap. But that also meant the Cavalry couldn't follow, at least not in groups.

They could make it if they were careful.

Oliver turned around to fetch Isolde and Sabrina, but someone was there. A shadow blocked his path. No. Two shadows.

"Ahhh, we were hoping it might be you," the shadows said, they spoke as one, but their voices somehow slithered. A brushing, hissing sound like a handful of snakes moving over one another's scaly skin. Something about it gripped Oliver's gut, made him feel like he might vomit.

The shadows stepped forward, into a slice of moonlight.

Oliver's grip on his sword tightened.

The Highborns. But they looked...different.

He'd seen them a few times, parading down the streets of the Capital, dead-eyed and bored. Now... they looked like something else. They seemed bigger, taller. They still looked like men, but not. Their features were all horrible angles, and their teeth, visible behind thin lips, looked sharp. And their eyes... Oliver was certain he'd seen their eyes before, but these eyes were not the same. They were purely black, no pupil, no iris, no white. Pure black from lid to lid. Black as ink.

Black as the nothingness promised in death.

They reached for him.

And Oliver suddenly mourned the garden he would never tend. He suddenly mourned the joy he would never see his friends experience. He mourned what could have been.

They reached for him.

And Oliver was afraid.

60

Killian followed the fiery white glow. He knew he'd find her there.

And he did.

All of the snow and ice had melted in this part of the battlefield. The ground smoldered and steamed. Plumes of smoke and soot billowed up around his feet as he walked into a clearing that could only be described as utter decimation. The earth was awash in a thin white light that spread out from the center in a wide, perfect circle.

In that center stood Neve, and the sight of her stole the breath from Killian's chest.

She was glowing with the light of her power. Not only that, but there were stars in her skin, glittering in her hair, at the tips of her fingers. Killian had never seen anything so devastating in his life. His knees buckled, but he forced himself to slowly advance toward her. Neve stood tall, her blades all put away, as if she hadn't needed to use them once. All around her lay piles of ash, charred and forgotten weapons, sparks of power still crackling in the winter air.

Without asking, he knew what had happened here. And gods, did he wish he'd witnessed it.

Neve's gaze was fixed on the sky, which still danced with falling stars. Killian moved slowly, as one might approach an animal in the wild, cautious so as not to startle. He did not want to end this night as a pile of ashes at her feet.

"I'm all right," she said, her voice quiet, steady, almost serene. "I won't hurt you."

Killian relaxed his shoulders, releasing a thick coil of tension he hadn't even realized had settled over him upon seeing her there. She was somehow like the night itself, both bright and dark all at once. He covered the space between them in a few long strides. Up close, she was even more magnificent. Stars stuck like snowflakes in her hair, which had unraveled from her braid and now swirled around her face like a black cloud. Stars in her skin. And her eyes, oh gods, her eyes sparkled like moonlight on sea waves.

He opened his mouth to speak but closed it almost immediately. He barely trusted himself to whisper a single word to her without weeping. The relief that she was unharmed was one thing, but the sheer depth of power that pulsed from her felt like she could ruin him.

She could ruin him, and he would say "thank you".

"Can I…" he tried to speak. The sound lodged in his throat. He tried again. "Can I touch you when you're like this?"

Neve pulled her gaze from the sky and looked down at herself, holding out her hands, turning them to watch the way the stars blinked along the length of her fingers. She then took those hands and brushed them down her neck, down her chest, over the dip and curve of her waist to her hips. Killian tracked every single move she made. It was as if she was reassuring herself that she was there, that she was real. Neve released a shaky sigh in a puff of frost-frothed air.

She looked at him and nodded.

It was perhaps the most gentle he'd ever been with her, the way he slid his fingers up her arms, her jaw, cupping her face in his hands. Her skin was warm and inviting, and there was a curious, dull humming that vibrated through her. Killian stepped closer, feeling her chest graze his. He pulled her into him and buried his nose in the top of her head, kissing her there, breathing in her scent. His arms curled around her, and he felt her hands slither up his biceps and grip his shoulders. Killian brushed his fingers through the silky yet tangled ends of her hair.

"Looks like you've been productive," he joked quietly.

Her rigid back softened. She leaned closer to Killian. "Did I frighten you?"

"Yes, but you always frighten me. Scariest woman I've ever met, remember?"

Neve pulled her head back to look up at him. The sharp edge in her eyes told him that she was serious but that she also didn't have the energy to admonish him for his ill-timed humor. The glow was beginning to fade from her, from their surroundings. The stars in her skin began to softly wink out. Killian wasn't sure if his touch, his presence, was dulling her shine or if she felt safe enough with him that her power could rest. He hoped it was the latter.

"The others?" she asked.

He shook his head. "I haven't seen them. The moment I could, I came looking for you."

Her gaze cut behind him, to the battlefield beyond the protective circle of destruction they stood within. "How many are left?"

He turned his head, squinting in the dark. "At least half. Probably more. Although it seems like you made a pretty good dent."

When he turned back to her, Neve grabbed his face and kissed him. Hard. Delicious tension crackled at the base of his spine with the force of her mouth on his. Her lips were silky and hot and moved with expert demand. Killian clutched her to him, feeling the way her soft breasts pressed against his torso. Her kiss was a claiming and a conversation all in one. He could feel her relief, her need, her love. A love that would last until he was in the ground.

The sound of a horn blared through the night, pulling Neve back from him. His entire soul felt the absence of her kiss.

"Cavalry, fall back! Fall back!" a voice shouted. The command was heard on the battlefield. Killian watched as soldiers ran and marched back toward the mouth of the maze.

Fall back? What reason would this army have to fall back?

Killian reached for Neve's hand and held it, intertwining his fingers with hers. There was a shuffling of bodies, and Killian tried to count how many Cavalrymen gathered. One hundred. There were at least one hundred soldiers left. They formed lines of defense again, regrouping. However, this time they left a space. A path that led straight from the maze to where Killian and Neve stood in the ash–littered clearing.

"What are they doing?" Killian muttered under his breath.

"Nothing good," Neve replied.

The Command General stood blocking the entrance to the maze, and the soldiers flanking him were at attention. Killian glanced at Neve. She was no longer incandescent, but a glow hovered around her edges. Her stance and her body were the picture of ease, of boredom even. But he saw the predator in her eyes, felt it in the low pulse of magic that radiated against the palm of his hand.

It was when her fingers tightened that he knew something was wrong.

Killian watched as the Command General stepped aside and three massive figures emerged from the darkness of the maze. The Highborns, dressed in Cavalry white, moved deliberately into the glow of the moon. Their features were stark and ghostly, fingers too long and gnarled with blade–like claws at the ends, cheekbones too sharp, eyes too black. Graying skin the color of cobwebs. Dark mouths with black lips and gums, teeth pointed like animal fangs. Even from a distance, they looked like monsters, like what wraiths might resemble if they had skin stretched over their skeletons. Whatever glamour that kept the Highborns looking human all these years was long gone. Killian had a feeling that what he was seeing now was what they truly were. Ghastly, terrifying creatures bred from hate.

Between them stood Oliver.

Killian's stomach dropped.

Oliver was trembling. The Highborns each had an arm looped through his, like the three of them were going to stroll down Main Street in the Capital. Oliver clasped his hands in front of him, and when he raised his face, tears glistened on his strong cheeks in the dim light.

Next to Killian, Neve went terribly still.

"It looks like she finally learned to wield," one of them said, though his voice contained multitudes, layers of sound like old whispers, the scrape of paper against paper, the hissing of something ancient and cold.

"Took her long enough," said the other. That same voice, identical to his brother's, emerged from his mouth.

Killian knew they were talking about Neve, the power she'd leveled the battlefield with. Her face didn't change as she watched them from afar; she remained cool and unbothered. But Killian could feel it. Her rage was hidden and dreadful, just beneath the surface like the infinite root system of an old tree.

This was bad.

He clutched her hand tightly. She did not move. Her gaze was locked on the Highborns, on their unnaturally long hands, casually draped over Oliver's corded, tense forearms. Oliver's panicked gaze cut to the side, and Killian followed it. In the shadows, hiding between the outer edge of the maze and a cluster of curving brambles protruding from it, Killian could see two women, a blonde and a brunette. Sabrina and Isolde.

Sabrina was holding Isolde, gripping her as Isolde struggled against the strength of Sabrina's arms. The librarian did not look well. Even from this distance, Killian thought she looked pale, and there was an arrow sticking out of her chest. Sabrina had one arm around her waist, the other clasped over Isolde's mouth as if to prevent her from screaming, to prevent them from being found there in the darkness.

Isolde was trying to break free, to get to Oliver.

Killian watched as Oliver's eye widened, as he clenched his jaw and gave Isolde and Sabrina a nearly imperceptible shake of his head. No. He did not want them to risk themselves for him. His eyes were wet and pleading, but not for himself. For them. Lifting his chin, Oliver turned his face forward. He found Killian for a moment and then settled his gaze on Neve. His Queen. He kept his eyes on her, and the look in them changed from panicked to resolute.

He knew. Before anyone else did. Oliver knew.

From that point on, everything moved so, so fast.

The Highborns each pulled a long knife. They were curved, serrated, wicked-looking things. In the space of a panting breath, they flicked their arms out, as easily and absently as a person might flick away a buzzing fly.

The battlefield was quiet, silent.

Killian heard Oliver's gasp.

A deep slice of red bloomed across his chest. Another one across the column of his throat.

The only mercy was that Oliver went quickly.

Sliding their arms out from the crooks of Oliver's, the Highborns let his body fall. First to his knees, then, with a gruesome and final thud, Oliver died on the icy ground, his red blood petaling out like roses on the snow.

Killian's eyes stung with tears, and his throat was thick. He barely registered the way that Neve gently slipped her hand from his, that she took a step away from him. Then another.

The Highborns were grinning at her, playful, like they'd won a game.

A memory scratched at the back of Killian's brain. Stories he'd been told about the bramble maze. It always came back to stories, after all.

He could remember the way it was phrased easily. Because it was told the same way, no matter who wrote it, no matter who recited it. It was always the same.

It was said that the brambles themselves were cursed and that no weapon forged would be strong or sharp enough to cut through. No man had ever managed to make it through the maze to the palace doors.

No weapon forged, but what about a weapon that was born?

No man had ever made it through, but what about a woman?

It was a trap. A setup. This was all just to get her to...

"Neve, no!" Killian screamed.

But he was too late.

Neve D'Aeth Lyra erupted in an explosion of starlight.

61

There was nothing. Nothing but the light. She was lost in it. It was infinite and cataclysmic. Neve knew, in that bright moment, what it was to be a god.

It felt like knowing you were both a part of the universe and that you were the whole universe itself. It felt like the cresting wave of a climax. It felt like ending life and giving it at the same time. It felt wonderful and terrible.

She sensed each heart that stopped as she pushed her power across the battlefield. Every last breath as it shuddered through withering lungs. Every body that dissolved into cinder. She felt the brambles as her magic brushed against them like a taciturn lover. She felt the earth and the sky and life and death.

All of it.

The flickering began around the edges of her power, like clouds in her vision. It faltered. Stuttered. Then the instability grew. Neve had the vague sense, from somewhere outside herself, that she was draining. Her power was finite after all. There was only so much of it she could hold in her body, only so much she could wield at once.

When she'd first felt the power within her, it was like an unbearable pressure, expanding and expanding. Now, on this cold winter's night at the foot of Lyra Castle, she was releasing it all.

Down to the dregs. She needed to stop, to give it time to rest, rebuild.

Pulling it back was much harder than letting it go.

Neve could feel her body shaking, sweating, and *weeping.* She knew that if she didn't stop, it would drain her completely, and she, too, would be nothing but ash on the breeze.

She thought of the library.

She thought of her friends.

She thought of Killian.

And she thought of what awaited the kingdom, her kingdom, if she let herself die here.

Neve would not perish under the weight of her arrogance. And she would not doom Eodia because of it either.

With a scream, she made it all stop. Agony ripped through her body, tore into that space where her power often rested.

It burned her. Cold fire.

In the absence of her light, the darkness was deep.

When she came back to herself, she had to make sense of what she saw.

Everything was ash. There was no more Cavalry. They were all dead.

No more bramble maze. The hedges shrank to nothing. The once fabled thorns were simply green-black powder on the ground.

No more stars or moon, the sky was blotted out by thick, dark clouds.

Her body trembled.

She turned her head to the right, where Killian had held her hand moments ago, an eternity ago. There was a second of fear that she'd blindly obliterated the man she loved. But he was there, crouched and covering his head with his arms.

"Killian," she managed to say.

Without hesitation, he was on his feet and at her side. He yanked her into an embrace, fisting his hands into her hair, cradling the nape of her neck.

"Fuck," he breathed, as if it was the only word he could muster, the only word that made sense. He was right.

Over his shoulder, Neve searched the battlefield. Two people remained. Isolde and Sabrina, looking rattled, like they'd just narrowly escaped death. They were also right.

Movement caught the corner of her eye, shadows in the distance, amidst the smoldering brush that was once the bramble maze. The Highborns, making their way toward the Castle.

She understood then why Killian screamed her name just before she'd unleashed herself upon the Cavalry. The Highborns killed Oliver to get her to use her power. The magic destroyed the bramble maze, leaving the path open and easy for the Highborns to reach Lyra Castle.

This was their plan all along.

She'd played right into their hands.

Neve wasn't sure what they planned when they reached the Castle, what they would do, or what they thought would happen. But they wanted to take it, conquer it as much as she did. She knew that deep in her bones.

She also knew she couldn't let that happen.

It did not bode well that the Highborns were seemingly unaffected by her power, not when she'd just ended everything in sight except Killian and her friends. Not when her body felt like it was breaking, failing in the aftermath of what she'd done. She couldn't afford to be weakened, not now. Not when she was so close and there was so much at stake.

Neve breathed past the pain, the burning. Her head swam, dizzy and light in a way that made it hard for her to see straight. She blinked a few times to try to clear her vision, but it didn't help.

Inside, it felt like her organs were cooking.

She swallowed. Closed her eyes. Neve tried to reach deep, to the place where her power lived. She found it. Instead of a mighty sleeping giant, it now felt like a plant without enough water: dry and limp.

Killian held her in his strong arms. Neve wanted nothing more than to let him bear her weight, to let him love her. But they were out of time. Regretfully, she pulled away.

"I have to..." she began, watching as the Highborns moved closer and closer toward the Castle.

"I know," Killian said. "Let's do this."

Neve took a step forward and wavered. Her entire world felt like it was off its axis, tilted. Dark blotches bloomed on the perimeter of her vision. She felt Killian's arm go around her again. The concern on his face was sharp and immediate.

"What's wrong?" he asked, his voice low and full of grit.

She drank down a steadying breath. "I drained my power, and it drained me."

He touched her forehead with the back of his hand, swept his knuckles down her cheek.

"You're burning up. It's like you have a fever." He slipped his hand under the neckline of her leathers and pressed his palm against her chest. The cool strength of his touch felt incredible against her heated skin. "Your heart is racing." His jaw tightened. His eyes searched hers. She had no answers for him.

"I know," she said. "We have to go." Neve stepped forward, but he held her back.

"No," he said.

The wilted remnants of her power prickled, and Neve raised an eyebrow. "No?"

He shook his head. She recognized the look on his face. She'd seen it enough times by now. She was almost as familiar with it as she was with his smile. Protective panic, thick and drenched in worry. His face was all angles in the moonlight.

"You're in no condition to fight. You can barely stand."

"There's no other choice, Killian. This will be our only chance to take the kingdom."

"Fuck the kingdom," he cursed. "I would watch the whole Island burn if it meant keeping you safe."

She shook her head. "No one can keep me safe."

"I can!" he replied, with such earnest insistence that it cracked something in her heart. "I can keep you safe, Neve."

She knew if she let him, he'd abandon the mission in an instant. He'd take her hand and run in the opposite direction. But that was not the way this story was supposed to end.

So, Neve dug deeply into herself and pulled on every ounce of strength she had left. She pulled from her pain, from her pleasures, from her history. She pulled from the battles she'd already won. She pulled from the ground and the sky. She stroked her power and told it, *commanded* it, to wake up. Neve rooted herself in the knowledge of who she was, who the people of Eodia would remember her as.

Lady Nightmare.

The Woman on the Plains.

Heir of Nyx.

Queen of Death.

She settled her resolute gaze on Killian's frantic face. Whatever he found in her eyes melted his resistance. Neve watched as he patched himself back together, pushed down the panic, and swallowed his worry.

"It's time," Neve said.

Somehow, she forced her trembling body into motion. One foot in front of the other. Killian was at her side, close, just in case. She ignored the heat trapped beneath her skin. She ignored the thick, dizzy cloud in her head. She pushed it all away, locked it down. Her eyes were set on the Castle. Her feet carried her.

She began to run.

As she reached the edge of what had once been the bramble maze, she met the wide gazes of Isolde and Sabrina. Wordlessly, despite their injuries and exhaustion, they fell in line with her and Killian, keeping their pace. The four of them ran through the dark, feet slipping on the ice and snow.

The cold air was as sharp as razors as it screamed into Neve's lungs. The Castle gates drew closer and closer, the towers loomed endlessly above, piercing the sky. She'd lost sight of the Highborns, which she assumed meant that they'd entered the Castle. The thought forced an extra pulse of speed into her legs.

Faster, she needed to move faster.

The only sounds were the violent drumming of her heart in her ears, her ragged breath sawing in and out, her boots crunching and battering the slick terrain. Neve forced herself not to feel. She couldn't let a speck of pain in, a whisper of worry. She focused on the sounds, the frigid air, and the sight of the Castle moving closer and closer with every wild stride.

After what seemed like hours, excruciating and interminable, they finally reached the Castle gates. Neve was first, and when she crossed the threshold into the open courtyard beyond, there was a rumble in the earth and the sky once again brightened. She looked up. The clouds dispersed, revealing the dancing stars and the glowing crescent moon, even brighter and more alive than they'd been during the battle.

And then there was a massive grinding noise and a rusted metal clunk.

The Castle gates slammed shut right behind her, leaving Killian, Isolde, and Sabrina on the other side of them. Magic. Neve could feel it, ancient and deeply rooted to this place. She reached out and wrapped her hands around the golden railings. The metal was warm and vibrating. She tried to push the gates open. They wouldn't budge. She tried pulling. Tried prying the seam apart.

Locked.

Whether it was the Highborns' magic or the will of the Castle on its own, the gates were sealed.

Whatever it was, it wanted Neve all to itself.

Killian shouted and yanked on the gates with all his considerable might. Sabrina joined him.

But Isolde stayed still. She was beautiful as ever. A light sheen of sweat glossed her brown skin, and dark circles blossomed under her eyes. The arrow in her chest looked angry. Isolde was tired, but a serene and knowing look brightened her eyes. She reached a hand through the rails. Neve grasped it.

"This part you have to do alone," Isolde said quietly. "Just like *she* did."

She. Nyx.

Suddenly, Isolde closed her eyes, and a vision filled Neve's head.

High in the bell tower of Lyra Castle, Eodia's Queen, blood spilling and near death, stretched her arms and reached her delicate fingers towards the ancient metal bell pull. Using her last rasping breath and all the strength left in her body, she tugged the chain. Nesting white birds exploded into panicked flight from the tower at the sound of the bell, a sound that had not been heard on the continent for over an age.

She felt the bell's peal deep down in her bones, it vibrated from her head to her feet, down into the stones of the castle itself. It resounded into the kingdom, into the violent waves of the sea, and beyond– into the very world.

And finally, the Queen lay herself down on the cool floor. Her blood quickly spread around her, carrying what was left of her life and her legacy into the cracks between the mighty rock that built the castle. Seeping down, down, down into the foundation of the mightily built fortress, her blood flowed even into the yawning earth below.

"When my blood returns," she whispered, "so shall the power and glory of this throne."

Isolde opened her eyes, and the vision faded from Neve's mind.

Neve finally knew what it all meant, what the journey was for.

Everything that was in motion inside of her went completely still. For the first time in what felt like hours, maybe even days or months, a particular quiet settled over her. A sense of rightness. It blurred out the rest of it: all the pain, the fever lighting her on fire from the inside out, the concern, the fear. It all went away because *this*... this was what mattered in the end.

What she'd been born to do.

Lyra blood had returned to the Castle, and now Neve would go to the place where Nyx was killed and change the story. This time, instead of the Queen's demise, it would be the half-brothers, the Highborns.

She needed to right a wrong made three hundred years ago.

Restore the balance.

Take what belonged to her.

Neve raised the librarian's knuckles to her lips and kissed them. "Thank you," she said. "For everything."

"It has been my honor," Isolde replied.

Neve took a step to the side, found Sabrina's hands where they were clutching at the gate, and covered them with hers. Sabrina stopped tugging on the rails, slowed down, and looked at Neve with watery eyes.

"I'm sorry I tried killing you that one time," Neve said with a smirk.

An unexpected bark of a laugh that turned into a sob punched out of Sabrina's mouth. As if even her body couldn't decide whether or not she should laugh or cry.

"Finally. I've been waiting for that apology for ages." Tears spilled down Sabrina's wind-raw cheeks. The tiniest smile curled her lips. And for once, something besides annoyance lit Sabrina's eyes. Neve thought perhaps it might be the warmth of affection, or, at the very least, a little bit of respect.

She took two more steps to the side and came face to face with Killian, the glinting golden bars of the gates between them.

The desperation on his face was clear, in his wide eyes, the set of his jaw, the bobbing of his throat.

Neve's chest hurt. She looked at him, and he looked at her, and for the space of a mere moment, there was nothing else.

Neve saw it all in his eyes. The night they met. The morning he watched her washing in the river, and thought she didn't know. The nights they held each other in sleep, before they'd even kissed. And then the rampant need to never stop kissing once they started. The quiet mornings, the sweet afternoons. All of the tender moments that supplied wealth to the love they bore for each other. It was there, in his eyes.

"I'm supposed to be your Knight," he said quietly, reaching through the gates for her. "Of all the moments I should be by your side, it's this one."

Neve stepped closer and let him take her face in his hands. "You brought me to this moment, Killian. Without you, I never would have made it here."

"Please," he said.

It was the "please", the way he said it, that broke her heart into pieces. She knew there was nothing she could do. But, gods, the sorrow that overcame her nearly brought her to her knees. Neve choked back the tempest within her that threatened to break free. She stood tall, raising her chin, gritting her teeth. She showed him the strength in her. She showed him that she would fight her way to the end, and let him see the unwavering love she had for him. She took his hands in hers and kissed them, then reached over and ran her fingers down the side of his handsome and desperate face.

"You are mine. I am yours. There will never be anything else."

A single sob released from his chest, she swore the relief and love in that sound cracked the great stones of the palace itself.

"But now," she continued. "You need to kiss me and let me do this. Kiss me and let me go."

He shook his head, as if to say no. As if to refuse to let her go. But then the refusal, the denial, turned into a nod. He straightened his back, settled himself, and yanked her against the gate. His mouth was on hers, hungry, needy. His lips memorized hers, his tongue tasted her, his breath mingled with hers until the air belonged to both of them.

His love for her was a brutal, living thing. An immortal thing.

Killian gently broke the kiss but kept her pulled close. "You can do this," he said. "I know you can do this."

"I can do this," she repeated.

Neve kissed him again, quick and forceful, then pushed out of his grasp and walked away.

The Queen strode toward the Castle, and she did not look back.

She couldn't bear to.

62

Neve was out of time.

She could not stop to take in the impeccable majesty of the Castle as she ran through the halls, searching. The hidden, sentimental part of her wanted to slow down and look at every piece of art, every tapestry, and explore every room. She'd read so many stories about this magnificent palace that it rankled her romantic sensibilities to be unable to marvel at the columns and the domed ceilings with their intricate filigree and paintings.

The only time she slowed, the only time she stopped, was when she passed a massive open doorway.

It led into a huge, open room with alabaster walls, all carved with impossibly delicate scrollwork depicting stars and suns, the moon in all moments of its lunar cycle. Moonlight streamed in from the leaded glass windows in the cathedral ceiling, illuminating what sat on the dais, lonely and waiting. A long crimson rug led from the entrance to the end of the room, to the raised platform with gleaming white stone steps.

To the throne that waited.

It was big, upholstered in cream damask. The seat was deep, the arms curved and inviting. The back of the throne was spiked with eight points, much like the star on the gods-room door in the library. Much like the crown she'd found there. Around the throne on the dais lay swaths of ivory gossamer, undulating piles of the whisper-thin fabric. It gave the effect, when looking at it from the entrance, that the throne was floating in a small sea of silky clouds.

It was not easy to turn away.

Neve let her instincts lead the way. She followed hall after hall until she reached an alcove that led to a staircase spiraling upward.

The bell tower. There were splatters of old blood all along the entrance, darkest on the first few steps. She knew that this was where Nyx's knights, including Gawyn Grey, lost their lives trying to protect her. She could feel their presence in this space, their noble deaths immortalized in stone.

High above, there was the sound of shuffling feet. A chill moved in a cascade down Neve's body. They were waiting for her up there. The Highborns. This was it.

Taking a dagger in one hand and the winding railing in the other, Neve climbed the stairs. Each step she took echoed up to the top of the bell tower. There would be no surprise attack, no moment where she could gain the upper hand. They knew she was coming; they could hear her ascent. And they waited.

When she reached the top, the Highborns were casually leaning against a pale stone wall, as if they were simply waiting for a meal to arrive at their table in a pub: unbothered but hungry. There was nothing in their black eyes as they watched her step onto the platform. Splatters of blood stood out in stark relief on the white cuffs of their shirts. Oliver's blood. The rest of their clothes were clean, unwrinkled, and in perfect condition. Which made the blood near their wrists all the more malevolent. This close, they no longer looked like the men who'd run their hands and tongues along her skin. They no longer looked human at all.

Their cheeks were sunken, skin gray and papery. Thin lips covered mouths that had gone black. Black tongues. Black gums held sharply pointed white teeth. The Highborns seemed taller, longer-limbed, their hands and fingers stretched out like skeletal claws. They still retained minor differentiating features, Neve could determine which was Balor and which was Cael by the slopes of each nose and the curve of each jaw. But for anyone who'd never spent time with them before, they would look identical.

"You're standing where she died," Balor said, his voice hissing and strangled. "If anything was left of her, you'd be stepping in it."

Neve looked down at her feet. There were no bloodstains beneath her boots, only a faintly sketched outline in the vague curving shape of a woman on the hardwood. Even in death, Nyx left art behind.

"So, what's your plan? Repeat history and see if it gives you a different result this time?" she asked, more out of her curiosity than anything else. But conversation would give her time, a chance to observe.

"Something like that," Cael said, black eyes sliding to his brother, a smirk on his puckered mouth.

Neve took a careful step. They barely noticed. So she took another. The Highborns seemed utterly and completely unthreatened by her. They were relaxed, arrogant. Anyone else would be tracking each of her movements, ready to defend, especially after they'd watched her lay waste to their entire army mere moments before. Their absolute nonchalance rivaled even her own.

It would have been impressive if the circumstances were different.

"*When my blood returns...* that was Nyx's curse," they said. They spoke in eerie, perfect unison. The layers of their voices multiplied, a whispering sound like tearing paper and metal grinding against metal. The sound set Neve's teeth on edge and made the pain in her head worse.

"If you needed my blood to take the throne, why did you try to have me tortured and killed?" She took another step, getting a feel for the space, the floorboards, and the direction the wind blew when it came through the open window of the tower. She sized them up, remembering their weight against her body, wondering how much that weight changed in their taller, stretched forms. Would it be the same? More? How much effort would it take to get them on their backs? She touched her tongue to the corner of her mouth.

"We knew Rory Grey wouldn't be able to kill *you*," Cael said.

A ghastly grin spread across both of their mouths. "But you needed to be punished," Balor added.

Neve didn't respond. She waited. Watched.

Cael's hand moved to his shoulder to scratch an itch, it seemed, with talon-like fingers. A second later, Balor's hand rose to do the same, nails skating over the same spot on his shoulder. They looked at one another for the briefest instant, something Neve would have missed if she weren't paying attention. But she was.

"The minute you stepped foot on this Island, you set this all in motion. We felt it when you arrived. It was always going to end like this," Balor explained, patronizing.

"It was time," Cael said.

"It was time," Balor repeated.

Neve observed the way their throats both bobbed with a swallow in unison, the way their chests rose with a breath. She took another step. They didn't care. Then she took the dagger in her hand and put it back in the holster at her hip. That... that they saw. Now they were watching, straightening.

She forced herself to breathe slowly, to smile a little as she used both hands to gather her unruly hair and twist it into a tight knot at the back of her head.

"So, what happens now?" she asked. She leaned her back against the wall across from them, mirroring their apparent boredom. Neve crossed her arms at her chest.

They looked at each other again.

"You're the last of the Lyra line. Nyx's curse will end when you do," Cael said.

"All we have to do now is take the throne," Balor added. He grinned again. They both did.

"Confident talk considering you sent an army for me…
and I ended them all," Neve replied. She made a show of absently
inspecting her fingernails, all while keeping her peripheral
vision on them. Her body was still throbbing, begging for rest,
burning. But she didn't let it show.

"They were men," they said at the same time. There was
something darker, malevolent in their tone now. She'd struck a
low blow, it seemed. "But we are gods."

She tilted her head, shrugged.

"Only half-gods," she said. A razor slice of silver flared in
their eyes, and she knew she had them; she was finally under
their skin. She flashed them a smile. "Just like me."

"We have centuries on you, girl. You are untested," they
hissed.

Her hands went to her hips. She unsheathed her daggers.
She stared into the endless black murk of their eyes and said, "So
test me."

They pulled those long, curving knives and came for her,
the serrated edges of the blades glinting in the moonlight. Neve's
hands tightened around her daggers. She willed her power to
rise. It shifted and curled in her, like a wounded fighter trying to
gain their feet after being taken to their knees. It was trying. *She*
was trying. But there wasn't enough magic left, at least not yet,
to do anything but add the thinnest dull glow to her fingertips.

Cael's blade swung in a wicked arc, aiming for Neve's
throat. With a fluid motion, she deflected the blow and retaliated
with a swift counter strike, drawing blood from the Highborn's
twisted flesh, just below his arm. The blood stank like rotten
meat and sloughed thickly from the wound. Balor hissed, and
Neve's eyes cut to him, noticing that he now had an identical
wound, fresh yet already festering, beneath the same arm.

Interesting.

With no magic, Neve's daggers were an extension of her
will instead. She moved quickly, twisting, ducking, spinning just

out of reach. She took every opportunity to cut into them. When she slashed across Balor's thigh, the same injury appeared on Cael. Whatever was done to one of them also happened to the other a moment later. It gave her hope. If she could land a fatal blow on just one of them, this would be over.

As she straightened from dodging another strike, an arm snapped out, its hand slamming against the center of Neve's chest. The force of it sent her flying backwards, where her back crashed against the wall, narrowly missing the edge of the window. For a moment, she couldn't see. For a moment, she couldn't breathe, the air having been entirely knocked out of her by that massive, awful hand. She opened her mouth, wheezing, fighting for a single breath. Her hands curled into white-knuckled fists around the daggers she somehow managed to hold onto.

Just one fucking breath, please.

Someone, something, must have heard her plea.

A breath screamed down her throat, filled her chest, and belly. She opened her eyes to see the Highborns hovering above her, waiting. This was a sport to them, one they weren't ready to stop playing. It was Balor who reached down and touched her face with long fingers that felt as if they were covered in dried candle wax. A cringe rattled Neve's spine.

"Are you feeling tested enough? Or shall we continue?" he whispered, gentle like a father, like a lover. Like a lie.

"I'm not done yet," she said.

Neve was fast as she thrust her daggers into him, just above his hips, one on either side, like she was skewering him. But it was Cael who let out a scream, like the sound of a dozen crows. They were both bleeding from their flanks by the time she pulled her blades out. The odor was cruel and overwhelming.

She scrambled to her feet, and the Highborns began circling her. Neve's breath was raggedly recovering from the blow, but she didn't have time to be tender with herself. Both

Highborns were leaking that thick, rancid blood, but they were undeterred.

They slashed at her with blades, they slashed at her with those terrible, gnarled hands. Neve knew that she was bleeding. She couldn't feel any of it. Her focus was solely on the movement of her body, the internal screaming at her power to *wake up, wake up.*

But it did not wake. Her power remained locked inside, on its knees.

The Highborns were strong, inhumanly strong. The fever burning beneath Neve's skin had not subsided. The more she fought and the more she pulled at her power to ignite, the more dire it became. Her dizziness was made worse by the way they circled her, keeping their speed constant so that she had to spin with them. At some point, she was no longer able to differentiate between the two brothers. But it didn't matter. They were the same deep down.

Still, her daggers weaved a deadly dance. She felt it when her blades sank deep into their waxy flesh. Their breath as they surrounded her became an incessant snarling. Her heart thrashed wildly behind her ribs, her body throbbed with the force of it.

Just one. She just had to take down one of them.

They crowded her, but she warded off their arcing knives with her daggers. The metal sang and slid as the blades met over and over again. But she needed more. Twisting and spinning, she dropped a dagger back into her hip sheath and reached behind her back to grab the sword.

It took a mere second too long.

A mere second of her arm stretched back, and the expanse of her ribcage was exposed.

It was Balor who struck.

A deep slice up her side, opening her from hip to underarm. The pain was immediate and senseless. She felt her heated blood spill from the wound like water from a kettle. And then Neve fell. Before the darkness came for her, she turned her head and saw the faded outline of Nyx's death on the floor next to her.

Poetic, indeed.

~

The night was quiet except for the sound of blades colliding. It came from the bell tower and echoed far and wide. Killian was pressed against the Castle gates, clutching the rails with sweating hands that were at risk of freezing to the metal. He stared up at the dark, empty eye of the tower window, hoping to get a glance of Neve, proof of life, something. He told his panicked heart to take the sound of fighting as evidence that she was still alive, but he wouldn't be satisfied until he saw her, touched her.

Behind him, Sabrina and Isolde were huddled together. Killian had tended to Isolde's wound, removing the arrow and field dressing it as best he could. It didn't hit anything vital, and by the time he was done wrapping it, the injury had already started to clot. Making use of his hands for the sake of someone else briefly calmed his worry. But now there was nothing to do but wait.

Killian felt like he could choke on all this waiting.

Then, the echoes of blade-against-blade abruptly stopped, and so did Killian's heart. Fruitlessly, he tugged on the gates, his muscles coiling, but they didn't budge. The only reason for the fight to end was if someone was dead.

Burning fucking gods, he hoped it was the Highborns.

He stood there, panting as the silence stretched on and on.

Until a burst of warm white light, bright as the sun, poured from the tower window and lit up the night.

63

Darkness never came. Only light.

As her blood pooled beneath her, Neve saw the glow of her power rising around her. It came from her like a sigh. And next to her on the floor, instead of the stain of Nyx's ending, Neve saw a face. A beautiful face that looked a little like hers. Dark hair. Green eyes. Smirking lips. A golden light rested over the woman like a shroud.

"I knew you'd come," Nyx said, her voice ethereal, barely there, but sweet and strong.

"I'm dying," Neve replied.

Nyx shook her head. "No."

"How can you be so sure?"

"Because I died in this very spot. You're not going to."

Neve couldn't move, but she could see, she could feel. Her body was full of magic, so full that it pooled out of her and drowned the whole tower. Time appeared to be... stopped. The Highborns were there at her sprawled feet, but they were frozen, the only movement was the whisper of wind in their brittle hair.

"I thought my power was drained," Neve mused.

Nyx shook her head again. "It was never gone. Because it's not just yours. It's *ours*."

"Ours?"

There was a knowing, playful smile on Nyx's lips. "We share power in this family."

Family. Something that Neve never thought she had. Something that existed for other people but never for her. Bittersweet emotion squeezed tight in her chest at the word.

"The power belongs to you, to me, to our mothers. It was a gift from the first of us, Celesta. And now you, the last of us, wield it."

"The last of us," Neve repeated.

Nyx nodded. "You were inevitable. It was always going to be you."

There was a tingling in her side, where the long slash from Balor's knife split her open. A distinct, stinging sensation bloomed, the feeling of her skin being sewn back together, but instead of a needle and thread doing the work, it was strings of starlight. Through her blood, a cooling rushed, devouring the fever and the burnout from what she'd done on the battlefield. Inside her, the power no longer felt like a giant trying to break loose. Now it felt like a caress, nurturing and kind, yet impossibly lethal. Its vastness was stunning.

It was no longer just the cold burning of starlight that she felt when she touched the magic. Within it, she could sense the memories of the women who had come before her. She could feel their joys and sorrows. She could feel the wild depths of the Great Sea. She could smell the rolling hills of grass and clover. She could feel the entire kingdom within her glow.

Tears sprang to Neve's eyes. "It's time to end this."

"When it's finished, ring the bell. Tell the world we've won." Nyx said with a wicked smile as her image dissolved into a sparkling vapor, and then into nothing at all.

Slowly, Neve stood. Not because she was weakened or afraid. No. She rose slowly because the Highborns were watching.

And she would give them a show.

The bell tower was bright, almost blindingly so. *She* was bright. The Highborns regarded her with bored expressions, but Neve knew they were uneasy. She could smell it.

"All this light is a cute trick," Cael sneered.

She said nothing. Keeping her eyes pinned to their faces, watching their creeping hands, she bent forward and took the daggers out of her boots. She dropped them to the floor and used her foot to absently kick them off to the side, out of reach. Neve straightened, dragging her hands up her legs, her thighs, as she rose. She took the daggers from her hips and cast them aside into the pile with the others. Did the same with her sword.

Balor laughed, a rasping sound. "Haven't we proven that you're no match for us, even with your arsenal of weapons?"

She didn't reply, but she sent a snap of her power at them, quick and cracking like a whip. It lashed at their hands, grabbed hold of those gruesome knives, and sent them clattering into the heap with her weapons in the corner.

The Highborns snarled in unison and made to lunge for her. But she took a step forward, pushing her power ahead of her and using it to lock them in place. Just like she'd done to Rory, like she'd done to the Cavalry on the battlefield.

Her magic curled like vines around their feet, twisting up their legs, growing thorns that sank into their flesh. Their black eyes glinted silver with fury. They struggled against her power as it climbed up their bodies, but nothing they did could shrug her off of them. Soon, the Highborns were wrapped in her light from toes to neck.

Horrible, hissing growls came from their rageful mouths. Balor snapped his teeth at her as she approached. She could taste their wrath, and underneath that anger, she could taste their fear. Its sourness coated the roof of her mouth like lemon juice. A flavor she could drink down forever if only to know that she was the one who finally introduced them to terror.

She stepped close to them. Close enough to kiss. Close enough to feel their acrid, dusty breath. Neve pressed a hand to each of their cheeks, like she would caress them, but she raked her fingernails down their skin instead. They growled and screamed. She was vaguely aware of them tossing slurs at her, like *bitch* and *whore*, as powerless men often did when they knew they were going to die.

Neve looked the Highborns in the eyes and said, "I am going to unmake you."

She held the power of the gods inside her. The power of her ancestors. The power of the entire kingdom: the earth that held it and the sea that fed it. She was made for this.

She looked at Cael.

"You first," she said, then slid her deadly gaze to Balor. "I want you to watch your death before it comes."

They both went silent at that. Whether because they didn't believe her or because they did, she would never know. Neve held Balor's gaze as she rested her hands on his brother's heaving chest. She thought of what it might be like to suck the life from him, from the inside out. And then she reached out with her power. His agonized scream split the silence as her magic found the life inside him, wrapped around it, and *squeezed*.

Sweat beaded on Balor's forehead as he watched. The effects of what she did to his brother were starting to touch him, too, delayed by merely a moment. After all, what happened to one of them happened to the other. Beneath her hands, she felt Cael's chest cave in, his skin sagged, his bones began to twist and snap. His scream went gritty and ragged. And still her power pushed. Punished. Ruined.

Then what was beneath her hands began to feel less like a man and more like sand. Cael crumbled. First into clumps, then into dust that powdered her fingers.

Balor was sobbing, choking on the sound. She stood face-to-face with him and watched him wither. He turned gray and hunched, old and worthless.

At the final moment, Neve leaned close.

"I am inevitable," she whispered.

He opened his mouth to speak, but all that came out was a rasp. Then Balor disintegrated into nothing.

All that was left of the Highborns was dirt on her boots.

Neve turned.

She reached her fingers towards the ancient metal bell pull. She tugged the chain.

Nesting white birds exploded into panicked flight from the tower at the sound of the bell, a sound that had not been heard on the continent for over an age.

She felt the bell's peal deep down in her bones, it vibrated from her head to her feet, down into the stones of the Castle itself. It resounded into the kingdom, into the violent waves of the sea, and beyond– into the very world.

Ring the bell. Tell the world we've won.

64

She stood tall in the center of the throne room.

The windows in the domed ceiling reflected the changing color of the sky. Pastel purple, pink, amber. The dawn of a new day.

It cast a watercolor light down onto the ivory throne, hugging the curls and layers of gossamer on the dais. Neve breathed deep to take it all in.

Stomping, running feet on stone echoed in the hall behind her. She smiled.

Isolde and Sabrina were the first to clamor through the doorway. They came running for her at full force, faces wet with tears. The women barreled into Neve and wrapped her in their arms. She hugged them back, her heart was full and grateful, warm.

"Thank you," she whispered to them. She said it over and over as they held her.

After a moment, they both pulled back slightly, looked at each other, and then Isolde gave Neve a knowing smile.

"He's been very worried," she said quietly.

Sabrina rolled her eyes. "Annoying. He's been very annoying."

Neve pressed her lips together to curb a laugh.

Isolde and Sabrina moved to the side, and all sense of joking suddenly disappeared.

Killian stood in the wide doorway, bracing himself against the frame with one arm as if he couldn't trust himself to stay on his feet. His face was a mask of beautiful relief, painted with love and awe. He pressed a hand to his chest, swallowed, then looked down at his boots.

After a moment, he moved toward her. Slow and steady, eyes shining. Neve had to suck down a plentiful breath. When he reached her, she thought he might pull her into his arms. Instead, he stood before her, searching her face, tears lined his eyes.

"You did it," he said in a cracking voice.

Neve nodded. "I did it."

Killian Grey fell to his knees before her. He set his sword on the floor at her feet. He bowed his head.

"I am yours, my Queen."

Neve was so full of emotion, she thought she might not be able to breathe around it. But she did. She ran her hand through his hair, and he sighed. Killian looked up at her. She smoothed her hand down his cheek, to his chin, and then to the collar of his shirt. She grabbed hold of the fabric and pulled. He smirked and rose to his feet.

Hand still wrapped around his collar, knuckles grazing the warm skin at the base of his throat, she hauled him to her.

His mouth met hers in a tangle of lips and tongues and teeth, his big arms wrapped around her waist and tugged her so close that he pulled her off her feet entirely. Neve let herself melt into their kiss, absorbing every bit of love and devotion he was offering her. It was perfect. It was everything.

But Neve had one more task.

Reluctantly, gently, she drew back from the kiss.

"There's something I have to do," she said. She heard a nearly silent groan of regret in his chest, but he set her back on her feet and released her from his embrace.

She stepped forward. The crimson carpet muted the sound of her approach. She took the steps softly, reverently. One, then the other. The clouds of gossamer on the dais were so deep that they puffed up around her calves. She turned, feeling the cushioned seat of the throne against the back of her legs. She closed her eyes.

Neve D'Aeth Lyra lowered herself onto the throne.

Acknowledgements

Thank you to my husband, Jeremy, for being my true champion, and to my daughters, Harlow and Autumn, for being my cheerleaders, despite being too young to read the content herein.

Thank you to my critique partner Emily Larson for being honest, loving, and just as excited as I was about the story. Truly, I could not have finished this project without you. You validated me, reassured me, and went out of your way to support and care for me. Your friendship is a fate that befell me, and I couldn't be more grateful that you're in my life.

Thank you to my mother, Naomi, for always encouraging me to pursue this dream, and to my dear friend Ana Fatturi, who has believed in me for over thirty years.

Thank you to my amazing beta readers: Kayce, Rana, Ashley, Sarah, Britni, Anna, Libby, and Rachel. You helped shape this story.

Ever since I could pick up a pencil, I wanted to be a writer. I cannot begin to express the magic of realizing this dream. From the very bottom of my heart, thank you.